MAIN

The Hardscrabble Chronicles

The Hardscrabble Chronicles

Laurie Bogart Morrow

With illustrations by the Author

BERKLEY BOOKS, NEW YORK

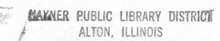

B

A Berkley Book
Published by The Berkley Publishing Group
A division of Penguin Putnam Inc.
375 Hudson Street
New York, New York 10014

This book is an original publication of The Berkley Publishing Group.

Copyright © 2002 by Laurie Bogart Morrow.
Cover art by Rick Johnson.
Illustrations copyright © by Laurie Bogart Morrow.
Text design by Tiffany Kukec.

All scripture references are taken from the King James Version of the
Bible, unless otherwise noted.

PRINTING HISTORY
Berkley hardcover edition / May 2002

Visit our website at
www.penguinputnam.com

Library of Congress Cataloging-in-Publication Data

Morrow, Laurie.
   The hardscrabble chronicles / Laurie Bogart Morrow.
      p.   cm.
   ISBN 0-425-18462-5
   1. City and town life—Fiction. 2. New England—Fiction. I. Title.

PS3613.O695 H37   2002
813'.54—dc21

2001056549

PRINTED IN THE UNITED STATES OF AMERICA

10   9   8   7   6   5   4   3   2   1

❧ A NOTE TO THE READER ❧

William Faulkner said, "It is the writer's privilege to help man endure by lifting his heart, by reminding him of the courage and honor and hope and pride and compassion and pity and sacrifice which have been the glory of the past. The writer's voice need not merely be the record of man, it can be one of the props, the pillars to help him endure and prevail."

To endure: That's the reality we live. To prevail: That's the thing that gives heart to fuel the soul. May *Hardscrabble* bestow upon you these truths and be as rewarding for you to read as it was a privilege for me to write.

—Laurie Bogart Morrow

With love to my sons and grandson—
Who, like this book,
Were born in Hardscrabble

CONTENTS

Contents

The Hardscrabble Chronicles is about a rural village in northern New England. Unlike Brigadoon, Hardscrabble does not disappear into the mist of dusk. It does not lie in a secret valley guarded by treacherous, ice-capped peaks, like Shangri-la. It isn't a seed that sprouted from a fertile imagination, such as Lake Wobegon. Hardscrabble is real; but like these fictitious places, it has been detained by Time and neglected by Progress—and that makes it enchanting.

I know. I've lived here for thirty years.

To capture the essence of Hardscrabble, I sometimes take license and roll several separate incidents into one story. On the other hand, there are stories I tell as close to the bone as I can. The same goes for the characters. One character may be a patchwork of personalities based on several people, while another may be cut from whole cloth. Most names have been changed, but a few are as true to this work as they were in life. These are men and women who traveled Destiny's road with dignity, grace, and kindness, and I honor them. They are the best of a disappearing breed called Yankees, and God broke the mold when He cast the last batch.

Their stories should be told so you may know, and so no one will forget, that common people lived uncommon lives in a remarkable place that I call Hardscrabble.

Introduction

Welcome to Hardscrabble

The town of Hardscrabble is arguably the most charming in the county, if not the entire North Country. However, relatively few people would know enough to agree, since Hardscrabble is off the beaten path. You have to have a reason to come here, or it's unlikely you will find us, unless you take a wrong turn. To put a point on it, "You can't get there from here," as the old Yankee saying goes, and as I have already pointed out, Hardscrabble has happily been ignored by Progress and Time—two conditions that have been the ruin of outlying communities that abut state roads. Those of us who are privy to the workings and machinations of the outside world find this a very great blessing. Those whose lives are being played out within its perimeters are content not to know any better, and they are the most blessed of all.

When I first came to Hardscrabble, I was a young, very pregnant wife and became so overwhelmed by motherhood that I never paused to absorb the culture shock of having moved from the hub of the universe, metropolitan New York, to Hardscrabble, the heart of rural New England. How I came here and why is part of my mystery, though I have a clue; but to this day—three decades and the whole of my adulthood later—I have never once looked back. Granted, I leave from time to time, but only for as long as is necessary to travel for a story and eke out a living as a journalist. It is enough and keeps food on the table for my family, logs in the woodstove, and the roof of the sprawling nineteenth-century farmhouse that we call home over our heads without leaking much.

Hardscrabble is no secret, though the late, great writer Corey Ford would surely disagree. For thirty years, from 1923 until, coincidentally, the year of my birth in 1953, he owned the Lower Forty, a sprawling field flecked with grazing cows and horses and oftentimes deer, which spilled from his doorstep and mine. He was the one who conjured up the name Hardscrabble to shield our town's identity. A passionately private man, Ford cloistered our whereabouts from his millions of readers while delighting them with stories about our eclectic, eccentric, colorful townsfolk.

I, however, am not so guarded and don't mind telling you how to get to Hardscrabble. I think if you knew, it would give you a real appreciation for our Town and the stories you're about to read.

How to Get Here

Likely as not, you're coming from the south, so head north about two, two and a half hours. You'll know your first turn when you see the lake on the right, but keep your eyes peeled between May, when the trees are in bud, and October, when the leaves are falling, because you can't see the lake for the trees. Once you have your bearings, look for a right—not the one that ends at the old Demeritt farm, but the one that goes past the fire-pine swamp. A stone's throw after the spot where Clydie Mason hit the twelve-point buck that wrecked his Ford pickup, hang a left. (Don't look for Clydie's truck. They towed it away an hour or so after it happened, about six years ago.) Finally, you come to the bridge. Cross over, but if it's nighttime, you might not realize you're on the bridge because it looks just like a road with a river underneath. You can make a right after that, but the next one is better because it takes you onto Brush Hollow Road and over Daniel's Hill, which gives you a lovely view of the Village. You'll know you're on the right track when you see the big field with the pond. When you see the field, then you're just down the road apiece.

One word of advice: Don't look for road signs. There aren't any in Hardscrabble because everyone knows where they're going. Oh . . . and another thing. If you ask a man who's wearing denim overalls, a plaid shirt, a soft-brimmed

felt hat called a crusher, and he's chewing tobacco, then you're asking a native. A native is a dyed-in-the-wool Yankee, and Yankees are plain-speaking folk. Ask him where the road goes, and he'll probably say, "Wal, I reckon it jest stays where it is."

If you get turned around and all else fails, your best bet is simply to head north by northeast as the crow flies and go straight.

You'll get here . . . eventually.

The Village

The Village—which is what we call downtown Hardscrabble—consists of two streets: Maple Street and Elm Street. Maple, as the name implies, is lined with maple trees, but sadly it is no longer true that Elm Street can say likewise, since Dutch elm disease destroyed the elms back in the summer of '68. There are, however, a great many lilac trees along Elm, and these are especially beautiful when in fragrant bloom in spring, but are a nuisance to the Hardscrabble Water Precinct, since lilacs' insidious roots strangle pipelines and must be dug up.

Elm and Maple meet at the Town Square, which boasts a flagpole, streetlight, and a watering trough whose usefulness ceased when automobiles replaced horses, and oxen were swapped for trucks, around 1940. But it was Miss Davinia Floyd, a crusty old spinster whose parlor window overlooked the Town Square, who was responsible for draining the trough and filling it with dirt. She complained so stridently, so bitterly, so unceasingly that small boys were terrorizing horses by sneaking in fish and frogs from the Village Brook, that she took it upon herself to drain the trough and fill it with pink geraniums and English ivy. The selectmen in their great, good wisdom felt it was better to turn a blind eye than confront the old biddy. Interestingly, the incident gave birth to the Hardscrabble Horticultural Society, whose Village Beautification Committee to this day maintains the trough with seasonal plantings from Easter until Thanksgiving. The Saturday after Thanksgiving, the trough becomes a stand for the Scotch pine that the McGregor family donates each year. It is festooned with strings of twinkling colored lights and trimmed with glittering glass balls. A silver star shines up top, mindful of Bethlehem. On a winter's night when the silent snow is falling, I do not believe there is a more beautiful Christmas tree in all the world.

A signpost tilts slightly askew at the edge of the Town Square to indicate the miles to faraway familiar places, such as Boston, 125, and Portland, 47. From here, Maple Street runs east to west and perpendicular to the Village Brook, while Elm runs north to south and parallel. On the leeward side stands the imposing Gothic Revival residence of the renowned intellectual eccentric, Professor Charles Markham, and his charming, gracious, gently suffering wife, Mab. The Professor, long since retired from decades of waxing lyrical over Chaucer at one of the more prestigious universities in New England, is a portly, wire-haired gentleman who resembles Mein Host in *The Canterbury Tales* and wears a tweed Norfolk jacket on all but the hottest summer days. In Hardscrabble, however, he is best known for the mulled brandy punch that he serves from a copious, rather dangerous looking cut-crystal pedestaled bowl in his study. Here he and Mab host the remarkably popular Wednesday night meetings of the Hardscrabble Literary Society, a book club the Professor himself established, and whose meetings he alone refers to as soirees.

At the edge of the Markhams' property, a bridge crosses the Village Brook. It is generally referred to as the Bridge That Crosses the Village Brook, not to be confused with the Bridge That Crosses the Pine River, which is on the opposite end of Town. Then, of course, there is the Huntress Bridge, which crosses the Ossipee River, but we haven't gotten there yet.

Directly on the other side of the Bridge That Crosses the Village Brook is the Hardscrabble Volunteer Fire Department. Mert Grant is our Fire Chief. He and his wife, Marianne, own and operate Mert's Grocery, just this side of the Huntress Bridge. That's where everyone buys their gas and beer. You'll generally find the Volunteers playing poker at Mert's while they wait for a call to put out a fire or rescue Libby Tyler's cat from a tree again, and in the pitch of night, if the lights are aglow at Mert's, it's usually the men just back from fighting a fire, having one beer for the road before setting out for home.

Talk at Mert's centers around who almost landed the biggest rainbow trout, who nearly got a double on pa'tridge, and who just missed a twelve-point buck, or a wild turkey, or a bear. There's the usual friendly rivalry, too, such as who has the birdiest bird dog, the most forgiving fishing pole, and the truest-shooting shotgun.

Mert, as you'll come to know, is one of the great personalities of Hardscrabble. He stands five foot four from the tip of his steel-toed work boots to the top of his spherical bald head, yet he towers over taller men in every other way. I saw him the other day at the Old Home Week Parade and asked him how he was doing.

"Not good," he said, chomping on an ever-present unlit cigar. (Mert gave up smoking years ago.) "Not good t'all. Backed my truck into a tree. Second time this week. Don't know how I'm going to explain to the insurance company that someone must have moved that tree again."

Across the street from the Firehouse, you'll see a cluster of houses that long ago were useful places of business: a blacksmith's, a wool trousers factory, a harness and bridle shop, and a printer's. These were once hustling, bustling centers of commerce that supported a population tenfold the size of Hardscrabble's today. But the internal combustion engine changed all that, and that whore, Progress, lured people to the cities and seduced them with creature comforts unknown hereabouts at the time, such as hot running water.

Farther on is the Hardscrabble Ten-cent Savings Bank, where a brass plaque in the foyer states that Mrs. Sarah Hodsdon opened the first account in 1868 with the princely sum of $17.35. Next to the bank is the Village Drugstore where Joe Pease, the druggist, dispenses prescriptions, advice, and old-fashioned ice cream sodas. His father-in-law, Dr. Bradford Fulton, affectionately known as Doc, has delivered Hardscrabble babies since time immemorial and lives across the way from Joe and his wife, Kay (Doc's only child), and Joe and Kay's three children. Doc's is a grand house with a first- *and* second-story balcony. He was divorced long before I moved to Hardscrabble. No one talks much about Babe Fulton, who left her husband and baby daughter for a banker down in Boston that kept regular hours and a yacht. Doc never remarried, though plenty of women have desperately tried to rectify what they perceive as an atrocity. Anyway, if you want to consult Doc, just go in, no need to knock. The first door on your right leads to his office; the one on the left, the kitchen. If you're troubled about your health, go through the right-hand door, and Doc will fix you up. If you're troubled with a problem, go through the left-hand door, and he'll fix you a cup of tea. Either door, he'll cure what's ailing you. No, you don't need an appointment, but it's a good idea to call ahead. Doc's a real outdoorsman and grabs what spare time he can muster to fly-fish in the spring, bass-fish in the summer, and bird-hunt in the autumn. In winter, he holes up in his icehouse on Loon Lake, pulls out fish when the flags release, and fiddles with his CB radio. His handle is Doc. You can raise him on channel one-niner, but speak up. He's a little deaf from years of shotgunning for pa'tridge and so is his English setter, Frost. If you can't reach him on the

CB, then head over to Loon Lake. His icehouse is the one with the sign over the door that says Liar's Den.

Now Maple Street rises to meet the Hardscrabble Elementary School, a tall, somber sort of building that sits high on a knoll and is reminiscent of the workhouse in Dickens's *Oliver Twist*. Behind the school is the Masonic Lodge, where the venerable Freemasons gather weekly in brotherhood to plan for deer season or turkey season or trout season or whatever season's about to be in season; but mostly, to take welcome respite from their wives.

The first Wednesday of each month, the Masons reluctantly surrender the Lodge to the softer sex, the Freemasons' better half, known as the Sisters of the Eastern Star. The ladies recite esoteric rites while dressed in Grecian togas fashioned from white bedsheets. Their ritual, I am told, is a very secret and sacred affair that is performed by candlelight.

Next is the Village Bandstand. Every summer Saturday evening, weather permitting, an ice cream social is held. The Hardscrabble Barbershop Quartet, which always takes the blue ribbon at the Fryeburg Fair, serenades us with such old-time favorites as, "Just a Song at Twilight" and "Sweet Adeline." The tenor is Charlie, owner and proprietor of Charlie's Cut & Shave, which is just down from Snead's Automotive. The quartet always closes the evening with a quiet little hymn called "Thank You, Dear God, for Summer." Then everyone folds their lawn chairs, rolls up their beach blankets, bids one another good night, and goes home in a contented sort of way.

Over there is Margie's Lunch, one of the social Meccas of Town, where you can get two eggs any style, toast, bacon, all the coffee you can drink, and fresh gossip for a buck twenty-five, seven days a week. Margie's never closes, even on Christmas Day. ("What else have I got to do?" she'll tell you.) She is married to George Allard, who runs the

Town Dump. You'll get to know George soon enough. And there's no way you can avoid Margie, who makes it her business to know everyone else's.

A stone's throw away is the Hardscrabble Public Library, where unwanted books are sold for ten cents, unwanted spinsters discreetly take out romance novels, and school-children study books on the American Revolution and George Washington, and stick their bubble gum underneath the reading table.

A row of stately homes lines Maple, each one an architectural jewel that occupies several acres of meticulously landscaped lawns and lovingly cultivated gardens. Two houses have widow's walks, which is a particularly fascinating phenomenon, since Hardscrabble lies forty-five miles west of the sea.

Along Elm Street

Let's return to the Town Square now and head down Elm Street. Overlooking the Village Dam is the Hardscrabble Village Store, which is run by Tilt Tilton, proprietor. Go to any emporium in any city in any part of the world, and you will not find a store quite like Tilt's. Where else can you get slab bacon sliced on No. 5 on the meat slicer, sirloin steaks as thick as the county phone book, extra-sharp cheddar cheese cut to order off a wheel as big as a wagon's, and tubs of fresh-dug worms for fishing, all neatly arranged under the beveled glass of a ten-foot-long meat counter? Lumberjack shirts and boiled wool pants in red or green plaid are neatly folded in tall, teetering stacks next to quart cans of baked beans. *Real* Yankee cooks bake beans from scratch. Tilt keeps individual barrels of dried pea, navy, kidney, red, and pinto beans next to Canning Supplies. Carol Mayhofer, who has won the blue ribbon for Baked Beans at the Hardscrabble Farm and

Home Fair five years running, always buys her dried beans from Tilt. "I wouldn't think of getting them anywhere else," she'll tell you, if you ask. (Carol's recipe is on page 308.)

Vegetable seeds for planting your kitchen garden come in in February. Go for a Canadian-bred tomato variety that yields after fifty days, because our growing season is short.

Fresh milk with cream on the top so thick you can eat it with a spoon still comes in glass bottles delivered daily from Huntress Hollow Farm, and brown eggs in cardboard crates on the checkout counter are still warm from sitting hens. Tilt's store has that delicious aroma of fresh-ground coffee, sawdust, woodstove smoke, and Hoppe's No. 9. One whiff restores the soul.

Tilt, a lifelong bachelor and self-proclaimed philosopher when it comes to understanding women, is fond of saying, "If you can get along with one woman, you can get along with more."* When a man has woman trouble, he generally

---

* Attributed to Bugs Baer.

confides his burdens in Tilt. Why, just the other day, John Milliken came in for some supplies. John is the father of twenty-one children—all his, all legitimate, and all by the same woman, his wife Beede, who at four foot six is fully two-thirds of a yard shorter than her husband. The Milliken farm has been in the same family long before the Civil War. Ask John what crop he cultivates, and he'll say, "Rocks," which sheds significant light on why New Hampshire is nicknamed the Granite State.

Anyway, John came into the Store one day and Tilt said to him, "John, you're looking mighty weary. Bet you're glad your workday's over."

John just shook his head. "Tilt," he lamented, "when I hang my pants up on the end of the bed at night, my day's work is just begun." That's Yankee humor for you—tossed with a pinch of wit and a dash of truth. You can always find plenty of both at Tilt's Store, too.

Across from Tilt's is the First Christian Church of Hardscrabble, where the venerable Reverend George T. Davidson delivers moving sermons (and private prayers that the Boston Red Sox will recapture the pennant). There is no other church in Hardscrabble, though back in the last century, there were actually two. That was before Liberty, then known as South Hardscrabble, raised the immortal battle cry, "Liberty from Hardscrabble," and seceded for no reason anyone can remember. However, Al Harmond will maintain to his dying day (which should be any day now, seeing old Al's ninety-nine years old) that his forebear, Zebulon Harmond, wrote this chapter in Hardscrabble history. Seems Zeb stole the bell from the steeple of the First Christian Church one dark and stormy night and hoisted it up into the steeple of the Second Christian Church (now the First Baptist Church), which had no bell because the twenty-eight-member congregation couldn't afford one. All hell broke loose, and that's when the Town divided in two, right down the Ossipee River. Of course, seven-eighths of the land lies on the Hardscrabble side and only one-eighth on the side that became Liberty, and this is probably why the First Baptist, which has enjoyed a twenty percent increase in membership since then, still can't afford one. And while this appears confusing, it makes all the sense in the world to the kind folk of Hardscrabble, who take great pride in our Town's deep-rooted and rather colorful history.

God shares His house of worship with the Ladies' Guild of the First Christian Church of Hardscrabble—aka, the LGFCCH for short—a formidable, well-meaning group of blue gray–haired widows and almost widows who bake, sew, and sell their wares at holiday bazaars held every month in the Church's Fellowship Room, whether there is a holiday that month or not.

Spitting distance and a driveway apart from the Church stands the Town Hall, which was strategically designed with two staircases, one on either side of the front foyer, so that crowds don't crowd when they go up or down the staircase, as it were. The second floor, you see, is where all large public gatherings are held, such as Town Meeting, Wednesday night bingo, dog obedience class, Friday night contra dances, and Tuesday morning aerobics, which are conducted by Nat Felton, seventy-two, who recently celebrated her fiftieth year as Hardscrabble High's girls' gymnastics coach.

In the foyer of the Town Hall is a glass display case, originally built to house Hardscrabble's crown jewel, the Children's Fishing Derby trophy. The trophy is a rococo concoction of dripping sterling silver crafted when Tiffany & Company was run by Louie himself. It fits, uncannily, as all things and people inevitably do when they've been part of Hardscrabble for a long time.

Ruth Soames, the Town Clerk, has the office by the left-hand staircase. She issued Corey Ford's car registrations and mine, albeit twenty years apart. Next door is the office of Alfred "Scrooge" Geoffrey, Town Tax Collector, who cheerfully relieves us of our taxes every second week in December.

The Selectmen's Office is by the opposite staircase. This is where Hardscrabble's three highest elected officials hold hours Monday, Thursday, and Saturday mornings to orchestrate Town business. Thundering decisions pass across their desks, such as what to charge for dump stickers ($5.00 a year), dog registrations ($2.00 a dog), and passes to the Town Beach on Loon Lake ($3.00 for an individual, $4.75 for a family, good between Memorial Day and Labor Day, guests free). A selectman serves a three-year term. Take Elmer Floyd, for instance. He's serving his eleventh consecutive term. Our selectmen are sort of like Supreme Court judges. Once they've got a foot in office, they're there until they've got a foot in the grave.

The selectmen preside over the annual Town Meeting, which is held the second Tuesday of March. It's the purest and purist's form of democracy. Every voice is heard, and a vote cast is a vote counted. As Aristotle wrote, "Democracy arises out of the notion that those who are equal in any respect are equal in all respects; because men are equally free, they claim to be absolutely equal." All, that is, except Joe Burgess, the dog warden, who caused quite a ruckus when he stood up last Town Meeting and asked for a title. We don't know why he got so full of himself, but Joe maintained that a man in his position should have some Respect, and after a long dissertation, announced that he wanted to be called "Animal Control Officer." When the Moderator opened the floor to discussion, there wasn't any; so, we voted him down, 289 to 1, after which Joe pouted for a week and then got over it.

Goes to show how strongly people feel about the issues. A dog warden is a dog warden, no matter how you say it, and that's important in a town like ours, where we call a spade a spade, and dogs are integral to our lives. It has something to do with a profound necessity of rural living, and that is the need for companionship. This is especially true here, in northern New England, where winters are harsh, miles are wide, and the black, empty nights are long.

For the elderly, the widowed, or the alone, a dog is a companion. For the young, a dog is a playmate, a wet lick, and a warm body to snuggle up to at bedtime. A working dog watches a farmer's flock by night and shepherds it by day. He is a wingshooter's partner in the field. A dog will protect the life of his master without a care for his own. The love of a dog can crack the most hardened heart. Toss a dog a scrap of love, and in return, he'll give you a lifetime of devotion. Sir Walter Scott summed it up when he wrote, "Recollect that the Almighty, who gave the dog to be companion of our pleasures and our toils, hath invested him with a nature noble and incapable of deceit." You can't talk about Hardscrabble without talking about our dogs. That's just how it is.

Now, about our Town Moderator . . . that's Dave Trenton, and his office is next door to the selectmen's. Dave was born and bred in Hardscrabble. He quietly and effectively runs the Town behind the scenes and without ever getting nearly enough credit, but he likes it that way. It's Dave who issues public notices, moderates Town meetings, strings Christmas lights on the bushes around the Town Hall and the Church, too, where he's Head Usher. And it's Dave who lowers the flag to half-mast when America mourns. He does it all . . . with the help of his Jack Russell terrier, Jack.

In the rear of the Town Hall on the first floor, there's a large, bright kitchen that's fitted with commercial appliances. People are always in the kitchen preparing for some gathering or other, such as the Firemen's Lobster Supper (held the second Saturday of Old Home Week), the monthly Community Club dinners (the second Thursday of every month), or Church suppers (every other Friday). Any resident of Hardscrabble can use the Town Hall for wedding and anniversary receptions at no charge, so long as you schedule ahead of time with Marianne Grant, Mert's wife. Marianne not only keeps the Hall spotless, but she keeps the calendar organized, too. Give her a call at Hardscrabble 253, but don't call past eight. She goes to bed early because she gets up at the crack of dawn to open Mert's Grocery by six.

Diagonally across the street from the Town Hall is the Post Office, where Lettie Connor has been postmistress for as long as anyone can remember. She was a young, willing woman when she put all those letters from Hollywood into Corey Ford's box, and an old, set-in-her-ways spinster when she put mail in mine. Always check your mail when you take it out of your postal box. You're apt to find a letter or two that's gone astray. Lettie's not the postmistress she used to be; but then, she's had to have her eyeglass prescription changed twice this year already.

Past the Post Office, Elm Street is lined entirely with quaint white houses that are more modest than the grand ones on Maple Street, but equally charming in their way. Why all the houses in the Village are white is a cherished story that goes back to the Great Depression, when spirits were low and poverty was high. The Weed family, Hardscrabble's landed gentry, purchased buckets of whitewash enough to refresh all the houses in the Village—and brighten townsfolks' spirits, besides. As a tribute to a good deed done in dire times, Hardscrabble remains a cheerful white to this day.

Our Valley

Hardscrabble is cradled in a wooded valley thick with pines, studded with crystal-clear lakes, bisected by rushing rivers, and surrounded by the rolling hills and majestic mountains of the northern Appalachian Range. Once a volcanic crater, these hills are stepmaidens to the great Mount Washington, which towers over the Eastern Seaboard, yet it is only spitting distance from our Town. The gentle slopes that embrace Hardscrabble are dotted with homesteads that were built by the first loggers and early subsistence farmers. Logging put Hardscrabble on the map.

Back in the days when the territory that is now New Hampshire was a royal province, the giant pines grew straight and mighty. They were felled, dragged many miles south to Portsmouth, and used for shipbuilding in the name of England and King George III. The shortest distance between two points is indeed a straight line, which is why the logging trails of Colonial times ultimately became state turnpikes. In those early days, the forests were called the King's Wood. In token to those distant times, there are places in these parts that are called King Pine and Kingswood. New

England's forests helped build America. Today, a few patriarchal pines and olden oaks remain. You can only wonder what history they have witnessed down through the ages.

New England was cultivated by a heartier breed of men than, I daresay, we know today: men who physically dared to challenge the harsh winters and unforgiving springs and broke their backs clearing away rocks and boulders to coax the barren, unyielding soil to seed. They are long gone, these courageous, steadfast souls, and with them their fields. The forests have since regained their glory, the lofty pines and noble maples are Nature's mantle. The loggers who felled the trees with ax and handsaw, and the farmers who tilled the soil with ox and plow, cultivated the Yankee lineage.

The sacrifices they made were the price of their dreams—and the dreams they realized, our legacy.

The Founding of Hardscrabble

The founding of Hardscrabble can be traced without documentation to the year 1630, when a Scotsman named Orlando Weed sailed with Sir Richard Saltonhull to *Mass-ad-chu-set* (Abinaquis for "near the green mountains") with a dog of "hevy cote, longe legge, intelijent temperment, keen to hunt wilde fowl." Shortly after he disembarked, Weed set out to cut the first cart path north through the wilderness, his sole companion being his "intelijent" and faithful dog.

No one knows quite why Weed chose to venture north into the wilderness, since Massachusetts was then wilderness, too. But venture he did, heedless of the fact that he was trespassing through perilous Iroquois territory. So savage and vengeful were the Iroquois that a Jesuit priest named Father Ragueneau called them the "Romans of the West," and in his classic and virtually forgotten work, *Révélations des Hurons*, wrote: "My pen has no ink black enough to paint the fury of the Iroquois." The fury of the Iroquois surely would have descended upon Weed during his long and arduous trek had it not been for the great good luck that would insulate him from harm throughout his entire life. And so, Orlando Weed passed through Iroquois territory oblivious to and unscathed by danger.

His journey came to an end when he encountered two of the most formidable adversaries of all—Mother Nature and Father Winter—during a season of such extreme severity that the snow lay six foot on a level. Unable to cross the raging Ossipee River, he claimed this beautiful place as his own and was content to remain here until his dying day. It was during his first spring, as he struggled to till the rock-laden soil, that Orlando was inspired to name his holding Harde Scrabble, or "difficult struggle." Two centuries later, on June 18, 1832, the community that sprang up around his farm became the Incorporated Town of Hardscrabble.

Anticipating that others would follow after he staked his claim, Orlando Weed built a footbridge that spanned the Ossipee River. Being a resolute and practical man, he charged a toll to every traveler who wished to cross. Weed christened it the Huntress Bridge, probably after his beloved hunting dog. Soon, out of necessity, he was able to build a bigger bridge. The cart path he cut by hand with a scythe and the bridge he built with the sweat of his brow was now the main thoroughfare between Boston and the White Mountains and beyond, to the Northern Territory. His resourcefulness made him a very wealthy man. He married three times, became a widower twice, and was survived by a wife seven decades his junior who, three months after her husband's death at the exalted age of eighty-nine, was delivered of a healthy baby boy, Weed's twenty-third child.

Orlando Weed was indisputably the father of Hardscrabble.

Townsfolk

Hardscrabble has a permanent population of 623. About half live in the Village, and the other half are scattered over an area of approximately fifty square miles. This number has hardly fluctuated since the Depression, when virtually all the textile mills shut down and people migrated to the cities in search of work. In its heyday, before Alexander Graham Bell made the world smaller and Edison lit up the night sky, there were over 6,000 people living in and around Hardscrabble.

I got lost once in the woods and came upon a cabin. It was abandoned but eerily intact, as though the family just stepped out on an errand. Homemade preserves in dusty Mason jars lined the shelves of a cupboard whose door hung by one brittle hinge. A squirrel was curled up in eternal sleep on a mildewed mattress that slouched on a rusted metal frame. Tucked politely around the kitchen table were four wooden chairs. Three place settings awaited a meal that never was served. A withered copy of *Time* magazine lay open to ashen pictures of Pearl Harbor. A few of the old-timers up in the hills remember a family named Blake or Drake, but no one knows what happened to them, and they never returned to tell.

These are the forgotten places, like Tinkhamtown. Tinkhamtown was a thriving community before the Civil War summoned and slaughtered so many men and boys. Then came the plague. And then there was no Tinkhamtown at all. Cellar holes overrun by juniper bushes and alders are reminders that once a village was alive and there. Yet Hardscrabble nonetheless endures, propelled by the human spirit, protected by the mercy of Nature, and nourished by faith in—and the grace of—God.

And there's a reason for this.

You see, Hardscrabble isn't a town. The Lower Forty isn't a forty-acre field. It's a chance—a chance to discover Who you are.

Hardscrabble is catching your breath over a soft summer sunset or catching the first trout on opening day of the season.

It's smiling into the eyes of a child and catching your reflection in their sparkle. Or having blueberry pie hot from the oven with a dollop of ice cream melting on top.

It's walking down an unremembered road to a forgotten place called Tinkhamtown with your dog at your heels and the scent of rotting apples sweetening the crisp autumn air, while rustling leaves whisper their secrets in your ear and the wind runs its fingers through your hair. Hardscrabble is a chance to take a risk and live and love beyond the limit, no matter what.

That's what Corey Ford really wrote about, and I'm picking up where he left off, that's all.

◈ ONE ◈

Coming Home

The only thing that one really knows about human nature is that it changes. Change is the one quality we can predicate on it.

— *Oscar Wilde*

I came to live in Hardscrabble when I was seven months pregnant with my first child. My husband and I both were city born and suburbia bred, and probably would have lived out our days on Long Island had Kip not inherited a sprawling, gently deteriorating farmhouse in northern New England where he had spent magical childhood summers. He was determined to recapture that magic for our children and raise them in the country. I was for it. We would live the tranquil life. We would fix up the farm and make it into a home. We would live happily ever after.

At least, that was the plan.

And so, long before country living was fashionable and rustic was chic, I came to Hardscrabble, where I would embark upon a life that was the antithesis of everything I had ever known or imagined, and would change the very nature of who I was, right down to the core. There was something romantically appealing, I thought, about sailing off in our Toyota Land Cruiser to some faraway and unfamiliar place. There was something Cary Grant and Myrna Loy in *Mr. Blandings Builds His Dream House* about restoring an old New England farmhouse and filling it with antiques and family and friends. In my mind's eye, I envisioned a rambling place with big bay windows, just like the ones in another cherished movie, *Holiday Inn*. Snowflakes would be falling gently from the sky, settling on towering treetops, covering the ground with a wintry blanket; and inside, dancing flames crackling in the hearth would reflect off the windowpanes and cast a golden glow upon frosted snow that glistened like pavé diamonds. A dozen Windsor chairs would surround a long Parsons table in a candlelit, wood-paneled dining room brimming with good, wholesome talk of growing children and much-loved dogs, fly-fishing, hand-made beers, and good books, seldom politics. There would be antique highboys and lowboys, and tall four-posters with a podium of steps to climb to get in and out of bed. The sheets would be Egyptian cotton, heavy on the starch. The aroma of cinnamon and hot apple pie would waft through the happy house, and there would be music, always music: Tina Turner and B.B. King, mostly Eric Clapton and, perhaps, on a gray November day, a Verdi opera or a Beethoven symphony. It was so delectable, so Currier & Ives, so imaginably tangible that if I strained my ears, I could almost hear Bing Crosby crooning "White Christmas."

Certain my friends would be envious of such idyllic prospects, I decided to feign casualness over my great, good, imminent fortune and said, "By the way, we're moving to the country."

They were utterly incredulous.

Had I said, "By the way, we're moving to Siberia," the reaction would have been the same. To them, the country was a three-day weekend and two-hour drive to a wayside

inn specializing in fine dining, as featured in *Architectural Digest*. It was a day trip to a calendar-quaint roadside stand, where you bought a bushel of apples, a pumpkin, a quart of maple syrup, and a bunch of Indian corn to hang on the front door, thus proclaiming to the neighbors that you had been to The Country.

My parents, on the other hand, took the news in an entirely different manner. They gave it some thought between cocktails and dinner, and at dessert announced that I was disowned.

Kip and I sold or gave away all of our furniture, packed our car with the remainder of our worldly goods, and with our black Lab, Bess, set forth on our highway voyage north on I-95 to Hardscrabble—and a new life.

We knew we were in store for a change. We just didn't realize that Change had plenty in store for us. It was the end of a chapter.

And the beginning of my story.

TWO

Nothing That a Few Nails
and a Bulldozer Wouldn't Fix

For a man's house is his castle, et domus sua cuique tutissimum refugium.

—*Sir Edward Coke*

In the summer of 1898, the Carroll County Court House burned to the ground along with all its records. Among these was the original deed to our property. We knew the house was around a century old, but we didn't know exactly how old until shortly after we moved in. A painting came crashing to the floor when the rusted wire on which it hung gave up the ghost. It was the first of a veritable myriad of things that would give up the ghost and come crashing, breaking, bursting, or falling in. Wedged behind the painting was a document that shed some serious light on our antique, antiquated house. It was a surprisingly crisp sheet of paper headed "Abstract of Title," stating that Edson W. and Jennie B. Tyler appeared on June 28, 1882, before George I. Philbrick, Justice of the Peace, and two witnesses in order to engage in a legal covenant regarding:

> *A certain spring of water, on the North side of the road leading
> from Hardscrabble Village to Daniel's Corner, so called,
> together with the privilege to construct and lay an aqueduct
> across my land, under ground, to convey the water from said
> spring to said Joseph S. Mills buildings, together with the priv-
> ilege of entering and repairing said aqueduct whenever repair-
> ing is necessary, said spring of water is the same that said
> Joseph S. Mills and Wid. Joseph L. Mills now draw the water
> from by their aqueduct pipe, said Mills to pay all reasonable
> damages done by repairing said aqueduct to said land. By
> reserving a chance to water my cattle and other stock out of
> said Spring, or my assigns the same right.*

This seemed to suggest that the Tylers had been long
established here. (In fact, years later, during construction on
the house, an earlier foundation was exposed, indicating a
structure existed on this very spot prior to 1800.) But we
didn't need an Abstract of Title to tell us that Hazelcrest—
for that was and is the name of our house—had been
around a very long time.

Ah, the Simple Joys of Country Living

"That house of yours is built like a brick shithouse,"
Frank Moulton, the local contractor, assured us. But whenever a nor'easter blew, gusts would pound the shingles,
break through the walls, and send the kitchen curtains flapping like the wings of an agitated duck. Once a breeze
coursed through the kitchen and blew out the pilot light
while I was basting a chicken in the oven. But it really
became clear that we had serious problems when, after one
blustery night, we woke up to find the front door on the
front lawn. This motivated us to embark upon a regimen of

preventative maintenance in anticipation of Any and Everything, come what may. We bought stainless steel buckets to catch the rain when it poured through the roof. We tacked plastic over the drafty windows to forestall the inevitability of replacing scores of windowpanes. We caulked, sealed, sanded, and patched. We rifled through barn sales for kerosene lamps and handmade quilts which, at the time—and this will knock your socks off—were commonplace, cheap, and useful because whenever it rained, or snowed, or the wind gusted to more than two miles an hour, the power invariably went out.

Christmas Eve found us huddled under a couple of those quilts by the light of the kerosene lamps as we sat in the kitchen next to the big, black vintage wood cookstove that was surely burning when Sherman was doing likewise to Atlanta. We had been feeding the pitiful, fluttering blue flames with torn packing cartons in a futile attempt to coax the wood to catch.

"What do you think our families are doing right now?" I asked Kip, as I stretched the quilt over my baby-swollen tummy.

"Sitting down to a hot, delicious supper," Kip muttered.

Our own plans for a merry little Christmas had, quite literally, been thrown to the wind. An early winter blizzard had swept in that morning and wiped out the power and phones. We couldn't cook, couldn't keep the house warm, and couldn't even boil water for a cup of tea. Our car was buried under Himalayan snowdrifts. If a plow had come through, its path was long since covered. We had been without electricity for ten hours, and the household thermostat was hovering around the forty-degree mark. There was no telling how much longer we would be powerless since there was no way of finding out. With no telephones and no neighbors, we were as isolated as Robinson Crusoe, only our island was snow, not sand, and our trees were pines, not palms.

This was our first encounter with a New England snowstorm. The reality far outweighs the perception, and there's no describing the sheer magnitude of a real nor'easter. The wind howls in B-flat. The snow swirls like miniature tornadoes and pummels the ground. It is relentless, it is raging, it is Mother Nature with PMS.

Our first order of business after moving in was to buy firewood. "Cordwood—cut—seasoned—delivered," proclaimed a painted shingle hammered to a big oak tree in front of the house of our nearest neighbor, a half mile down the road. But when we mentioned this to Frank Moulton, he warned us that our neighbor was Ken Tibbetts, a native of Hardscrabble and "no-good crook" who charged top dollar.

"Your best bet," Frank said, "is to check the *Gazette*. You can get a mighty good deal in the classifieds."

So we checked the classified ads in the *Hardscrabble Gazette* and found, "Wood, $35.00 a cord, delivered."

"Why, that's half the price that Frank said Ken Tibbetts charges!" I exclaimed. Of course, we didn't know the wood was green and would be perfectly seasoned . . . in time for next winter.

And so, there we were: alone, cold, and without family, friends, or dinner on Christmas Eve.

A Stranger Appears

Bess had managed to crawl under the woodstove and curl up into a ball. "How about a bone, Bessie?" I asked, reaching for a tin of dog biscuits. The clever girl didn't budge an inch, but she did arch an eyebrow as if to say, "If you think I'm going to move from the only place in the house where there's heat, then think again."

"Speaking of dog biscuits," Kip said, "is there anything to eat that doesn't need cooking?"

"Well, we could toast marshmallows over the kerosene lamp," I suggested.

"No, we can't," Kip replied. "They'll taste like kerosene."

"There's peanut butter and jelly," I said, "but there isn't any bread."

"No bread?"

"I was going to bake bread, but then the power went out," I said.

"You don't know how to bake bread," Kip quite astutely pointed out.

"I know," I replied defensively, "but people who live in the country bake bread."

"I'm sure they do, but they also go to the grocery store and buy it." Suddenly there was a terrifying explosion.

"What's that!" I shrieked. We didn't have to wait long for the answer. A blast of water flung open the swinging door that led to the living room and came crashing into the kitchen. The house had grown so cold that the water in the pipes had frozen and the radiators had burst.

"Do something!" I cried.

"What the hell am I supposed to do?" Kip hollered, as he flung open the basement door and ran downstairs. "There's got to be some way to shut off the pipes!" Meanwhile, the water was rising, and soon I found myself standing in a shallow pool.

"Call the fire department!" Kip yelled from downstairs.

"I can't call the fire department!" I cried.

"Then call Frank Moulton!"

"I can't call Frank," I screamed. "I can't call anyone! The phones are dead, remember?"

Bess began to bark. I turned to calm her and caught my breath. I was facing a stranger and a large German shepherd.

"Hope we didn't startle you, m'am," the man said, rubbing my so-called watchdog between her ears. He was unremarkable in appearance: average build, average height, looked to be on the leeward side of sixty, and dressed in traditional, seasonal Yankee finery: a red lumberjack plaid hunting coat and green boiled-wool bib overalls. His eyes, though, *were* remarkable. They were warm and laughing, with tiny lines that pinched and crinkled the corners and ran down the sides of his weathered face to meet his cold-blushed cheeks. The German shepherd, somewhat jealous of the attention Bess was getting, nudged his muzzle into his master's palm. This put Bess's hackles up. The stranger soothed both dogs with a few caressing words, then returned his attention to me.

"I tried knocking, but I guess no one heard me. Sorry to intrude," the stranger said, politely removing a shapeless felt hat from his head and stuffing it in his jacket pocket, "but I was just driving by and noticed a stream of water flowing down your driveway. Know you're new to Hardscrabble and thought you might need a hand."

"Oh, thank you, thank you," I wept. "My husband's down in the basement. The pipes burst, and we don't know how to turn off the water . . . and it's Christmas Eve . . . and . . . and *I'm going to have a baby. . . .*"

"Right now⸮" the stranger asked, alarmed.

"No, not *now*. Next *month,"* I wept.

He was perceptibly relieved. "I think I can help you. I used to know this old house pretty well. My grandparents lived here a long time ago—folks by the name of Tyler."

"Tyler⸮" I said, recognizing the names in the old Title.

"*Ay-yuh.* Ed and Jennie Tyler. But they've been gone, lemme see, near on fifty years." He pointed his flashlight at the cellar door and followed the beam downstairs. Both dogs trailed at his heels. Within moments, the water had stopped gushing and began to recede through the swollen floorboards.

"We don't know how to thank you," Kip said over his shoulder as he and the stranger came up from the basement. "I just couldn't figure out all those knobs and cranks down there."

"Not surprising in a house like this," the stranger replied. "These old farmhouses were built before plumbing. And when plumbing was added, there was no such thing as insulation. That's why you've got all them shut-off valves. When it got cold, folks simply shut down the plumbing. *Ah-yuh.* That's how it worked."

"Seems that's how it still works," Kip replied, offering his hand to the stranger. "I don't believe I caught your name.

"Mine's Kip, and this is my wife, Laurie."

"No, I don't suppose we had a chance to introduce ourselves in all the ruckus. "My name's Ken Tibbetts. I'm your neighbor just down the road apiece. And this here is my dog, Prince. . . . Prince?"

Prince was nowhere in sight. And for that matter, neither was Bess.

"They must still be down in the basement," Kip said.

"I'll go down after them," our neighbor offered.

"Ken Tibbetts!" I whispered to my husband.

"Yeah," Kip whispered back, "who would have thought."

Ken Tibbetts came up from the basement with both dogs in tow. "These two dogs were getting along awfully well downstairs," he said. "Prince is a real Casanova, but he can't do much about it anymore, just in case you have worries about your little gal getting in the family way."

"I've heard about you, Mr. Tibbetts," Kip said. You sell firewood. . . ."

"Call me Ken," he replied. "Wal, yes . . . wood in the fall, painting and roofing in the spring and summer, and plowing in the winter. Who told you about me?"

"Oh . . ." I hesitated, "Frank Moulton."

"Frankie, eh? Doubt he had anything good to say about me," Ken sniggered. "After all, he's my brother-in-law."

"Well you know," Kip broke in uneasily, "we've been meaning to call you. But what with moving in and all, we just didn't get around to . . . uh . . . ordering some wood."

"That's mighty green wood you're burning," Ken said, eyeing the black smoke that was oozing out of the seams of the woodstove. "Smells like poplar. How much of this you got?" He glanced at the stack piled high in the woodbin alongside the stove. "Don't look like this wood will dry before next winter, and even then, it won't be much good."

"Why not?" Kip asked, surprised.

"Like I said, this here is poplar. Poplar burns poorly, and

besides, it gives off a sickly sweet kind of smell. Can't you smell it?"

"I was wondering what that was," Kip grunted.

"I *was* feeling a little sick, but I thought it was the baby," I moaned.

"Nope. It's poplar, all right. Most people would pay you to haul off poplar," Ken's eyes smiled. "There are a few scoundrels hereabouts who advertise in the *Gazette* that they sell firewood cheap. Then these flatlanders, they come up from the city and think they're getting some sort of deal. But they find out sooner or later that it's poplar when they try to burn it!" Ken gave Kip a Meaningful Look. "Hope you don't happen to got too much of this here poplar, Kip."

"Oh, no," Kip choked, skirting the truth like a hare being pursued by a hound. "Ken, I think we're going to need about . . . four cords."

Ken paused a moment. "Four cord, eh?" he replied pensively. "Wal, this is the end of season for me, folks. May not be quite four cord left, but I think I can muster up enough wood to get you through the winter. Good stuff, too. You can practically light it with a match, it's that nicely seasoned."

"How much are you charging, Ken?" Kip asked with feigned nonchalance.

"Wal, it's going to be forty dollars a cord, I'm afraid. But like I said, it's first-quality firewood."

Forty dollars! Ken Tibbet's price was only five dollars more than that green, useless poplar!

"How soon do you think we can get it?" Kip asked with an urgency that betrayed a desire to be warm and fed.

"Wal . . ." Ken muttered, stroking the stubble on his chin. "Let me see. It's Christmas Eve. . . . Tomorrow's Christmas Day. . . . That's a mighty big storm we're having, and it don't look like it's about to go away anytime soon. It'll take some shoveling to get at my woodshed . . . but I reckon I can get you a half cord or so in about an hour. And I can deliver the rest in the morning."

"An *hour!*" Kip and I cried in unison.

"Wal, I'll be as quick as I can. Besides," he grinned, "the little woman here has to keep warm for two."

"Ken," Kip said as our neighbor turned to go. "Let me help you get that wood."

"No, not a problem, Kip. Prince and I are a pretty good team. We got loading wood down to a regular science."

Sure enough, Ken came back in less than an hour with the wood—and a quart of his homebrew beer, besides. In no time flat, the house was warm and dry. An hour after that, the three of us sat down to a hot dinner that I cooked on the woodstove by the light of the kerosene lamps. Just as we were getting started, the old pendulum clock on the kitchen wall struck midnight. It was Christmas Day. At that precise moment, the power came back on. Kip got up from the table and turned off the lights.

"This," he said, in the warm glow of the oil lamps, "is how it was meant to be."

Later that night—closer, actually, to dawn—Kip and I finally crawled into bed. As I drifted between awake and asleep on that holiest of holy nights, it struck me that we hadn't moved to the country. We had come home.

And that was how it was meant to be.

THREE

The New Town Reporter

When a dog bites a man, that is not news, because it happens so often. But if a man bites a dog, that is news.

—*John B. Bogart*

Clem Lovell fed me some advice once that stuck to my ribs like oatmeal.

"Laurie," he said, dragging pensively on an unfiltered Camel, "if there's one piece of advice I can give you, it's this: Nothing remains the same except change."

I was struck as forcefully by his wisdom as if he'd hit me between the eyes with a two-by-four. Plenty about my life had changed in the four short months since I had moved to Hardscrabble, all of which was overshadowed by the wonderment of becoming a mother for the first time. Several lifetimes have passed since Clem imparted this confidence to me. My baby now has a baby of his own. And as the years folded one over the next, I know now that Clem said nothing new or original. He was merely stating a basic principle expressed by ancient Greek philosophers, the Bible, by poets such as Shelley and Swinburne, and in the stories of Hemingway or anyone, for that matter, who ever explored the human spirit through words. After all, change is a prescript of human nature: The very act of being human compels change. But I am content even still to attribute this philosophy to Clem for my own purposes and a whole parcel of reasons. In the dark nights, these are some of the words I hold close when I need to grasp onto something solid.

Clem shared this wisdom with me shortly after I had taken over Doris Almy's job as Town columnist of the *Hardscrabble Gazette*. Doris was an impossible act to follow. She was a short, plump, jolly woman with a pompadour of silk-spun, Sedona-red hair dyed to match her Pomeranian, Little Doris. Age and eras were no deterrent to Doris, who at seventy-something still wore overly arched, drawn-in eyebrows à la Marlene Dietrich, and a smear of screen siren–red lipstick generously and somewhat unevenly applied beyond the natural outline of her thin lips. She dressed like a dowager duchess and conducted herself like one, too, holding court at every Church social, tea party, coffee klatch, bridge party, community gathering, public meeting, funeral, and wedding during her reign as Queen of Gossip. Her collection of hats rivaled that of another queen, the Queen Mother of England, and likewise she never left her house without a pair of gloves: white cotton between Easter and Labor Day, white kid between Labor Day and Easter. Doris's shoes matched her handbag, her lipstick matched her nails, and had the makers of Barbie desired a geriatric version complete with wardrobe and accessories, Doris Almy would undoubtedly have been the inspiration.

For twenty-five years, Doris ended her weekly column with the now immortal line, "A good time was had by all," which gave Hardscrabble the same comforting assurance that Walter Cronkite bestowed upon America with his *CBS Nightly News* sign-off, "And that's the way it is." One particularly immortal Doris Almy column is tacked in a place of prominence on the bulletin board in the office of the *Hardscrabble Gazette*. The last paragraph reads:

After the conclusion of the funeral, we all paid our last respects to the Deceased, who even in Death looked ravishing against the white satin lining in that pink chiffon dress that I always so admired, God rest her soul. Then Reverend Davidson invited everyone to join the family in the Fellowship Room in fellowship and cucumber sandwiches that were particularly delicious. Thank you, Ladies' Guild, for such a delicious reception as usual. I am sure we will all miss dear Kathryn Portnoy now that she has finally gone. A good time was had by all.

"That's classic Doris," chucked Judge Parker, county magistrate, consummate sportsman, and sole stockholder and editor-in-chief of the *Hardscrabble Gazette*. "I never changed a word she wrote. She was a peacock in a barnyard full of hens, was our Doris."

The theoretical rooster in Doris's barnyard was her forbearing husband, Hank Almy. Hank had long since moved out of their conjugal bedroom for the peaceful tranquillity of the guest bedroom on the opposite side of the house, where he sought respite in mysteries by Agatha Christie and whiskey by Jack Daniel's. One day, Hank woke up dead. At the funeral, Doris rose dramatically from her place in the first pew just as Reverend Davidson was about to impart the Benediction. The merry widow faced the packed House of God, flung her black feather boa around her neck, dabbed at a dry tear with a white Belgian lace handkerchief, clutched Little Doris to her mountainous bosom, and dramatically announced that she, too, was leaving on an eternal journey—about two hours downstate, where she was going to live with her son and his family. For the first time in the course of the funeral, there was sobbing and a cloud of grief descended upon the assembled mourners. Whoever would take Doris's place? Whoever *could?*

That is when Fate pointed its twisted finger at me.

We Meet Doris Almy

"Look at this," I said to Kip, pointing to an ad in the *Hardscrabble Gazette*. "Here's something I could do." He took the paper from my outstretched hand.

" 'Wanted: Town columnist. No prior experience necessary. $15 a week. Contact Editor.' You could do that with your eyes closed," my husband replied. "And an extra sixty bucks a month wouldn't hurt the family coffers."

"I can't see that it would take up too much time. I mean, how much can go on in a small town like this?"

I would soon find out.

*E*very first Sunday of the month, the Ladies' Guild hosts a coffee after service. This usually doubles as an occasion for the Church family to welcome visitors and, in infrequent instances, new neighbors—like us. Kip and I had received a call from Fran Forsythe, the president of the Ladies' Guild. "Do come to church on Sunday," she invited warmly. "We didn't want to bother you earlier, what with the baby on the way. But now that he's arrived, we'd love to welcome you into the Church family. There will be a coffee afterwards. Please join us." It was the end of February, and Tommy was barely a month old. We wrapped him up in an alpaca-lined bunting that had been mine when I was born, and drove through the plowed aisle of snow that covered the road to Church. We were singled out from the congregation during announcements and introduced by Reverend Davidson. After the service, we attended the coffee in the Fellowship Room, where quite a pleasant fuss was made over the baby.

Kip and I had read Doris's column with amusement from the moment we moved to Hardscrabble, and between giggles, we speculated on what she looked like. However, we weren't prepared for the whirlwind in pistachio green that pushed her way through the Fellowship Room to meet us.

"I'm Doris Almy," she announced in a way that implied she needed no further introduction. A spherical ball of fluff poked its shiny black nose out from under Doris's frontal precipice. "And this is Little Doris." She snuggled the Pomeranian against her cheek. "Say 'how dee-do,' Daw-ree," her mistress cooed like Betty Boop. Daw-ree gave a high-pitched yap that exposed tiny, surprisingly pointed teeth. The little dog was wearing a pistachio green coat designed to match her mistress's, down to the buttons and white rabbit fur collar. We exchanged the usual pleasantries before Doris dismissed us and moved on to work the crowd.

*   *   *

*T*he following week's edition of the *Hardscrabble Gazette* showed how smooth the seasoned Town columnist was at her craft. A paragraph about us read like this:

> *It is always delightful when people move to Town who are young people like Mr. and Mrs. Kip and Laurie Morrow, who have the old Tyler place which Kip inherited from his grandparents who, as we all know, bought it from Myra and Colby in 1957, though many of us didn't know Kip's grandparents, who were summer folk, as well as we would have liked to. They are new parents of a brand-new baby infant! A little boy! The young family attended the church coffee hostessed by the Ladies' Guild. Thank you, Ladies' Guild, for a delicious coffee as usual. Linnie Miles, shame on you! Your crumb coffee cake just ruined our diet! A good time was had by all.*

"I'm sure I could do as good a job as Doris Almy," I said to my husband, after reading the column out loud.

"If you can't write better than that blindfolded, then you're in trouble," he chuckled.

"It couldn't take a whole lot of time."

I couldn't be a whole lot more wrong.

Easier Said Than Done

A week later, Judge Parker called to say I had gotten the job. I was pleased until he mentioned that I was the only applicant. "You have to attend a couple of meetings and functions each week and write about them," he explained on the telephone. Mention a few names and report what went on—nothing complicated about that. Just don't be surprised if it takes the Town a little while to get used to you. Remember that Doris was a fixture in this newspaper for a quarter century. When someone takes up a little of your time every week for a long time—even if it's just reading a column—then a personal attachment forms. Doris was tied to a lot of townsfolk, so be patient. It will take time to untie that knot."

A new mother nursing her baby takes up twenty-five out of twenty-four hours a day, so I had to carefully schedule the times I could go out. No matter how hard I tried, I never managed to be where I should be, when I was supposed to. My debut as Hardscrabble's Town columnist was at the February meeting of the Hardscrabble Literary Society, but I got there late and missed Professor Markham's lecture. Then I missed the Planning Board meeting to discuss whether the dirt road that led to the Town Dump should be paved. And I skipped the First Grade play when I found out that chicken pox was going around at school and my mother couldn't remember whether I had had them or not. Plenty had been going on in Town, but I hadn't been there to cover it, so I put together my first column the best I could:

> *The monthly meeting of the Hardscrabble Literary Society was very well attended. Members hung on every word of Professor Markham's dissertation entitled, "The Impact of Chaucer in His Day on the Proletariat of Canterbury." The Professor's famous mulled brandy punch took away the chill of the February air, members said. The First Grade play was a great success despite the fact that half the cast was home with chicken pox. The Planning Board voted unanimously not to pave the Dump Road. The Farmer's Almanac says there will be above-average snowfall in the month of March.*

"No one wants to read about snow or chicken pox," Judge Parker reproached. "You infer that the members of the Literary Society are a bunch of lushes, which they are, and school was canceled yesterday because parents got frightened that there was a raging epidemic. The Planning Board has its nose out of joint because you gave lip service to a four-hour meeting. "Snow? Why did you write about snow? That's what it does in February. We don't have to tell our readers. All they have to do is look out the window."

I took the Judge's criticism bravely, left his office with a promise to do better next time, and quite literally ran into Clem Lovell, who at that fortuitous moment was walking his beagle, Stan, past the *Gazette* building.

"Good mawning, Laurie," he said in his jolly, cigarette-rasped, Yankee drawl.

I flung my arms around his grandfatherly shoulders and sobbed.

Clem said, "Now, now." This would become our standard salutation over the course of the years of friendship that followed.

"Clem, the Judge didn't like my first column."

"Why?" Clem asked.

"Because . . . I wrote about . . . snow and chicken pox."

"Snow? That's sort of like bringing coals to Newcastle, isn't it. And chicken pox, eh?"

"I don't know anything about Newcastle," I wailed, wiping my nose on the back of my mitten, "but I do know I shouldn't have taken this job."

Stan pawed at my leg in canine sympathy. Clem took out a pack of unfiltered Camels, gingerly selected one, and tapped the tip on the back of his hand. He lit the cigarette, took a long draw, and imparted to me the second most valuable piece of advice I have ever received. "Laurie," he said, dragging on the Camel, "if there's one piece of advice I can tell you, it's this: Grow a thick skin."

"What do you mean?" I asked, bewildered.

"I mean, be like a duck."

"A duck?"

"You know, let water run off your back just like a duck's. Don't let little things get to you."

"You mean, don't sweat?"

Clem paused and took another draw. "No, you don't have to perspire. Just don't trouble over things that really don't matter."

Clem did it again. Here was another piece of wisdom that would stay with me through the years, and to this very day, it is an objective I still aspire to achieve.

*T*he following week, I arrived at the offices of the *Hardscrabble Gazette* full of exhilaration and proudly handed my second column to Judge Parker.

"Laurie," he said, tilting backward in his chair and putting his feet on the desk. "We can't print this."

"What?" I exclaimed. I had dedicated my entire week in pursuit of the social life of Hardscrabble at great expense to my family, laundry, housecleaning, and freelance writing career. Certainly I had written a column that even Doris Almy would have been proud!

"Judge, I went to Mrs. Forsythe's tea party and Mrs. Hawke's tea party, I even wore a hat—well, a woolen scarf—and I made sure I mentioned the name of each and every woman that attended each tea party!"

"That's the problem," the Judge said, tamping a wad of tobacco from the bowl of his pipe. "You could have gotten yourself—and, I might add, this newspaper—into a potentially volatile political situation." The Judge looked at me with genuine pity. "It's really not your fault, Laurie. You haven't lived in Town long enough to know our ways. Here's the lay of the land: Fran Forsythe and Peletiah Hawke are first cousins by marriage. About five years ago, Fran's mother's sister—who at the same time was Pellie's mother-in-law's sister—passed after a long illness. She had no children and died a very wealthy woman. Frannie was her favorite, but in the end, it happened that Pellie was at her side when she slipped away." Judge Parker struck a match, lit his pipe, drew a few puffs, and continued in a tone that suggested handing down judgments from the bench. "Now, Pellie maintains that just before she died, Elsa gave her the diamond ring—big as an acorn—that she always wore and was wearing right to the end. Frannie knew that the ring was meant for her and claims Pellie slipped it off the deceased's finger before the body was cold. But there was no proving that, and nothing was down on paper, so even I couldn't intercede in my capacity as an instrument of the law. Pellie refused to give the ring to Frannie, and neither one has spoken to the other ever since."

"But they live next door to one another!" I pointed out in amazement.

"That's right, they do. And they belong to all the same clubs, their husbands play golf together every Saturday morning, and their children are best friends. Fran and Pellie just don't speak to one another, that's all."

"What has this got to do with my column?" I asked, still unable to make sense of why I was potentially a sociopolitical incendiary.

"It means that if we published who was at which party, then it's likely our door will be knocked down by a gaggle of hysterical women. You see, the ladies of Hardscrabble don't like anyone to know whose side they're on. This way they can change sides whenever they change their minds."

"I don't understand. . . ."

"You will, in time. Look," the Judge continued. "I know you can write. You just can't write like Doris, and frankly, she couldn't write at all. But she was a first-class gossip." He grew quiet for a moment. "Tell you what we'll do," he said.

"I'll get my wife to fill you in on what's going on in Town—she's always on top of things—and you write them down. That's how we worked it out when Corey Ford wrote the Town column, before Doris came on the scene. The happenings in and around Town then became the inspiration for his "Lower Forty" columns in *Field & Stream*, and the rest is pretty much history. No reason you couldn't write stories, like he did."

"Do you really think I could?"

"Sure. You'll find there's plenty to write about here in Hardscrabble. Stay to the facts, and you'll see that the stories will write themselves. Yep, that's what Corey did. And he was a lousy Town columnist, too."

And that, dear Reader, is how *The Hardscrabble Chronicles* came about.

~☙ FOUR ☙~

The Special Town Meeting

Democracy means simply the bludgeoning of the people by the people for the people.
—Oscar Fingal O'Flahertie Wills Wilde

That welcome lull after the holidays was sorely interrupted when the selectmen called a Special Town Meeting for January 23rd in response to a petition that had been filed by a group of residents who had recently moved to Hardscrabble from out of state. They were new to the peculiarities of country living and wanted road signs posted, a luxury the town had never seen fit to afford. Townsfolk couldn't make head or tail of the fuss. After all, they knew the byways and back roads in and around Hardscrabble without markers telling them where they were.

"Dang flatlanders," cursed Melvin Snead of Snead's Automotive, "want to change everything."

"Road signs! Such a blemish to the Village," moaned Mab Markham, as she poured afternoon tea for herself and her husband, Professor Charles Markham, who was seized by a quote from Chaucer.

"'O wynd, o wynd, the weder gynneth clere,'" Charles recited as he savored a cucumber sandwich.

However, it was Orion Brooks, a native son of Hardscrabble and one of our most colorful residents, who voiced the opinion of the general consensus when, in his distinctive Down East drawl, he mumbled, "I'm agin' it."

Mike Zalinski Has Had It

It all began last August. Mike Zalinski, a newcomer from Massachusetts, went up to Officer Oak as he was coming out of Tilt's Store with his yellow Lab, Tess, his ever-present companion.

"Explain to me this, Officer Oak," Mike Zalinski confronted Hardscrabble's sole emissary of law and order. "How does a stranger who's coming to Town know which is Maple Street and which is Elm?"

"Wal," Officer Oak reflected, drawing deeply on an unfiltered Camel. "Maple Street is lined with maples, and Elm Street used to be lined with elms, but they got the Dutch elm disease and were cut down."

"But there are maples trees on Elm Street, too," Mike Zalinski argued.

"Ah-yuh," Officer Oak observed, taking another draw on his cigarette. "So there are."

Thus, one of the great disputes in the history of Hardscrabble took root.

*M*atters only got worse when Mike Zalinski went to the Post Office and asked Lettie Connor, the Postmistress, for the legal mailing address of his new home on Elm Street.

"Oh, yes," the septuagenarian spinster said. "Yours is the old Harmond house, isn't it? Let me see. . . . As I recall, it was built by Zebulon Harmond in 1862, then his son, Dulton, inherited it, but he died in Panama and left it to his son, Al Harmond, who sold it to you before he moved into the County Home. . . ." The old lady flipped through her card file. "Ah, here we are. Your address is 'Elm Street.'"

"What street number on Elm?" Mike Zalinski asked.

"Oh, we don't have any street numbers here in Hard-scrabble," Lettie demurred.

"No street numbers?"

"Well, no . . . but if you'd rather, you can use 'Portland Road,' or 'Old Portland Road,' Or 'Porter Road,'" she suggested, trying to be helpful. "Elm Street is called all of these, depending upon who you speak to. Tell me, which one do *you* like best?"

Mike Zalinski responded with a blank stare. "Well, I wouldn't worry," the Postmistress beamed. "I promise you'll get your mail, no matter which street name you choose. I know everyone in Hardscrabble, and I never forget a name." Lettie paused. Confusion veiled her eyes. She smiled sheepishly. "Now, then. . . . What did you say yours was again?"

With that, Mike Zalinski went directly home and started drafting the petition.

The Selectmen Call for a Special Town Meeting

The following morning, Mike Zalinski marched into the Town Office with Tess trotting briskly at his heels. He slapped the petition on Elmer Floyd's desk.

"When I ask how to get somewhere," the irate flatlander complained, "you locals say, 'Down the road apiece' or 'You can't get there from here.' This town needs road signs. Where I came from, we had road signs on every street corner, and I'm going to make sure we get them here." And with that, he stormed out of the office and slammed the door, which nearly caught Tess by the tail.

"Maybe he should just go back to where he came from," Elmer Floyd, the chairman of the selectmen, muttered as he picked up the paper that Mike Zalinski had left on his desk. The three Town officials huddled over the petition. Their responsibility was clear. Twelve signatures were scrawled at the bottom of the page, enough to warrant a Special Town Meeting. Elmer reached for the telephone. "Lucille," he yelled into the mouthpiece to the operator, "Get me Dave Trenton." He could hear Lucille manipulate the switchboard wires and ring through to the Town secretary. "Dave, that you? Elmer here. Look, them dang flatlanders served up a petition. *Ah-yuh* . . . about the roads. So listen, you get word out that we're calling a Special Town Meeting . . . let me look at the calendar, here . . . January 22nd . . . no, that's Bingo Night at the Masonic Lodge. Let's make it January 23rd. *Aaah-yuh*. . . . Usual time."

According to Town law, an announcement had to be posted two weeks in advance of a Special Town Meeting. "Special Town Meeting," Dave Trenton carefully typed out on his Royal manual, "to determine whether to assign names to the roads in Hardscrabble and erect road signs accordingly. All registered voters, please attend. Business will be called to order at seven o'clock sharp. By Order of the selectmen of the Incorporated Town of Hardscrabble." Dave carefully took the sheet of paper out of the old typewriter, set it on his desk, and threaded an envelope into the machine. "Editor, *Hardscrabble Gazette*," he typed. "There," Dave said to himself, as he folded the notice and put it in the envelope. "Now that should stir things up in Town. . . ."

Word Gets Out

"'Assign names to the roads in Hardscrabble!'" bellowed Major Fred Ford, who for twenty years had been retired from the U.S. Army and still insisted on being addressed as Major by everyone in Town, including his wife. He threw the *Hardscrabble Gazette* onto the floor. A cloud of shaved hair rose around the barber's chair where Charlie, of Charlie's Cut and Shave, was giving the Major his usual high-and-tight. "Thought we had names for our roads."

"Yeeesss, we do," replied Charlie, as he deftly mowed the Major's egg-shaped head with an electric razor.

"Well, doesn't it seem like a waste of time to call a meeting to discuss something we don't need to discuss? Whoinell cares whether or not we have road signs? Everyone knows what the roads are called!" the Major exclaimed.

"Yeeesss, we do," Charlie drawled.

"That does it. I'm going right over to the Town Office and give those selectmen a piece of my mind." The Major jettisoned his formidable girth out of the barber's chair, thrust a fiver into Charlie's hand, snatched his camouflage Army cap from the hat rack, and marched out the door.

"Yeeesss, I'm sure you will," Charlie grinned as he watched the Major hurdle down Maple Street like a bull in the streets of Pamplona.

The Word Is Out at Margie's

Meanwhile, Margie's Lunch was also buzzing with the news.

"Why, we've always called the road Libby Tyler lives on, Daniel's Corner Road," Ethel Rimsford moaned.

"You mean Andrew's Hill, don't you, dear," Gertrude Gordon corrected her.

"Well . . . yes," Ethel conceded. "If you mean just above the Village but below Daniel's Corner, that's . . ."

". . . Bennett Road," chimed in Marianne Grant, who was knitting a sweater for her newborn grandson.

"Daniel's Corner used to be called Flacker's Bend," Rachel Malvery offered. "Oh, that was years ago, when Mother and Father were first engaged and old Farmer Flacker had his farm stand, you know, at the bend. It was one of those romantic things. I remember how Mother would whisper to Father, 'Do you remember that time at Flacker's Bend?' and they'd look so dreamy at one another." Rachel sighed.

"What happened at Flacker's Bend?" the ladies chimed in unison from the edge of their chairs.

"Oh," Rachel replied. "I don't really know. In those days, you didn't presume to ask your parents delicate things like that."

"Ah . . ." The ladies nodded knowingly, though they weren't quite sure what Rachel meant. There was an uncharacteristic lull in the conversation while they mulled over this obscure revelation.

"More coffee?" Margie interrupted briskly. And the ladies all eagerly held up their cups.

The Opposition Rolls Out

Meanwhile, Mert Grant had called a special meeting of his own. Seated around the woodstove were the members of the Hardscrabble Volunteer Fire Department and Flame, Mert's Irish setter and ever-present companion, and official mascot of the Department.

"Whyinell," Mert fumed as he chomped his never-lit cigar, "didn't the selectmen consult me first? After all, who knows this Town better than me? Heck, I been Chief twenty-two years! It is my sworn duty to know every square inch of Hardscrabble!"

"Remember that time there was the fire up Green Mountain ways over t' Alec Roy's place, behind the old Tanner orchard?" Jeff Hornsby recalled wistfully.

Mert's eyes lit up at the memory of one of the great challenges in Hardscrabble Volunteer Fire Department history. "Old Thompson place. I remember that call as if it were yesterday. Snow so high we couldn't get up the drive. Had to radio ahead and tell 'em to put some wood on the fire till we got there."

"Or when Libby Tyler's cat got stuck up in that tree over to Smith's Pond, below the culvert across from the old beaver dam?" Bo Goss chimed in. "Got there in jig time," Mert preened. "A little mouth-to-mouth-resuscitation, and that cat were as right as rain." His thoughts returned to the trouble at hand and the half-chewed cigar ping-ponged from one side of his mouth to the other. "Now some goddang flatlanders want to name our roads for us? Hell and damnation! We don't tell 'em their business, they shouldn't tell us ours!" The jangling of the phone cut the Chief short. Mert caught it on the first ring.

"Right! We're on the way!" he roared into the mouthpiece. "There's a fire up to Jim Douglas's place," Mert bellowed to the volunteers as he reached for his Chief's hat, "top of Swett's Hill, over to Beacon's chicken farm, down that lane past the trout pond where Duncan Grimes caught that thirty-inch rainbow trout last May. C'mon men!"

The fire alarm pealed. The volunteers pulled on their bright yellow waterproofs and strapped on their helmets. Mert, chomping on his cigar, gunned Fire Engine Number 1 with Flame by his side and tore down Elm Street, sirens wailing, lights whirling, shattering the calm of the bright, star-encrusted, wintry night.

There wasn't a moment to lose if Jim Douglas's outhouse was to be saved.

The Special Town Meeting Is Called to Order

A foot of fresh-fallen snow heralded the much-anticipated day of the Special Town Meeting, but this did not deter the hearty folk of Hardscrabble—or the flat-landers, for that matter—from shoveling their way into the Town Hall. A ribbon of water from snow-caked galoshes streamed down the center aisle. Hot tempers and cold glances steamed the windowpanes. The selectmen sat solemnly at a long table on the stage. Women swaddled in tweed coats were waving greetings, while men in plaid lumberjack coats conferred earnestly with one another. The Major was standing at the doorway, scrutinizing the crowd and taking stock of the opposition as though they were the enemy which, of course, they were. Mike Zalinski, surrounded by his fellow petitioners and with Tess at his side, held court under a framed antique engraving of George Washington. Margie Allard and Tilt Tilton were having an animated discussion about rising meat prices while Margie's husband, George, who was quite content to have Tilt separate him from his wife, was lost deep in thought over his favorite pastime, raccoon hunting.

Dave Trenton, in his capacity as Town Moderator, walked up to the podium. "Five minutes till the meeting is called to order," he yelled over the din. "Everyone, please take your seats."

Every seat was taken. The aisles were packed like sardines. The flatlanders, bundled in trendy down parkas, made a suburban show of unity in the eighth row. Everyone had just settled down, when the members of the Hardscrabble Volunteer Fire Department, led by Mert Grant and their mascot, Flame, marched down the aisle single file, filling the front row, which had been roped off.

"You can't do that!" Mike Zalinski objected, bolting out of his chair. The firemen, to a one, had boycotted his petition.

"Who says so?" Mert bellowed in defiance. "If we get a call, we got to be ready case someone's house's burning . . . even if it's yours." Laughter erupted from the crowd but was quickly stifled by a sudden clash between Mike Zalinski's Lab and Mert's red setter. The instant the dogs made eye contact, Flame took off down the aisle and dug his teeth into Tess's ruff. A cheering crowd encircled the dogfight like spectators at a Coliseum. Mike Zalinski was waving his arms wildly over his head. Mert Grant got so heated up that his cigar almost lit itself, ricocheting from one corner of his mouth to the other, like the hand of a metronome.

"C'mon, Flame, c'mon!" he hollered. "Show that bitch a thing or two!"

Mike pushed through the crowd and was rooting from ringside, "Go get him, Tess! Go get him, girl!" Like Moses parting the Red Sea, Selectman Elmer Floyd pushed his way through the crowd to the flailing mass of dogs, dove in, and grabbed each by the scruff of the neck. Amid low growls and brushing tails, he handed Tess and Flame to their respective owners and warned, "Keep these dogs in line, or I'm calling in the dog warden!" Elmer glanced up at the hall clock. "Awl right," he hollered at the aroused assembly. Let's get on with our own dogfight." And with that, the portly selectman waddled back onstage, raised his gavel, and struck the table so hard that it shook like leaves caught up in a late November breeze.

The Meeting Comes to Order

The meeting was called to order. Dave Trenton read the article, and the floor was opened to discussion. Lettie Connor, the Postmistress, was the first to be recognized. "I'm finding it difficult enough remembering everyone's names," she confessed, "without having to remember street names, too."

A tall, lanky man in a bearskin cap raised his hand and was acknowledged by the chair. "No one knows where I live," Gus Hallowell intoned, "unless they know the old beaver pond up by Huckins's, down the road from Miller's farm. I'd surely like a name for my road. Hallowell Road," he mused. "Yep, that would work jest fine. Then everyone would know where I live."

The Major was recognized by the chair and spoke for ten minutes on how he had led his troops through France during the War without encountering a single road sign and never once got lost. Professor Charles Markham was recognized next and began an enthusiastic interpretation of "Til crowes feet be growen under youre yë" from Chaucer, which had nothing to do with road signs or anything else, for that matter. Tess started barking again.

"I'm telling you one last time, Mr. Zakinski," Selectman Floyd warned, "keep that dog quiet, or else I will excuse you from the meeting."

By now, Mab Markham had gently persuaded her husband to sit down. George Allard started to snore, and Margie leaned over Tilt and hit her husband with her handbag.

At half past eight, a recess was called, and everyone poured into the dining hall, where hot coffee and sandwiches were being served by the Ladies' Guild. In all the commotion, no one noticed Flame and Tess skulk down the fire escape and disappear together into the cold, blue black January night.

The Meeting Resumes

A half hour later, the meeting was again called to order. Everyone, it seemed, had something to say. Dave Trenton looked at the hall clock. The tension was heavy in the air. The meeting had been going on far too long. He stood up, praying someone would move the question, when suddenly George Allard raised his hand.

"The chair recognizes . . . *George Allard!*" Elmer Floyd bellowed. A hush settled over the crowd. George Allard seldom had anything to say—but when he did, it was Important.

"Wal," George began slowly, "seems to me that all the hemming and hawing that's wanting to be said, 's' been said, so I says we get on with it and vote and go home to our beds."

"Do you mean you want to move the question, George?" Dave Trenton asked.

"If that's what it takes, that's what I'll do." George yawned and sat down to a thundering ovation.

"Splendid, splendid," the Professor applauded. " 'Oon ere it herde, at tothir out it wente,' " he quoted to no one in particular, yearning, too, to go home to bed and his much-thumbed bedside copy of *The Canterbury Tales*. "I second the motion!"

"Thank you, Professor," Dave yelled over the crowd with a sigh of relief. "Question moved and seconded!"

"All in favor . . ." The Town Hall resounded with a unanimous "Aye!"

"Now, to the vote!" Elmer exclaimed, hammering the gavel with all his might. "By law, this petition can be passed by a simple voice majority. Dave, please read the petition again."

Dave obliged. " 'To determine," he read clearly, "whether to assign names to the roads in Hardscrabble and errect road signs accordingly.' All those in favor, say 'Aye.' "

"Aye!"

"All those opposed . . ."

"Nay!"

Bedlam burst forth. It was impossible to tell whether the "ayes" had it or the "nays." Elmer Floyd lunged for his gavel and hammered on the table so hard that the head flew off like a missile, hitting the back wall with a hollow thud. "Order, order!" Elmer bellowed, grabbing his chair and thumping it on the floor. "Written ballot! We'll have a written ballot . . . *written ballot, I say!*"

"Everyone, line up!' " Dave Trenton, ever the voice of reason, ordered as he herded the crowd into some semblance of a line. He signaled to his longtime girlfriend, Ada Frump, to get out the ballots and pencils. Scrooge Geoffrey, Ruth Soames, and Clem Lovell, our Supervisors of the Checklist, were consulting over the procedure, which consisted of setting up two wire-frame wastepaper baskets, one marked Yea and the other tagged Nay with cardboard squares, and getting out pencils, ballots, and most important, the Checklist of Registered Voters.

The voters were forming a line in orderly confusion when Tess and Flame crept back into the Town Hall, unnoticed by the milling crowd. *They had not been missed—not even by their masters.*

The line moved as slow as molasses. People were tired, and nerves were frayed. One by one, the Supervisors of the Checklist ticked off each voter's name against the checklist as they passed one by one to the front of the line and handed over a ballot. One by one, each voter checked "yes" or "no." And one by one, the pieces of folded paper were deposited in the antique wooden ballot box that had been used on voting days since the town of Hardscrabble became incorporated in 1832.

After the last vote was cast, the selectmen began to sort the ballots into the wire wastepaper baskets.

"Democracy in its *purist* form," Mike Zalinski sniggered to his wife.

Everyone took their seats and watched as the white slips mounted up in the baskets. The Yes basket filled up fast. Then the No basket took on a commanding lead. Finally, all the ballots were sorted. The baskets appeared exactly even.

Mike Zalinski and Mert Grant rose from their seats and walked onto the stage with Tess and Flame at their heels. The father of the proposition and the defender of the opposition could contain their anxiety no longer.

"Seems mighty close," Mert commented, looking down at the wire baskets heaping with ballots.

"Too close to call," Dave Trenton said. "Well, they have to be counted anyway, Mr. Chairman, if you're ready to do the honors."

"Ay-yuh," Elmer replied and set his metal chair down between the two baskets. Just as he was about to reach into one to start the count, Tess flicked her tail. Flame, who had fallen for the pretty little Lab during their undetected rendezvous, was determined to now stake his claim. He uttered a lovelorn howl, lifted a hind leg, and a perfect arch streamed into one of the baskets, saturating the pile of ballots.

You could have heard a pin drop.

Elmer looked down at the drenched, yellow ballots. He looked over at the amorous dogs nuzzling against one another. He looked up at the horrified faces of Mike Zalinski and Mert Grant, and at Dave Trenton, who could barely contain his laughter. Then, with a solemn expression, Elmer stood his full height of five foot six inches, looked out over the good people of Hardscrabble, and in a clear, loud, official voice declared: "The 'nays' have it!"

Not one person dared dispute Selectman Elmer Floyd's call.

"Meeting adjourned!" And with the thundering of the chairman's order, the Special Town Meeting came to a right and proper end.

*T*hings pretty much settled down after that, and from that day to this, there has been no more talk of road signs in Hardscrabble. Townsfolk are content, and flatlanders are resigned, which is as it should be. By summer, Mert Grant and Mike Zalinski were making plans for opening day of pa'tridge season with Flame and Tess. You see, the night of the Special Town Meeting produced more than a resolution to an issue: It produced a litter of promising Lab and Irish setter cross pups.

"This little pup o'mine has a lot of her dad in him, I can tell." Mert beamed as the pretty yellow female that he kept from the litter played with his bootlaces.

"And if you don't mind my saying, Mert," Mike grinned with pride as he stroked the sleepy copper red puppy in his arms, "this little lad of mine looks more and more like his mama every day."

So, when you come to Hardscrabble, remember: Maple Street is lined with maple trees, and Elm Street has maples too, just not as many. And if you want to know where Libby Tyler lives, ask anyone, and they'll be happy to point the way.

After all, it's just down the road apiece.

FIVE

Jet of Huntress Bridge

Probable nor'east to sou'west winds, varying to the
southard and westard and eastard and points between;
high and low barometer, sweeping round from place to
place; probable areas of rain, snow, hail. . . .
       —*Mark Twain, on New England weather (1876)*

No sooner had things begun to quiet down after the Special Town Meeting, when one of the worst nor'easters ever to descend upon New England struck Hardscrabble. It snowed and it snowed. For five days and six nights, the relentless tempest hovered over farmland and forest, city and town, before it swept out to sea. And when it was finally over, three feet of beautiful, brutal snow blanketed the mountains and vales, paralyzing the vast territory that stretched east of the Connecticut River across Vermont, New Hampshire, and Maine. There was no power, no telephones, and no heat. Road crews and volunteers plowed and shoveled, day and night, to rescue people from their crippled homes and the danger of freezing or starvation. Neighbor stretched out a helping hand to neighbor. Houses with woodstoves and a full larder were open to the cold and hungry. Young people shoveled the walkways of the old, and old folks baby-sat children while parents tended to the toilsome routine of making do without modern amenities. Good deeds averted many a potential disaster, but Time stood in the way of an ill-fated few.

One terrified couple abandoned their home during the worst of the blizzard only to fall, freeze, and die at the foot of their rural road. A young boy escaped his mother's notice, grabbed his sled, and coasted into the deadly path of a snowplow. The Captain Bradford House, our town's most historic homestead, burned to the ground after its owners lit a long-disused fireplace. All that the Hardscrabble Volunteer Fire Department could do was look on hopelessly and helplessly from the foot of the long, winding, unplowed drive.

After the snow, after the stunned residents of Hardscrabble digested the damage, after the power and a semblance of normal life were restored, the bell in the Church steeple rang. Reverend Davidson, that elderly and most holy minister, stooped over the heavy oaken pulpit and, bearing the burdens of age and sorrow, surveyed his flock, then said, "Where there is need, there are no differences between good men." A muffled sob sounded from somewhere in the congregation like a hollow wind whistling through the winter woods, and then everyone rose, and wept, and embraced one another.

The annual Town Meeting was postponed for the first time in Hardscrabble's history. School was canceled indefinitely, and Margie's Lunch was closed because there were no deliveries to replenish her cupboards. True to form, that elderly coterie of widows that constitute the indefatigable Ladies' Guild of the First Christian Church of Hardscrabble put their collective shoulder to the wheel. They augmented their regular Monday afternoon work sessions with Tuesdays and Thursdays to treble their efforts to stitch quilts and knit caps and mittens for those in need.

Just when we thought the worst was over, more tragedy struck.

The Collapse of the Huntress

Spring came in like a lion, not a lamb, after the ground-hog sought his shadow. An abrupt, extreme rise in temperature thawed the valley. Snow melted as fast as it had fallen, flooding the roads, engorging the rivers, and burdening our town with a new set of problems. Dirt molted into streams of mud, wrenching houses from their foundations. Roads washed out, mud slides slicked the hills like hot fudge dripping over a scoop of ice cream, and ancient trees were uprooted as easily as corn in the clutches of a hungry bear. The bold, swift, tumbling Ossipee River battered and buffeted the stone supports of the old Huntress, a bridge that was new long before Paul Revere forewarned his fellow patriots that the British, indeed, were coming. When the old dame could stand it no longer, she fell into the river that she had spanned for so many years. So complete was her devastation that fallen timbers, carried downstream, choked the dam at Parsonsfield. Some drifted to the Kennebec, and a few got as far as the Saco, where they set out to sea for distant, foreign shores.

The collapse of the Huntress triggered a human calamity, for on the far side of the bridge was Huntress Hollow Farm, a once-prosperous dairy holding upon whose banks the Huntress Bridge stood. The Farm, as everyone hereabouts calls it, had been in the Gilpin family since Josiah Gilpin first settled there after the Civil War. He designed and supervised the rebuilding of the bridge, erected a colony of barns that housed his celebrated herd of Guernsey cows, and improved the rambling, white clapboard farmhouse that would shelter five generations of

Gilpins. But now The Farm only had one resident—old Harold Gilpin, a quiet, hardworking man who maintained and actually improved upon the family's legendary line of Guernseys. Harold ran The Farm for over fifty years, and at the end of his long and prosperous occupation sold the herd with a view to retire. Then his wife, Flo, died. No one expected it, least of all Harold. Flo had been so hale and hearty. But working a farm can sap the lifeblood out of the strongest of men and women. Two days before their fiftieth wedding anniversary, Flo died in her sleep. That was almost a year ago.

There was to have been a big party. All of Hardscrabble had been invited. Everyone planned to go. After all, Harold and Flo were special to all of us. The schoolchildren had decorated the Town Hall with crepe paper streamers and brightly colored balloons, the Ladies' Guild made tea sandwiches and baked pies, and the Hardscrabble Volunteer Fire Department arranged to put on a fireworks display. But there would be no celebration. Instead, on the day of their golden anniversary, Harold Gilpin kissed the cold, pale cheek of his beloved wife and bid her a final farewell as Reverend Davidson consecrated her body to the Earth and her spirit to God.

The Situation Worsens

Since Flo's passing, Harold lived a solitary life along with Jet, his black Lab and constant companion. "We manage just fine, Jet and me," Harold would tell townsfolk when he would come into the Village on errands. Yet a veil of loneliness clouded the old man's eyes, and at times a tear would prick the corners. He missed Flo. And he missed the hard but satisfying work of tending to his herd. Sometimes it is harder to manage with less when you have to manage alone. Never did Harold Gilpin feel so alone as he did now. He stood on the bluff high above the river, Jet by his side, watching the timbers of his beloved bridge tumble into the raging waters. Jet whimpered and pawed the ground. Harold was anxious, too.

For now, master and dog were completely cut off from Hardscrabble—and from help.

"Wal, Jet," Harold murmured as he watched the river swallow what was left of the bridge, "I guess that's that. It's over."

Master and dog trudged up the lawn to the farmhouse that had sheltered so many Gilpin kin through the generations. Once they stopped and turned to look over the devastation, but when they resumed their short trek home, Harold's pace was slowed by the burden of his heavy heart. Jet looked into his master's eyes and again whimpered. "Not a thing we can do," Harold said sadly, shaking his head. The wind roared through the pines, and a sudden, harsh chill gripped the old, gaunt man as his eyes scanned the darkening horizon. "More snow, I'm afraid, lad," he murmured to Jet, and he huddled deeper into his fleece-lined coat.

They reached the house and walked in. Harold bolted the front door behind them, then crossed the slate-floored foyer to the living room, neglecting that his boots were caked with snow and mud. He flicked on a light switch and chuckled. "Forgot," he said to his dog. "No power." He reached for a kerosene lamp on the Parsons table. Harold struck a match, lit the wick, and gingerly held the lamp out in front of him as he shuffled across the spacious, wood-paneled living room with Jet at his heels. The house was cold. The companions pushed through a swinging door at the far end of the room and entered the kitchen. "We must have been outside a good long time, Jet," Harold said as he held his hands over the old wood cookstove, only to summon the faintest sense of warmth. "Fire's just a glow." He opened the cast-iron door, prompting a puff of gray ashes to sprinkle to the floor like flour from a sifter. Then he bent over a stack of wood and carefully fitted several logs on top of the smoldering embers in the firebox. Jet raised his nose to the kettle on the stovetop, then turned away. "You're right, old man," Harold smiled sadly. "Stew's gone cold, what's left of it."

Harold lit another kerosene lamp and held it high as he made his way back into the living room. He sat down at his desk, took out a sheet of paper from the top drawer, and began to write. He wrote slowly, and for a long time. When he was finished, he folded the paper carefully, sealed it in an envelope, and propped it on the desk. His hand was cramped with cold and arthritis. He shook it as he shuffled back into the kitchen and slumped into the rocking chair beside the stove. Her chair . . . Flo's. He took to sitting in it after she died. He could feel her presence in that chair somehow, and it comforted him. He had loved Flo, and she loved him. "We're like two oxen in the same yoke," he would say to her often, and she'd always laugh. He chuckled at the recollection and wondered how many times they had had that same silly banter in the half century they were hitched together as husband and wife. "Well, almost fifty years." Harold sighed. And then, for the second time that day, he said aloud, "I guess that's that. It's over."

Harold tried not to think about missing Flo, but as the chair creaked on the uneven pine floorboards that had been burnished and softened by the feet of countless Gilpins, all long gone, he could not put a halter on his contemplations. Mother and Dad, Harold thought, recollecting his thick-skinned, softhearted, hardworking Yankee parents. And his only sibling—his younger brother, Jim: Jim, just eighteen when he and his mates on the USS *Arizona* were swallowed by the black burning brink of Pearl Harbor. There was Aunt Effie and Uncle George, his mother's brother, who lived on the farm and managed the milk business, while Harold and his father tended to the cattle and the rest of the farm. Uncle George and Aunt Effie had a daughter named Sarah, the black sheep of the family, who moved to California and died young from good times and bad booze. Then there was Harry, their own Harry, Harold and Flo's shining light and only hope. The boy should have lived to inherit The Farm. But it happened so quickly, the encephalitis that wrenched him from his parents' loving arms at the tender age of nine.

These thoughts, and the emotion of the day over the loss of his bridge, overtook Harold, and the creak of the floorboards became fainter and fainter until the old man drifted off into a half slumber of memories.

"Get off your toffer, you old coot," he heard Flo urge in the distant mist of his half consciousness. Jet whimpered, but the dog seemed so far away. Harold felt cold, so very cold. The logs mustn't have caught, he thought. But he was too tired to get up and stoke the woodstove, too tired for anymore empty loneliness, too tired to think about being cut off from Hardscrabble and help. Again, Jet whimpered. Harold wanted to lift his hand and pet the dog's noble head and assure him that it would be all right, but his hand felt too heavy to move, and the growing pain in his arm made him feel weaker and weaker. Then the rocking chair stopped rocking. The floor ceased to creak. Harold's hand fell lifelessly to the side of the chair.

The howling wind and Jet's frantic barking shattered the silence inside the deathly cold house, and the lowering darkness enfolded the old man as he drifted into unconsciousness.

Jet Goes for Help

No gentle stroking came from the paralyzed fingers when Jet thrust his muzzle into his master's palm. No smile shone on the expressionless, ashen face when the big dog stood upon his haunches and licked the old man's cold, clammy cheek. No quiet words were forthcoming, as the big black Lab looked pleadingly into Harold's closed eyes. Jet howled, but the only reply came from the buffeting snow-laden wind outside. Then, with all his weight, Jet lunged against the swinging door that led from the kitchen, causing it to spring back and forth on its hinges like a quivering bow. He bounded across the living room. The mighty wind crashed against the windowpanes, and Death pounded on the front door, but the dog was not deterred.

As many a great writer has testified, man's unswerving companion is his dog and none other; and the unseverable tie of devotion that fuses the heartstrings of one with the other is a blessed and mysterious chemistry. Perhaps it was that; perhaps it was the resolute loyalty bred of three generations of Hardscrabble Labs by the man each loved and who loved them in return. Whatever it was that alerted Jet to the danger that was creeping closer and closer to his master is confined to the wonderment that Kipling called the power of a dog. With head down, shoulders squared, and propelled by a powerful determination, Jet hurtled the full force of his hundred-pound frame through the bay window in the living room and vaulted into the wrath of the raging storm.

Sleet-tinged snow pricked Jet like needles as he bounded across the lawn. The wind rammed the side of an ancient oak that came crashing down; a callous branch caught the hurtling dog, tearing his flank. His wounds left a blood trail as Jet broke through the crusted snow. He got to the bluff above the Ossipee River. Below raged the boiling, suicidal rapids. The dog paced up and down, calculating a jumping-off point. Then, chest forward, he jettisoned into the night air like the release of a coiled spring. Jet crashed into the frigid, angry river. He struggled against the possessive, grasping current, broke free, and with all his might, swam across toward shore. The dog's strength began to ebb when, without warning, a massive timber that had fallen from the Huntress broke free from where it had lodged behind a boulder and floated like a life raft to save him. Jet threw his body over the timber and rode it to shore. His feet touched the shallows. He pulled himself from the river, sore and exhausted, and shook splinters of ice from his coat.

Jet knew where he was! Across the lawn was Mert's Market! A single light burned brightly out back, where Mert Grant and his wife, Marianne, lived. Jet jumped up against the window and began to howl. Mert looked out and exclaimed, "By Gawd, it's Jet, old Harold's dog." Marianne bundled her bathrobe tightly around her and ran to the back door, calling Jet by name. He came running to her. "The dog's hurt bad," she said, petting the frantic, bleeding animal while trying to dab the blood from an open wound on his neck with the hem of her terry cloth robe.

"Poor fellow, he is," Mert replied in a troubled tone. "Look, something's wrong. Something's not right up at The Farm. Jet wouldn't leave Harold's side if he was shackled in iron chains to an eight-wheeler." He reached for the telephone. "Lucille," he hollered to the Town operator, "get me The Farm."

"Sorry, Chief," Lucille replied. "The lines are down on

the other side of the river. I can't ring through." With that, Mert ordered Lucille to start the chain of calls that would summon the members of the Hardscrabble Volunteer Fire Department. Then the portly, deceivingly agile man dove into his overalls, flung on his yellow coat and, grabbing his fire chief's hat and his trademark cigar, raced next door to warm up Fire Engine No. 1. In no time flat, the volunteers had mustered and were ready to go.

"Ralph, you take the Sno-Cat," Mert hollered through the fury of the storm to Ralph Tasker, who raced snowmobiles as a hobby and knew how to run them hard.

"Chief, what about the dog?" John Framer yelled. Mert suddenly remembered Jet. He opened the driver's-side door and hoisted the frantic dog onto the seat beside him. "You ride shotgun, boy," the Fire Chief said to the Lab as he revved the engine.

A terrible shock immobilized the firemen when they came upon the devastation that was the Huntress Bridge. No one had known that the Huntress had collapsed. Who would? No one passed this way unless they were going to The Farm, and no one would attempt to go there on a night like this. Mert backed up the fire engine and made for Effingham Road. "There's only one way we can go," he hollered. "We'll have to take the Effingham Road and follow that old logging trail to The Farm."

"No way, Mert," Tom Gardiner yelled over the screaming wind. "That road hasn't been used in years. It's more'n a mile from there to The Farm."

"I know," Mert said. "But it's the only way. If we can't push through it, we'll send in the Sno-Cat, and the rest of us will hike in. Alan," the Chief called over to Alan Jones, who was a medic, "you got your emergency kit? I have a feeling you'll be needing it. Tom, you call Rescue and tell them we need backup."

The logging road was impassable by fire engine or Sno-Cat. The narrow dirt road was a maze of fallen trees that clutched at the men and tripped them as they struggled to reach The Farm by foot. Now it was a blizzard, a veritable whiteout driven by the turbulent, fractious, evil nor'easter.

"Follow Jet! Follow the dog!" Mert commanded, and the men lined up behind the canine leader. They pushed their way through a web of tangled trees, sinking into ankle-deep mud hidden under heavy, crusted snow. Roots grabbed at their feet like tentacles. Tree branches ricocheted and cut their faces. Finally, the men could see the outline of The Farm. "Break down the door," Mert ordered as they reached the house. Ken Sergeant smashed the lock with his ax and kicked in the door. Jet raced for the kitchen, and the men ran behind him.

Harold was sitting in Flo's rocking chair, just as Jet had left him. The dog rubbed his muzzle into the stiff, unresponsive hand, looked imploringly into the closed eyes, lay down, and rested his head on his master's feet. There was no need for Mert to kneel down alongside Harold to feel the old man's pulse.

Jet had already told them that his master was dead.

Jet Goes Home

Harold Gilpin was laid to rest next to his wife and alongside young Harry in the granite family mausoleum that Josiah Gilpin, wary of hard, frozen winter ground, had the foresight to build on The Farm. Everyone from Hardscrabble came to pay their last respects. Mert held Jet on a leash. Reverend Davidson raised his hand and uttered the same words he had spoken barely a year before for Flo.

His prayer was interrupted by the hollow, empty wail of

the heartbroken dog. Reverend Davidson closed his Bible and lowered his head. It was fitting that Jet had the final word.

The Farm was boarded up. Bob Dempsey, a young schoolteacher who lived on the logging road that led to The Farm, offered to take Jet. Several weeks passed.

Then one day Bob came through the door of Mert's Market wearing a dismal face.

"Jet's dead," the young man announced sorrowfully.

"What happened?" Mert asked in alarm.

"I did everything I could," Bob continued. "Jet chewed through his lead, so I built a yard for him, but he'd just get out. Every chance he could, Jet would make his way back to The Farm. I trekked in time and time again to get him, but this afternoon, when I got to the house, I found him dead. He was where I always found him, lying down by the rocking chair in the kitchen.

"How did he get in?" Mert asked in amazement.

"Never saw anything like it. He pulled away a board that had been hammered over that big window he crashed through the night Harold died. I gave up hammering it back in place, because Jet would just tear at it again, and his mouth would get all torn from pulling at the wood and nails."

"I wonder what he died of?" muttered Jim Towle, who was sitting in one of the rocking chairs around the woodstove.

"I think I know," Mert whispered in a half-choked voice. "Harold always said Jet was a one-man dog."

The Farm Is Sold

The news traveled like lightning through Hardscrabble: Huntress Hollow Farm had been sold. Bill Briggs, a successful dairy farmer from Sandwich and an old friend of Harold's, bought it. "Harold and I talked about me buying The Farm one day. After all, I got three sons," he told Mert. "None of 'em are keen on books, and none of 'em like being indoors. Put aside a wad of money over the years, thinking they would want to do better than their old man and go to college, you know. But none of 'em want any part of it, so I bought The Farm for them. They will make a go of it, they're hardworking boys. And I'll keep an eye on them.

"Who gets the money from the sale of the place?" Mert asked.

"Beats me," Bill Briggs answered. "Lawyer's handling the whole thing."

Harold Leaves a Legacy

On the first Tuesday of May, the annual Town Meeting was finally held. The day blossomed warm and soft. The turbulent ravages of the late-winter storms were a faint and forgotten memory lost in beds of daffodils and the medley of a chorus of swallows, robins, and blue jays. Chairman of the selectmen, Elmer Floyd, rapped his gavel, and the Town Hall, filled to bursting with townsfolk, settled down.

"We have put off our annual meeting long enough, so I don't think you'll mind if we put it off a little longer," Elmer addressed the crowd while adjusting his glasses. "Before we tend to business, I have a letter that I want to read to you. As you all know, Harold Gilpin died last month. He left no heirs. However, he left this letter—a letter addressed to you, the people of Hardscrabble. It was found propped up on Harold's desk. He must have written it just before he died. I am going to read it now, 'cause that's what he wanted. The Hall fell silent.

Dear Friends,

I wish I was here to shake each one of you by the hand to thank you, but this will have to do. Because I have a lot to be thankful for. You people been like family, especially since my dear wife Flo was called Up Yonder. Now I reckon it's getting on my time, too. I want to join her—I'm ready. I leave no regrets except one—my dog, Jet. But if I know my Jet, he will be running Home to me soon. That's just the way it is with dogs. You love 'em, and they love you more. I don't have any kin to leave The Farm to, but tonight I had an idea. A little while ago, the old Huntress fell into the Ossipee. She was a grand old gal, that bridge, and a lot of you loved her as much as me and my family did. You men, you fished off her when you were boys. Then you brought your children and your children's children to fish there, too. You ladies crossed her to come to The Farm to get fresh milk for your families. Flo and me, we always looked forward to your stopping by. And of course, every year when we gave our Christmas eggnog party, you all came. Those were the best times for me and Flo.

I spoke to Bill Briggs t'other day, and he says he will buy The Farm when I am ready to part with it. Well, I think that I'm jest about ready. I reckon my time's running out.

So here is my last request. State won't rebuild the Huntress. They say she's a private thoroughfare. So, I want the money that comes from Bill buying The Farm to be used to build a new Huntress. Your children and grandchildren can fish off her again. And you womenfolk can buy fresh milk at The Farm. And maybe, just maybe, Bill's family will throw an eggnog party come Christmas. That is where the money is to go. Flo would like that, and so would my boy. Why, he used to catch three-pound rainbow trout off that bridge, that boy o' mine.

I'll be going now. Why, I can almost hear Flo hollering for me. She says it's been awful heavy work pulling that yoke without me. So God bless and be happy. I am.

I guess that's that. It's not over—why, it's just the beginning.

All of Harold Gilpin's hopes came to pass. The Huntress was rebuilt, stronger and sturdier than ever. Children cast their lines from the bridge into the

Ossipee, people crossed over to The Farm for fresh milk, and the Huntress came back to life once more. The Briggs boys built up the herd, and soon Hardscrabble Guernseys were once again winning blue ribbons at the Sandwich Fair. Come Christmas, the townsfolk gather at The Farm for the annual eggnog party. The first toast offered, always, is to the memory of Harold Gilpin and his dog, Jet.

Harold's letter was indeed found propped on his desk— on a book, in fact, that was opened to a well-thumbed page and this poem:

Crossing the Bar

Sunset and evening star,
  And one clear call for me!
And may there be no moaning of the bar,
  When I put out to sea.

But such a tide as moving seems asleep,
  Too full for sound and foam,
When that which drew from out the boundless deep
  Turns again home.

Twilight and evening bell,
  And after that the dark!
And may there be no sadness of farewell,
  When I embark;

For though from out our bourne of Time and Place
  The flood may bear me far,
I hope to see my pilot face-to-face
  When I have cross'd the bar.

—*Alfred Lord Tennyson*

When you cross the Huntress, look for a modest brass marker. It's nailed to the corner post on The Farm side and is inscribed:

"For Harold and Jet, who cross'd the bar."

SIX

The Simple Pleasures of Country Living

Alonso of Aragon was wont to say in commendation of age, that age appears to be best in four things—old wood best to burn, old wine to drink, old friends to trust, and old authors to read.

—*Sir Francis Bacon*

We now had a good supply of seasoned firewood, thanks to Ken Tibbetts. He was and would become as good a neighbor as we could ever have hoped, and we came to realize that this sort of selfless generosity of spirit prevailed throughout Hardscrabble. It seems to me, at least, that the closer people coexist with one another—as they do in and upon the shoulders of cities—the more privacy-protective they become. And yet in the rural places, where the distance between one home and another is often measured in miles, sheer distance is the dividing factor, and the invisible boundary imposed by want of privacy is virtually unknown. I know and you do, too, of neighbors who, year after year, exchange only the barest of greetings. Perhaps it's to do with survival *in* nature, not *by* nature. But then again, I am no philosopher.

And so, we stoked the woodstove day and night, and that kept the kitchen wonderfully warm. However, the oil burner heated the rest of the house. Our waking hours centered around the kitchen, so we lowered the thermostat to a cool fifty degrees in the rest of the house to save oil and money. At night, we raised it to a comfortable sixty degrees. This worked well for about three months.

Then one fine day, a sound like a Tibetan gong clanged through the house. The aged oil burner gave one, last, stentorian heave and cracked beyond repair—yet one more thing to give up the ghost. This was terrible! A self-employed craftsman with an infant son and a wife that boasted an unguaranteed weekly income of fifteen staggering dollars could not readily come up with the kind of money needed to replace the antiquated heating system of such a rambling house as ours. Our only recourse was to convert one of the heat-sapping fireplaces into an energy-efficient furnace by installing a woodstove into the opening. Now we were in "country living" right up to our necks. It's curious how quickly we often forget the unpleasant things we encounter on the Road of Life. At the time, our circumstances were surely bleak, but harking back across three decades, it all seemed such High Adventure then. Indeed, Time rubs memories to a pleasantly dull patina when the memories are good.

"Look," Kip reasoned, "back when this place was built, they had no oil burners! They had no electricity! They had no insulation, and we don't either, but the old-timers managed, and by God we will, too!"

Ah, but we were cocksure then, full of the blind confidence that comes with youth's inexperience, confident we could handle anything that came our way. We bundled Tommy in the alpaca-lined bunting that had been mine as a child, depleted our meager bank account, and set forth on a crusade for a brand-new woodstove. The plan was to convert Kip's study and adjacent bathroom into winter living quarters for the three of us. This, plus the kitchen with the antique Magee Oxford of Boston wood-burning cookstove that was new when the house was, too, would meet our modest needs until we could afford a new oil burner. We had the rest of the house drained and shut down so there would be no repeat performance of the frozen pipe ordeal that had made Christmas Eve so unforgettable—or, should I say, memorable. Then, clenching our parkas and purse strings tightly about us, we headed to the Hardscrabble Cashway where we found a Herculean woodstove that would have done justice to the Coliseum in Rome had it had a roof.

Mel Shaw, who owned and operated the Cashway along with his wife, Harriet, the Church organist, ushered us into the back of the store, where a display of woodstoves, cookstoves, and refrigerators were lined up in a row. "This is a mighty powerful apparatus," Mel explained. "Now, it's not your most powerful unit, neither is it your least. But it can throw a lot of heat and, if you're handy, you can install it yourself."

"Kip is terribly handy," I said with wifely pride. Kip and Mel consulted earnestly with one another for a few moments, went back and forth on price, and then shook hands to close the deal.

"Well, Kip," Mel said, "if you want, I'll give you a few pointers on How To Do It."

We listened carefully to Mel's easy instructions. Why, it was child's play. "Take this dolly with you and return it when you come by next time," Mel said, as he wheeled the stove out to our Land Cruiser. "It'll make offloading a breeze."

We drove happily home, poor in pocket but rich in spirit at the prospect of a partially toasty house.

Kip Installs the New Woodstove

The woodstove fit snuggly into the fireplace opening. Kip had skillfully chipped a hole in the masonry to vent the flue.

"It's really quite simple," he said, fitting the stovepipe into the back of the woodstove. "You put this end here, like this, and the other end there, like that. Now, a little newspaper . . . some kindling . . . a few of these perfectly seasoned logs . . . Okay, hand me the Strike Anywhere matches." He struck one on a hearthstone. The wooden match broke in half. He struck another. No flame.

"Let me see that box," he said, as I handed him the matches. "These aren't Strike Anywheres! These are the kind you have to strike on the box." He took out another match, struck it along the side of the box, and held the flick-ering flame under the pyramid of firewood.

"Frankly, I can't see any reason why we'll ever need an oil burner again," I cooed. "See, Kip, this is one of the simple pleasures of country living."

Tommy slept the Sleep of Innocents in his bassinet, Bess snored in canine contentment, and Kip and I snuggled together, basking in the warmth and glow of our accom-plishment until we, too, drifted off into contented sleep.

Call Out the Fire Department!

It had been a grueling day—financially, physically, and emotionally grueling—and I was dead to the world, so I can't say how much time passed when I heard Bess's bark-ing. She sounded a million miles away until I was jarred from my sleep to find her standing on my chest, barking into my face. I sat bolt upright. The fire was crackling like a freight train barreling down the track. Smoke was pouring out of the woodstove from all sides. Kip was already on his feet, smacking at the smoke with a pillow to no avail. Smoke and sparks were spewing down the chimney like spent fireworks.

"Grab Tommy!" Kip yelled as he lunged for the tele-phone to summon the Fire Department. I bundled the baby in his bedclothes and fled from the house with Bess at my heels as the room filled with thick, gray, billowing smoke.

"Take Tommy over to Fran Forsythe's," Tom yelled, refer-ring to our elderly neighbor who lived just down the road. A light snow was falling as I backed the car out of the driveway and into the glare of the whirling yellow lights of Hardscrab-ble Engine No. 1 as it came wailing around the bend.

During the handful of minutes that I was gone, the

Hardscrabble Volunteer Fire Department had the situation well under control. The baker's dozen of firemen were swarming around the house like bees on a honeycomb. Officer Oak was there, too, standing by the swirling blue lights of his police cruiser talking to Clydie Mason and Orion Brooks, who always followed fire engines. An ambulance, there In Case, was parked in our driveway. Its pulsating red lights, along with the police blues and fire engine yellows, lent a carnival atmosphere to Hazelcrest. Atop a tall ladder leaning against the roof, a solitary fireman resembling Santa Claus in a yellow rain slicker was lacing a fire hose down the chimney. "Turn it on," he yelled down to someone below. Moments later, a stream of water cascaded down the front steps. Curls of black smoke billowed out of opened windows like portieres over the balcony of an opera house. A tightness came to my throat. I began to cry.

"It's going to be all right, Laurie," Mert Grant said as he champed on his cold cigar and put his arm around my shoulders. "It could have been worse." Black soot streaked his round cheeks like Indian war paint, and beads of water dripped off the rim of his fire chief's hat.

"*Ay-yuh,* just a little chimney fire and a bit of a mess. Seems your flue was packed with pine needles from that giant white pine right there. I was just telling Kip: 'Kip,' I says, 'when a tree gets that big and branches hang over a chimney like that, you got to cut 'em back.' *Ah-yuh,* that's what I told him. When you lit that fire, them pine needles caught like a Chinese lantern. You have that chimney cleaned?"

"Honey," I said to my husband, who had just come out from the house wearing a soot-caked Barbour jacket. "Did we have the chimney cleaned?"

He looked sheepish.

"Well, folks," Mert said, "you ain't gonna be using that

fancy new woodstove of yours until the sweep comes to clean your chimneys. Unless, of course, you want to throw another bonfire!"

Kip and I moaned in unison. It was obvious we weren't quite ready to enjoy the simple pleasures of country living.

A Missing Lab

"Do you realize," I said to Kip, "that if it hadn't been for Bessie, we might not have woken up at all? We could have been asphyxiated by the smoke!"

"Where *is* Bess?" Kip said, looking around.

We called her. She didn't come. We looked around. She was nowhere in sight. I went over to Officer Oak; Kip canvassed the firemen. "Have you seen our dog?" we asked.

But no one had.

The firemen were gathering up their gear and winding up the hoses. "If I see her, I'll let you know," Mert said as they prepared to leave. "She probably got scared off by all the commotion."

"I'll patrol around the neighborhood and see if I can't find her," Officer Oak offered. "She couldn't have gone far." It was a comfort of sorts to hear from others that our dog had probably simply taken herself for a long walk to get away from all the commotion. But in the back of our minds, we knew that that was not like her, and worry festered as we mopped the floor before going over to Fran's to get Tommy. By now it was almost ten o'clock, three hours since Bess had warned us of the chimney fire—and she was still missing.

"What do we do now?" I asked Kip.

"There's nothing we *can* do but hope she shows up," Kip replied with serious worry written on his face. "Let's go get Tommy."

Seeing Kip worried like that only exacerbated my own concern. We walked slowly to the car, burdened by worry. I had parked at Kip's workshop at the far side of our property, about a hundred yards from the house.

"When did you last see her?" Kip asked, as we traipsed through the snow and bitter cold. The stars popped out of the crystal-clear night sky like a diamond necklace against the bodice of a black velvet gown.

"The last time I saw Bess was—"

Suddenly we heard barking.

"The last time I saw Bess was . . . *in the car.*" I forgot I had left her in the car when I returned from Fran's.

Tom opened the car door, and Bess came bounding out.

"Here we are, girl," Tom said, rubbing her vigorously along her flanks as she swayed back and forth with delight at being found. "Bet you thought we had forgotten you. We did!" Kip looked at me with a half-cocked eye. "Well, Mommy forgot you."

I winced at my stupidity. "With all the confusion, can you really blame me?"

"No," my husband replied. "We'll just chalk another one off to the simple pleasures of country living! C'mon, Bessie," he chuckled, "let's go get Tommy so we can all go to bed."

And we did just that.

SEVEN

Spring Comes to Hardscrabble

For winter's rains and ruins are over,
And all the season of snows and sins;
The days dividing lover and lover,
The light that loses, the night that wins;
And time remembered is grief forgotten,
And frosts are slain and flowers begotten,
And in green underwood and cover
Blossom by blossom the spring begins.
　　　　　　　—Algernon Charles Swinburne

A crashing wave gains the shore and gradually ripples into a thread of shimmering foam; likewise, the harsh, merciless winter that took Harold Gilpin and his faithful dog Jet unfolded into a soft, benevolent spring. Time and the advent of warm weather brought on flowers and forgetting, and Hardscrabble returned once again to its bucolic, unassuming ways.

I met the arrival of spring with the anticipation of a bride greeting her betrothed at the altar. Winter had been a hard taskmaster that whipped us till we were bone weary. Splitting and stacking wood to keep warm and fuel the cookstove day in and day out requires a strength and stamina that is foreign to city-born-and-bred people, as we discovered soon enough. No longer did we take for granted basic things, like hot running water. In the course of our enlightenment we lost our innocence, for the simple pleasures of country living are in truth exceedingly complex. Nonetheless, we established some semblance of a pattern to our new and basic life, drew enormous pleasure from our efforts, and were happy in ways we had never known before.

And so, like all things, winter, too, finally came to an end. The crocus, Mother Nature's harbinger of spring, raised its sprightly head from the greening ground to proclaim the first day of May like a town crier ringing his bell. To the consummate angler, this is the sacred, long-awaited opening day of trout season. Under the cloak of dawn, the diehard fly-fisherman will steal away to his secret trout pool. He'll pull up his waders, pull on a fishing vest so stuffed with artificial flies and fly lines and tippets and assorted tackle, and wade into the water with the countenance of Moses parting the sea beside Pihahiroth. He waddles deep into the river and loses his footing; and when he emerges he looks like the Michelin Man bobbing in the current, waving his arms like a conductor, his baton a No. 5 fly rod.

For the thirteen members of the Hardscrabble Volunteer Fire Department, the first Sunday in May is the Children's Fishing Derby, which they sponsor each year for boys and girls, ages five to fifteen. In early April, the Village Brook is stocked with pen-raised trout that taste, no matter how delectably seasoned or sautéed, like sawdust. But they provide good sport and great fun for the children, which is all that matters.

For Tilt Tilton, our good friend at the Hardscrabble Village Store, it is his time to repaint, yet again, the Fresh Worms sign that he'll hang under the shingles that say Gasoline, Cold Beer, and Guns Bot & Sold, a sign so caked with years and layers of paint that it has taken on the girth of a brick. It is one of the many signs that Tilt takes pleasure in repainting, like the one that says Gone Fishing, which he hangs on the door whenever he gets a hankering below the belt to visit one of his lady friends.

And for the Ladies' Guild of the First Christian Church of Hardscrabble, it is time for their Spring Rummage & Bake Sale, especially popular particularly among sportsmen. Months ahead in anticipation, they'll scour the obituaries in the *Hardscrabble Gazette* to see who has passed on to the Happy Hunting Grounds. Some of the finest sporting gear turns up at the Spring Sale. Come spring-cleaning time, you can always count on a freshly widowed woman to intrude upon the holy inner sanctum that in life was denied to her: her dearly departed husband's rod and gun room. Deliberately, cheerfully, she will dismantle it with the intent of turning it into a long-coveted sewing room, oblivious to the fact that she is committing sacrilege by destroying a veritable Sistine Chapel of hunting and fishing gear hung from the ceiling and walls, dedicated to the worship of sixteen-gauge Parker shotguns and five-weight fly rods.

The Children's Fishing Derby

This May Day in Hardscrabble broke to calendar-cobalt skies, a cacophony of warbling robins, fields of rippling yellow daffodils, and held the double distinction of falling on a Sunday. The town was all astir. Anglers were whipping the waters with Royal Coachmen painstakingly tied to the sheer tippet tips of their fly lines. The ladies of the Guild were putting out iced lemon squares, walnut fudge brownies, and fresh strawberry rhubarb pies—all homemade, of course—on the Bake Sale table. And children, up since the crack of dawn in anticipation of the derby, were dressed, ready, and pestering their parents, who clung to their beds like a newborn pup to its mother's teat.

And on the outskirts of Town, Reverend George T. Davidson was sitting at his desk in his solitary cottage on Davidson Lake, going over his usual sermon on Matthew 14:17 about the fishes, the loaves, and the Red Sox.

Saint Matthew and the Red Sox

He was, alas, no fisherman. But he surely was a baseball fan. In truth, the Most Reverend George T. Davidson, Jr., was the most ardent, devoted baseball fan the Boston Red Sox ever had. Between Lent and Easter, when Spring Training rolled around, he would take some well-deserved time off, drive his 1968 Buick to Florida, and sit in the bleachers to cheer on "the Boys." He sat in the front row center, always. They all knew him—every single pitcher, catcher, baseman, and outfielder, through the years. And in the summer, several of the Boys would turn up at Reverend Davidson's summer baseball camp to pitch in with coaching Hardscrabble High's team, state champion twelve out of the last sixteen years. The Boys did it as payback for the support and encouragement that the elderly man of the cloth heaped upon them and their teammates season after season. They loved him, and believed The Rev had a personal telephone line to God. But then, we all did.

And so it was customary for Reverend Davidson to preach Matthew 14:17 on the first Sunday in May. There was a message to be had somewhere betwixt and between the fishes and the loaves, and the fishing derby, and opening day of season, despite the fact that the fish that Saint Peter fished were sardines and tilapia, not trout. And when it came time for the Benediction, Reverend Davidson always managed to slip in a petition on behalf of the Red Sox. Sunday's Benediction would hold particular importance. You see, there was an outside chance that year that the Red Sox could take the pennant.

And frankly, a little Divine intervention wouldn't hurt.

Getting Ready for the Derby

The deep-throated bell, high in the steeple that has summoned Hardscrabble's Christians for nigh on two hundred years, pealed the Primary (that is, the first call to worship). In an hour, the devout would take their seats in the white, puritanical pews, rise to the strains of the Processional, and sing at the top of their lungs—but not today. Except for Low Sunday, the Sunday after Christmas—which hardly anyone attends except Fiona Hogg and her irascible 102-year-old mother, Gerty McNab—only a handful of pious parishioners would be in Church this day. The children of Hardscrabble would be at the Fishing Derby. The Ladies' Guild would be in the Fellowship Room, tending to the final details of the Spring Sale. And fly-fishermen were ardent disciples of Saint Peter the Fisherman, to whom they prayed for a trout to land that was worth boasting about.

Meanwhile, Fire Chief Mert Grant and the members of the Hardscrabble Volunteer Fire Department had finished staking the boundaries along the Village Brook. They were milling around a horseshoe arrangement of card tables swathed in colorful crepe paper. This makeshift affair was the Judges' Stand. In the center stood a sterling silver trophy by Tiffany & Co., ordered in 1949 by Hardscrabble's benevolent but rather eccentric benefactress, Lila Hornbeam, mistress of an enormous estate called the Republican's Hideaway, to commemorate the very first Children's Fishing Derby. Lila Hornbeam instituted the derby after the premature death of her husband, Ronald, who adored fishing, children and, alas, single malt Scotch. The child who caught the biggest fish would take home prize money and a citation, but the Tiffany trophy was returned to its glass case in the lobby of the Town Hall, where it spent another year under heavy lock and key until the next derby.

Over the years, conflicts had arisen that fractured bones of contention over the interpretation of the fishing derby rules. To avert misunderstandings and the occasional fistfight, the rules this year were clearly printed in black marker on large sheets of oaktag paper, posted in front of the Judges' Stand for everyone to see.

"Awl right," Mert addressed his men, champing on his ever-present, never-lit cigar, "listen up and let's review the rules here." He pointed a short, stubby finger to the rules. "Rule number one," he read. " 'You must fish with a rod and a reel. No sticks and twine, BB guns, butterfly nets, tennis rackets, or anything else like that can be used to land a fish.' That clear, everyone?"

"Ay-yup," the group declared in unison.

"Number two. 'You got to fish a barbless hook. If you don't, you don't fish.' Now, you boys keep an eye peeled when you check them hooks," Mert cautioned. "We all remember how Jack Bartlett got all lathered up after we disqualified his son last year for fishing a barbed treble-hooked silver spoon. Hadn't been for Tom, here, who exposed this dishonesty, that boy would have taken the prize. Shame, though, to see the boy cry."

"Shame to see Jack cry, too," Tom Gardiner chuckled, pushing his hook-studded fishing hat back from his brow. "That was a trophy trout in anyone's book."

"Rule three," Mert continued, chewing his cigar. " 'Worms and artificial lures are just fine.' "

"But no bits of steak," Ralph Tasker interjected.

"No," Mert confirmed. "And no shrimp tails or licorice, neither. That's just plain cheatin'." The Hardscrabble Volunteer Fire Department nodded in collective agreement.

"Finally," Mert pronounced, pausing to spit out a piece of masticated cigar, "rule four. 'No keeping fish. Fish must be taken to the judges in a bucket of water and tossed back as soon as they're measured.' We lost a truckload of fish last year 'cause we didn't make it clear that this is now a catch-and-release derby. Everyone took them fishes on home. Even some adults did."

"Yeah, and they tasted like sawdust," Ralph remarked.

Mert darted Ralph an accusatory look.

"Wal, any real fisherman knows that farm-raised fish taste like sawdust," he added sheepishly.

"Now, as to the judges," Mert concluded, checking his watch. "In a half hour or so, they will arrive. Remember, these people are our honored guests. So I want you to watch them like a hawk and check every fish they measure, 'cause these folks don't know which end of a fish bites and which end—"

"Beats me why we invite judges at all," John Framer muttered. "We end up doing all the measuring anyways."

"You have to have judges," Ralph replied.

"Yeah, but why can't we be the judges? After all, it's our derby." John shrugged.

"Wal, now, John, you know how it goes," Mert explained. "Fire Department's always invited judges. That's jest the way it 'tis. Community spirit and all that."

"Damn if any of them ever sent us a decent judge!" Alan Jones remarked.

"Who knows," Mert replied. "Mebbe this year we'll get lucky."

And with that, the members of the Hardscrabble Volunteer Fire Department shook their heads and solemnly sipped their lukewarm coffee, because they knew better than that.

And so did Mert.

The Judges Arrive

By nine o'clock, all but one of the judges had arrived. The first to show up was Mrs. Fran Forsythe, always punctual, who represented the Ladies' Guild. She was much loved by everyone in Town and lived alone at Towledge, one of Hardscrabble's oldest and most distinguished homes, built in the Federal style by her great grandfather, Elias Towle, who founded the Hardscrabble Ten-cent Savings Bank, and was widely believed to haunt the Town Cemetery. Today she was wearing a sprightly hat of violets, which brightened her rather drawn face, for in the past year Fran had suffered a great and tragic loss. But this is a happy story, and Fran herself would take exception to the telling of it here. This, though, will explain the deepened lines on her face and the heaviness of her stride. Fran Forsythe tucked her grief into a corner of her heart and never wore it on her shoulder, like some. After all, she came from old Yankee stock and was as stately and stalwart as the old homestead in which she lived.

Representing the Order of the Eastern Star was Marie Antoinette Hampton, a retired college drama professor who was fond of pointing out that she inherited her talent with a needle from her Parisian grandmother, a couture seamstress. This was apparent in the flowery dress and matching cloche that she wore with certain flair. At her elbow hovered her husband, Levis, a gentle and sweet-natured man who was always poised to obey the stream of orders that flowed from the lips of his adored and adorable wife.

"Lev," she said, "I can't seem to find my reading glasses. I must have left them in my purse, in the car."

The slight, subdued man bobbed his wild, wire-haired white head in connubial concord and proceeded on his mission for the missing eyeglasses.

Professor Charles Markham assumed the duty of judge by proprietary right, since he owned the land binding the Village Brook except along the northeast corner, where it abuts the Town cemetery. A vicarious angler through the readings of Izaak Walton, the Professor dressed the part of lordly landowner. With him was his springer spaniel named, appropriately, Chaucer. Chaucer possessed the same amiably distracted demeanor of his master and was a devoted audience for the Professor's illimitable soliloquies. Whenever the Professor finished reciting something from his namesake, Chaucer the dog would spring high into the air.

"I wouldn't be at all surprised," the Professor confided to no one in particular, as he tucked his thumbs under the lapels of his belted Norfolk tweed jacket, "if Walton himself wore similar apparel when he went 'a-fishing.'"

"A-woo," Chaucer agreed.

At that moment, the deafening clamor of a beaten-down 1952 Ford pickup truck barreling down Elm Street attracted everyone's attention. It screeched to a halt alongside the Judges' Stand. The driver's side door opened like the report of a shotgun. Out clambered a thin, gawky man in a worn plaid flannel shirt and oil-stained denim coveralls that hung like a sack from his spindly shoulders. A shapeless crusher with cigarette burns on the brim was pulled low over his forehead; underneath stared a pair of bleary red eyes that burned like red coals. A nose such as you would see on the marble bust of an ancient Roman general hovered over a deeply dimpled chin that was crusted with several days' growth of beard. The aroma of tobacco and beer permeated the air like cheap aftershave lotion. As the dubious character sauntered over to the Judges' Stand, a look of supreme delight spread upon the assembled countenances of the members of the Hardscrabble Volunteer Fire Department.

"Looks like the Freemasons sent us a real judge after all!" Ralph Tasker chuckled with glee.

The fourth and final judge was none other than Perry Towle, native son of Hardscrabble, jack-of-all-trades, long-time Freemason, and the most famous poacher in all of Carroll County.

Mert Is Delighted

"Now we're cooking with gas," Mert whispered under his breath as he rubbed his hands together with glee. "If anyone can judge a trout, it's Perry."

"Good morning, Perry," people were saying as he tipped his hat to the crowd.

"'Mornin' yoursel'n," Perry mumbled through a cigarette that was dangling from the corner of his mouth. "Mornin', Fran," he nodded to Fran Forsythe, his extremely distant cousin, who was also his principal employer. Fran replied with an affectionate nod.

With the formalities over, the judges were ushered to their seats, and Mert, having difficulty suppressing his delight, took hold of himself to explain their duties.

"Each child must be registered by name and age before he's given a number. The number has to be pinned to the back of his shirt, like this." Mert demonstrated on Ralph Tasker.

"Ouch!" Ralph exclaimed, as Mert accidentally pricked him with the safety pin.

"Maybe I should do the pinning," Marie Antoinette

Hampton—known as Tony—announced with presumed authority, taking the tin of safety pins away from Mert. "I am extremely good at pinning."

"Okay, Tony, you do the pinning," Mert allowed. "To continue," he resumed with an official tone in his voice, "we've marked the boundaries along the brook, as you can see, with orange flags. The children must fish within the boundaries. If a child don't, he's disqualified. Any questions so far?"

"Oh, Mert, could the Ladies' Guild borrow those little orange flags for our Fourth of July Bake Sale?" Fran Forsythe asked. "They would look so cheery with the red, white, and blue decorations we put out, don't you think?"

"Well, sure, Fran," Mert shrugged, plainly unhappy with all the female interrupting.

"How big are these trout supposed to be?" Perry drawled.

Mert brightened up. "Well, Perry, that's a very good question. We don't like to see fish come to the Judges' Stand much under six inches 'cause they were six inches when we put 'em in. But there's plenty of adult trout coming down from winter runoff. With any luck, one of the kids will hook one and show us seasoned anglers a thing or two!"

"How big does a fish got to be to be a keeper?" Perry asked with a glint of mischief in his hooded, bloodshot eyes.

"Well, that's the thing, Perry," Mert countered. "None of 'em are going to be keepers. That's the new rule. Fish gotta be thrown back in."

There was a terrible silence. Perry looked like a bolt of lightning had hit him. "Wot kinda deal's that?" the poacher exploded.

"Well, it's just the way it goes, Perry," Mert replied. "You catch 'em, then you release 'em back to where they come from. Lot of people are fishing that way nowadays. It's called catch-and-release. It's about conservation."

"Constipation?" Perry scowled. "It sure'n," and he continued to mutter so incredulously that the only word Mert, or anyone else for that matter, could make out was "bunk."

With that, Mert advised the judges to assume their duties, since the children were now beginning to arrive.

The Children Register for the Derby

By ten o'clock, Maple and Elm Streets were lined from end to end with cars.

"How many children have signed up, Fran?" Mert asked the smiling woman. Fran was always at her best around children, like a mother hen.

"Sixty-three," she replied, ticking off a long list with the point of her pencil, "not counting the Clemmons boys." Her voice trailed off as three barefooted boys came running toward the Judges' Stand. Close at their heels bounded a dog so big and so shaggy that it looked like a Shetland pony in full winter coat. Perry got up with a violent start.

"Where you going, Perry?" Mert asked, as the derby's most colorful judge headed down to the brook.

"Checkin' on them lures," Perry mumbled, casting a dark, sidelong glance at the approaching brothers and their formidable canine companion.

"Oh, my," Tony Hampton whispered sadly. "What bedraggled boys."

"Good morning, boys," Professor Markham said as he bent down to calm Chaucer, who was cowering between his legs. "And good morning to you . . ."

"Bear," the eldest boy said. "Our dog's name is Bear."

Bear bared his teeth, exposing canines that would do a Kodiak bear proud, and growled. "Quite right," the Professor remarked, as Chaucer feverishly scrambled onto his lap. Bear's growl deepened, and streams of drool dripped from his jowls. "Right, then," the Professor continued. "One at a time. Your names and ages, please. You first, young man."

"I'm Mark, sir," the eldest boy announced, "and I'm eleven." The boy politely removed his cap, revealing a mop of unruly brown curls. The cap had been stitched in many places, and the makeshift lining was cut from a burlap potato sack. That cap spoke of poverty, like the worn-out boots that were several sizes too large and the threadbare clothes the boy wore; but a proud, sad maturity gleamed from the his rich, brown eyes that belied his youthful years as if to say, *I was born old, and that's my lot. I've accepted that.* The boy paused, made a motion to his brothers to remove their caps, then politely introduced them. "These are my brothers, Jim and Seth."

"And how old are you, Jim," the Professor asked.

"Ten, sir."

"No you ain't," the youngest boy contradicted. You're only nine."

"I'm going to be ten next month!" Bear growled and shook his head, spraying drool all over the crepe paper cloth that draped the Judges' Stand.

"Well, we'll put down ten, then." The Professor winced. "And what about you, young man?"

"I'm Seth. I'm eight."

"Eight! My, my," Mrs. Hampton commented, keeping the youngest boy between herself and the formidable dog as she pinned a number on the back of Seth's tattered shirt. "Now run along and good luck!" Bear uttered a loud bark and, with one sweep of his tail, toppled the coveted trophy. Ralph Tasker, standing nearby, caught it before it could crash to the ground.

A fallen pine straddled the throat of the stream that

feeds the brook and it was here, on the far side by the cemetery, that the boys chose to fish. They had to cross over this precarious natural footbridge, and Bear attempted to follow. However, he crashed into the water, provoking a clamor among the young contestants and their parents.

"That dog's a'scared all the fish away!" a small boy cried; but the Clemmons brothers took no notice and didn't stop until they reached the farthest boundary flag. In contrast to the Professor's carefully manicured property, this corner of the pond was heavily wooded and provided perfect cover for Perry, who had been hiding behind a clump of scrub bushes awaiting the boys' arrival.

"Pssst!" he hissed.

"Hallo, Uncle Perry," the boys answered in unison.

"Wal hallo, nephews," Perry the Poacher whispered with a grin. "Keep it down, now, boys. I don't want anybody to see me with you. You ready to win the derby?"

"You betcha, Unc," the boys grinned.

"Did you remember to bring your Top Secret lures?" their uncle asked.

"Right here, Unc," Mark replied, gently opening the lid of his treasured tackle box. He reached in and took out three round crystals, the kind that hung on fancy chandeliers. They sparkled like gemstones in the darting rays of sunlight that pierced the canopy of pine branches overhead.

"You boys know what to do."

"We sure do, Unc," the boys replied in unison.

And with that, Perry shook each nephew by the hand, patted Bear on his dripping-wet head, and disappeared into the bushes.

On Your Mark, Get Set, Go!

Mert had his grandfather's Colt single-action army revolver in one hand and a megaphone in another and was about to fire the starting shot when he saw Perry emerge from the bushes.

"What are you doing, Perry?" Mert asked suspiciously.

Perry didn't miss a beat. "Answerin' the Call of Nature, a' course, Mert." He grinned as he yanked up his fly and pushed his way through a gaggle of parents to the Judges' Stand.

Mert shrugged his shoulders. "Boys and girls," he bellowed into the megaphone. "I'm going to count to three. When I say 'three,' I'll fire my gun. When you hear the gun go off, start fishing. You have until noon—that's only two hours to catch the biggest fish you can. Is everyone ready? Awl right, here we go. One . . . two . . . three!" BANG! Sixty-six fishing lines coursed through the air like flying spaghetti.

The water was dimpled with rising trout; the air was pierced with children's shrieks and cheers and took on the enthusiasm of a World Series tied in the final inning.

"Joey's got a big one on," someone hollered, and another shouted, "Angela hooked a beauty!"

Boys and girls were hooking fish right and left, running to the Judges' Stand to have them measured, tearing back with them as water sloshed over the sides of their pails, tossing the fish back, and casting again—all as fast as they could. But by eleven-thirty, the trout had grown wiser and weary and failed to rise as rapidly to the bait. A steady stream of children lined up at the Judges' Stand with their buckets and last catch, eyeing one another's trout, hopeful that theirs was bigger. Meanwhile, the Clemmons boys, along with Bear, continued to fish at the end of the brook, far away from the other children.

"They're up to something," Mert muttered suspiciously to Ralph Tasker. "What kind of lure are they fishing?"

"I don't know," Ralph replied. "I thought Tom was going to check their poles." He shouted over to Tom Gardiner, "Did you check the Clemmons boys' poles?"

"No," Tom hollered back. "Mert said he would."

Tom looked accusingly at Mert, Mert looked sheepishly at Ralph, and Ralph looked back and forth between Tom and Mert. Then all three men gazed uneasily across the brook at Bear. The dog was so big that all three of his young masters could easily sit upon his back.

"Seems to me," Mert suggested, "that someone must have checked them boys' poles already."

"Ah-yuh," Ralph said. "I'm sure someone has."

"Yep," Tom concurred. "No question about it."

And with that, the three men went back to whatever it was they were doing, confident that someone had the courage to check the Clemmons brothers' poles.

And the Winner Is . . .

All but a few children were left on the water as the hands of Mert's pocket watch rapidly approached noon. Just as Mert was about to fire the closing shot, a sudden cry went out from across the brook.

"We win, we win, we win!" the Clemmons boys cried.

Perry jumped out of his chair. "What did they say?" the Professor asked.

"They won!" Perry exclaimed. "They said they won!"

All eyes turned to the far end of the brook. An enormous rainbow trout was flapping wildly in Mark's arms. The fish was so big it wouldn't fit in the boys' bucket, so Mark took off his shirt, immersed it in the brook, and wrapped it gently around the majestic, glistening fish. Gingerly, almost reverently, the older brother cradled the mighty fish in his arms and raced across the pine log footbridge with his brothers at his heels and Bear charging alongside in the water. Out of breath, he gasped, "Here is our fish! Ain't he the winner?"

The entire crowd fell silent. No one had ever seen such a glorious fish.

"Hurry, sir, and measure him," Mark begged Mert. "I got to get him back into the water."

Mert lunged for a ruler. "I don't think I need to measure him to declare him the winner, but let's see . . . thirty-six and a half inches!" he bellowed. "The WINNER!" Everyone roared.

"Just a moment!" Jack Bartlett hollered. A hush spread over the crowd. Not one person, adult or child, was unaware that Jack Bartlett held a mighty big grudge over his boy's disqualification at last year's derby. "I want to see what these kids caught that fish with." A hush settled over the crowd. Jack Bartlett and his son pushed their way forward with chips on their shoulders. "Seeing as how you were so particular about my son's lure last year, I think we got a right to demand to see this kid's lure."

Mert shifted uneasily from foot to foot. "Wal, son," he said kindly to Mark, "can you show us what you landed that fish with?"

Mark reached deep into his pocket and took out the chandelier crystal. He held it in the palm of his dirty, work-coarsened hand and looked up at Mert with wide, worried eyes that were familiar with hardship and unused to getting a break.

"I used this, sir," he whispered and showed him the crystal in a trembling, outstretched hand.

"You back off, Jack," Perry bellowed, coming to his

nephew's aid. "Wot's wrong with that? There's nothing in the rules that says the boy couldn't fish with that doodad. Got nothing but a wire for a hook, no barb. It's legal as hell, I tell you."

"Oh, yeah?" Jack Bartlett shouted. "What makes something crazy like that doodad legal and my son's silver spoon lure not legal? I say this fish is disqualified!"

"Back off," Mert said quietly to Jack. "This boy won the derby fair and square. That's a helluva fish—bigger than any fish you or I ever caught. Don't ruin the occasion for the boy. He deserves the prize money, and Lord knows he and his family could use it."

Jack looked down at Mert, his face red and swollen, and shot out, "I say that boy's a cheat!"

With that, Perry stepped forward and dropped Jack flat to the ground with a right hook to the jaw. All bedlam broke forth. Just when things couldn't get any more out of hand than they already were, the giant trout flapped its enormous tail and catapulted into the crowd, landing right in front of Jack Bartlett. Jack, who was still on the ground, lunged for the fish, but instead of wrestling with the trout, he found himself wrestling with Bear. The enormous dog grabbed the prostrate man by the front of his pants and shook him like a rag doll. Terrified for his manhood—as well he should be—Jack screamed and was about to collapse when, with a shake of his enormous head, Bear tossed the coward into the brook. Then, with the gentleness of a lamb, Bear took the rainbow trout in his mouth, ran up the hill, and raced down Elm Street.

In Hot Pursuit of Bear and the Rainbow Trout

"Bear!" Mark and his brothers hollered, "Bear! Come back!" For the first time ever, Bear did not obey. He cushioned the struggling trout against his thick, water-soaked ruff and continued to run down the street. The entire crowd followed in hot pursuit.

"Look!" someone hollered. "He's going into the Church!"

The double doors of the First Christian Church of Hardscrabble had been left wide open to let in the warm May morning. Bear ran into the Church, down the aisle, right up to the altar—and dropped the trophy trout at the feet of the Most Reverend George T. Davidson.

The minister was on the verge of offering his special petition to the Almighty about the Red Sox and the coming baseball season when this phenomenon occurred. He looked down at the giant trout in utter disbelief. The crowd from the derby was streaming into the church, filling the pews, and the back and sides of the Church to capacity. With his hands still raised, Reverend Davidson looked upon a crowd that would have broken the record for Christmas Eve attendance. Perhaps it was because his hands were raised in an attitude of prayer; perhaps it was because people were in disbelief and out of breath. Whatever the reason, you could hear a pin drop except for the flapping of the tiring trout's tail against the altar steps and Bear's panting as he sat protectively beside it. Mark Clemmons came slowly forward, his tattered cap held tight in his hands, and knelt in front of Bear and the fish.

"Is this your fish, son?" Reverend Davidson said.

"Yes, sir," Mark whispered.

"And, I assume, your dog?"

"Yes, sir."

Then the holy man bent down, took the tired fish gently in his arms, and placed it in the baptismal font, which was full of water. He turned to the congregation and again raised his hands:

"And Job said, 'But ask now the beasts, and they shall

teach thee . . . and the fishes of the sea shall declare unto thee. Who knoweth not in all these that the hand of the Lord hath wrought this? In whose hand is the soul of every living thing, and the breath of all mankind.' Thus endeth the word of God."

"Amen," the congregation said.

Not willing to end it with Job, Reverend Davidson continued, "Now let us assume an attitude of prayer. Oh, Lord, whose sons, the Boston Red Sox, have come once again to the beginning of their long and arduous trail as they approach the new baseball season . . ."

Meanwhile, Perry was standing in the back of the church with his cousin, Fran Forsythe.

"Perry," she said. "Those chandelier crystals the boys used as lures. They look awfully familiar."

"So they should, Fran," Perry answered. "They came off of the one hanging over your dining room table."

"I see," Fran replied pensively, "that's very interesting, Perry. Maybe next fishing derby, we should give a crystal to each child as bait."

"Mebbe we should, Frannie," Perry smiled. Mebbe we should."

The Legend of Big Boy and George Allard's Dog

*The animal shall not be measured by man. In a world
older and more complete than ours they move finished
and complete, gifted with extensions of the senses we
have lost or never attained, living by voices we shall
never hear. They are not brethren, they are not under-
lings; they are other nations, caught with ourselves in
the net of life and time, fellow prisoners of the splendor
and travail of the earth.*

—*Henry Beston*

Summer in Hardscrabble is Mother Nature's way of
apologizing for what she does to us from December
through March, but if she could put a voice to it, she'd
probably blame it on her paramour, Father Winter, whose
temperamental winds and bone-chilling temperatures are
responsible for making life in general such a pain in the
neck and other places. But even after our first winter in
Hardscrabble, I soon realized that the soft months of spring
and summer have a way of soothing the hard memories of
winter.

I continued to write the Town column, but a week didn't go by when I didn't hear about some mistake, omission, or criticism that I had failed/succeeded to make. Taking over Doris Almy's job wasn't as easy as the Judge said it would be, even when I took to heart Clem's advice that I should "grow a thick skin." Take, for instance, this scintillating news-packed item that I wrote:

Excitement is rising as July 6th approaches and internationally acclaimed psychic, Howard C. Doyle, visits the Hardscrabble Literary Society and discusses his experiences and conjectures with regard to psychic research and haunted buildings and places. This very special evening will begin at 7:00 P.M. and will be held at the home of Professor and Mrs. Charles Markham on Maple Street, not at the Town Hall, which was previously reported in error. All are welcome to come and hear Mr. Doyle speak and to partake in the summertime version of Professor's Markham's celebrated punch.

Instead of the accolades I received condemnation:

"How could you report that our monthly soiree would be held at the Town Hall, Laurie, when you know that the Literary Society always meets in our home?" Professor Markham said tersely from the other end of the phone. "You should know by now that our soirees are never held anywhere but here."

"I'm sure I don't know what I was thinking," I apologized into the receiver. "I'm terribly sorry, Professor, and I promise this won't happen again."

"I'm sure it won't," he softened a little, "but you know, my dear, you must always get your facts straight. Chaucer always got his facts straight, and you should apply that same standard to yourself, by his example."

I hung up, upset with myself, the Professor, and Chaucer

and decided to take my mind off matters by taking Bess on her leash, and Tommy in his stroller, for a walk the mile or so into Town. It was a beautiful summer's day, and I wasn't going to waste a single ray of sunshine or thought on the Professor's displeasure. Just as I got to the Post Office, however, Clem came out with his dog, Stan. It was all I needed. Tears welled up in my eyes, and I threw my arms, as usual, around his shoulders.

"Oh, Clem," I sobbed. "I just had this awful phone call from Professor Markham, and he's terribly upset with me for writing in the Town column that the Literary Society meeting was going to be at the Town Hall when I should have written that it is going to be at his house and—"

"Now, now," Clem interrupted, as he took a draw on his Camel. "Why are you getting so upset? Charlie's house is three doors down from the Town Hall. People would show up at his house anyway, out of habit. I guarantee you, those Literary Society people can smell Charlie's punch a mile away! But Laurie, if there's one word of advice I can give you, it's this: 'Don't take life too seriously. You will never get out of it alive.' "*

"I'm sure you're right, Clem," I said as I wiped my nose on my shirtsleeve and the humor went right over my head. "But it's upsetting, all the same."

"Take a look at old George Allard, for instance," said Clem, trying to drive in his point. "He never takes life too seriously. He goes about his business and doesn't mind anyone at all—not even Margie. You should take a page out of his book."

Then Clem told me a story about George, a story I've never forgotten.

And neither will you.

*Attributed to Elbert Hubbard.

George Allard and His Dog

George Allard has managed the Hardscrabble Town Dump longer than anyone can remember. You can depend upon George and even set your watch by the hours he keeps. George opens the Dump at nine every morning, except Mondays and Thursdays. At noon, he latches the gate and goes to Margie's for lunch. Then he returns precisely at one to continue to conduct the business of assisting Hardscrabble residents dispose of their garbage. At four o'clock he locks up and goes fishing or hunting, depending upon the season. People make a ritual of going to the Dump, a social Mecca of our town. Those who are housebound—spinsters, shut-ins, the sick, and the inactive elderly (which number only a few, as the vast majority of Hardscrabble's senior population is, by and large, incredibly energetic)—can arrange a weekly trash date with George. Say that George is scheduled to come to you at seven on a Tuesday morning. He'll be there, rain, snow, or sleet notwithstanding except for Christmas Day or—more sacred—opening day of pa'tridge or trout season.

As Clem says, "The only thing that stays the same is change," but George is an exception to this rule. Nothing ever changes with George except, I suppose, his clothes. The '49 Ford pickup he drives is the only vehicle he's ever owned. He lives in the house in which he was born. As you know, he's married to Margie, his childhood sweetheart. And he's been breeding coonhounds since forever and always has one riding shotgun beside him in his truck.

As you know, Margie's Lunch is not only the town coffee shop but also a major Hardscrabble hub for gossip. For as much as George is a man of few words, he gets even fewer in when he's with Margie. Margie is always busy at lunchtime, cooking and gossiping with her customers, but good wife that she is, she always has a hot lunch waiting for George when he comes in at noon. George listens to the chattering, eats his meal, drinks his coffee, then leaves to reopen the Dump. Clem says he's observed George over the years, and that the couple of words he gets in edgewise when he comes in for lunch are, "Hello," "Be seeing you," and if someone talks to him, "Ay-yuh," which serves as a good, general, all-purpose response to most comments and questions. Try it yourself.

George's coonhounds were famous. They could scent and tree a coon quicker than any dog in the county. But there was one in particular that was called George's Dog because folks were hard put to it to say what the dog's name really was. The only time I ever heard George call his dog, he said, "Here." George's Dog was sleek with a silky, buttery chestnut coat and alert, cheerful eyes. He had a soft, sensitive muzzle and floppy ears that twitched every time something or someone caught his interest. He wasn't overly friendly; in fact, he was a little aloof with strangers, like his master was, but his devotion to him was unconditional. As I said, George's Dog rode shotgun everywhere in that old Ford, and when Margie was in the truck, George's Dog rode between them. Where there was George, there was George's Dog—never farther than spitting distance away.

Raccoon season, which is in the summertime, was and still is a big deal around these parts. Raccoons aren't desirable eating nor particularly valuable anymore for their pelts. Nonetheless, there's a bounty on their heads. They are quite simply, vermin-pests and the bane of every farmer's or home gardener's existence. Raccoons can ruin a crop of corn faster than anything else . . . faster than a drought or flood, and are more thorough than a hungry bear. Open season on raccoons runs year-round, but late summer has always been considered the height of season. That's when farmers load their shotguns, let out the dogs, and proceed to demand retribution from the varmints for the damage they inflict on their crops. To a farmer and even a family that relies on the produce from their gardens to help shave down the grocery bills, hunting raccoon isn't sport. It is survival. In a modest household, a good crop means a family can get through the winter.

Culling the neighborhood of raccoons is no mean feat. They are clever creatures that know when and where to make themselves scarce. As soon as the coast is clear, a raccoon will sneak out of its den and feast on young corn to the point of repletion. A good harvest comes from good weather, good rain, good luck, and a good coonhound. A keen coonhound makes all the difference in the world.

George's Dog was a helluva coonhound. But it was George's Dog's grandfather, a dog also known as George's Dog, who was the most famous coonhound of all.

Hunting Up Big Boy

Before George married Margie, he lived with his parents and his brother, Jim, up on Swett's Hill down Parsonsfield ways, where they maintained a large, well-to-do farm. The summer before produced a bumper crop of corn, but this year didn't look good. Spring and early summer rains drowned the seeds and made mud of the fields. Throughout July and August it had been like a hothouse—wet and sweltering hot, like a furnace—and the young corn that did survive was in constant danger of root rot. The humidity was so heavy in the air that it wore on you like a wet raincoat. The nights were so still, you could hear a lonesome owl moan forlornly across the valley and coyote call to one another in the woods. After dark, it was too hot to do anything but sit on the porch and drink cold lemonade. This particular night, however, the Allard brothers had plans. Jim and George were after raccoon: Actually, they were after one raccoon in particular—a huge old varmint known throughout Hardscrabble as Big Boy.

He was as ornery a coon as ever was born. You could stand guard over your cornfield, eyes peeled, and Big Boy still would manage to burrow into a dark corner, quiet as a church mouse, and wreak havoc on a patch of young, sweet corn. He was so elusive that some farmers gave up trying to corral him and planted extra corn, knowing the big coon would invariably be coming to dinner.

But enough was enough for the Allard boys. What with this year's crop looking pitifully scarce, it was going to be tight enough trying to make ends meet without having to hassle with coons—especially a coon like Big Boy. So, the brothers decided that tonight was going to be his last. Jim and George waited for the sun to settle before they shouldered their twelve-bores and headed to the creek below the farm. Beyond that was a swamp, and a little farther along, an abandoned apple orchard. That was where Big Boy was thought to hole up.

The Game Warden Interferes

The midnight moon hung like a pendulum in a sky flecked with twinkling stars. There wasn't a breath of a breeze, and the only sound came from a couple of squirrels squabbling over some household matter high up in an oak tree. The brothers stepped gingerly through the alder woods, but the footing was muddy, and each twig that cracked underfoot sounded like Chinese fireworks in the stillness of the night. "Big Boy's sure to hear us comin'," George whispered. "More likely he'll smell us first," Jim replied as an unexpected and unwelcome breeze betrayed them. Suddenly there was an ear-splitting cry. *Ou-eeee....* George's Dog raised his nose, and every muscle in his body became rigid—no doubt he'd caught Big Boy's scent! He lunged through the dense underbrush and crashed into the stream. *Ou-eeee....* George's Dog plunged through the water and leapt onto the far shore, tail high and at a dead run right toward the grove, all the while *ou-eeee*ing and *wee-wail*ing. Suddenly the wild cry abruptly turned to utter silence. *"Aarghhh...help!"* someone suddenly shouted. *Ou-eeee...* George's Dog's shrill, murderous bark replied.

"Aarghhh...help! Someone get this gawdang dog offa me!"

The brothers pressed through the dense cover. Wait-a-bit thorns pulled at their clothes and tore at their arms until they finally came upon the scene. High in the bending branches of an old, gnarled apple tree was none other than Bill Burns, the county's notoriously unpopular game warden, hollering and kicking his heels as high as he could to keep them from the gnashing teeth of George's Dog.

Strapped to the warden's back was a game pouch, which held a young, dead raccoon.

"Wal, hallo, Warden," Jim grinned matter-of-factly.

"Fine evening to be up a tree," George chuckled.

"Get your grimy dog outta here," Bill Burns hollered. "He's gonna tear off my leg!"

"Gee, Warden," George replied. "Seems my dog thought you was a coon. You smell awfully like one." George called off his dog.

"Next time, don't go strapping no coon on your back, Bill," Jim called out after the angry warden, as he climbed down from the tree. "Partic'urly at night during corn-growing season!" The warden turned heel and ran into the night. "Wal, guess that's that," Jim continued. "No point going after Big Boy now. He'd a heard us clear across Maine by now."

"Aa-yuh," George agreed.

Big Boy at Last!

The brothers headed up the hill for home. An insomniac cow mooed in a nearby pasture, and chirping crickets sang harmony with a chorus of bullfrogs, conducted by a particularly deep bass. The boys crested the hill when suddenly, George's Dog raised his wet, black nose and sniffed the sultry air; again he took off like a bat out of hell . . . this time, toward home!

Ou-eeee, ou-eeee. . . . Again the slumbering silence was shattered by George's Dog's strident cries. A single row of corn down the center of the Allards' field was waving wildly, as if the stalks were caught by the tail of a tornado. It was Big Boy, and in hot pursuit was George's Dog! The corn parted, forming a clearing, and the two opponents, dog and raccoon, squared off. There he was all right: Big Boy, the biggest coon Jim and George had ever seen. The full moon illuminated the enormous animal's thick, glossy fur. Under his black mask glared beady, bright, alert eyes. Real harm could come to George's Dog if those ferocious, formidable white teeth sank into his flesh. Within seconds, dog and coon were wrapped up in one another, twisting, tumbling, wrestling, reeling, and spitting among the flattening cornstalks. Jim, who was a few paces behind his brother, leveled a bead on the raccoon and aimed to fire, but it was too close to see where one animal ended and the other one began. Fur rolled into a blur, seconds rolled into minutes, and the minutes rolled into what seemed like hours.

Then came a thunderous *bang. . . .*

There stood Pa. He'd been awakened by all the commotion. A ring of smoke encircled the bore of his Parker shotgun. He looked at his sons. He looked at George's Dog, panting hard and exhausted in the dust. He looked at Big Boy, who lay beside his adversary, panting hard, too.

Neither animal had taken a single pellet! Pa had shot into the trees! The blast had broken up the fight, as it was meant to do.

"Well, I'll be dang," Jim whispered.

"Never saw the like," George said in awe.

"That's one goldurn big coon," their pa replied, rubbing his chin.

George's Dog got up. Big Boy got up, too, and for a moment, the men thought that the two animals were about to square off for Round Two. For a long while the two animals just stood there, barely a tree branch width between them, staring one another down. They didn't growl. They didn't spit. But somehow, in a way that neither George or Jim or Pa could ever explain, it was clear that dog and beast were saying, "Hey, let's call it a draw." With that, Big Boy scampered off into the cornstalks, and George's Dog got up and nudged his master's hand with his muzzle as if to say, "Don't worry, boss. All's well."

The End of Big Boy

The story of George's Dog and Big Boy swept through Hardscrabble like wildfire. No one questioned why the Allard men had allowed Big Boy to go free. After the story got around, everyone agreed that letting the bandit raccoon go somehow seemed like the right and proper thing to do.

The wily Big Boy was never heard from again. Some say he wandered off into Maine in search of new horizons to climb and cornfields to conquer. Others say he got in between a bear and her cub. Just a couple of months ago, however, Orion claimed he saw Big Boy coming down the lane toward his chicken coop—but we all know that Orion can't see a thing at night, so no one took heed.

No, Big Boy was gone and gone for good. No one ever encountered him again. But the legend of Big Boy and George's Dog is firmly bound into the laurels of Hardscrabble folk's lore. Not because what happened was a great story. Because what happened was a great lesson.

Samuel Clemens, in his autobiography, wrote: "Of all the creatures that were made he [man] is the most detestable. Of the entire brood he is the only one—the solitary one—that possesses malice. That is the basest of all instincts, passions, and vices—the most hateful. . . . He is the only creature that inflicts pain for sport, knowing it to be pain. . . . Also—in all the list he is the only creature that has a nasty mind."

I wonder what the man that the world knew better as

Mark Twain would have said had he witnessed the brawl between Big Boy and George's Dog. But were I to wager a guess, it would be something like: Now, *those* creatures could teach Man a thing or two.

And indeed, they did.

NINE

The Return of Doris and Little Doris

Looking back on that first summer in Hardscrabble, I remember we shoveled horse manure, tilled the soil, and planted a wondrous vegetable garden that wild animals—including a bear with an attitude and one particularly persistent family of blue jays—pretty much devoured. Bit by bit, we started to replace the old windows with new and install insulation where it mattered most to avoid the pratfalls that we, out of innocence, had had to deal with too well over the course of that first winter. We attended Church on those Sundays when guilt overcame the desire to sleep in, and went to Saturday night ice cream socials at the bandstand along with everyone else in Hardscrabble. This, in tandem with the daily routine of going to the Post Office for mail, Tilt's Store for groceries, and Mert's for gas and beer, soon integrated us into the fabric of Hardscrabble and ingratiated us to the townsfolk. In the short time since we moved into Hazelcrest, we city orphans had been adopted into the Town family. Why we enjoyed such uncharacteristically swift acceptance among Yankees—a breed of people universally known for their heels-in-the-ground reticence—was because we were a young family.

Hardscrabble, like most rural New England communities of the day, was largely made up of women over childbearing age and men over the desire to put a woman in that position. And so, we were coddled and cuddled like baby chicks by a mother hen and loved every bit of the attention. Nine out of ten times, whenever there was a knock at the door, we could expect to find a grandmotherly neighbor smilingly on the threshold with a casserole or just-out-of-the-oven pie or a man with a saddle of bear or venison. "The missus don't like bear," or "That deer packed so much weight it nearly broke the icebox," was a mere pretense. Here were people who shared what little they had with a struggling young family. (Call me a cynic, but to this day, I have yet to see that caliber of selflessness among gatherers of material wealth.) We were part of a family, albeit a large one—the family of Hardscrabble—and as in any family, it came with security of belonging. Being Town columnist even failed to impinge negatively upon the affection and support we came to enjoy from our neighbors.

Things Settle Down

No matter what the beat, journalists throughout the ages have always entertained a certain reputation, and I was no exception, even in the finite universe of Hardscrabble. With the exception of a few confrontations and outbursts, such as the one with Professor Markham, writing the Town column now progressed at a fairly consistent snail's pace. There was never any headline-breaking news. No earthquake convulsed the ground, no one of importance passed through, and nothing out of the mundane troubled our sleepy town. In the column, I announced meetings, thanked the Hardscrabble Volunteer Fire Department yet again for getting Libby Tyler's cat out of a tree, and reported whose children and grandchildren were visiting whom. There were always murmurings—even from the kindest and most polite of people—that Doris Almy was still sorely missed. No matter how thoroughly I thought I reported the comings and goings of Hardscrabble, or how well I wrote about them, something was missing—something that never quite meas-ured up to the Doris Almy standard. True to her word, Mrs. Parker, the Judge's wife, called every week and gave me the Cliff's Notes version of the social happenings of Town, most of which—at least to me—seemed rather tepid. Apart from being a loving wife and mother, gracious hostess, and a green-thumb gardener, Mrs. Parker had a natural talent for extracting the most boring news, such as who just returned from visiting her daughter, who attended his thirtieth Army regiment reunion, or whose dog just had a litter of puppies. But this was precisely what people wanted to read, and goodness knows, my columns would never have passed muster had it not been for Mrs. Parker and her wealth of knowledge concerning Town trivialities.

My little Tommy was at that wonderful, portable age where I could take him with me just about anywhere. The balmy summer weather permitted us to get out without the encumbering, half-hour routine of donning down parkas, boots, mittens, scarves, and other winter survival gear and paraphernalia, necessary in the dead of winter even to go down to Tilt's for a gallon of milk. Now that I was able to attend more events and functions, I could wax lyrical about the apple brown betty served for dessert at the Chuch sup-per, and the brilliance of Professor Markham's latest dis-course on the consequence of creative thinking and enlightened philosophy in the age of Chaucer. Yet Doris's memory still hovered over my column, and there would be little sunshine illuminating even my best efforts to alter the general consensus.

It Begins to Get to Me

I was at the Post Office one day talking to Dave Trenton and his girlfriend, Ada Frump.

"You're a breath of fresh air, Laurie, after being strangled by Doris's wordy columns for a quarter century!" Dave laughed.

"I know how tough this must be for you, though," Ada added sympathetically. "People talk so."

I recounted this conversation a short time later to Clem, who I met up with on my way to the *Hardscrabble Gazette* office to deliver my most recent column. "You know what bothers me most?" I said. "It's that Dave and Ada feel the same way as everyone else does. No one will ever accept me as Town columnist. Not as long as I live, thanks to Doris."

"People talk," Clem replied wisely, lighting an unfiltered Camel while Stan curled up at his feet. "It's all about small town mentality"—he took a draw and looked philosophically at a sparrow dancing on the spent blooms of a lilac tree—"and from what I've seen, you bump into small town mentality wherever you go—especially in the cities. It's human nature." Again, Clem paused for another philosophical draw. "Laurie," he pondered, "if there's one piece of advice I can give you, it's this: 'Don't let people get to you. No doubt Jack the Ripper excused himself on the grounds that it was human nature.'"*

As usual, Clem was right.

Old Home Week

Old Home Week was drawing near. For over a century, the annual celebration that begins the second Friday in

*Attributed to A. A. Milne.

August has never been missed, not even during the Great Depression or either World War. Old Home Week is to Hardscrabble what the Feast of San Genaro is to New York's Little Italy. The atmosphere is ripe with laughter and merriment. It's a backslapping time, a time when our Town declares silently to the cosmos that All is Well, We're Okay, and Life is Grand, whether it is or not. Old Home Week is a time to take pride in who we are as a community, where we've been, and reaffirm that wherever we're going, we're going together, arm in arm. Old Home Week is as Yankee as maple syrup and apple pie and almost as sacred as Christmas or the opening game of the season for the Red Sox. As I write, I look back over thirty Old Home Weeks to my very first. As with any Significant Event in life, there's nothing quite like the first time.

And yet, not much changes between one Old Home Week and the next except, perhaps, the faces—and those that are missing generally have departed to live in the House of Many Mansions, where I'm certain they have Old Home Weeks, too. If you were born and raised in Hardscrabble but no longer live here, you come home for Old Home Week, unless an Act of God gets in the way. Children who are off at college, grown children whose paths have led them away from the four corners of Town—anyone who has roots in Hardscrabble—comes home for Old Home Week. Old Home Week is many families reuniting for a gathering of the Town family.

The Old Home Week Committee publishes a roster of events that comes out Memorial Day weekend. These are diehard volunteers who plan the festivities with an intensity that rivals Macy's Thanksgiving Day Parade. It virtually takes a whole year, and after one Old Home Week has ended, preparations for the next begin almost immediately. Just take a look at the Roster, and you'll understand why. It is single-spaced, printed front and back on a legal-sized sheet of paper in letters so small that you need a magnifying glass to read it. The schedule is jam-packed with plays and concerts, sports events for young and old, teas, suppers, story hours, bazaars, sing-alongs . . . and on and on.

The festivities kick off with the Firemen's Carnival at the Hardscrabble Ball Field. A traveling concession sets up a Ferris wheel, merry-go-round, and all sorts of other rides and entertainment. There's a shooting gallery and a wonderful ladderlike contraption that, if you throw a ball and it hits a gong, a hapless member of the Hardscrabble Volunteer Fire Department—usually Bo Goss—falls from a high platform into a pool of cold water. There's candy cotton, hot dogs and hamburgers, and that great New England delicacy, fried dough.

Old Home Week Parade

Everyone comes out for the Old Home Week Parade, which is held the first Saturday. Participants and floats gather at the Ball Field around nine in the morning, which is where the parade route begins—and ends. At ten o'clock on the dot, the parade starts, wending its way down Maple, over the Bridge That Crosses the Dam, and down Elm all the way to the road that leads to the Town Beach (not to be confused with the Hardscrabble Community Club Beach), turns around in front of the Town Cemetery (the big one, not the small one), and heads back. This gives everyone a chance to see the parade twice.

The Judges' Stand is set up on a scaffold above the postage-stamp size front lawn of the Town Hall. Each group or float has sixty seconds to perform a routine, song, dance, or show off a highly polished antique car or a preened pair of oxen. The Hardscrabble Volunteer Fire Department buff

Engine No. 1 and retired Engines No. 1 and 2 to a mirror shine and drive them along the parade route with sirens wailing so loud that the people have to cover their ears.

The Church float always features a group of performing parishioners called The Hardscrabble Players. They wear full, homemade, colorfully hilarious costume. The Players write and produce original plays that are only ever performed during Old Home Week, with titles such as *Uncle Jacob's Jug of Bootleg Gin, Sweet Cassandra the Virgin Slave*, and *Mathilda's Innocent Mistake*, which they perform Wednesday evening on the stage on the second floor of the Town Hall.

Next there's the Hardscrabble High Kickers, a contra dance club that reels and jigs down Maple and Elm, always careful not to step in the fragrant piles of dung that the horses and oxen leave along the parade route. The Girls' Soccer Team is led by Nat Felton, who became coach the year Eisenhower was elected president. The Hardscrabble High football team and the school's marching band are led by the cheerleaders, who mimic the routines of the Dallas Cowboy Cheerleaders and pull their shorts up and tops down despite the warnings of the principal. The Town softball team, a group of men on the uphill and downhill sides of middle age, march the parade route with a banner that proclaims them regional champions over the half-dozen ball clubs in the county.

Then come the political candidates or incumbents: county treasurer, county sheriff, county clerk, state representative, and sometimes, if his popularity is low in the polls, a congressman. They wave and smile and toss penny candy to squealing, delighted little children. Sometimes in an election year, a candidate for state senate will sit somberly in the back of an open convertible and nod.

The parade, always led by Jim Chisolm's Model T Ford, is decked out in red, white, and blue crepe paper and carries precious cargo: the oldest resident of Hardscrabble. For the past five years it's been Kirby Walters, age 102. He waves cheerfully, even if he is a bit disoriented, from the backseat. It is at the Old Home Week parade that the oldest resident of Hardscrabble is presented with the Boston Cane, a solid-gold-handled walking stick that he or she will possess till death do they part, at which time the cane is repossessed by the Town selectmen and the deceased is repossessed by his Maker. Elmira Wiggins held the record for the Boston Cane. She was 107 when she passed to her just reward. Of course, the fact that she drank like a fish and smoked like a chimney doesn't say much for the merits of living a caffeine-free, smoke-free, alcohol-free, and fat-free life.

Members of the Shriners Club come out in force, cheerfully garbed in kaleidoscopic-colored clown costumes, donning orange wigs and white face paint with bright red noses that honk. Each squeezes into a tiny, roaring, battery-powered fun car that drives faster than you'd ever guess; and in precision configurations that thrill the spectators, the thirty-clown-man squad weave in circles and figure eights, barely missing spectators's toes. The Shriners take their act throughout the state to raise money for the Burn Unit at the Children's Hospital, and the donations that their clown antics generate give hundreds of boys and girls a new lease on life. Cities have rock 'n' roll groups that give benefit concerts; here in Hardscrabble, we have the Shriners.

The Sven Jorghanssen family brings up the rear of the parade and have for as long as anyone can remember. Not one of its members—which fluctuate between three and four dozen—is known to anyone in Town, yet every year they show up in traditional Swedish costume and sing folk songs to the accompaniment of guitars played by the family's aged matriarch and patriarch.

There isn't an hour during the day or evening when

something isn't going on during Old Home Week. Just check the roster—you can pick up a copy at the Post Office or the Hardscrabble Village Store. Children's activities include water sports day and land sports day, a marionette show, and a soccer game; and for teenagers, there's a dance at the Town Hall, complete with disc jockey. Then there's the Ladies' Guild Christmas in August Fair, which is a big draw; and local artists put on an art show; local craftsmen, a crafts show; and the Friends of the Library conduct a Dime-a-Book Sale. An adults-only lawn party, hosted by the Hardscrabble Literary Society, is held at the Markams' house, and yes, the Professor serves his celebrated rum punch—chilled, not mulled—because, after all, it's August.

There's the Firemen's Lobster Supper, where tables are set family style on the first floor of the Town Hall, and you get two lobsters, two ears of corn, Parker House rolls, cole slaw, a bottle of tonic, and a choice of apple or pumpkin pie, all for seven bucks fifty. The Hardscrabble Barber Shop Quartet performs at the bandstand, there's a garden tour of the Village that's conducted by the Hardscrabble Horticultural Society, and Lila Hornbeam opens her estate, the Republican's Hideaway, for an afternoon tea to benefit the campaign of whichever Republican has currently garnered her favor.

I can tell you anything you want to know about Old Home Week now, but back then, I knew absolutely nothing about it at all. It was this that led to the beginning of the end of my career as Town columnist.

Panic Sets In

It was two weeks before Old Home Week. I sat forlornly at the kitchen table poring over the first Old Home Week roster I'd ever seen. My column for the *Hardscrabble Gazette* was due the following morning. I was to tell everyone about Old Home Week. But how could I? I'd never been to one in my life. After all, we'd only been living in Hardscrabble since November.

I'd call Mert. He'd tell me about the Firemen's Carnival and the parade and all else that goes on. But when I called Mert's Grocery, Marianne told me he wasn't in and to try him at the Firehouse. Lucille, the Town operator, must have been eavesdropping on the line and interrupted Marianne to inform us that the volunteers had just left on a call, try later. I tried later. Ralph Tasker answered and said Mert was on his way back to the Grocery. I called the Grocery but Marianne said he hadn't pulled up yet, but she'd have him call when he got in. An hour later, Mert returned my call—five hours after I first tried to reach him.

"You called, Laurie?" he asked, and I told him I had, and why. "Oh, the usual," he said. "We got a Ferris wheel and all them rides like the merry-go-round, and the fortune-teller and there's the water balloons and the darts, and the ball game and Bo Goss, he'll be up on the platform again—and, of course, some pretty nice prizes at the shooting gallery. *Ay-yuh,* and a roulette wheel. That's about it."

I thanked him. Now I was even more confused than ever.

Something Unexpected Happens

I had just hung up with Mert when the phone rang. It was the Judge.

"Can you come to the office this afternoon, Laurie, say around four?" With his usual perspicacity, I suspected Judge Parker realized that I was out of my depth with Old Home Week. If that was the case, what was he going to do? I mean, what was the worst thing that could happen? The answer was pretty obvious.

That afternoon, I walked into the *Hardscrabble Gazette* offices, fully prepared to receive my pink slip from Judge Parker when, to my surprise, I found none other than Doris Almy sitting in the chair across from his desk.

"Doris Almy!" I exclaimed to the elderly cream puff swathed in layers of light-blue chiffon. She was holding Little Doris, who was struggling under a flouncy collar that matched her mistress's overdressed garb.

"Hello, my dear," Doris replied with an outstretched, gloved hand and a hint of regal condescension in her voice. In her absence, she had achieved legendary status in Town the way people do who were notorious in life after death, for in the hearts of Hardscrabble, she was now the Illustrious Doris Almy, the greatest Town columnist who ever walked down Elm and up Maple, her name etched in eternity alongside Hedda Hopper and Walter Winchell.

Doris took a deep breath. She clutched a lace handkerchief in her hand. "I have been following your columns, Laurie, and they are utterly delightful," she said wistfully, pausing to daub her eyes. "You have been doing such an excellent job, my dear, that you put my poor efforts of all these many, many long, hard years to shame. Doesn't she, Little *Dow-reet?*" she cooed to her Pomeranian. Little Doris replied by glaring at me with her beady black eyes and snarled, exposing her malicious, pointy little teeth. To this very day, Little Doris has a special place in my heart as the only dog I ever loved to loathe.

"It's so good to see you, Doris," I said with surprise coloring my face red. "How wonderful you look, and how nice to have you back in Hardscrabble for Old Home Week." Doris darted an uneasy sidelong glance at the Judge.

"Well, Laurie, you see it's like this. Doris isn't here for Old Home Week. She has decided to move back to Hardscrabble. . . . She's returned for good."

Doris flourished her handkerchief dramatically and explained. "You see, my dear, try as I might, it just didn't work out living with my son and his precious family. They live their own busy lives, and I felt like a fish out of water. I missed Hardscrabble so. I missed my friends and all the parties and meetings and socials that I used to attend. I never did sell the house, you know. I wanted to wait a year, to see how things worked out. But things haven't worked out as well as I had hoped, and so I'm moving back. I want my old life back. And I want—"

"You want the Town column back."

There was an uncomfortable silence.

"Yes," the elderly woman confessed, putting on her best Sarah Bernhardt routine. She was going to soak the moment for all it was worth. The Judge looked at me from under his heavy brows with amusement dancing in his eyes. He knew precisely what I was thinking.

"Well, Doris," I said slowly. "I certainly will not stand in your way." Suddenly, I felt an enormous weight lift off my shoulders.

Doris tottered to her feet, hugged Judge Parker and then hugged me, squeezing Little Doris between us. "Oh, thank you, thank you, my dear," Doris cried, as I pulled away from her suffocating embrace. "I am forever grateful. Little *Dow-ree,* what do we say to the nice lady?" She held the small dog dangerously close to my face.

"It's quite all right, Doris," I said magnanimously, taking a cautious step backward before Little Doris had a chance to sink her razor-sharp little teeth into my nose. "I know everyone here in Hardscrabble will be delighted to read the news of your return when you write this week's column."

"Oh, my dear," she said, wagging a finger. "I don't know about that."

I know, I said to myself. *Boy, oh boy, do I know.*

The Happy End to a Very Short Career

Doris's triumphal return did indeed come out in the next issue of the *Hardscrabble Gazette*, sparing me the terrible burden of having to preview Old Home Week and all of the festivities. Her column announcing her triumphal return—arguably her greatest effort—commanded the front page. After all, Doris Almy's columns sold papers. It began:

> *It is with great and enormous happiness that this Reporter is writing to you, my dear friends, to say that we have returned to Hardscrabble as your Town columnist and we are very happy about this, as I hope you are too. It is because I missed our friends and our home and most of all you, our newspaper friends, so much that I am back home for good. These past months away were happily spent with my son and his family, and although I spent many happy times with my son and his family, home is really Hardscrabble. Which brings to mind something somebody once said, and that is, there's no place like home, isn't there, because home is where the heart is. This Reporter has resumed our duties immediately and what happier time to do so than Old Home Week, which is such a fabulous time of the year for us all. This Friday, the Firemen's Carnival will be held as usual at the Ball Field with the usual rides and refreshments. . . .*

Doris ended her column with a gracious tribute to me:

> *The Ladies' Guild will have their annual Old Home Week coffee, which they give every year after Old Home Week Service on the last Sunday of Old Home Week and I would like to say one more thing. Thank you, thank you, Laurie Morrow, for writing the Town column during my absence. You did such an outstanding job and I am sure almost everyone thought so,*

even if they didn't say so. Now, everyone, do not forget, tonight's meeting of the Hardscrabble Literary Society, which Professor Markham assures me will delight all the Members and their guests, as his talk tonight is entitled, "The Impact of the Cleric on Religious, Social, and Political Morality in the Age of Chaucer," and of course his delicious punch, as always. I am sure a good time will be had by all.

Yes, Doris Almy was back.

TEN

The Adventures of Tom and Archie

Keep gude company, and ye'll be counted one of them.
—Scottish proverb

And so, the seasons unfurled like a mainsail on the mast, and Nature in her good grace obliged the good folk of Hardscrabble with balmy, cornflower-blue days and serene, indigo nights. Winter worries had melted with the snow, and a stream of bliss flowed from April through August like a tripping mountain brook. Autumn coaxed a lingering Indian summer to move on, as leaves tinged with jewel colors embarked upon their final journey and fell to the ground.

It was the first of October, opening day of grouse season: to a wingshooter, as holy a day as Christmas, though many an old pa'tridge hunter would liken it to a Day of Atonement. At an altogether reasonable hour of the morning, two friends stood shoulder to shoulder at the throat of a woodland path that led to forgotten fields. Their hunting coats were seasoned by the seasons: the waterproofing without luster, tears patched by an awkward hand, the corduroy collars pleasantly frayed. A brace of handsome sporting dogs flank the men: one, a black Lab; the other, a "snow Belton," as Evans called mostly white English setters. The canine adjutants were poised for fowl warfare, eager to receive their commands: withers quivering, nostrils quivering; keen for the scent of pa'tridge, a fragrance they had longed to inhale since twilight on the closing day of the previous season.

The friends mustered here thirty opening days before and every one since: Tom, with the pre-War Winchester Model 12 that Jim Gibbs sold him cheap with money he'd saved from his paper route; and Archie, with the Parker VH 16-gauge that he inherited from his grandfather. That first season so many lifetimes ago marked their rite of passage to manhood: two sixteen-year-olds on the cusp of adulthood, their eyes shining like the sunlight that glinted off the barrels of their sporting guns, their hunting coats embarrassingly new and unsoiled, their excitement barely restrained. Since those virgin days, every opening day brought something new, some golden reminiscence to deposit in the memory bank. Tilt Tilton called Tom and Archie "those fine young lads" from the time they bought their first root beer for a nickel, to the present day, thirty years later, when Tilt still charged them a nickel for a tonic, for old times' sake. During their growing up years, they'd barrel into Hardscrabble every June to devour summer vacation with the appetite and eagerness peculiar to adventuresome boys. Together they'd fish for trout, pot feral cats and crows with homemade slingshots, climb the hillocks, and explore the dark recesses of the forest—all the things boys, once released from the shackles of the suburbs, do to set their imagination, curiosity, and spirit free.

Both were born into modest privilege, both had roots in Hardscrabble, both carried a legacy and love of the outdoors that had been handed down to them by their respective forebears. Fishing, hiking, and hunting were the fundamental things that bonded them to Hardscrabble and one another.

Tom would eventually inherit his family's farm, start a family and business of his own, and fulfill his dream of making Hardscrabble home. Archie, too, would marry and raise a family, but his universe orbited around the city. Nonetheless, he came back to Hardscrabble at important times, such as Thanksgiving and Old Home Week, and religious occasions, such as Christmas, and the opening days of trout season, grouse season, and deer season.

And so, on yet another opening day, the lifelong friends stood again in a place so familiar, so necessary, so part of their brotherhood, at the lane that led to the fields: a pair of middle-aged men who had spent their college years studying law, the classics, and women; who stood for one another as best man at their respective weddings; was godfather to the other's firstborn; and whenever they could, still fished, hunted, hiked together, and potted crows with single-shot rifles that had taken the place of their boyhood slingshots.

Their guns were oiled; the dogs, in peak condition. Tom had broken in a new pair of hunting boots. Archie recently had the stock of his Parker bent because he knew, just knew, that it was gun fit, not his swing, that kept him from hitting grouse; and this season, by God, he was going to finally get a double. They were ready. It was time to set out on another opening day for another showdown with the wily ruffed grouse.

The Proper Time of Day

It took several opening days before Tom and Archie accepted the old-timer's proverb, "Pa'tridge don't wake up till after the sun rises and they've had their second cup of coffee, so there's no point you getting out of bed till you've had yours." Those green years, when stories of whitetail deer saturated their imaginations from the pages of *Field &*

Stream, they assumed that all wildlife lived by the same timetable. And so, Tom and Archie would stalk grouse a half hour on the dark side of sunrise, listening through the curtain of daybreak for a pa'tridge to flush from a poplar thicket, a gorse bush, a low-hanging pine bough, an olden stone fence swallowed by the woods, all the likely places; but, of course, one never did. By their midtwenties, the comrades-in-arms mellowed to the advice about pa'tridge and other worldly things, and realized that their predawn ritual in the hunting fields held the dubious distinction of alerting their feathered foe to their presence as surely as if an alarm clock had gone off.

An Inauspicious Morning

"Are you ready?" Tom asked Archie with the solemnity of a Shakespearean actor about to make his entrance.

"Yes, I suppose so," Archie replied, though he could have said, "Alas! Poor Yorick. I knew him, Horatio," with equal compunction.

"C'mon, Bess," Tom said to his Lab, whose excellent genes largely compensated for her master's amateurish training skills. The black dog took off into the woods like the release of a coiled spring.

"Find a bird, Frost," Archie ordered, and the setter held her nose high in the air, nostrils twitching, eyes straightforward and radiant with the warmth of autumn, and bounded down the lane.

"They scent 'em!" Tom said and loaded a couple of cartridges into the chamber of his shotgun.

The crunching footsteps of determined hunters and the rushing of swift dogs through dry ferns and low brush sounded like the crashing surf against a rocky coast. An explosion of songbirds burst from a bed of gorse bushes. Frost's clanging cowbell pealed above the ruckus.

"Get ready," Archie said.

"For what? Tom asked.

"I feel a grouse."

"Where?"

A cloud of concern hovered over Archie's brow. He stopped dead in his tracks. "Hear that?" he whispered. A cantankerous squirrel was scolding them from nearby.

"A goddam squirrel? Tom hissed back.

"Don't you hear that Frost's bell stopped ringing?" The men saw a flash of white in a thicket of alders. "There she is," Archie continued softly. "You go left, I'll go right." And the hunting partners assumed the light footfall of Indians of yore, an exercise in woodscraft inspired by the novels of Kenneth Roberts, which they had consumed in their youth.

Suddenly, a blast pierced the woods. For one terrible moment, Archie thought Tom's gun had misfired, and likewise, Tom thought Archie's had. But Archie had merely stepped on a stick and alerted a fine, fat grouse, which took off like a rocket. You could speculate that the seasoned wingshooters knowingly withheld firing their guns at the thoroughly impossible shot. But that wasn't so.

"Does that to me every time," Tom confessed.

"Yeah, me, too," Archie confessed back.

"That first pa'tridge of the season always takes your breath away."

"Oh, I was going to shoot," Archie allowed, "but it was your shot."

"The bird was in your quarter."

"No, Tom, it was in yours."

"Well, even so, your dog was on point."

"Yes, that's true. Damn good dog. C'mere, Frost. Frost?" Archie blew his dog whistle. Soon the situation was clear. Frost hadn't found the bird. She was answering the call of nature when her master stepped on the stick and the grouse took flight. Bess, in the meantime, was nowhere to be seen. "With our luck, she's flushed all the grouse between here and Maine," Archie mumbled.

"I don't think so, Arch." Tom grimaced as they rounded the bend. Bess was scraping leaves over her fresh mark. "There's one thing I've observed about dogs, Arch. Where one leads, the others follow."

"And they say dogs aren't human." Archie chuckled.

The Old Lower Forty Covert

Tom and Archie were now approaching the second of the three hidden fields, a forty-acre patch that was home to the Lower Forty covey, which had sheltered generations of grouse. Archie dreamt of this place. Here he would get his long-coveted double.

"Bess, heel." Tom commanded and motioned to his friend to go it alone.

Archie nodded thanks and sent Frost in. The stylish setter looked like she came out of a nineteenth-century oil painting. She worked the thicket in a frenzy, then froze on point.

"Whoa, girl, steady," Archie said softly. Wait-a-bit thorns

tugged at his chaps. He maneuvered himself into a position parallel and slightly ahead of his dog, careful this time not to break the back of another tattletale branch. His trigger finger was poised along the guard; his muscles tense, alerted to shoulder his gun and swing at the first flurry of wings. It was warm for October, and Archie knew the grouse would sit until he was right on top of them. "Hunt 'em up," Arch encouraged Frost. She edged forward. Archie kicked up some leaves, took another step, and kicked up more leaves. Frost relaxed and flagged her tail.

Nothing.

That's it, Archie thought. *She's picked up old scent.* That flagging tail's a dead giveaway. "No bird," he said to Frost. He broke open his gun and shouted to Tom, "False point."

He glanced over at Frost. In those few passing seconds, she had stealthily inched forward to a rock-solid point. "Oh, geez, oh, no," Archie moaned. In the frenzy to snap his gun shut, he caught his cuff in the breech. Three grouse exploded five yards directly in front of him. It would have been a perfect crossing shot. Frost turned her head just enough to glare at her master with manifest disdain.

"Nothing here," Tom muttered.

"Nope," Archie sulked. "Nothing here."

This was one of those times when silence spoke fathoms.

A Grouse in Hand Is Worth . . .

The next lane led to the third hidden field. As kids, Tom and Archie named it the Enchanted Forest because it resembled the Wicked Witch of the West's woods in *The Wizard of Oz*. Even on the brightest day, this stretch remained cloaked in darkness. Once, they came upon a deer pelt with no sign of a carcass or bones, as though the animal had stepped out of its skin. Another time, they saw tracks that could only have been made by a mountain lion. Here, in the cool of the glen, they were sure to find a grouse.

"I'll send in Bess," Tom suggested. "She's bound to flush up a grouse, or even a 'cock."

Archie brightened at the idea of a double on woodcock. However, ideas—even good ideas—rarely produce a bird, and a good hunting Lab can only flush one if there's one to flush. Bess vaulted over fallen trees, burrowed into concealed crannies, searched stone fences, but not a grouse or a woodcock flushed.

"Let's head down to the old Beaver Dam covert," Tom suggested. But when they made their way into the bowels of the swamp, they were greeted with birds of a different feather: a flock of six mallards and a gaggle of seven Canada geese.

"It's just as well they took off," Tom allowed, as the men gazed forlornly after the departing birds, "seeing as we forgot our duck loads," whereupon the men took solace in a philosophical discussion about non-tox shotshells.

They emerged from the swamp around lunchtime, settled upon an inviting carpet of moss under an old oak tree, and took out their sandwiches. As you know, a sandwich that is eaten in the open air rivals the finest gourmet dinner, and root beer in a glass bottle bests champagne; and so, the hunting buddies ate their lunch under the shady tree, in the comfortable silence that comes with a friendship that fits like a favorite sweater. The warm sun, the carressing breeze, the moss bed that was as soft as an angora blanket, made them sleepy.

"Wouldn't mind stretching out for a minute or two," Tom said.

"Me, neither," Archie replied.

"Know something, Arch. Funny thing about pa'tridge," Tom reflected. "You see 'em even when they're not there."

"I know what you mean," Archie agreed.

"Take that rock, for instance."

"That rock?" Archie asked.

"Yeah, the one that's perched on that stone wall over there."

"Sure, I see it."

"Looks like a grouse, doesn't it."

"Yep. Looks just like a grouse."

At which point, the rock flew away.

Up in Arms

Unexpectedly reinvigorated, the men jumped to their feet and prepared to return to the hunting fields or, more appropriately, the battlefield, to wage war anew against the wily grouse.

"C'mon," Tom said. "Let's hunt the Old Churchyard covert," and they headed down a country lane to an old, abandoned cemetery.

"If only these stones could talk," Tom said.

Ghosts do haunt Hardscrabble, and a rash of cloud cover lent a pall to the graveyard. Frost crept between two headstones that had tipped over under the weight of time and locked on point. "Steady, girl, steady," Archie said, careful not to step on someone's grave. A brace of grouse lit from a low branch of an old apple tree and rocketed past the hunters. Tom withheld firing over ground where so many were supposedly resting in peace. To his surprise, two shots rang out well after the birds were out of range. Archie was red in the face. "Damn safety must have moved when the 'smith bent the stock."

The hunting buddies tried the Huntress Bridge covert and the old Trout Pond covert; they tried the old Blue Rock covert and the old Tiger Rock covert, but nary a bird was to be seen. Discouraged and rankling with disgust, they turned to familiar words of grief, such as, "It isn't the weight of your game bag, it's the sport," and, "We may have missed birds, but the birds didn't miss us. At least we were here for opening day." The sun, and their spirits, sank by the time they called it quits.

Nick Joins In

Tom and Archie had first met Nick shortly after college. Unlike them, Nick was lucky. He became a stockbroker at the height of the market, sold short, bought long, acquired a personal fortune, and paid taxes that were equivalent to Tom's and Archie's combined annual incomes. The friends never begrudged Nick his wealth.

They begrudged him his luck.

The first fish he ever caught was a trophy trout. He won the first regatta he ever sailed. Mount Washington was the first climb he ever attempted. And the year he took up skiing, he tackled Tuckerman's Ravine.

Nick bought a weekend home in Hardscrabble so he could spend quality time with his friends. For years, he decried guns, but Tom and Archie invited him to shoot sporting clays at the local club one day and, needless to say, Nick took to it like a duck to water.

So, when he expressed a desire to go bird-hunting, Tom and Archie agreed to take him the weekend after opening day. For once, Nick appeared unlucky. The weather was gray, cold, and gusty, with intermittent spits of rain. Birds wouldn't budge under conditions like this.

"Let's make it noon tomorrow, guys," Archie suggested on the telephone the night before. "No point going out before then."

They met up the next day. Nick had no gun.

"Where's your gun?" Archie said.

"Didn't bring it," Nick replied. "I limited out before breakfast!" Daggers flew from Archie's eyes. You could cut the thickening air that hovered around Tom with a knife. Nick, oblivious to the autumn of their discontent, rhapsodized, "My mother-in-law's with us this weekend, and she was having her coffee by the French door when she calls to me and there, on the deck railing, are four grouse lined up like a carnival shooting gallery."

"I don't want to hear this," Arch moaned to Tom.

"So I get my gun, go around front 'cause Paula would have killed me if I shot a gun in the living room, and—here's the best part—get two birds with one shot! And I only fired my right barrel!"

It was all Tom could do to restrain Archie from killing Nick. "Don't do it, Arch. It wasn't his fault that he took a Scotch double his first time on grouse."

Nick Does It Again

The rest of hunting season went steadily downhill from there. On the way to the Dump one day, Tom saw a grouse sunning itself smack in the middle of the road. Out of sheer desperation, he took his revolver out of the glove compartment of his car, aimed, and fired, scoring a clean miss. The grouse, he later told Archie, spat at him and waddled away.

There was hope. Deer season was looming on the horizon. Tom and Archie traditionally hunted deer early in the morning and late in the afternoon, and grouse in between; but it never seemed to fail: Whenever they carried rifles, they'd come upon a grouse; when they shouldered shotguns, they'd see a deer.

After burying the proverbial hatchet in a truly sporting gesture, Tom and Archie invited Nick to join them for opening day of deer season. This would be Nick's first deer hunt. As his immeasurable luck would have it, Nick got his hunting license the year before Hunters' Safety classes became mandatory. It was left to Tom and Archie to freely impart advice to their protégé, for which they credited his immediate proficiency to their talent as instructors.

Opening day arrived. The three were to meet at Archie's place at five o'clock in the morning, but by six, Nick still had not arrived.

"Let's go," Archie said. I'm not waiting all day." And with that, the two men began their customary drive to the top of Swett's Hill. Fifteen minutes later, the unmistakable crack of a rifle shot resonated throughout the valley. It had come near Archie's house. The men ran down the hill to find Nick standing in Archie's driveway—over a twelve-point buck.

"I can't believe it!" Nick burst out. "I got out of my car and heard this rustle—I thought it was you guys—and this deer comes out from behind Arch's house. . . ." Now it was Archie's turn to hold back Tom, who hadn't gotten a deer in twenty-two years.

Of course, Tom and Archie once again did the sporting thing and helped Nick get the deer to the weigh-in station; of course, the buck dressed out at 205 pounds; and of course, no deer came within the crosshairs of either Tom's or Archie's scope the entire season.

Then, the greatest insult of all occurred.

On the Wings of a Grouse

It was the day after New Year's and two days after the close of grouse season; that time of year when the exhausting festivities of the holidays are over and the ordeal of winter lies ahead. It was a quiet day until a resounding crash shattered the silence at Tom's house. He himself was at his shop; his wife was home with the baby and the dog. Certain of their safety, she searched for the cause of the commotion. On the living room sofa was a fat, dazed grouse. Stunned to find itself perched upon the unnatural habitat of a floral chintz slipcover, the bird soiled it, then sat back, content. Brilliant sunlight reflecting off the Tudor window obviously confused the feathered missile, which launched through a pane. Glass was everywhere, but the bird, surprisingly, was unscathed.

Tom's wife ran to the telephone to call her husband, but the line was busy. Seized with laughter, she called Archie in Boston. Her husband and his best friend had spent three months hunting in vain for grouse, and now one was sitting on her brand-new living room sofa!

"Archie," she giggled, "you won't believe this! There's a grouse sitting on our sofa."

There was a heavy silence. "Listen carefully," he instructed. "Don't go near her. She could be pregnant. If she's pregnant, she may attack you."

"She? Pregnant? Attack me? Archie, stop kidding. This isn't some Alfred Hitchcock movie!"

Moments later, her husband appeared—with a fishing net. "Where is she? Archie just called me. We have to be very careful. He suspects she's pregnant. He says only a woman would do a thing like that."

Tom's wife stopped laughing.

"Bess," Tom commanded the dog, avoiding his wife's glare, "keep away." The Lab was jumping in the air, ecstatic at finally seeing a grouse. Gently, Tom scooped the bird into the net, ran to the front door, and released her. The bird took off, circled back, and left a parting gift on the shoulder of Tom's new Barbour sweater.

There's Always Next Season

Even the deepest wounds heal in time. By next opening day, all was forgiven though not entirely forgotten. Tom and Archie never went grouse hunting with Nick again, who came to favor the local preserve where, he said, you could get more birds for your bang. However, the three friends gathered together for opening day of deer season. After all, Tom and Archie figured that Nick's luck would eventually put a deer in front of one—or maybe both—of them.

But then, that's another story.

"Well, what do you think?" I asked Kip. He had just finished reading "The Adventures of Tom and Archie." I could tell from his chuckles that the story struck his funny bone—and his cringes brought back how Nature's lesser children managed to foil him time and time again.

"You don't think anyone will ever see that this is about Ted and me, do you?" Kip was concerned. After all, reveling in a hunter's successful exploits is one thing; uncovering his failures is another.

"Look, Kip," I said, "you told me yourself that if I was going to write stories about Hardscrabble, then I had to draw from the truth."

"Yeah." Kip shrugged. "But did you have to be so truth-ful?"

"Okay, I'll tear this up if it hurts your feelings," I said, reaching across the sofa to take the story away from my husband. Kip put the sheaf of papers down on the coffee table, stood up, took my hands in his, and pulled me to my feet.

"You did hurt my feelings," he murmured, enfolding me in his arms. "But I know how you can make it all better."

ᘛ ELEVEN ᘚ

$\mathscr{E}$ach $\mathscr{Y}$ear $\mathscr{I}$s $\mathscr{S}$even

[Beauty is] an omnipresence of death and loveliness, a smiling sadness that we discern in nature and all things, a mystic communion that the poet feels—an expression of it can be a dustbin with a shaft of sunlight across it, or it can be a rose in the gutter.

—Charlie Chaplin

$\mathscr{H}$e was in the midst of dictation when he realized, out of a clear sky, what day it was. It might not have occurred to him at all if he had not happened to glance at the dog, curled asleep on an easy chair in the study. "I just happened to think, Miss Marsh," he observed. "This is Tober's birthday."

"Yours, too, isn't it, Mr. Hilton?" she asked with a smile.

He looked at her in surprise. "How did you remember that?"

"Because I—" She caught herself and said lightly, "A good secretary is supposed to remember dates and things."

He nodded. Mary Marsh was a good secretary; he had been lucky to find her, way back here in the country. She had left a good job in the city to take care of her widowed mother in the old family place down the road, and she was glad to pick up a little extra money typing manuscripts. Very efficient, very quiet: a little touch of gray in her dark hair, a low and pleasant voice, alert eyes. Sometimes when he was dictating he caught her eyes resting on him with a curious look, bright with secret laughter. She asked, "How old is Tober?"

"Let's see. Seven this year." He scratched the sleeping setter's ear; Tober unpeeled a lid and looked up at him for a moment. "They say every year in a dog's life equals seven, so actually that makes him . . . forty-nine." He realized for the first time: "We're just the same age."

Somehow he was not happy that he had thought of it. It depressed him. Maybe it was the gloomy afternoon, with the fall rain slashing at the windows and the leaves plastered against the glass. He didn't feel like dictating.

"I guess that will be all for today, Miss Marsh." He rose formally. Miss Marsh stood up, folding her notebook. "You can be working on those revisions on chapter four." Her bright eyes searched his face, and he added with business-like precision, "Thank you, Miss Marsh."

"Thank you, Mr. Hilton." She paused. "Congratulations."

The big house was quieter after she had left, and the rain on the roof drummed steadily. He strolled into the living room and stirred the coals in the hearth; the setter crawled off the chair, pausing to stretch his full length for a moment, and padded after his master into the living room and collapsed heavily in front of the hearth with a long sigh.

"We're both getting old, Tober," Jeffrey Hilton said.

"Tober" was short for October S. Hilton; he had been named after his birth month, and Eden had supplied the S. "After Harry Truman's middle name." She had laughed. Jeff could still hear the echo of her laugh, and it hurt him, as it always did when he thought of her. Everything had been an adventure when they were together. They had bought this old house on an impulse. "Jeff, the view. That way the lilac bushes frame it . . . and that adorable old well . . . and the barn down there." They had fixed up the place together, and it had been fun; everything had been fun. Eden loved to live so much, he thought to himself, and it was the thing she could not hold. They had bought the puppy on an impulse—"The same birthday, Jeff"—just the year before she died.

He walked out into the kitchen, and Tober followed him. Old Mrs. Farnsworth had left some cold meat and salad on a plate, and he carried it back to the living room. No sense setting the table just for himself. In front of the fireplace was Eden's favorite chair, and the flowered silk upholstery she had loved; no one ever sat in it since her death. The house was like a museum; his whole life was in the past, with an invisible velvet cord to keep the world out.

"Get a grip on yourself, Jeff," his hunting buddy, Mack, kept telling him. "It's no good. You can't bring her back."

Can't bring her back. But Jeff couldn't shake her. He wanted Eden back. It had been six years, and he wanted her more and more—more now than ever before. Tober lifted his head and looked at his master with soft brown eyes that understood.

Jeff had told her not to go out. The roads were icy underneath the early-winter snow. "Don't worry, Jeff. It's only a dusting. I won't be gone long, honest." Won't be gone long . . . but she'd left for a lifetime.

"Take the long way around then, honey," Jeff had said uneasily. "The hill into town can be pretty treacherous."

She'd given him a playful peck on the cheek. "Don't worry so much." She'd smiled, and he remembered the carefree way she'd swung her coat over her shoulders and closed the door behind her, leaving the house and him forever.

Tober cradled his noble head between his paws and halfway closed his heavy-lidded eyes, keeping a sleepy watch over Jeff. Jeff lit his pipe, sucked in the sweet smoke, and fell back into the softness and security of his easy chair. Why didn't she listen? She should have listened. He should have insisted.

The injuries had been too serious. The doctors had said no one could have come out of that kind of accident. "If by some miracle she does, she'll never walk or speak again, Mr. Hilton," they had whispered.

Jeff and Eden never spoke of their love. It was something that never needed words. It was always there. Even when they were apart. Even now, when she was gone. The sound of the rain beating on the roof grew louder and snapped Jeff out of the past, back to the present.

"You've got to get on with things," Mack had tried to tell him. "You've got to get on with living. Eden wouldn't have wanted you to give up. You know that." Sure, he knew. But he had given up. So what? He didn't go fishing anymore, and when he went out with Tober during bird season, they went alone. He didn't see much of Mack these days. He missed the company sometimes. He missed her all the time.

At first Jeff didn't hear the knock through the beating rain. Tober did and bolted from his slumbering sprawl to the front door, barking in his muffled dog voice. It was the only voice Jeff heard these days, except for Mrs. Farnsworth's . . . and Mary Marsh's.

She stood there, drenched, drawing her raincoat over a picnic basket she held close to her knees.

"Miss Marsh, come out of the rain," Jeff urged, surprised to see her.

"I should have called, Mr. Hilton, but I just wanted to drop off a present. It's a birthday cake of sorts. It just didn't seem right to let the occasion pass without one."

"That's very thoughtful of you, Miss Marsh, but I've gotten in the habit of passing over my birthday."

"Oh, it's not for you, Mr. Hilton." She smiled, setting the basket down as Jeff helped her out of her dripping coat and hung it in the foyer closet. "It's for Tober. After all, it's his birthday, too."

Mary Marsh opened the basket and took out a pie still steaming from the oven. She knelt down and put it on the floor in front of Tober. The setter wagged his tail furiously. "Hamburger pie, Mr. Hilton," Miss Marsh explained. "After all, it's only once a year." She petted Tober, who was intent on savoring his birthday present.

Funny, Jeff thought. *That's something Eden would have done. . . . She even scratched Tober's ears the way Eden did. Funny how I never noticed that before.*

He looked at Mary as if for the first time. She didn't look at all like Eden. Eden's hair was blond; Mary's was almost black. Eden had shining blue eyes like the sky on a cloudless summer day. Mary's were . . . She suddenly looked up at him, and he saw hazel eyes shimmering like the sun-lit leaves of autumn. Eden's laugh was different, like a soft April breeze. He listened to Tober's bell jingle as he ate his birthday pie, and the ring of Mary's gentle laughter made a sweet melody.

She stood up. "I'd better go. . . ."

"No," Jeff said into her warm eyes, which sparkled now like the deep waters of a trout pond. "After a rain like this, the roads get slick. That hill into town can be pretty treacherous."

"Don't worry," she said, reaching for her raincoat. "I'll take the long way around."

"Why don't you wait awhile," Jeff said. "Besides, I think I'd enjoy some company on my birthday."

Mary looked at him quizzically. He had never asked her

to stay before except to finish a manuscript. Jeff felt her hesitation. She turned and put back her coat. Suddenly the rain stopped, and rays of sunlight passed through the large picture window in the living room like beams from a lantern.

"I think it's finally going to clear up," Jeff said, and Mary smiled as they walked together through the shafts of light to the pair of chairs in front of the fireplace. Jeff gestured to one. Mary settled comfortably in the chair with the flowered silk upholstery.

Somehow it suited her.

$\mathcal{L}$ost

You gain strength, courage and confidence by every experience in which you really stop to look fear in the face. You are able to say to yourself, "I lived through this horror. I can take the next thing that comes along. . . . You must do the thing you think you cannot do.

—*Eleanor Roosevelt*

$\mathcal{S}$he knew the tears would come. They didn't come often, and she hated it when they did. But she was lost, really lost in the woods, and she was beginning to get frightened. She had never been frightened before, at least not like this—but it came from the same place, the fear. It came from within, that helpless place in her soul, the dark compartment she kept securely locked. She knew too well what it was to feel helpless. Helpless, like the day she lost her only daughter. She didn't want to think about that right now; she couldn't. She had to find her way out of the woods and get home. Home to her family. It was going to be dark in a couple of hours, and she was completely turned around.

They would be getting worried. Even her little springer

spaniel seemed concerned as she stood alongside her, looking up expectantly. Her husband knew where she had gone, or at least where she was going. Her sons knew this place well, too. They learned to hunt here. That was . . . what? Ten years ago . . . "Don't worry," her husband had assured her. "I'll take care of them. No, they're not too young. I was eight when my father took me bird hunting for the first time. . . ." Now their sons were at the cusp of adulthood, and yet it seemed like only yesterday. She wouldn't have been lost if they were with her; she shouldn't have gotten lost in the first place. After all, she learned to hunt here, too, all those years ago. But then she gave it up, had the children, kept the home fires burning. Then the baby died. Afterwards, when she learned to live with the terrible emptiness in her heart and tried to get on with it, she took up hunting again. Bird hunting, and now this fall she was going after deer with her husband and their boys. She loved the woods; it was so peaceful. And the hunting, well, that was a good way to fill the place her daughter was meant to fill, to dull the loss, to understand that expectation always falls short when you want something so very, very much.

No, she shouldn't have gotten lost, but she did. These woods went on and on for miles, through swamps and hills and valleys and on to nowhere, for all anyone knew.

Once it had been a thriving New Hampshire village with homesteads and even a meetinghouse. You could still make out the road that led to it, but now it was only forested trail. Here and there lay foundations of old houses and barns. A stone corral for sheep had tumbled with time, barely an out-line, bordered by ancient lilac bushes. Apple trees marked the foundation of an outlying farmhouse, out here, another there; they were overgrown and gnarled and shouldn't, but did, bear fruit, still, in the fall. She picked a ruby-red apple and pierced it lightly with her teeth, expecting bitter juice. But the apple was sweet, and she was hungry, and she ate it and picked another. Her pup jumped up, begging for a bite, and she gave her the core to devour. She stopped crying because the apple was comforting and she felt revived.

The leaves were brilliant, more brilliant against the blanket of darkening gray sky than they ever are on a cloudless, peacock-blue day. Good artists never attempted to paint autumn, she thought, because only nature knew how to mix the right palette. She used to paint, but she had given it up. When the baby died, she lost her inspiration. She couldn't deal with joy unrealized after she had been robbed of her only chance to raise a daughter. She wanted her so much. As time passed, it hurt more, and she didn't understand why. Tears again pinched her eyes, and she tried to fight them back.

Would she have raised her little girl to hunt? Probably not. When her sons and husband went hunting, she and her daughter would have gone shopping and done girlish things together. It would have become a joke. She would have threatened her husband with a big credit card bill as he and the boys took off for yet another weekend hunting deer. And he would have put her over his knee and pretended to spank her, and the children would have laughed. Yes, he and the boys would have gone hunting, and she and their daughter would have gone shopping, and everyone would have had a good time and lots to tell over Sunday night supper.

But her husband couldn't hold her over his knee anymore, not since he got sick. That was just after the baby died, when his legs got weak and he couldn't go hunting anymore, at least not like he used to. Now that the boys were older, they would drive their dad to a promising place, and he'd sit and wait for a deer while his sons went stalking in the forest. Last year, he took a fine buck that way, just under two hundred pounds dressed. Lately he felt better, and he could walk a mile sometimes. Last Sunday grouse season opened, and they took their hot little springer pup out for her first opening day. She put up four grouse. It was such a delight to finally have a good dog to flush their favorite coverts that they missed every single shot; and laughed, like they used to.

How did she get so turned around? She hefted her shot-gun, breech open, over her shoulder and headed out of the old orchard, away from the once-was town. Stupidly, she left her compass in her other jacket, but the sun was setting, and she made that her marker. Her dog became lively again, as if to say, "Good, let's go home." But that wasn't it, she thought, that wasn't it at all. She brought her gun down, loaded a shell in each chamber, and no sooner had she closed the breech than her dog pounced on a fat grouse hen. The bird exploded from the forest floor with a whirrrr, hell-bent for safe haven. She swung her gun to her shoulder, pointed the barrels, and felled the bird with the second shot.

A sudden gust like a tailwind lifted the spaniel high over a crumbling stone wall as she bounded to retrieve the grouse. So majestic, the grouse, and she remembered the legend her husband told her of how Indians would say a prayer over their game, thanking their brother of the forest for sacrificing his life to sustain theirs. She whispered a tender prayer. She needed to speak to the silence; and the mighty pines arched overhead like a forest cathedral. The brisk evening wind blew her damp cheeks dry. It was at dusk eight Octobers ago today that her baby died in her arms.

Now she found herself in a fern-covered glen. The forest floor was awash with that golden cast peculiar to autumn sunsets. It reminded her of a happy time—how many years ago?—it must be going on twenty-five, when she and her husband first hunted together here. Here? Yes! She knew this place: She was at the beaver pond. They had brought a picnic and had drunk wine and then made love in the soft grass there, at the shoulder of the pond. The leaves shivered and shook loose the memory of a long-ago soft summer breeze that caressed their bare bodies, warmed by the sun, warmed from the loving. She wanted those days back, she wanted her daughter, she wanted to go home.

She saw the hill beyond the beaver pond and knew that uphill was the forgotten cemetery and beyond that, the road. It was a hard climb, but she was sure about it now, and it gave her renewed strength and hope. Her pup took the hill with trouble, for the ground was thick with brambles. She kept up with the little springer, her eye marking a birch tree that had splintered and fallen into the fork of a giant maple. Out of nowhere, a limb suddenly slingshot and cut her above her chin. She felt it sting, and a drop of blood trickled onto her red turtleneck, against her black hair, and she grabbed at the branch that dared injure her and broke it off with a snap. High above she could see the horizon through the pines, and she lunged forward, her arm bent to shield her face as tree limbs tore at her clothes as if trying to hold her back. There it was, the little cemetery. Seven head-stones, that's all. Only seven, but they told the whole story. *"Their name was Eldridge,"* her husband's voice spoke to her across the years, *"and they owned that farm over there. Look. You can see the foundation."* She again turned her eyes in the direction he had pointed. It was still there, just a vestige of a place and a time that was no more.

"A father, a mother, and their five children. See this little

marker with the lamb? She was the first, she died at birth." Just like my daughter, *she thought;* just like my own baby. *"And next to that,"* the memory voice of her husband continued through the past, *"three, all in a row. Two boys and a girl, ages two, three, and five. All within a week. It was smallpox. The epidemic took the whole village."* She thought, Oh my God. I lost just one child. How did that mother survive? *Then she saw the fifth stone and remembered the mother hadn't. "Within a year,"* her husband's voice trailed, *"the mother . . . they say she died from grief."* And the sixth? The sixth tombstone was the last child, a son, killed in the First World War. Just turned eighteen. The last stone, the seventh. It was less tarnished by years than the others, dated six years after the soldier boy's. The father's. He was helpless. There was nothing he could do but watch each of his loved ones die. They say he finally went mad from grief. . . .

Helpless . . .

She didn't know how much time had passed, how long she sat pondering over the fate of the poor farmer and his family, how long she mourned for them, for herself. Her pup was asleep at her feet, and the autumn air was now cold with damp, the sky dark. This was a good place to leave her grief, she thought. Let it go, get on with it, find the road. But she felt the weight of her soul heavy upon her as she stood up to go.

She left the cemetery through the stone posts, squeezing past a sapling that had grown smack between them. How tremendous, she thought, as she realized it was a Gilead tree. She picked a leaf and rubbed it on her hand, aching for some balm to heal the wound within.

And ahead was the road. After that she knew her way. Her pace quickened as each step brought her closer to familiar ground. *It's time to get on with it,* she thought. Not to sorrow. She had blessings to enjoy, far more blessings than sorrows.

And then, with utter disbelief, she saw them. Ahead of her on the road were three grouse, dancing up and down and beating their wings all for joy, dusting the dry dirt road with their tails. Even the pup paused to look at the pageant. The birds continued to whirl and flutter, and the shiver of gold and red and orange leaves accompanied them like delicate music. All she could do was watch in wonderment.

The cover of night was gently descending upon the forest when, from a distance, there shone a light. Headlights. "Mom? Mom!" voices cried. "Are you all right?" Her sons raced toward her, scattering the grouse, which then pirouetted high into the air like fireworks and disappeared into the woods. Not far behind was her husband.

"Yes . . . I'm here. . . . I'm all right!" she cried as she ran to her family. Each step felt lighter. Each step carried her closer to the shelter of her loved ones. Each step took her farther and farther from the burden she left behind. For she had finally unlocked the compartment in her soul and gently, lovingly, laid her sorrow to rest in the holiness of the woods.

This episode is out of timing with the rest of this book. From cover to cover, *The Hardscrabble Chronicles* accounts for a mere two of the thirty years I've lived here. "Lost" happened to me about fifteen years ago.

Losing a child is hope dashed. The loss of hope, no matter how great or for what reason—whether for a brief time or for a period that lingers, festers, and disintegrates into blackness—is a cruel and heavy burden. I carried mine to Tinkhamtown where unexpectedly, a light filtered through the forest, and through my grief, and illuminated the dark place in my heart.

Loss is part of living. The Whys are seldom understood, often never known, but we can profit from loss. I was lost. I had lost faith. But in a single unplanned moment, I found it once again—or perhaps it found me. The rediscovery of faith is an act of grace.

Remember, in your own journey you don't have to look for a tranquil place like Tinkhamtown. Just search for the tranquil place in your heart. It's there, if you look hard enough.

You'll know when you find it.

THIRTEEN

The Sheep Killer

If you forgive people enough you belong to them, and they to you, whether either person likes it or not—squatter's rights of the heart.

—*James Hilton*

There was no reason not to believe Bert Ramsdell except for one thing: He couldn't possibly have seen what he swore he saw. Still, there was no question about what had happened. The proof was as clear as the blood-stained snow in his barnyard. Six sheep—four ewes and two lambs—lay dead, their throats ripped open by a savage animal that Bert insisted was a wolf.

"You say your dog began barking," Officer Oak of the Hardscrabble Police Department reiterated.

"That's right, Officer," Bert replied, as he stroked the velvety ears of his yellow Lab, Belle. "She got so excited, I thought she'd bolt through the window. Then the sheep started to bleat, and I grabbed my shotgun."

"And Belle?"

"I didn't let her out. She's going to have puppies, and besides, it was dark, and I didn't want to shoot her by mistake. Don't know what I'd do without my Belle. . . ."

"And you say you saw . . ."

"A wolf. Clear as day."

"Sir, how can you be so sure on a night like this?" the officer asked, looking up at the starless sky.

"I'm telling you, Officer. It was a wolf."

"Mr. Ramsdell," Officer Oak muttered as he penciled some notes into his logbook, "there haven't been any wolves in these parts since the night old Al Harmond's great-great-grandfather stole the bell from the First Christian Church and hoisted it into the steeple of the First Baptist Church."

Bert waited for the rest of the story, but the tall, gaunt officer only seemed intent on scribbling his notes. "What about old Al Harmond's great-great-grandfather and the wolf?" Bert asked at length.

Oak lifted his eyes from his logbook, arched a grizzled eyebrow, and replied with a hint of disdain, "Well, son. That's the difference between a townsfolk and a flatlander, isn't it." And with that, he cast his eyes and attention back to his note taking.

For a moment, Bert Ramsdell thought the crime wasn't the savage slaughter of his sheep but the fact that he was indeed, through no fault of his own, a flatlander. Now, you well know that there are two unequal factions in this Town. But Bert Ramsdell was wrapped up in his newly acquired farm and as innocent as a baby when it came to Town politics. As far as Bert was concerned, he exchanged plenty of pleasantries with native townsfolk at the Post Office and at Tilt's Store. He'd even been to a Church supper and was surprised how cordial townsfolk were toward him. All well and good, but there are limits. For instance, a native never bought a flatlander a cone at the Old Home Week Annual Ice Cream Social. A native would never show a flatlander his secret pa'tridge covert, or tell him which fly the trout were biting. There was only one time when the line was crossed. That was eight years ago, at the Masons' Ball when Ralph Tasker, who runs Tasker's Septic & Well Drilling ("Our business is going in the hole") got in his cups and fox-trotted that Boston Brahmin, Mrs. Claude Wilkins II, to "Chattanooga Choo-choo" to the consternation of Mr. Claude Wilkins II, who cut in, collapsed, and died on the final choo-choo as a result of a stroke.

You saw what happened when the flatlanders wanted road signs. I didn't tell you what happened when the flatlanders stood up at the annual Town Meeting before last and moved to have the Dump renamed the Hardscrabble Recycling Center. Or when they thought the dog warden should be called the animal control officer.

"They move here complaining they didn't like the way their own towns have been changing," Major Fred Ford fumed as he was getting shaved over to Charlie's Cut & Shave, "so they come here and set out to change ours."

"Wal," Charlie replied, "we been doing pretty good these last two centuries. Daresay we can handle it for another couple more."

These are the differences, and more, that Bert did not understand. So, no matter how vehemently he insisted upon what he saw or how solid the evidence may prove, neither Officer Oak—or any other native, for that matter—was about to believe him. There was no use pressing the point. The jury was out and wasn't coming back. The silent, high court of born-and-bred Hardscrabble townsfolk would invariably ignore Bert's claim and even censure him.

After all, a wolf hadn't set foot in Hardscrabble since old Al Harmond's great-great-grandfather stole that bell—but that's another story, and we should get back to ours.

* * *

$\mathcal{T}$he adjuster from Carroll County Reassurance & Trust carefully tore the check along the perforation and handed it to Bert. He forewarned him not to expect much, but Bert wasn't prepared for so little.

"I'm sorry," the faded man in the gray suit said, "but in situations like this—"

"Look, Mr. Cassidy," Bert interrupted, smacking the check with the back of his fingers, "this hardly covers what I've got into raising those ewes, and the lambs were already spoken for!"

"I understand," the faded man answered nervously as he straightened out his drab tie. "But our policy clearly states, 'In the event of a dog attack, the Insured will be reimbursed the replacement cost of livestock at market price—'"

"Dog attack?" Bert exclaimed. "It wasn't a dog that killed my sheep. It was a wolf!"

"Well, now, I don't know about any wolf, Mr. Ramsdell. I have to go by the police report that was submitted to my company." Mr. Cassidy adjusted his bifocals on the bridge of his beaklike nose, then leafed through an oaktag file. "Yes . . . it says right here in black and white that your sheep were killed by a dog. . . ."

Dog! Bert stopped listening to the dull drone of the pallid insurance man. He knew that Officer Oak hadn't believed him. What he didn't know was that Oak had purposely misstated Bert's account on the official police report. This cast a different light on the matter. Not believing his testimony was one thing. Covering it up was another.

$\mathcal{A}$ll that night, Bert tossed and turned in bed, weighing his options and trying to figure out what to do. He could lodge a complaint against Officer Oak and demand that he set the record straight. He could turn a blind eye and forget the situation. Or he could confront Oak himself.

He chose the latter.

The next morning, Bert called the Hardscrabble Police Department only to learn that Officer Oak was on patrol. "Would you please ask him to come up to Horse Ledge Hill Farm?" he asked the dispatcher.

"I'll make sure he gets the message," a nasal female voice replied, pronouncing *message* like *massage*.

Later that afternoon, Bert was leading a colt out of the stable when Belle started to growl. Officer Oak appeared around the corner. The Lab snarled and bared her teeth.

"What's got into you, girl?" Bert admonished Belle as he tethered the colt to a granite post. "Calm down, now. You know this man." But as Oak walked closer, Belle got even more agitated. Bert raised his hand to signal to Oak. "Hold off a minute, Officer," Bert said, raising his voice over Belle's barking. "I don't know what's come over her. Perhaps it's because she's almost ready to have her pups. Let me get her inside." He grabbed Belle by the collar and took her into the house. "I'm sorry about that," Bert said, returning. "I've never seen her do that with anyone before."

"No problem, sir. It happens. She's just protecting her own."

"Officer Oak," Bert resumed. "My insurance man was here, and he showed me your report. It seems you made a mistake."

"A mistake, sir?"

"Yes, a mistake. You wrote that my sheep were attacked by a dog when you know quite well that I stated it was a wolf. I'm asking you change your report."

Oak pulled himself up to his full height of six feet. Staring Bert straight in the eye he said, "I reported what I believe is the correct assessment of the situation. Unless you have proof to the contrary, my report stands."

"Look," Bert said, raising his voice a little. "I don't like being called a liar. I know what I saw, and I saw a wolf."

The policeman paused, and a change of expression came over his face. Calmly, quietly, he said, "Son, just be grateful your dog didn't get out. That animal you saw was no wolf. It had to be a rabid dog. It was dark. Anyone could have mistaken what they saw. If your Belle had gotten into a dogfight, chances are she'd get hurt pretty bad and infected, even killed. Have you ever seen a dog with rabies? It's not a pretty sight."

"I'm telling you, it was a wolf."

"All right. But I'm sorry, I'm not changing my report." And with that, Officer Oak nodded his head good-bye and walked back to his patrol car. Bert heard the engine start and didn't move until the sound of the motor grew fainter as Oak drove down the long drive and out of earshot.

It was dusk by the time Bert had finished his chores and remembered the mail. He got onto his John Deere and bounced down the drive to his red mailbox. Among the bills and flyers was a plain white envelope postmarked "Hardscrabble, March 23." There was no return address, and he didn't recognize the handwriting: "Mr. Bertram Ramsdell, Horse Ledge Hill Farm, Town." He gingerly opened the envelope. Written on a single sheet of paper was: "Hope this helps. From a friend."

Inside the note was a bank check made out to Bert for one thousand dollars.

* * *

A week passed when again Bert was awakened by Belle. She was standing on her hind legs at the window, scratching at the sill, her lips curled over her teeth in frenzied rage. Unlike the last time, this night was brightly lit by a galaxy of iridescent stars and a full moon. Bert looked out the window, and sure enough, advancing deliberately and stealthily toward the barn was the wolf. His coat glistened like silver under the luminous cast of the evening sky, and his black eyes burned like two live coals. Jumping into his boots, Bert grabbed his gun and bolted out of the door, but it was too late. Like a thunderbolt, Belle burst from the house and charged at the wolf, but before she reached him, a gunshot pierced the terrible still of the night. For a moment Bert was startled, fearing his gun had blindly discharged. But then he realized the shot came from another gun—Oak's. The wolf fell to the ground.

The officer dropped his smoking gun, ran to the fallen animal, and fell to his knees. Gathering the lifeless body in his arms, he buried his head in the silver fur, and sobbed. Bert hurried to Oak's side and froze in shock. The animal before him wasn't a wolf. It was a dog—a Siberian husky.

Officer Oak's dog.

"He got out again, and I knew he'd return to your place," Oak whispered. "That night he attacked your sheep. I looked all over for him, but I didn't think he'd get this far. Then I got the call to come to your farm, and I knew. When I got home, Scout was waiting for me on the front porch, covered in blood, acting like nothing had happened. Even then, I couldn't bring myself to putting him down. He's all I had. My wife died last May, and my boy, he's far away, stationed out at Kaneohe Marine Corps Base in Honolulu." Slowly Oak got up, took a red bandanna out of his back pocket, and wiped his face. "I know what I did was wrong, but I thought I could save Scout. I'd been medicating him, and the symptoms seemed to go away. But tonight, when he got away a second time, I knew what I had to do." Shakily, Oak stood up and hoisted the body of his beloved dog over his shoulder and said, "Now you do what you have to do, son." Oak walked away, paused, then turned around. "I tried to tell you," he called back to Bert. "Your sheep were killed by a dog. I couldn't lie on that report."

*T*wo weeks passed before Bert Ramsdell showed up at the police station. Officer Oak saw him come in and rose solemnly from behind his desk.

"Officer, I've come to lodge a complaint," Bert stated. "I'm sorry it's taken so long to get down to the Village, but you know how it gets on a farm during lambing season."

"I expected that," Officer Oak replied like a man prepared to hear his sentence.

"I've come . . ." Bert stopped to clear his throat. "I've come because you never told me the end of that story."

"Story?" Oak replied with surprise.

"You know, the one about old Al Harmond's great-great-grandfather and the wolf."

There was a pause. Oak sat down, tipped back his chair, crossed his feet on his desk, and chuckled.

"And another thing," Bert continued. "About that check . . ." Oak turned red. "You didn't know that Melanie Wells at the bank and I have been dating, did you?" Bert stretched out his hand. "Thanks," he said warmly. "That check went a long way." He turned to go, then stopped. "Oh . . . one more thing." Bert reached into the pocket of his waterproof jacket. "Belle sent you a present."

He took a black ball of fur and placed it gently in Josiah Oak's large, veined hands. The officer held the puppy close to his face and smiled as a wet, pink tongue licked his cragged cheek.

"He seems to like you." Bert said. "He's yours if you want him. Needs to be with his mom for a while, but he'll be ready in about a month."

Oak didn't say a word. He ran his hand over the back of the black Lab pup, said, "I think I'll call him Scout. Should grow up to be a pretty good water dog, I bet."

"I bet he will." Bert smiled.

"You know," Oak said, resuming his usual demeanor, "I have this secret pa'tridge covert . . . Maybe this fall, Scout," he tussled the little pup's ears, "and I will show it to you."

"Now, Officer Oak," Bert grinned, "I'd like that very much. But please . . . would you finally tell me what the hell happened to old Al Harmond's great-great-grandfather and the wolf the night he stole the bell from the First Christian Church!"

"Son," Officer Oak replied. "I reckon it's time you knew."

FOURTEEN

At the Hardscrabble Village Store

I remember old Tilt, who used to run the country store in town. Tilt was a typical New Hampshire man, independent, small-spoken, scowling over his spectacles at all intruders. He would sit in his rocking-chair by the stove, and growl at any customer who came in: "Naow, whatinell do you want?" His attitude toward the world was best expressed one morning when I found him washing the big window in front of the store, removing the winter's accumulation of grime.

"Cleaning the window so people can see in, Tilt?" I asked him.

"Naw," he grunted, "so I can see out."

—Corey Ford

*J*udge Parker told Corey Ford stories that he, then, put on paper, and that's how I got some, too. Here's one that took place before my time, but I'm retelling it as it was told to me. Men and women, husbands and wives . . . some things just never change.

* * *

he regular September meeting of the Lower Forty Shooting, Angling and Inside Straight Club was held the other afternoon in the rear of Tilt's Store. All the regular members were present. Judge Parker, the self-appointed president of the Lower Forty, opened the meeting as usual with a twenty-minute report on fly-fishermen's wives, using his own as an example, and informed his fellow members that wives were thieves when it came to fishing things and, as it turned out, this was the second time he had to salvage his old fishing jacket with the ripped lining from the Ladies' Guild's rummage sale.

"This is a very serious situation," the Judge said. "You know how long it takes to soak a fishing jacket good with bug dope? Six years? Mebbe seven? Just when I get it ripe so the moskeeters stay away, my wife rifles through my closet and smuggles it clear out of the house!" The Judge bristled.

"Goldurn wives are always interferin' with a man's business," Tilt grumbled.

"Unfortunately, you can't live with them, and you can't live without them," sighed Mert Grant as he chewed on his unlit cigar.

"Lucky thing I dropped by the Ladies' Guild's little fete. Got some pretty good feathers off some of them women's hats they had lying on the sales table. Perfect for tying flies," the Judge gloated.

"You don't mean to say you plucked the feathers right off the hats, do you?" Dave Trenton asked.

"Sure," Judge Parker replied casually. "Them women look like a covey of pa'tridge in Church on Sundays in those hats. Makes me itch for my 12-bore right around the Doxology. This'll compensate me for all the aggravation I have to put up with from Patience whenever I want to go fishing. Besides, these feathers will make some pretty fine trout flies."

The next order of business—even though there was never any order or, for that matter, any real business—was to decide the location and strategy for opening day of bird season which, as we all know, opens the first of October and is second only to Christmas Day. Judge Parker asked for the report by the Committee on Plans and Procedures, and Doc stood up.

"I make a motion we follow that old logging road down by Nason's farm. Saw Farmer Libbey yesterday. Said he hit two pa'tridge with his truck last week along by there and never ate meatier fowl, though he did crack a tooth on some birdshot," Doc said.

At that moment Patience Parker, Judge Parker's wife, accompanied by two other women, came barreling through the door of Tilt's Store with the fire of battle in her eyes.

"Merrow Parker!" his wife stormed. "Lettie here says she saw you from the Post Office window plucking the feathers off of the hats on the sale table, and I believe you'd do such a thing. Admit it!" She gestured toward the white-haired postmistress, who was bobbing her head as though she were bobbing for apples.

"Patience, you know you gals look like a gaggle of geese in those hats," Judge Parker said uneasily, as Tilt reached for the jug of Old Stump Blower and took a swig to calm his nerves. He handed it over to the Judge, but Patience glowered even hotter, if that was possible. "Not now, Tilt," he whispered. "That'll only fuel the fire." Then Judge Parker stood up and with outstretched hands, said to his wife, "I was only doing you a favor, dear."

"Favor!" Patience Parker exploded.

"Wal, yes," the Judge replied. "Why, without them feathers, we men can focus more on your lovely faces—"

"Enough is enough, Merrow!" Patience said. "This time you've gone too far!"

"Patience," Doc interrupted, "you ladies can see we are having our regular meeting now, and of course, as you probably know from your own rules when you have your Ladies' Guild meetings, only members can have the floor."

"Except on Ladies' Day," Dave Trenton interjected.

"Well, Dave," Patience replied angrily, "I won't hold my breath, because there has never been a Ladies' Day in all the time you men have been calling yourselves the Lower Forty. But that's about to change."

"What d'ya mean?" George Allard, who hardly ever said a word, spoke up.

"What do you mean, Melanie?" Bert Ramsdell puffed over his pipe to his newlywed bride, the youngest member of the female trio.

"We mean just that, Bert, dear," the young wife replied. "You men go hunting and fishing whenever you like with no notice of us. We're fishing widows half the year, and the other half we're hunting widows."

"Well, not quite, Melanie," Officer Oak pointed out. "Pa'tridge only goes three months, but then again, there's ice fishing after that. . . . I'd say five months fishing and five hunting."

"Oak's right," Judge Parker observed, happy to have the support of his fellow members. "March and April is mud season and not good fer much, so we sort of set about at Doc's camp and tie flies in anticipation, so to speak. After all, trout season's just round the corner then, come May."

"O' course, we have made a few concessions," Tilt interjected. "Like promisin' you wives we'll stay home one Saturday a month, f'rinstance."

"And when was the last time you were home on a Saturday?" Patience Parker demanded of her husband.

At that moment, Margie Allard and Rachel Malvery came into Tilt's Store, and more than dust was flying as they hastened down the aisle, past the coffee and canning jars, practically toppling the rack of fishing poles.

"George Allard, you demon, how dare you take those feathers!" Margie demanded.

"Mar-r-rgie," George stuttered. "I'm sorry."

"Don't listen to him, Margie," the Judge intervened. "George was simply trying to keep me out of Harm's Way. I am the guilty party. I took the feathers." The Judge stood up to his full height of six two and was white as a doe's breast. And then, clearly shaken, Judge Merrow Parker did something he had never done before—something, in fact, that had never been done in the history of the Lower Forty Shooting, Angling and Inside Straight Club. He reached for his fishing creel and took out the tin cup he used to keep worms, wiped it with his shirttail—and poured himself a cup of Old Stump Blower.

"Naow, hol' on a minute," said Tilt, who had been sipping pretty continuously at the jug since the women had stormed his fortress. "See what you done to the Judge!" Never in the history of the Lower Forty has any member taken a cup of Old Stump Blower! We swill it! Direct from the jug!"

With that, everyone began talking and hollering all at once. Finally, Melanie Ramsdell succeeded in quieting the commotion by tapping a lead sinker on the meat counter.

"I have written a poem," she announced when the din and dust had settled. "And I believe it speaks for every woman here." Bert cocked his eyebrow and looked with grave concern over at this wife, who was waiting for everyone to be seated before she began.

"I call it, 'Lament of a Fisherman's Wife.'"

Margie Allard applauded.

Melanie nodded in appreciation and cleared her throat. "'Lament of a Fisherman's Wife,'" she repeated. "By Melanie Ramsdell."

> *When I speak, he mutters and mumbles.*
> *He is deaf, and acts as if blind*
> *If I cooked up some hay for his dinner*
> *He'd never notice or mind.*
>
> *Royal Coachmen perch on the mantle,*
> *Hooks are caught in my very best chairs.*
> *When I reach for my brush on my nightstand,*
> *Line and tippet get caught in my hair.*
>
> *Fishing tackle is strewn on the counter,*
> *I trip over fly rods and reels.*
> *My spouse talks fishing, sleeping and eating,*
> *We have it for every dang meal.*
>
> *Whenever I miss him, he's fishing;*
> *The children cry, he disappears.*
> *Oh woe is the angler's wife's burdens*
> *For her husband knows not of her tears.*

Melanie's lower lip began to quiver, and Patience Parker ran to her side with a handkerchief. "That was beautiful, dear," she cried. "That's just exactly how I feel."

"Me, too," Margie Allard added.

You'll excuse me," interrupted Lettie, who was a spinster, and obviously overwhelmed by It All. "I have to get back to the Post Office."

Patience Parker looked down her aquiline nose at her

husband, who at that moment decided to pour himself another cup of Old Stump Blower.

"Ladies, ladies!" Corey Ford, the secretary of the Lower Forty, pleaded. All eyes settled on the handsome man in the tweed jacket who sat by the woodstove, an English setter at his feet. Corey seldom spoke, since he was always busy taking the minutes of the meetings. "Really, that was lovely, Melanie, but look . . . who's minding the rummage sale? Besides, we were right in the middle of an important report on opening day of pa'tridge season."

"Oh, be quiet, Corey," Patience demanded. "You're just a bachelor."

You could have heard a pin drop on the floor if it wasn't for the sawdust. "Sorry, Corey, dear," Patience apologized. "But frankly, we think it's high time the Lower Forty admitted women."

The shotguns and rods hanging behind the meat counter practically fell off the wall in the storm of protest that followed. Finally, Corey blew his dog whistle, silencing everyone. He stood up, took a long pull from his pipe, looked around at the gathering, and said, "Never have I seen, heard, or been asked to consider such tomfoolery as to have women members in the Lower Forty. Good God, ladies— you must be wet behind the ears to even suggest such a thing. The way I see it, you can't predict a woman any more than you can predict a pa'tridge. But Patience is right. I'm just a bachelor. I don't envy you boys when you get home tonight. As for me, Cider here would never forgive me if I gave my consent. Who knows. Maybe, just maybe, it's time women were admitted to the Lower Forty. Clem's right: 'The only thing that stays the same in life is change.' Perhaps it's my time for one."

Judge Parker stood up and with a visible tear in his eye, banged his tin cup against the almost-empty jug of Old

Stump Blower and said: "Gentlemen, I give you Corey Ford."

"Hear! Hear!" the members roared.

The ladies, however, were utterly silent. They didn't want to get soaking wet waiting for some fish to bite a bunch of feathers. They didn't want to come home cold and exhausted and dirty after a dreary day hunting birds in the woods. All they wanted was to prove a point. They didn't know what to do with Corey's poignant endorsement. In fact, they didn't want it at all.

Meanwhile, Corey nudged Cider with his foot and got up to leave.

"Are you going home, Corey?" Officer Oak called after him. "Shall I drive you home in the cruiser?"

"I was thinking," the Judge suggested, "of coming up after dinner to your place to tie some flies."

"No, Judge," Corey replied. "I think Cider and I will go check out our secret covert for opening day."

"Where?" Melanie Ramsdell asked innocently.

"Melanie!" her husband, Bert, admonished. "There are some things a man will share: his car, his tobacco, and maybe . . . maybe even his wife. But you never ask a man to share the whereabouts of his secret pa'tridge covert!"

Corey waved his pipe as if in salute to the Lower Forty Fishing, Angling and Inside Straight Club. He knew where he was going—up beyond the beaver dam to the stream, where the lilac trees grow by the old bridge and where, by some divine miracle, a copse of elm trees are in full leaf. Corey Ford was going to Tinkhamtown—but he didn't want to say. Then his right eyebrow shot up to his hairline, as it would do whenever he was about to say something witty. He turned to his friends, the motley brotherhood of the Lower Forty, and saluted them. "As Wellington said at Waterloo, 'That was a damned fine-run thing.' " And with that, Corey took the last belt of Old Stump Blower, tipped his tweed hunting hat, and walked out of Tilt's Store with his ever-present English setter, Cider, at his heel. Officer Oak watched Corey walk down Elm Street until he turned the corner of Maple and disappeared out of sight.

"Wellington said something else," Officer Oak said quietly, breaking the heavy silence. He said, 'Nothing except a battle lost can be half so melancholy as a battle won.'"

The wives didn't win that warm September day. They lost, and they knew it.

"I've been trying for forty years to change my husband," Margie Allard said. "I guess I'll have to keep on trying."

"Bert?" Melanie asked. "Bert, I was wondering—could I go fishing with you on Saturday?"

"Sure," her husband said. "Providing you carry the rods."

"I suppose we'd better be going now," Patience said apologetically.

"A very good idea," the Judge replied. "And Patience . . ." he added tenderly, "I'll be home for dinner, dear."

And so a chapter ended in the life of our Town.

But a new one had begun.

FIFTEEN

Just a Dog

We are all of us in the gutter, but some of us are look-
ing at the stars.

—Oscar Wilde

The phone call came out of the blue. An aged, crackling voice wrapped in a slow, undulating Southern drawl came blasting across the line. Kip put his hand over the receiver of the phone and smiled broadly. He pulled me onto his lap and held the earpiece between us. "It's old Fort Falls," he whispered. "I haven't heard from him in a couple of years!" Then Kip took his hand off the mouthpiece and said, "Fort, you don't have to yell! I can hear you loud and clear."

The voice on the other end hollered back, "Can you hear me now, Kippy?"

"They can hear you clear 'cross to Maine, Fort. You don't have to talk so loud."

" 'S that better, Kippy?" the old man said without any perceptible decrease in his decibel level.

"That's just fine, Fort," Kip laughed, resigned to listening to what the earsplitting voice had to say. He knew it would be a short phone call. Fort came from a generation that counted the seconds on the telephone because a long-distance call could cost a morning's wages. "He's deaf, too," Kip whispered to me as I got off his lap to move a saucepan that was boiling over on the wood cookstove.

A minute later, my husband came into the kitchen. "Good old Fort," Kip said. "He practically raised me. Taught me to hunt and fish when I was a kid. I learned everything I know about the woods from Fort."

"He lived here in Hardscrabble?"

"Yep. He and his wife lived next door in the stone house and took care of Corey Ford for years. Before that, Corey had a plantation, and Fort was his estate manager. Then Corey moved here, and Fort and his wife, Louise, followed. When he left Hardscrabble in '53 for Dartmouth, Fort and Louise drew the line. They said Hanover was too fancy a place for country folk like them, so they opted to stay in Hardscrabble. They bought the farm down the road—the one beyond Ken's place—and lived there about fifteen years before moving back to Carolina when Louise's health started to fail."

"That's a funny name, Fort," I pondered.

"His full name is Fort Sumter Falls. There's a great story behind it. You'll have to have Fort tell you when he gets here."

"Oh, is he coming to Hardscrabble to visit?"

"Oh, didn't I say? Yes . . . he's coming for a visit."

"That's nice. Where's he staying?" I asked.

"Here. With us."

"With *us?*"

"Sure. He's only coming for a month."

"A *month?*" I couldn't believe Kip didn't ask me first. Here I was, with a large house, a small child, and more work than I could handle, and now I had to take care of a house guest for a month! I reined in my temper about as unsuccessfully as an unbroken stallion getting his first taste at a bit.

"Are you kidding?" I screamed.

"Sure . . . I mean, no," he continued, oblivious to my outburst or what it meant to have another person under our roof to feed and pick up after. "He's flying in on Saturday."

"This Saturday?"

"Laurie, that's three whole days away . . . plenty of time for us to get ready. *("Us?"* I thought.) Besides, he's no trouble at all. You'll love Fort."

"How old is he?"

"Fort? Why, I guess he's pushing eighty by now."

This was one of those special moments in married life when I happily would have hung my husband by, uh . . . the thumbs.

Fort Arrives

Saturday arrived. Kip, Tommy, and I got ready to leave for the airport. The guest bedroom was all set, the refrigerator was stocked with food, sherried beef was simmering in the Crock-Pot for dinner, a batch of my homemade bread was rising in an enormous earthenware bowl on the kitchen counter, and some Joe Froggers were cooling on a wire rack out of Bess's reach.

I was prepared, and in the comfort that comes anytime you feel the contentment of having your own universe in order, I began to actually look forward to meeting the man that meant so much to my husband. Shortly after Fort had called a few days before, we got another phone call—this time, from Fort's granddaughter, who Kip had known since childhood.

"I'm sorry about Granddad," she said. "I don't know

what got into him. Suddenly he announced that he wanted to go back to Hardscrabble one last time, and the next thing I knew, he was on the phone with you. I'm sure it has a lot to do with Grandma dying."

"Louise is dead?"

"Yes, Kip. She died about six months ago. But she'd been awfully sick for a real long time."

"Send Fort on up," Kip told her. "God knows he took care of me plenty when I was growing up. Laurie and I can surely take care of him for a mere month. Besides, it would be good for him to come home to Hardscrabble and be among his old friends."

"There can't be many left."

"Oh, you'd be surprised," Kip answered. "Hardscrabble doesn't surrender its own to the Grim Reaper graciously."

"Let me speak to her," I whispered to Kip, and after saying, "Of course it's all right, we'd be delighted"; and, "It means so much to Kip to have Fort visit"; I asked a battery of questions. The answers were consoling: "No," his granddaughter said, "he has no special dietary needs. He eats whatever you put in front of him." "Yes, he's entirely self-sufficient. Just give him a good book or a fishing rod and . . ."

So here it was, Saturday, and we were ready to leave for the Airport. As I said, everything was ready for Fort's arrival. I wasn't, however, prepared for the robust, elderly man who walked off the airplane.

He must have been very handsome as a young man. The square, cleft jaw was firm, his smile wide, and his blue eyes twinkled from under white brows that were arched in perpetual amusement. He had a full head of snow-white hair, stood as straight as an oak tree, and had a handshake as firm as a logger's. The only thing that betrayed his age (which I soon found out was actually eighty-three) was a hearing aid in one ear and a gimpy leg. ("Leg quit working right when I was a kid," he later explained. "I got in the way of the intentions of a hotheaded bull that got lusty over the cow I was milking. I took a horn right through the kneecap.")

"Fort!" Kip threw his arms around his old friend's broad shoulders.

"Why, Kippy," he purred in his Carolina drawl. "Good God, boy, it's good to see ya."

"How long has it been, Fort?"

"Lemme see. . . . Been about ten years, I reckon. You was just getting out of that fancy college your pa sent you to in Massachusetts."

"Williams. Yeah, I know. Well, that's behind me, thank God. Fort, I want you to meet my wife, Laurie, and my son, Tommy."

Fort held a box tied with a fancy ribbon in his hands and gave it to me. "Jest a little something for you, Laurie—pralines, a specialty down South. My wife, God rest her soul, she used to make the best pralines in all of Carolina. These are store-bought. Not too bad, but I can't say I've had a really good praline since Louise died."

"I'm sorry about Louise, Fort," Kip said.

"She had all kinds of problems at the end, then her heart just stopped beating one day." Fort's eyes got teary. "I'd just come in from sowing the corn—"

"Tell me," I interjected, anxious to reroute the course of the conversation. "How did you get your name, Fort?"

He brightened up. "Well, now, that's quite a story, Laurie," he smiled. "You see, my daddy was born and bred in Carolina. He and his kin never quite got over losing the War. . . ."

Tom whispered to me, "He's talking about the Civil War."

". . . so when I was born—I was the last of twelve children—it so happened that I came into the world on the day that Fort Sumter fell. So my daddy—his last name were Falls, you see—he named me Fort Sumter Falls. . . ."

". . . because," I interjected, "you were born on the day that Fort Sumter fell."

"She's not only pretty, but she's smart, too." Fort winked at Kip. "You picked a good'un, Boy."

Maybe, I thought, having Fort for a month wouldn't be so bad.

We Meet Rebel

"How many bags do you have, Fort?" Kip asked as we made our way the short distance to baggage claim.

"Just one . . . and Rebel."

"No. . . ." Tom said, stopping in his tracks. "You didn't bring Rebel, did you?"

"Rebel?" I asked.

"Yes," Kip replied. "Why, he must be fifteen by now!"

"Sixteen, Kippy!" Fort beamed, and at that moment, an airport representative carried a small kennel into the baggage claim area.

"Rebel!" Tom cried. "How are you, old boy?" He opened up the wire cage, reached in, and took out a handsome beagle that, like his master, did not at all show his age.

"You didn't say anything about bringing Rebel," Tom said.

"Don't suppose I did, Kippy," Fort smiled, fondling his dog's ears, "but then I reckon I guess I didn't have to. You know I never go anywhere without my Rebel." Rebel pulled away from Kip to plant a series of wet kisses on his master's hand.

Tommy squealed with delight at the little dog.

"I don't know when there wasn't Rebel—that is, a Rebel," Kip explained to me. "Fort's been raising beagles . . . since when, Fort?"

"Since I was a tadpole myself, Kippy. One time, I had twelve beagles. Got Corey started on beagles for years and years before he took up with them high-hat setters of his. Though I gotta say, I did love 'em—Cider and Tober and, a' course, Trout. I always named one a my beagles, though, Rebel, and I've never been caught without one."

"This dog must be the great-great-grandson of the first Rebel I ever knew, right, Fort?"

"Yep, I reckon that's so. That was Rebel of the Wilderness. His son was Rebel of Gettysburg. This old boy is Rebel of Appomatox."

"He always named his Rebels after Civil War battles," Kip explained.

"Do you think he'll get along with Bess?" I whispered to Kip as we headed to the car with Fort, his bag, and Rebel in tow.

"Sure, if she ever wakes up long enough to get to know him. Besides," Kip added, "it's not like anything is going to happen."

"I see what you mean," I grinned. "I guess the most they could ever be is really good friends."

Fort Settles In

Fort and Rebel fit right in. Kip was delighted to have his old friend with us, who proved to be like a favorite uncle, not a guest. Rebel and Bess hit it off immediately and spent most of the day curled up, sleeping contentedly together like a couple of old folk, which in point of fact they were. It was hard to believe, but Bess was now getting on nine.

"Your dogs have always lived to a great old age," Tom asked Fort when we were sitting to dinner that evening. "What's your secret?"

"Can't say I do anything particular," Fort replied. Take care of 'em just like I take care of myself. We take a long walk every day, he gets a lot of loving and gives a lot of loving, and he eats what I eat." Fort took the side of his fork and shoveled some of the sherried beef and rice I had made over to the side of his plate. He could see I was concerned that perhaps he didn't like his dinner. *"Mmmmm,* that was a *reeeeal* good dinner, Laurie," he said. "That cow died good. I'm just saving a bit for Rebel. Like I said, he eats what I eat."

"There's plenty more, Fort," I said, lifting the casserole cover to offer seconds.

"I'm full, gal. Besides," he smiled, looking over to the counter. "I see them Joe Froggers sitting over there, and I'm particular partial-like to Joe Froggers."

Fort Reminisces

Fort told us stories, wonderful stories. About the plantation down South, and years before when Corey first bought it, and how back then some black folk wished the Civil War had never happened because the road to freedom was a hard road for them. "Corey was a great quail hunter," Ford reminisced, "and he bought the plantation so he could hunt birds. Of course, the business of the place was growing cotton, and there were black folk who tended to the crop just like their daddies and mammies had.

"They were poor folk. Corey was away most of the time in Hollywood, writing those movies for all those famous people like Hedy Lamarr and Robert Taylor and Greer Garson. He got mighty upset when he saw how poor people was. So he called me from Hollywood one day and he says, 'Fort,' he says to me, 'every week you butcher one of those big hogs we got on the farm, and you let the folk come down and give them some meat.' I remember how workers would gather round the slaughter yard, standing up along the ridge, waiting for the signal to come down for their pork parcels that me and my wife made up after some of the hands did the slaughtering. Corey made sure the families with children got the best cuts, then the sick and old people. Soon we was raising hogs like nobody's business and slaughtering three or four a week, just so the black folk that worked for Corey could have fresh meat.

"Well, then Corey gets another idea. You see, the nearest store was nine miles away, and folk had to walk to get their supplies. No one had a car back then, and only a few black folk could afford to keep a mule. One day, Corey calls me up from Hollywood and says, 'Fort, you go build us a store. That way the folk don't have to walk so far to get their supplies. And while you're at it,' he says, 'you go and build a school, for the youngsters. They need some education, too, you know.' He had a heart of gold, Corey did, and no one never gave him near enough credit, but he didn't want gratitude. He was rich and famous. 'I had a lucky break,' he'd say to me. 'If I can give other people a break, well then, that's payback enough for me.'"

Fort's Visit Sails By

And so the days melted into weeks, and Kip and I reveled in Fort's company. The two men went off just about every day to their old, secret trout streams and dark holes on the lake, fishing with Bess and Rebel in tow. They never came home without at least a couple of handsome rainbow, or a salmon, or a string of smallmouth bass.

All the while, Fort told us stories. There was the hilarious one about how the septic system got stopped up when Corey's mistress came from Hollywood to visit him at Stonybroke, his home in Hardscrabble; or the time when Corey's best friend, W. C. Fields, came to stay with Corey at Christmas and how people here in Town took no notice. After all, Hollywood types didn't impress people in Hardscrabble. Now, a ten-point buck . . . *that* was a different matter entirely.

Years later, when I started working on Corey Ford's literary archives, I discovered how deep the friendship was that he shared with Fields. Ford, a lifelong bachelor, always had difficulty coming to grips with Christmas and, until the day he died, gathered friends and friends' families about him and positioned himself as the benevolent Ebenezer Scrooge. Fields, likewise, had a great difficulty at Christmastime, but for a different reason. He was quoted as saying, "I believed in Christmas until I was eight years old. I had saved up some money carrying ice in Philadelphia, and I was going to buy my mother a copper-bottomed clothes boiler for Christmas. I kept the money hidden in a brown crock in the coal bin. My father found the crock. He did exactly what I would have done in his place. He stole the money. And ever since then I've remembered nobody on Christmas, and I want nobody to remember me either."

There was Fort's story about how Judge Parker and Corey founded the "Love the Little Kitty Society," a club complete with printed membership cards and a charter dedicated to "tiger hunting for the man with modest means." The two friends would sit on Corey's stone porch every night after supper and pot feral cats because, as Fort pointed out, "feral cats kill most of the wild birds, including pa'tridge—and the Judge wanted to pronounce and execute the sentence against those feline offenders."

But there was one story that Fort told us. It would take a number of years before I gathered up all the pieces and I could put the whole puzzle together. It is one of the most poignant stories I've ever known—and I daresay, I'm not alone.

Just a Dog

Farmer Boyden was tending to his chickens and pigs when he heard a shot ring out from below his barn. It was deer season. Fearful that one of his cows had been hit, he dropped what he was doing, grabbed his shotgun, and ran as fast as he could to the pasture. Gratified, after a quick glance, that his small herd appeared unscathed, his relief turned to outrage when a second shot was discharged not fifty yards away. It came from an adjacent field, which belonged to his neighbor, a country gentleman and a writer. There, beyond the stone fence, by the apple tree, stood a hunter. The farmer did not recognize the man. A cloud of dissipating smoke encircled the muzzle of a 30-30, freshly fired at point-blank range at what the farmer assumed was a small deer or coyote. But when he came upon the scene, he saw to his horror that the fallen animal was his neighbor's English setter.

"Whatinell do ya think yer doin'?" the farmer hollered at the hunter.

"Thought it was a deer," the hunter said offhandedly, as he unloaded the unspent bullets from the chamber of his gun. "I heard a rustle in the brush and saw a flash of white. Thought it was a whitetail deer. Honest mistake. It was an accident. . . . Anyone could have seen that white through this heavy cover and thought the same thing."

Indeed, the brush was heavy; and the dog was mostly white—a snow white English setter with orange ticks. But now she was a pitiful, lifeless heap. The farmer knelt down, hopeful of finding a sign of life, but finding none, he gingerly hoisted the poor animal onto his shoulder. As he was doing this, he caught a glimpse of the hunter turning heel and making his way to the road, where a car with Massachusetts license plates was parked.

"Mister," the farmer called. "Come back." The hunter turned around with a smirk on his face that was wiped clean when he realized he was looking into the shooting end of the farmer's double-barrel gun. "You come with me," Farmer Boyden ordered quietly, as he motioned toward his neighbor's house with the persuasive point of the gun muzzle.

"Look, I said it was an accident," the hunter mewled, turning pale. He groped for his wallet. "Here. . . ." he offered with hands shaking. "Here's five bucks. That should settle the matter."

The farmer replied with the determined cock of the right hammer of his gun.

"This dog was my neighbor's," the farmer said. "You owe him some explaining, not a darn fiver."

"Hell . . . it was just a dog," the hunter pleaded.

"You tell that to my neighbor," the farmer replied bitterly.

The farmer marched the hunter across the road and up the long, winding drive that led to an imposing stone lodge.

"Knock on the door," the farmer ordered, as he gently lowered the body of his neighbor's dog onto the front lawn.

A moment later, the country gentleman answered the door, beheld the scene—and fell to his knees.

Mabel, the housekeeper, related what happened. She had been in the kitchen baking pies when she heard a hollow cry. Running to the front door, she came upon her employer on his knees, cradling the body of his beloved setter, Trout. Sitting stiffly on the ledge of the stone porch, looking blankly over the valley vista, was a stranger. Standing nearby with a loaded shotgun trembling in his hand was Farmer Boyden.

"The stranger got up," Mabel recollected, "and said, 'It was just a dog.' Then Charlie Boyden said to the stranger, 'Get the hell outta here.' The man ran down the driveway like a frightened hare. Charlie carried Trout behind the house and buried her. Corey was too broken up. He went to his room and didn't come down for dinner."

The day was November 23, 1940.

Farmer Boyden's neighbor was the legendary outdoor writer Corey Ford, who wrote a monthly column for *Field & Stream*. From 1952 until 1969, the antics and misadventures of an eccentric Down East group of hunters and fisherman known as the Lower Forty Shooting, Angling and Inside Straight delighted and captured the hearts of readers the world over. Not only were dogs an integral part of the fictitious Lower Forty, but they were fundamental to Corey's real-life existence. A lifelong bachelor, Corey's beloved setters were his family—and Trout especially was like a favorite child.

The night his little setter died, Corey made an entry in his diary that I happened upon but can't divulge. After all, a man, when confronted with the handiwork of the Grim Reaper, is due the privacy and respect of his sorrowing, and I found his diary unwittingly. Suffice it to say, the man mourned deeply, as you who have loved and lost a dog well know; and afterwards, he wrote a letter to his hunting buddy, chief editor of *Field & Stream* Ray Holland. Corey asked him to publish the following letter, and Holland stopped the presses to get it into the December issue of the magazine. It read:

Dear Ray:

I know this is a kind of unusual request; but I'd like to borrow some space in your columns to write an open letter to a man I do not know. He may read it if it is in your columns; or some of his friends may notice his name and ask him to read it. You see, it has to do with sport—a certain kind of sport.

The man's name is Sherwood G. Coggins. That was the name on his hunting license. He lives at 1096 Lawrence Street, in Lowell. He says he is in the real estate and insurance business in Lowell.

This weekend, Mr. Coggins, you drove up into New Hampshire with some friends to go deer hunting. You went hunting on my property here in Hardscrabble. You didn't ask my permission; but that was all right. I let people hunt on my land. Only, while you were hunting, you shot and killed my bird dog.

Oh, it was an accident, of course. You said so yourself. You said that you saw a flick of something moving, and you brought up your rifle and fired. It might have been another hunter. It might have been a child running through the woods. As it turned out, it was just a dog.

Just a dog, Mr. Coggins. Just a little English setter I have hunted with for quite a few years. Just a little female setter who was very proud and staunch on point, and who always held her head high, and whose eyes had the brown of October in them. We had hunted a lot of alder thickets and apple orchards together, the little setter and I. She knew me, and I knew her, and we liked to hunt together. We had hunted woodcock together this fall, and grouse, and in another week we were planning to go down to Carolina together and look for quail. But yesterday morning she ran down to the fields in front of my house, and you saw a flick in the bushes, and you shot her. You shot her through the back, you said, and broke her spine. She crawled out of the bushes and across the field toward you, dragging her hind legs. She was coming to you to help her. She was a gentle pup, and nobody had ever hurt her, and she could not understand. She began hauling herself toward you, and looking at you with her brown eyes, and you put a second bullet through her head. You were sportsman enough for that.

I know you didn't mean it, Mr. Coggins. You felt very sorry afterward. You told me that it really spoiled your deer hunting the rest of the day. It spoiled my bird hunting the rest of a lifetime. At least, I hope one thing, Mr. Coggins. That is why I am writing you. I hope that you will remember how she looked. I hope that the next time you raise a rifle to your shoulder you will see her over the sights, dragging herself toward you across the field, with blood running from her mouth and down her white chest. I hope you will see her eyes.

I hope you will always see her eyes, Mr. Coggins, whenever there is a flick in the bushes and you bring your rifle to your shoulder before you know what is there.

—Corey Ford

A furor followed. Mail poured into the New York offices of *Field & Stream* the likes of which the magazine had never seen before or possibly since. Hundreds of newspapers, magazines, dog and sportsmen's clubs, businesses, and community groups across the country seized upon Corey's poignant open letter and reprinted it to the same effect. Anyone who ever loved a dog understood. Most wept. Today the message garnered from Corey's letter is no less potent or poignant than when the ink and tears were still wet on his paper, and "Just a Dog" stands alone in the laurels of American sporting dog literature.

I wanted to tell you what happened because you understand. You understand what it is to love and be loved by a dog.

You know what it is come autumn to ramble in the woods with your canine companion by your side, under a shower of golden-tinged russet leaves; and catch a whiff of ripened apples warmed by streaks of sunlight filtering through a cathedral of lofty pines. If you hunt, you take more pride in your dog's retrieves and frolicsome flushes or stylish points than you do in the weight of your game bag come dusk.

You fall asleep at night to the rhythm of dog-snores and slumber-barks that come from the foot of your bed—or more likely, on it.

You know that a wet dog-kiss can lick your troubles clean.

And the warmth from his soft brown eyes can melt your worries.

We have them for such a short time, in the great scheme of life. Our four score and ten are a mere twelve or thirteen years to a dog. Dogs pack a lot of love into the time they share with us.

But then, you know.

Because you, too, know the love of a dog.

SIXTEEN

Bill Plover's Funeral

*Life's meaning has always eluded me and I guess
always will. But I love it just the same.*

—*E. B. White*

Harry Bixby was pacing up and down the antique
Oriental carpet that Lila Hornbeam donated to the
First Christian Church of Hardscrabble after she acquired an
even more valuable Persian for the foyer of her country
house, the Republican's Hideaway. A threadbare path
bisected the rare silk Tabriz as though a river had, quite literally, run through it. This is the only sin, perhaps, that
Harry Bixby had ever committed, and it filled him with
remorse; but it was an honest sin, if such a thing is possible.
The damage emerged gradually as an outward symptom of
Harry's nerves which, along with the carpet, frayed a little
more with every passing Sunday, holy day, wedding, chris-
tening, and funeral.

Harry was Church secretary, with the self-appointed job
of maintaining the well-being of the Church. Of his own
volition, he tended to every detail, such as centering the
flowers on the altar, polishing the brass collection plates,
and straightening the hymn board, which had a propensity

to tilt somewhat to the right. These and countless other minutiae had to conform to Harry's and God's standards. As far as Harry was concerned, nothing was ready until everything was perfect; and until everything was perfect, Harry was a nervous wreck.

"Man's going to give himself a heart attack," Clem Lovell remarked to his wife, Louise, one Sunday as Harry scurried down the aisle like the March Hare when Lila Hornbeam signaled that her hymnal was missing from her front pew (it was under her scarf). He nearly went into apoplexy the Sunday Lila came to Church with several prominent Republicans in tow and motioned to Harry that there were not enough hymnals in her pew (they were under her mink coat).

Harry never married, which was a very good thing, according to Margie Allard, who said there wasn't "a woman alive who could live with that Harry Bixby except for his dear mother, Wanda, God rest her soul." God rested Wanda's soul the day after she reached the exalted age of ninety-two, and though Harry missed her terribly, his work at the bank and the grueling ecclesiastic demands he put entirely upon himself kept him extremely busy. Financially, he had done very well and lived modestly, invested modestly, kept a modest but lovely home, and preferred the pleasure of his own modest company. He altogether ceased entertaining after Olsen Leavitt put a glass of ginger ale down on Harry's Chippendale coffee table without a coaster. It left a white ring, and the table had to be refinished at considerable expense. (Harry, who sympathized with the way Scrooge was before Marley's visit, sent Olsen the bill.)

Which brings us to this particular Sunday, and why Harry Bixby had a very good reason to pace.

Today, you see, was Bill Plover's funeral.

Bill Plover, Salt of the Earth

Bill Plover was a native son of Hardscrabble who worked on the Town road crew from the day he graduated from high school at the then-mandatory age of fifteen, until his retirement at the now-mandatory age of sixty-five. In snowstorms so bitter that even the dawn was reluctant to rise, Bill would plow the roads so people could get to where they had to go in the morning. In the heat of summer, he'd shovel piping-hot asphalt into potholes so people could drive the roads without breaking an axle. If a tree branch was precariously low to a power line, he'd trim it. If a stone fence needed mending, he'd mend it. Bill was sort of our municipal handyman.

Bill had been looking forward to retirement. He was going to plant a new vegetable garden with his wife, Madeline. He and Madeline were always gardening, and the fruits of their efforts produced the most beautiful garden in all of Carroll County. A couple of years ago, a photographer from *Yankee* magazine happened upon the Plovers' house at the peak of summer. The picture was published, and Harry and Madeline became local celebrities. But no picture could capture the incredible beauty of their garden. Climbing trellises of morning glories and old-fashioned roses were so laden with blooms that they concealed the porch pillars. Zinnias, petunias, scented geraniums, daylilies, snapdragons—every variety of flower seed available through the Burpee catalogue—blossomed in the garden. Flowering trees and shrubs embraced the property. The garden flourished from the moment the crocuses peeked through the last of the winter snow in April, through November, when autumn's mums finally lay their heads upon winter's shoulder. That was when Bill and Madeline brought out baskets and wreaths of cheerful red and white poinsettias of the plastic species, which brightened even the bitterest days of winter until growing season returned with spring.

However, the old upholstered sofa that sat on the open-air front porch was the hallmark of the Plover homestead. Every evening after supper in all but the most loathsome weather, Bill and Madeline would sit on the sofa and wave to each and every passerby, friend or stranger. This is a time-honored custom in Hardscrabble. People wave because it's the neighborly thing to do. Somehow, such a simple gesture can make a person feel as though he isn't traveling the long, lonely, Road of Life entirely alone.

And yet, Life takes some people down a fork that brings them to the end of their road when they least expect it. That's what happened to Bill. He was working in his vegetable patch when the Grim Reaper took out his scythe, cut Bill down in the full blossom of his retirement, and ushered him to the eternal garden. Doc said the only thing Bill would have felt was the dirt between his fingers and the sun on his back.

Just When You Least Expect It

Harry paused from his pacing to check the time. It was one o'clock, and already people were arriving. The church was brimming with potted plants, because people knew it would give Madeline pleasure to plant them afterwards in her garden. By half-past, the church was also brimming with people, confirming Harry's worst fears and worsening his rash of worry. His mind was reeling. Everything was ready. No detail was left undone. There were more than enough hymnals in Lila Hornbeam's pew.

However, even Harry couldn't have been prepared for what happened next.

It is a custom in Hardscrabble that funerals are of the open casket variety, and this was the case with Bill's. It is also tradition that the immediate family is the last to be seated, and this, too, was the case with Bill's. And so, at two o'clock precisely, Harry led Reverend Davidson from the sacristy to the altar. He signaled Joey Miller, one of the young acolytes, to ring the church bell. As the mournful bell pealed, Harry slowly, solemnly, led the grieving family down the aisle. The family consisted of Bill's poor widow, Madeline, their daughter Susie, Susie's husband Elmer, and Susie's poodle Cheré. Susie, an only child, was "Daddy's little girl." She was also a rather large woman, and a large woman in grief can be rather a handful. It was all Madeline and Elmer could do to carry the great burden of grief in Susie, who Harry feared would have to be carried down the aisle. So great was his worry that he took out his white starched handkerchief to daub beads of perspiration from his forehead. Harry was feeling light-headed from the intense heat, profound emotion, and the sight of Lila Hornbeam fidgeting for her hymnal (it was under her handbag).

Let us pause briefly from this highly charged scene to describe the structural support that holds up a casket. Hidden under the crimson velvet drapes is a collapsible metal contraption of surprisingly flimsy construction. Upon this the coffin sits. I mention this so that you understand that such an apparatus is not designed to also support a collapsing, hysterical, 290-pound woman clutching an excitable French poodle to her massive, heaving breast.

It all happened so suddenly.

Harry was ushering the family into the pew across from Lila Hornbeam's (who still had not found her hymnal) while Madeline tried to calm her bereaved daughter. "Don't worry, darling, he's only asleep," she whispered. Susie turned to look at her deceased father lying peacefully in the casket. Whereupon Susie gave out a bloodcurdling cry, fainted, and fell into the coffin.

Harry's quick response saved the moment from certain calamity. He grabbed Susie by the nape of her mourning attire, threw her aside, lunged his full weight against the teetering coffin, blocked the contraption from skidding forward, and steadied the shifting corpse with his shaking hands. Elmer and the pallbearers jumped to his assistance, but the damage had already been done. Cheré the poodle leaped into the coffin and was licking the makeup off Bill's face. Only after the commotion died down did Harry discreetly make his way into the privacy of the vestry and have his heart attack.

Harry Copes with Change

Harry was in the hospital for two weeks. A hospital bed and heart monitor had been moved into his home, along with a full-time nurse.

"You're going to have to have someone around to take care of you for awhile, Harry," Doc said.

"That's the way it is, no discussion. Olivia Reading's going to move in with you for awhile. She's a wonderful woman, and she'll take very good care of you."

"What about the Church?" Harry asked.

"To hell with the Church. The Church will have to do without you for awhile," Doc replied. He saw the worry—the culprit of his patient's troubles—cloud his friend's brow. "Look, Harry," he continued. "There's nothing you can do. Besides, it's funny, but things have a way of getting done. You'll be amazed, but the Church will go on with or without you. I don't mean to sound callous or like the voice of doom, but this is a critical time for you. You're going to have to redirect all that energy you put toward worrying into healing yourself. It's a tall order, and Olivia and I are here to help, but this is something that you are going to have to do for yourself. Look out for yourself for a change, Harry."

And so the Sundays came and went, but Harry barely improved. He became depressed when he saw that Doc was right: The Church managed fine without him. He lost interest in his house. He lost interest in his flower garden. He used Kleenex instead of his starched cotton handkerchiefs. He didn't even bother reading the magazines that came in his mail. But it was the day that he put his glass of ginger ale down on the Chippendale coffee table without a coaster that Olivia realized that Harry's depression had gotten out of hand. She called Doc.

Early the following morning, Doc arrived with a large smile on his face. "Harry," he said, "I've brought you something that I think will get you back on your feet in no time flat. He reached into the deep pocket of his hunting coat, took out a Brittany puppy, and put it on Harry's lap.

"What's this?" Harry asked.

"It's your puppy," the doctor replied.

"My puppy?" Harry said and looked at it in disbelief. "I don't want a puppy. I've never owned a puppy. I wouldn't know what to do with one!"

"Well, it's about time you did," Doc said.

"Look, Doc, I can't keep this . . ." at which point, the little creature cuddled into the hollow of Harry's arm, licked his hand and, looking up at him with wide eyes, yawned and fell asleep.

Gently, tenderly, Harry ran a fingertip along the puppy's silky ears. It wasn't true that he had never had a dog. He had a little cocker spaniel named Butch when he was growing up. Butch was his best friend, but after he died, Harry swore he'd never have another dog. He knew he would never be able to stand the pain of losing a dog again.

"How old is—"

"She. She's seven weeks old, and today is the first day she's been away from her mother."

"What did you say her name was?"

"I didn't. That's up to you."

Harry ran the palm of his hand along the back of the soft, honey-and-white pup. It all flooded back to him, the softness of a dog, the warmth, the joy of holding a living creature close. Then the reality of it all came tumbling down. What was he going to do with a dog? A dog was a lot of responsibility. He glanced at his wall-to-wall carpet and his highly polished furniture. A dog? Here, in his home? *Dogs leave messes,* he thought. *Dogs ruin carpets and furniture.* Then the little puppy took a deep breath, opened her warm, brown, round eyes, looked adoringly at Harry, released a sound of contentment, and fell back to sleep.

"I think . . ." Harry said. "I think I'll call her Honey."

From that moment on, Harry and Honey were inseparable. She was, he was quite certain, the smartest, the lovingest, the most beautiful dog on earth. And although she did the things that all puppies do, like scamper about and unwittingly scratch the furniture—and yes, leave an occasional accident—Harry somehow managed to cast aside concern. After all, accidents do happen, and as far as the furniture was concerned, he could always have it refinished after Honey had grown out of puppyhood.

Harry Takes on a New Lease in Life

It is a long-held, universal belief that dates back to the dawning of time that a person who loves, and is loved, by a dog can break the bonds of illness better than any medication or cure. This was exactly what happened to Harry. Whether it was the walks that he and Honey took several times a day, or the enjoyment of tossing a ball for her to fetch; whether it was simply the comfort of having a companion whose sole purpose in life was to adore; whatever it was, it was exactly what Harry needed.

Honey not only won Harry's heart, but she had mended it, besides.

Harry Returns

One day, Reverend Davidson came to visit. "I spoke with Doc, Harry, and he said you're as fit as a fiddle. We were wondering when you're coming back."

"Oh, you don't need me, George," Harry replied.

"Well, that's not entirely true, Harry," the minister replied. "Things aren't quite the same without you. I can't find half of what I need when I need it. Why, the other day, someone put the flowers in the middle of the altar, and I nearly knocked them over when I went to give the Call to Worship. The acolytes are never sure when to ring the bell, and well, I don't want to worry you, Harry, but the collection plates are tarnished."

Harry thought a moment. He had a condition. Not a heart condition—Doc assured him there was no longer a concern for that. He had a condition of coming back.

"George, I'll only come back if Honey can come with me."

"Of course Honey can come to Church with you," the kindly minister smiled. "After all, God loves all creatures, great and small."

Harry Bixby did indeed come back to Church and in no time flat, everything was back the way it used to be . . . well, almost. The flowers were in their proper place on the altar, but if they weren't exactly centered, that was all right.

If the hymn board tilted a little to the right, that was okay, too. And when Lila Hornbeam couldn't find her hymnal, Harry waited for her to find it herself, which she always eventually did—under her shawl, her coat, or her handbag.

Harry still paces up and down the Oriental carpet—not out of old habit, but because Honey loves to trot at his heels. And if her toenails clip and pill the carpet, so what?

After all, it's just a carpet.

SEVENTEEN

The Verdict

We should be obliged to appear before a board every five years and justify our existence . . . on pain of liquidation.

—George Bernard Shaw

*J*udge Parker was never late for court. Sometimes he cut it close, right down to the wire—like today. Nonetheless, not in all the years that he served as municipal court justice had he missed or been late for a single court date: not the winter he caught four rainbow trout and pneumonia ice-fishing on Loon Lake; or when either of his children were born; and even if he'd had a twelve-point buck in the crosshairs of his rifle scope, he would pass up the shot if it meant being late. Not once did Judge Parker delay the business of the people unless there was a blizzard, like the storm of '62. That was the deal when he took the oath so many years ago, and Judge Parker was a man of his word.

"If a man in my position doesn't keep to his word, then what kind of example is he setting?" he would say to people. And of course, he was right.

As I was saying, Judge Parker was cutting it real close.

He trudged through the foyer of the Town Hall, leaving puddles of water in his wake as he made his way to his chambers. He took off his fishing vest and threw his long black robe on over his waders. He'd just come off the water fighting a brute of a rainbow—thirty inches, at least— but the trout was clever and ran with the line into a thick, tangled bed of water lilies. There was nothing for it but to cut the line; the river bottom dropped sharply, and there was no way the Judge could wade out to unhook the scoundrel. Like all good fishermen, the Judge followed a creed: You leave no loose ends. Not in fishing or any other priority in life. To cut bait was sacrilege, but today of all days, this sin would have to be forgiven.

The Judge barreled through the door that separated his chambers from the courtroom. A black storm cloud over his head was brimming with thoughts of that no-good trout. The storm cloud darkened, however, when his thoughts shifted to the business at hand.

"All rise. . . ." the bailiff cried to the packed room. Judge Parker glanced over his reading glasses from one end of the room to the other. He had anticipated this crowd. After all, the news had struck like lightning throughout Hardscrabble. Casper Smalley's house had been vandalized.

And Jonas Foss's beagle had been shot in cold blood.

The Warrant Is Read

"Court will come to order," the Judge bellowed, the report from his gavel echoing over the packed, otherwise stone-silent room. Bailiff, will you please read the Warrant."

Daniel Lovering, a tall, thin, bespectacled young man who only recently was appointed clerk of the court, read:

> *Casper Smalley of Leavitt's Road complains that Jonas Foss of Darby Field, on or about the 17th day of August, with force and arms did willfully, maliciously and without right or license did enter upon the property of the said Casper Smalley and then did wrongfully deface, injure and harm the dwelling house of said Smalley by throwing or causing to be thrown fifty-two or more stones which did break, shatter and cause to deface seventeen windows in the dwelling house of said Casper Smalley, contrary to the form of the statute in such case made and provided and against the peace and dignity of the State.*
>
> *Wherefore the said complainant prays that the said respondent may be held in answer to this complaint and that justice may be done in the premises.*

"Let the record show that this Warrant has been submitted and read to the Court, and is hereby . . ." Judge Parker paused, pushed up the harness to his waders, adjusted his reading glasses, and held his hand up to command silence as he reread the Warrant to himself, slowing up to the part that dealt with the actual offense.

He put the papers down and again looked over the crowded courtroom, this time slowly, taking in each familiar face. Everyone was there: the entire membership of the Lower Forty Club, the Hardscrabble Volunteer Fire Department, Mike Zalinski and his fellow flatlanders, Professor and Mrs. Markham and the Hardscrabble Literary Society, Tilt Tilton with Margie and George Allard, Lettie Connor, Scrooge Geoffrey, all three selectmen, Doc—everyone in Town who had a dog—and of course, Doris Almy and Little Doris.

"Mr. Foss," Judge Parker addressed an old man who was sitting alone behind the defendant's table. He wore denim overalls, a plaid shirt, and a striped tie. "How do you plead? Guilty or not guilty?"

"Please stand up, Mr. Foss," Daniel Lovering whispered, and the old man nodded his head and rose with difficulty.

"Not guilty, your honor."

"You may be seated, Mr. Foss," the Judge said. He paused, turned, and addressed the plaintiff. "Mr. Smalley, the defendant has pleaded not guilty. You may proceed with your evidence. I will now swear you in.

The courtroom remained absolutely silent as a man with a beer belly that threatened to bulge out of his Hawaiian shirt stood up from behind the plaintiff's table with a sneer. "Raise your right hand," the Judge continued. "You solemnly swear the testimony you are about to give, relative to the case now on trial, shall be the truth, the whole truth and nothing but the truth . . ." The Judge paused and looked down at the slovenly man. . . . "so help you God."

"I do," the plaintiff replied.

"Mr. Smalley, do you recognize Mr. Foss?"

The heavyset man shrugged his shoulders. "He's my neighbor."

"That's not what I asked, Mr. Smalley. I asked if you recognized him."

"Well, no, Your Honor. I only just bought my place a few months ago. Plan to use it in the summers as a vacation home. My real home's in Rhode Island."

"I see. But Mr. Smalley, you were aware that your neighbor had a dog."

"Well, as a matter of fact, Your Honor, I sort of shot that nasty dog."

The Judge looked over the top of his glasses. "Can you describe the dog that you shot, Mr. Smalley?"

"Well, Your Honor, he was a nasty old rabbit dog, if you must know. Caught him scratching up my flower bed."

"How much damage did he bring about to your flower bed?"

"Well, I can't say, Your Honor. The point was, I saw him digging around out there."

"Where were you when you shot him?"

"Over by my house."

"And how far away from the flower bed do you figure that was?"

"I'd say a good twenty yards or so."

"At that distance it would be a little hard to see the if the dog had done any damage, wouldn't it?"

"Listen, Judge. That dog was on my property. If he dug up my garden or not, what does it matter? He was a nasty dog, I tell you, barking at eight, nine in the morning when a person's trying to get some sleep. . . . But that's not my complaint, Judge. It's what that man"—he pointed to Jonas Foss—"did to my house!"

"Mr. Smalley, I'll direct this line of questioning, if you don't mind. You knew that the dog you shot was a rabbit dog. . . ."

"Your Honor, that mangy dog was trespassing on my property!"

"Mr. Smalley, I'm going to ask you—one time, sir, just one time—to not interrupt me. Now, what did you say the dog looked like?"

"He looked . . . brown, black, I don't know. I'd only seen him once before."

"In other words, it wasn't his habit to trespass upon your property."

"Well, Your Honor, I can't say. I haven't been here all that much."

"Mr. Smalley, would you please relate what happened on Thursday, August 16th."

"I shot the dog. Then I was away all day and overnight in Boston on the 17th, that's Friday. When I came back that morning, I found all the windows of my house broken— every single one. Someone had thrown rocks and vandalized my house!"

For the first time, there was a rumbling in the courtroom. There had never been any desecration of property in Hardscrabble, not in the long history of the Town.

"Order!" Judge Parker said. "I'll have order in my court." He turned to Mr. Smalley. "Mr. Smalley, is there any reason why someone would vandalize your house?"

"Of course there is, Judge," Mr. Smalley retorted. "It's obvious to me and everyone in this courtroom that Foss, here, broke my windows just on account of that stupid old dog!"

The Judge pulled his glasses farther down his long, thin nose and looked down at Casper Smalley.

"You are not, Mr. Smalley, in a position to speak on behalf of anyone in this courtroom. Did you see Mr. Foss break your windows?"

"Well . . . er, no."

"Have you any witnesses you can produce who saw him break those windows?"

"Why . . . er, no, Your Honor."

"Then you have no evidence?"

"Evidence? Why yes, Your Honor—I have the evidence. My windows are all busted, and I can tell you for a fact that that man over there, Jonas Foss, is the one that did it!"

Restlessness descended upon the courtroom. There could be no doubt about the situation. Jonas Foss remained in his seat. The expression in his eyes told the Judge that the old man's thoughts were somewhere else.

Judge Parker reached across his desk for a pen and said, "The Court makes a finding of 'Not Guilty' and the Warrant is so marked."

Casper Smalley jumped to his feet. *"Not guilty?* What kind of justice is that? First that damn dog digs up my property, then his owner vandalizes my home!"

Judge Parker rose slowly from behind the bench to his full height of six foot three, removed his glasses, and looked down at Casper Smalley. "Mr. Smalley, you may consider yourself a very lucky man. By your own word, without question or solicitation by any man, you stated to this Court that you shot and killed Skip Foss."

There was a murmur in the courtroom. The Judge continued. "Skip Foss, sir, was a litter brother to my Drive. And if he was like Drive, I'll tell you what sort of a dog he was. He was probably one of the best rabbit dogs to ever comb these woods. Let me tell you something, Mr. Smalley. You didn't shoot a dog, no sir; you killed your neighbor's best friend and hunting buddy.

"Now, Mr. Smalley, I understand you're new to Hardscrabble. It's pretty clear you're not cognizant of our ways. Well, knowing the men of this Town as I do—and I think I know them quite well—I am somewhat surprised that no one drove over to your house with a Springfield bull gun and a hundred rounds of armor piercing. I am surprised that no one took that rifle, sighted it in for three hundred yards—which is the distance from the edge of the woods to your house—put down a bag of sawdust for a benchrest and . . ."

The Judge felt a lump in his throat and reached for a glass of water.

". . . and smashed your bathtub, the wash basin, the toilet bowl, and flooded the whole house.

"I am surprised," he continued, his gaze piercing, the tone of his voice as cold as granite, "that none of the men on the state road crew ran a Jeep up to your well house on the hill and dropped a half ton of rock salt into your well, or dumped a quart of shellac into the oil tank of your Cadillac.

"There is nothing within the interpretation of the law that demands punishment for killing a dog. I suppose I could demand that you pay restitution to the defendant, but nothing will buy Jonas Foss back his dog. Mr. Smalley, in my book you're a murderer. That's right, sir. You murdered Skip Foss in cold blood.

"You see, Mr. Smalley, I doubt very much that Skip Foss was digging up your garden. Since you're new to Town and I gather not a hunter yourself, you're probably unaware that right below your house is the finest rabbit swamp in the whole of the county. I rather expect that Skip was taking a shortcut, to go and check things out.

"Mr. Smalley, you obviously have never owned a dog. If you had, sir, you could not have leveled a gun on Skip Foss." The Judge paused for another sip of water. "Let me tell you a few things you don't know, Mr. Smalley, but what every other person in this courtroom does:

"You don't know that the first to greet you in the morning and the last one to bid you good night is your dog. If you had a dog, you'd know this as sure as you know the sun rises from the east and sets in the west.

"You don't know that you're never alone or lonely when you have a dog. Now, Mr. Smalley, if you had a dog, you'd know this as sure as you know where your next meal is coming from.

"You wouldn't know—in fact, Mr. Smalley, you probably will never know—that among the greatest losses you can suffer is the loss of your dog. No matter how hard you try, you can never love a dog as much as he loves you. So when you lose a love as big as that, sir, then you lose a piece of your heart. If you had a dog, you'd know this as sure as you know how to breathe.

"You'll never know these things, Mr. Smalley, and I'll tell you why. I'm drawing up a violation that will appear on your record as 'convicted of theft.' You not only stole a dog's life, but you robbed Jonas Foss of his companion. Unfortunately, it's not likely to happen, but if anytime, anywhere, you acquire a dog and this becomes known to an officer of the law and he calls up your record, it will clearly state that this matter is to be directed to my attention. Then, I swear, Mr. Smalley, that I will do everything in my power to deprive you of the ownership of that dog. There is nothing that you have told me to indicate that you deserve the privilege. And considering the grievous act you have committed, nothing assures me that you have the kindness it takes to possess and care for a dog.

"However, the thing that concerns me most, Mr. Smalley, is that maybe I've put some ideas into some of these folks' heads"—the Judged waved a hand over the crowd— "and if that is so, then so be it, and it will be up to you and your conscience to deal with whatever may come your way. Besides, a case can only be tried once, and I declare this one over."

With that, the gavel fell, the crowd rose to its feet, and the Judge left the room. There was no burst of thunderous applause as people filed out of the courthouse. They were satisfied that justice had been done.

The following day, Smalley put his house up for sale and left Hardscrabble, never to return. Not long after, Clem Lovell's beagle, Stan—who, like his owner, had a way with the women—accompanied his master on a social call to visit the Judge's Drive, who was in season. The visit eventually produced a fine litter of beagle pups.

The pick of the litter was given to Jonas Foss.

⚘ EIGHTEEN ⚘

New Day Dawning

The kiss you take is better than you give.
—Shakespeare

All that night and into the small hours of the morning, Jeff and Mary talked. How, he wondered, as he watched the reflection from the dancing flames from the fireplace kiss her dark hair, had he been blind to the simple sweetness of this woman? She was a breath of fresh air, a salve to his soul. For whatever reason, it had to be now and not before, that this had come to him. He was ready. For the first time in the months since Eden had died, he was ready to live again.

In the chair across from him, Mary was enveloped in an unfamiliar euphoria. She was captivated by his words, his handsome, dark good looks, the square set of his jaw, the warmth in his eyes. Yet in the background, her practical nature tried to apply reason to the emotions that were playing havoc with her heart. From the start, she had been attracted to Jeff. In the weeks that followed, she grew comfortable in his presence. In the dark confidence of night, she would think about him, then want him, then realize she had wanted him since the first time she saw him.

But the work stood between them, and again her practical nature intervened: It wouldn't have been right. And she was right, but for the wrong reason. Jeff was not ready. But he was ready now. Now, in front of the fire, sitting opposite one another, talking, freeing their minds and their hearts of pent-up thoughts and feelings—it was right, so right. But Mary didn't know what to do next.

She didn't have long to wonder.

The following morning, Mary appeared at the usual time to work on Jeff's manuscripts. They had parted the night before with the awkwardness that comes between two people who have shared so much, so suddenly, in so short a time. He had helped her into her coat, buttoned the top button, and pulled the collar up around her neck. He kissed her on the forehead. And she drove off with a cheerful wave that felt incomplete, like a loose end. But today was a new day, and she was determined, somehow, to recapture some of the magic of the night before.

However, when she got to the house, Jeff was not there. She walked in and called his name. No one answered. On the table in the foyer was an envelope with her name. She opened it with shaking hands.

The note said:

"Meet me in the field below the house, by the apple tree."

What a strange request, she thought. She couldn't imagine what this was all about.

The ground was wet from the rain the night before. The sun was shining with that slick-clean shine that comes after a rain, as though the sun itself had been washed and polished, too. She pulled on a pair of Wellington boots that she kept in her car, took off her tweed blazer, and put on her Barbour jacket instead. It would be a bit of a hike getting into the field.

The driveway was carpeted with damp autumn leaves, and the trunks of the trees were black from the rain. What few leaves remained on the bare branches shimmered like gold and rustled like jingling coins. Mary didn't bother snapping shut her jacket. The sun was warm. Or was the warmth radiating from her heart? She did not know.

She got to the end of the long, curving drive and crossed the country lane. Below lay the field. Dense brush lined the roadside like an unclipped hedgerow, making it impossible to see the field below. Mary was unsure how to enter the field, when a white balloon bouncing in the breeze caught her eye. It was tied to a tree. Something was written on it. She untied the balloon. It said, "Mary, enter here." The string slipped through her hand and for a moment, she watched the balloon dance with the wind and fly away. She negotiated a small clearing that opened into a rolling field, like a pastoral Secret Garden.

In the middle stood a twisted, overgrown apple tree that still bore fruit on the topmost branches. Under the tree was a tent like the one in the pictures on Jeff's study wall of African safaris he had taken. Mary was totally bewildered. An unexpected gust of wind whipped through her hair and uncoiled her secretarial bun. The long, glossy dark hair streamed behind her; she pushed it away from her face and made her way through the tall, dry, wheat-colored grass toward the tent. A dog was barking. It was Tober, who came bounding out of the tent toward her. He rubbed his soft, wet muzzle in the palm of her extended hand.

"Whatever are you doing out here, boy?" she asked, as she petted the handsome setter. A note was tied to his collar. It read, "I request the pleasure of your company. Please R.S.V.P. in the tent."

"C'mon, Tober," Mary laughed. Let's see what this is all about." Jeff stood in the doorway of the canvas tent, holding back the flap so she could enter. He was dressed in a tuxedo and Wellington boots.

"What's this all about?" Mary giggled, as he ushered her inside. A bearskin rug covered the tent floor. A small table set for breakfast stood in the corner. A camp stove was lit, and the tent was warm. Tober padded over to the stove, lay down nearby and, with a contented sigh, closed his eyes and drifted into a half sleep.

"I had to figure some way I could get you away from work, and the only way I could do that was to get you out of the house," he explained.

"And why the tuxedo?"

"Because today is a very special occasion."

"And what occasion, may I ask, is that?"

Jeff took Mary in his arms and kissed her tenderly and for a long time. "Today," he whispered, "is the occasion of our first kiss."

Jeff unbuttoned Mary's coat. "Don't say a word," Jeff said. He gently lowered her onto the bearskin rug.

"Isn't this going a little too—"

"Shhh," he replied. "And in answer to your one and only question, the answer is no. It's going the way it's supposed to go. Now be quiet and kiss me."

Outside, the wind whispered secrets to the trees, the sun wiped away the rain, and a new day dawned.

NINETEEN

Nipped in the Butt

Doc got the first call, then Officer Oak, and the third from the Republican's Hideaway was for Judge Parker. The three men pulled up the long, serpentine drive to Lila Hornbeam's secluded estate at precisely and coincidentally the same moment—first the police cruiser, followed by Doc's Army surplus Jeep, and the Judge's old Ford truck brought up the rear. Not one had a clue why he had been so urgently summoned. All anyone knew was that Something Terrible had happened at the Hideaway.

"Wothehell is this all about, Park?" Doc called over his shoulder to the Judge, as he reached into the backseat of his Jeep for his medical bag.

"Guess I know just about as much as you do, Doc," the Judge replied. "Which is nothing. Lila called hysterical and told me to come as quick as I could. She hung up before I could get a word in edgewise. And just as I was about to tie the hackle on a Royal Coachman . . ." the Judge said, referring to a fly he was tying that was a surefire summer hit with rainbow trout in Loon Lake.

"Same with me," Doc replied.

"A Coachman?"

"No, I was actually tying a Hare's Ear, but Lila was pretty hysterical when she called me, too. Of course, I assumed there was some sort of medical emergency. What do you know, Oak?"

"No more'n you do, Doc. I just got word from the dispatcher to get up here as quick as I could. I was out over t'other end of the Lake Road. Put the pedal right down to the floor. Cruiser kicked up a lot of dust."

"Road crew oughta be watering down that road," the Judge said. "When it gets as hot and dry as it has lately, the Lake Road is like the Sahara."

"I don't remember an August this dry," Doc contemplated. "Been a long, long time."

At that moment, the massive front door of the Republican's Hideaway swung open, revealing a short, stout, stern-looking woman. Molly Bradshaw, head housekeeper and self-anointed dictator of the Republican's Hideaway, stepped out onto the wraparound porch.

"Took you long enough," she scoffed.

"Now, Molly, we came as fast as we—"

"Don't give me any of your excuses, Oak," the elderly housekeeper admonished. "Me and my gamy leg could have walked clear to the Village and back in the time it took you to get here. Wipe your feet on the mat before you come in. Miss Lila's in a dither." The formidable woman led the way into the dark, wood-paneled foyer like a general leading his troops.

Lila Hornbeam, hearing their voices, called out from the library. She was wearing a vapid green shift and looked like a piece of wilted lettuce as she slouched against a chintz-upholstered armchair, listlessly batting a Japanese fan alongside her flushed cheek in a vain attempt to summon some cool air from the sweltering August heat. "Nothing like this has ever happened before," she cried. "Not in all the years I've lived here. Please go upstairs and see to him right away,

Doctor. I think he's lost a lot of blood. My nerves . . . I cannot cope . . ."

"A lot of . . . who, Lila?" Doc asked.

"And you, Officer Oak," Lila Hornbeam continued, turning her attention to the policeman, "he's in the kitchen. I think they tied him up . . ."

"Who's in the kitchen?" Oak replied, completely befuddled. "Who's in the kitchen?"

"And you, Park," she continued feebly through half-closed eyes, "I'm depending entirely upon you to make sure this doesn't get into the papers. If it does, it will cause such a scandal . . ."

"Scandal? Lila, what are you talking about?" the Judge implored.

A terrible wail resounded throughout the house.

"Where did that come from?" Officer Oak cried. "Upstairs or downstairs?"

"Yes!" Lila wailed . . . and fell into a dead faint.

*M*olly, who had never been more than a room or two away from Lila since her mistress had come to the Republican's Hideaway as a young bride three decades before, reached into her apron pocket and took out a tiny bottle of smelling salts.

"Stand away, you men," she ordered, and bent over the semiconscious woman to revive her.

"Let me take a look at her," Doc suggested, but he froze from coming closer at Molly's glacial stare.

"It's not like I haven't cared for her these thirty-one years, Doctor," the housekeeper retorted. "You know as well as I do that this is what she does whenever she has an attack of the vapors, and no harm ever comes of it.

She doesn't need you, but the gentleman upstairs surely does."

Again, a moan filtered down the corridor, and this time it definitely came from upstairs. Confusion spread over the three men's faces.

"Then who's in the kitchen?" Officer Oak asked.

"The dog, of course," Molly replied indignantly. "Now, be off with you and do what Miss Lila said."

Doc climbed the stairs two at a time, Officer Oak sprinted through the dining room toward the kitchen, and the Judge stood in the middle of the foyer next to the limp figure of his longtime friend. Lila took a whiff of the smelling salts, choked a little, and began to revive just as the phone rang.

"That'll be trouble," Molly forewarned. The Judge picked up the hall phone.

"Who is it?" Lila said vaguely as she swept a weak hand across her moisture-beaded brow.

"It's Tilt from the Store," the Judge said. "Just wanted you to know that Clydie's blown a tire on the delivery truck, and your groceries will be a little late today."

"Late? Groceries?" At that, Lila fell into another swoon, the Judge threw his hands up in the air, and Molly dove into her apron pocket again for the bottle of smelling salts.

*D*oc was walking down the long corridor. The groans sounded increasingly like something out of *Wuthering Heights*—eerie, haunting, and foreboding. Tentatively, he opened one bedroom door after another until he realized that the wailing was coming from a large room at the end of the hall—the room that years before had belonged to Lila's late husband. Doc turned the handle slowly and peeked in.

Sprawled upon an enormous, grossly ornate, Victorian four-poster bed was a rotund, bald, stark-naked man with a white bath towel coiled like a cobra on top of his private parts.

"Ohhh . . ." the man moaned. "Please get me a doctor! If you have any compassion, you'll get me a doctor! A dog has attacked me! Ohhh . . ."

"I'm a doctor," Doc replied, taken aback by the sight. He quickly gathered his composure. "Do you mind if I take a look?" Doc sidled over to the bed, gingerly unfolded the towel, and erupted into torrents of laughter.

*D*ownstairs in the kitchen, Officer Oak had confronted the alleged assailant—none other than Ben the postman's dog, Dash.

"He's a *canine indiscriminatus*," Ben explained proudly, ". . . a dog of indiscriminate genes. In short, Ben is a mutt."

"C'mere you mutt, you," Officer Oak said affectionately, tousling the familiar dog's long, floppy ears. "I always said that Dash had some sort of hound in him," Officer Oak said, squinting at the dog. He had known Dash since Ben had taken him home as a puppy from the pound, over eight years before.

"Very astute of you, if I do say so myself," Ben said, nodding his head vigorously. "His mother was a basset hound! And his father was a vagrant!"

"Well, he surely is a handsome fellow, no matter who his dad was." Officer Oak smiled as a river of drool streamed from the dog's smiling, panting mouth and onto the toe of one of Oak's meticulously polished boots. "So," he continued, "what exactly happened?"

"I'll tell you the truth, and you won't believe me."

"Give it a try," Oak chuckled. "I could believe just about anything that happens at the Republican's Hideaway."

Ben told his story and Lila, who finally collected herself, was able to fill in the rest. It seemed that the corpulent man that amused Doc in such an unabashed way was none other than a former state senator whose name, for obvious reasons, we will not divulge. He was a frequent visitor at the Hideaway, and having no current or recent wife (though there had been several) he took advantage of the kind hospitality of one of his most enthusiastic constituents—none other than Lila Hornbeam. Lila had been an ardent supporter many years before, when the Senator first ran for office. After he failed to win a second term, he found he had an abundance of time on his hands. So cordial was Lila's invitation that the Senator took to spending most of his summers at the Hideaway. The Senator was useful. He was a useful companion, dinner partner, and to top it off, he made it his daily habit to stroll down the long drive from the house to collect the household mail from the mailbox. He called this his "morning constitutional." There was nothing in the world, he said, that made him more relaxed than his morning constitutional.

So relaxed, in fact, that on sultry days, when he was Lila's only guest, would he saunter leisurely down the drive wearing nothing more than a cup of coffee and a doughnut. Since the Republican's Hideaway was miles from any neighbor, the risk of being seen by anyone was limited to Molly the housekeeper, the day maid, and Moses, who was handyman, butler, and chauffeur rolled into one. The staff knew that it would cost them their jobs if they divulged the secret of the Senator's rather startling habit.

This particular day had dawned hell-hot and steamy

with no promise of respite under the fiery yellow cannonball sun. A large weekend party was expected later that afternoon, so the Senator decided to take his morning constitutional a little early. He bathed and didn't even bother to towel off. The warm air would dry him soon enough, he figured. The only thing he slipped into was his golf shoes, which provided good traction on gravel and grass, and he blithely continued on his way. He got to the end of the drive, opened the mailbox, and found that he was too early—the mail had not arrived. At that moment, Ben rounded the corner in his mail truck.

Ben pulled up to the mailbox as usual. He slid open the door. However, the sight that greeted him silenced the usually chatty mailman. Ben couldn't think of a word to say. Just as he figured a "good morning" would be in order, Dash jumped out of the truck and lunged for a dripping raspberry jelly doughnut that the Senator had brought from the breakfast sideboard and now held protectively in front of his manhood. The dog aimed for the tasty morsel, missed, and instead closed his teeth around a nut of a different sort. Dash was a gentle dog with a very soft mouth. All he succeeded in doing was splattering the jelly on the Senator, which he proceeded to lick with great enthusiasm. But when the Senator looked down, he saw red and promptly fainted. Ben, who couldn't have weighed 130 pounds dripping wet, struggled to pull the heavy man into the mail truck. He tossed him on top of the mailbags and throttled the engine, catapulting the rickety old vehicle to its maximum uphill speed of fifteen miles an hour. Ben honked the horn the entire journey up the driveway, and Lila, who heard the commotion from her desk in the morning room, came running out. Dash didn't have an opportunity to finish licking the jam, and Ben didn't have an opportunity to explain to Lila through her hysterics that that was all it was.

"That's pretty much what happened," Ben explained to Officer Oak, who was doubled over in laughter. At that moment, Doc came guffawing into the kitchen. Tears were running down his cheeks.

"Do you know who that is upstairs?" he roared.

"Ah-yuh," Judge Parker said, following in on Doc's heels. "That's Senator————. Up to his old tricks again, though why Lila thinks he's news anymore beats me. Even if the papers got wind of this, what would they say? 'Senator gets licked'—why, that's no news at all! Happens every day."

"I gave him a sedative, all the same," Doc said, wiping his tears with the tail of his shirt. "He had a real shock when he saw all that jam, thinking instead he'd been bit. Funniest thing was, when Ben hauled him into the mail truck, he must have fallen on a pile of mail. That jam was sticky as glue, and a label came off a piece of mail and got stuck on his manhood.

"It said, Bulk Rate."

TWENTY

And This, Too, Shall Pass Away

What we anticipate seldom occurs; what we least expected generally happens.
—Benjamin Disraeli

Fran Forsythe rocked slowly back and forth on the porch, deaf to the congenial rhythm of the old wicker rocking chair, indifferent to the afternoon sun warming her face, blind to the breathtaking panorama that unfolded before her unseeing eyes. Sometimes she would sit and rock and contemplate how her forebear, Josiah Towle, had combed these foothills two centuries before in search of a purely perfect plot of land on which to build his home; how he amassed a large fortune, built Towledge, and produced a large family to fill it. Through the generations, the fortune thrived, but the family did not: Fran alone remained, the last of a distinguished line. She thought about that often. But she wasn't thinking about that now.

She was thinking about Death.

Had Death appeared on her doorstep, she would have let him in, willingly; it would have been the answer to her prayers, and for too long, her prayers had been unanswered. For too long, she tried to suffocate the sorrow, but the sorrow was suffocating her. Yes, she would gladly have taken Death by the hand, but not by her own. That was against everything she stood for, as a God-fearing Yankee.

A pair of blue jays quarreled in a nearby apple tree that was heavy with late-season fruit. A gray squirrel joined in the argument. A dog barked from somewhere across the valley. The tired motor of an arthritic truck panted up the hill, grew louder, and stopped. Someone called out her name. The old woman heard none of these things.

She was lost in some faraway place, deep in the outback of her soul.

Towledge

A baker's dozen of patriarchal houses graced Hardscrabble until that tragic winter of the Huntress Bridge episode, when the Captain Bradford house burned to the ground. That left an even dozen houses of that period and ilk, all of which were so well maintained, they appeared as though their original coat of paint was still wet. All, that is, except the Ezekiel Hornbeam house, which Lila Hornbeam rechristened The Republican's Hideaway after "the true political faith," as she'd say, and built a wing to accommodate the constant flow of eccentric houseguests she affectionately referred to as the "VIPs of the GOP." But it was Towledge, and its commanding view over the hills and dales that genuflect before the great Mount Washington, which surely was the jewel in the crown of Hardscrabble.

The sprawling white clapboard house and its embracing, wraparound porch was a stoic and grand celebration of New England architecture. Inside, it had been warm and welcoming and hospitable, right down to the overstuffed chairs that were pulled up to the fireplaces. And there were parties, wonderful parties, full of laughter and good people, good food, and good times. But there were no more parties at Towledge, not for almost a year, and the place had lost its warmth, as the heart of a house does when it becomes home to a single soul; and lonelier still, when the loneliness festers from the wounds of loss, as they had with Fran.

By making a busy life for herself, she had bandaged her invisible wounds, as though distraction would tourniquet the dull, throbbing pain in her heart. But a bandage cannot stop the hemorrhaging heart, and sorrow is a cruel bedfellow, so cold and comfortless. Not the plethora of preparations for the Ladies' Guild's Christmas Bazaar, nor the committee meetings for the new Library addition; not the monthly soirees of the Literary Society, at Charlie Markham's; not even arranging the altar flowers from the Forsythe Family Church Flowers Trust Fund, dispelled her grief.

The squirrel had ceased his chatter, since no one was bothering to listen; the blue jays flew away to continue their argument elsewhere; a cover of clouds blanketed the sun, and a soft, autumn breeze bussed Fran on the cheek. She closed her eyes and for a moment imagined it was her beloved husband kissing her from some eternal place, assuring her that he loved her still and forevermore, and that she was not alone: It would be all right one day. But the breeze didn't even linger long enough to dry away her tears.

Suddenly she sensed someone standing in the shadows. She did not know how long he had been there. It didn't matter. It was a familiar presence, and she didn't have to turn around to see that it was her very distant cousin and handyman, Perry Towle. Perry moved quietly out of a habit acquired over a lifetime of poaching whitetail deer, though now, in his dimming years, he did little of that anymore.

"Why hello, Perry," Fran murmured, as she turned her tearstained cheek away to avoid his worried gaze. As women past the full bloom of life are wont to do, Fran stood up slowly, stiffly, and keeping her back toward Perry, smoothed her dress with vein-knitted hands. Before turning to greet him, she put on her face—the one that kept the grief from lying close to the surface.

"Got somethun' in your eye?" Perry asked, knowing the real matter, and taking a red bandanna from his back pocket, pushed it into the palm of Fran's hand. She clutched it and lowered her head. A stream of tears poured from her brimming eyes. "It's okay to cry, Frannie," he said softly. The old woman buried her face in her hands and for a good, long minute, wept bitterly before Yankee fortitude broke in. Perry eased her back into the wicker rocker. He was the only person she'd allow see her come undone like this.

"Frannie," he said in a firm voice that helped turn the tide of emotion to something more pragmatic. "You know my great-nephew, Mark."

"Mark? He's the boy with that formidable black dog, isn't he? Is anything wrong with him?"

"Nothing uncommon wrong for a twelve-year-old, I reckon. Thing is, I could use a hand around this place. We need to get the property to bed, storm windows up, and you know, I'm not getting any younger."

"Neither of us are, Perry." Fran agreed. "A boy at Towledge, eh? It's been a long time since we had a young person around the place. When would he come?"

"Oh, a couple of days a week after school, Saturdays, mebbe a Sunday here and there. Depends on what needs doing."

Fran paused in thought. "I don't know, Perry." She hesitated. "I don't know that I can deal with having a young person here. It's been too many years. . . ."

"I already talked to him, and he's anxious to work. He's a good lad, Frannie. Says he can walk up the hill after school. I'll take him home at night and pick him up on weekends. He'd be no trouble."

"What would I pay him?"

"A glass of milk and some of your peanut butter cookies for a start; you know, the ones with the big chocolate chip in the middle. And mebbe a couple of bucks, besides."

"I don't know. . . . I assume this is all right with his parents?"

Perry answered the question with a brief nod.

"Perry, I'd just as soon hire someone like Raymond Jones to help you out. I really don't think that I could—"

"Frannie, you got to shake off these blues and get a grip on yourself. You need a jump start on life. Look, this boy needs the work. I need the help. This jest might work out well for everyone."

"Well, then," she said after some thought, "tell him I'll pay him two dollars an hour."

"That'll be riches to him, Frannie," Perry grinned. "What about the cookies?"

The old woman smiled. "I'll throw those in as part of the deal."

Mark and Bear Come to Work

The grandfather clock in the front hall struck three as Fran looked out the kitchen window to see if Mark was coming up the hill. To her surprise, he was sitting on the granite step at the foot of the driveway, and next to him sat that enormous black dog, Bear. The boy was putting on his shoes. "That's funny," she thought. "He must have walked up the hill barefoot. . . ."

From her hiding place behind the red checkered kitchen curtains, Fran watched in amusement as the boy picked up his book bag, slipped the strap over Bear's neck and, with an affectionate rub between the ears, they walked together, side by side, toward the house. The rich scent of rotting apples that travels on the heels of an imminent frost permeated the autumn air. Fran continued to peek from behind the curtain. She heard Mark talking to Bear, who replied with adoring eyes and a wagging tail. As the pair made their way up the lane, Fran saw that the boy wore no sweater or coat.

"Come in, dear," she greeted Mark at the kitchen door.

"Stay outside, Bear," Mark ordered his canine companion, who reluctantly obeyed. Mark swept his tattered baseball cap off from his head of thick, brown, undisciplined curls. Fran offered her hand and noticed the cuff of the boy's shirt, despite a row of darning, was badly frayed. "Always shake a person firmly by the hand, son," she instructed, and for a fleeting moment she was carried back across forty years, when she taught her own son the proper way to shake hands. The boy's grip tightened. "That's fine!" Fran beamed.

A batch of fresh-baked peanut butter cookies was cooling on the counter. The boy's eyes widened at the sight and smell, and Fran motioned to a place at the kitchen table set with a tall glass of milk and a plate brimming with warm cookies. But before he took his seat, he glanced outside, to check on Bear. Fran glanced outside, too. The dog had assumed a clownlike position, splayed along the steps with his head resting between his front paws on the topmost one. He looked up at his audience with sad eyes, and Fran could sense that Mark was sorry to see his companion outside, alone.

"Do you think," Fran offered, "that Bear would like to come inside?" The boy's face brightened. He ran to the door and beckoned to the dog. Bear wagged his tail, almost knocked over the umbrella stand, and planted a long, wet kiss on Mark's cheek. Fran drifted back again to a past time, to Muffie, her cocker spaniel who she adored, and how, when she died, Fran could not bring herself to get another. She went to give Bear a timid pat on the head when he, instead, gave her a long, wet lick on her hand.

With that, she went to the cupboard, took out a loaf of bread and a couple of jars, and proceeded to make Bear a peanut butter and jelly sandwich.

A New Lease on Life

Things worked out better than fine. Mark and yes, even Bear, gave Fran a new lease on life. What was to have been a few days a week soon became every day. Now a large glass jar filled with home-baked dog biscuits was next to the cookie jar. Mark worked as hard as an adult. As for Bear, he took to working, too. Fran found an old leather tool belt in the barn, took it to the leather shop, and had a canine version made for Bear, which strapped around his girth like a saddle. Wherever Mark went, Bear followed, keeping the boy's tools within easy reach.

Fran became concerned that all the time that Mark was spending at Towledge was taking away from his school-work, so she began to tutor him after he finished his snack. "A child is like a tree. If you plant it, stake it, and water it, it will grow tall and strong," the former schoolteacher told Perry. And so it was that the child was nourished with food and knowledge, and the sharp angles of hunger disappeared, and his appetite for learning grew.

Mark became consumed by reading. Tom Sawyer and Long John Silver were among his new friends, and the boy's circle of literary acquaintances grew and grew. Fran would watch the sparkle in his enthusiastic eyes as he'd pore over *Oliver Twist* and *Kidnapped* and *White Fang*. Often he'd stop and read passages to her, then tell her what he thought.

"Listen to this part, Miss Frannie," he said while reading *Adventures of Huckleberry Finn*. " 'We catched fish and talked, and we took a swim now and then to keep off sleepiness. It was kind of solemn, drifting down the big, still river, laying on our backs looking up at the stars, and we didn't ever feel like talking loud, and it warn't often that we laughed—only a little kind of a low chuckle. We had mighty good weather as a general thing, and nothing ever happened to us at all.' " Mark sighed. "Have you ever gone fishing, Miss Frannie?" he asked.

"Oh, a long, long time ago, when my husband and I were first married."

"Was he a good fisherman?"

"He was the best fisherman you ever saw. Why, he used to go down to the river just there, below the house, and study the insects that were hatching on the water and the bugs that were hiding under the rocks. Then he'd put some specimens in glass jars, study them, and tied artificial flies. They looked just like the real thing."

"Did they catch fish?"

"Ted caught a lot of fish with all sorts of flies that he tied. I remember one particular fly that he was convinced would be a real 'fish magnet.' That's what he used to call a good fly—a fish magnet. Anyway, he went down to the river and after awhile, came home all hot and bothered. 'That goldurn fly didn't catch a single fish!' he said, and I remember him holding it between his fingers and shaking it like he wanted to slap some sense into it."

"That must have been pretty funny," Mark laughed.

"Oh, it was," Fran smiled. "But it wasn't funny to him. Well, he wasn't going to let that fly lick him. The next day, he tried fishing with it again, and this time he got his limit in less than an hour!"

Bear, who was sleeping in his usual place by the woodstove, raised his head. "Hear that, Bear?" Mark said. "Trout!" Bear woofed once, put his head between his paws, and went back to Dog Dreamland. "He fished the same fly both days?" Mark asked. "He caught fish one day and didn't catch fish the other?"

"Yes, and he didn't understand why—at first. Then one day, he tried an experiment. He tied the exact same fly, but this time he tried two versions—one, in all dark colors and the other one in light colors. The next day, he went to the river just as the morning hatch was rising. He cast the light fly into the sunlight and—*wham!*—he hooked a great, big trout! Later, he returned to the river for the evening hatch, and cast the dark fly into a dark pool. *Wham!* He hooked another!"

"You'd think it would be the other way around," Mark pondered.

"Well, he tried that, too. But the fish didn't seem to like it that way. I remember he said, 'Trout are ornery fellows. You try to catch them every way you can think of, and they always decide to oblige when you least expect it.'"

Mark sat with his elbows on the kitchen table, his chin nestled in the palms of his hands, then said. "So . . . water in sunlight is light, water in shadow is dark. He fished the light fly in the sun and the dark fly in the dark pools. Did he ever name the fly?"

"Yes, he did. He named it the Towledge Tattler."

"I can sure see why. The Towledge Tattler lures the fish to tell it a tattletale. Everyone likes to gossip!"

"Clever boy," Fran laughed.

"No, Miss Frannie. I'm not clever. I'm just a fisherman."

Pride Before the Fall

Winter was breaking, and a hint of snow was in the air; nonetheless, Mark continued to walk up Andrew's Hill barefoot. Although the two had become fast friends, Fran stayed away from the subject of Mark and his shoes. She didn't want to humiliate the boy. But as the weather worsened, she couldn't bear looking out the window and seeing him stop to put them on at the granite step. When the first snow of the season started to fly, she couldn't hide her anxiety any longer. When she finally asked, Mark's head hung heavy with embarrassment.

"Because I'm the oldest, I get new shoes. I have to hand my shoes down to my brothers, and the less I wear them, the longer they'll last."

"But Mark, surely your family can keep you in shoes."

"Things haven't been so good since my pa had his accident, ma'am."

Later, Fran spoke to Perry. "Frannie, don't you think I've tried to help my great-niece and her family? It's just no good. Mark's father is a proud man. He won't even take a penny if he smells charity. Frannie, poverty isn't just empty pockets. It's an empty stomach and empty dreams."

"When pride forces a boy like Mark to suffer, then that's sheer stupidity. What happened to Mark's father, anyway?"

"Richard was involved in a logging accident a couple of years ago. A tree fell on his legs and crushed them something terrible. It took over 200 stitches to sew him back together, and they're still not right. He's in pain all the time. Can't afford medication. Can't get regular work."

"Surely your brother-in-law has compensation."

"No, that's the thing. He took his pay under the table, so there was no insurance. And he refuses to claim disability because, there again, he's so proud. On a good day, he helps George at the Dump and makes a few bucks. George used to look the other way and let Richard take the returnable bottles and cans over to the Recycle Center in Maine for the deposit money. But that dang woman who finished out Kev

Ralston's term as selectman after he had that stroke, got wind of it and threatened to cause all kinds of trouble."

"She was rather petty and unkind, wasn't she."

"Townsfolk called her worse than that."

"What happens with the money Mark earns?" Fran asked.

"He hands every cent over to his dad. He feels the responsibility."

"Why, Mark's only a boy."

"That boy was born old."

The following day was Saturday. Just before Mark and Perry were about to leave, Fran handed a large parcel to Mark.

"These are for you and your brothers," she said. "Don't open it until you get home."

Fran waved to Mark and watched as he hoisted the heavy package into the truck then pulled Bear by the collar to help him clamber into the cab. "I hope his father will keep his pride from getting in the way this time," she said to Perry.

"We can only hope, Fran," Perry said, shaking his head with uncertainty. "We can only hope."

The next day was Sunday. Perry and Mark arrived to tie burlap bags over the hedges to protect them against winter. Mark had a long face—and Fran's gifts.

"My father said we can't accept these, Miss Frannie. He said it's charity."

Charity! Fran was livid. Perry, who was helping himself to a cookie, put a restraining hand on her arm. "Don't get yourself worked up."

"Well, there's one thing I can do," she said. "While Mark is working for me, he can wear those new boots. If his father is that proud, then let him be proud in his home, and I'll be proud in mine. Put these on, dear," she said, handing the boots to Mark. He took them tentatively. The pungent, brand-new leather smell sweetened the air. He pulled them on. They were wonderfully warm, and his feet felt as though they were wrapped in pillows. No one had ever given him anything like this before. For the first time since he had come to Towledge, the boy ran freely into Fran's arms and gave her a hug. Bear jumped up and joined the happy pair.

"I guess," Fran said, "they call this a Bear hug!"

And so, the days unfolded into weeks, the weeks into months, and the heavy loneliness in Fran's heart was assuaged by the joy that Mark and Bear brought into her life.

Tragedy Strikes Again

Fran knew that Mark's family lived at the end of Brooks Lane, but she wasn't prepared for what she saw. A mountain of discarded tires was piled alongside the plywood and tar paper–roofed double trailer whose exterior could best be described as rust. Behind were the hulls of five or six cars, these, too, pockmarked with rust. Laundry hung sadly on a clothesline that was tied between two leafless trees. *How could clothes dry in this cold?* Fran mused, as she parked her car in front of the dented aluminum door. She got out, wishing this was not the place. She heard Bear moan inside.

The woman who answered the door was thin and gaunt, with a glimmer of former beauty still lingering around her high, chiseled cheekbones. Mark resembled his mother. Dark circles under frightened eyes betrayed a kind of fear that Fran had never known: the fear of not knowing where the next meal was coming from; the fear, perhaps, of being beaten by a frustrated husband; the fear of never knowing hope. She wore a cheap apron over a cheap, short-sleeved, cotton dress. The sleeves of her cheap sweater were too short and brought attention to her large wrists and small, red hands, worn from hard work and bony from malnutrition. She looked far, far older than her years. Fran was certain that in a household that made do with little, this woman, more often than not, made without.

"Please, come inside where it's warm," Marianne whispered. "I thought you might come." She could have said, "I had hoped you would come," from the tone in her voice, but a nervous glance sideways betrayed her fear of being overheard by someone she feared.

It wasn't warm inside at all. The only source of heat appeared to come from an old kerosene cookstove, something somebody threw away at the Dump when it ceased to throw much heat. The house was furnished with discarded chairs, a table, and a shabby sofa that was on the verge of uselessness. In the far corner of the room that served as living room and kitchen was a double bed, and in that bed lay Mark.

"Mark didn't come to the house after school," Fran said to his mother. "I was worried. He's had a terrible cough lately. I hope that you don't mind, but I called the school, seeing as you have no phone. They said Mark didn't come to school today."

A man emerged from a dark corner of the room. He was unshaven and wore clothes that had been new for someone else.

"I'm Richard Clemmons," he said in a friendless voice. As he came closer, Fran noticed that he limped, dragging his left leg badly behind him. He hunched his shoulders in a cynical way and looked at the world through defiant, untrusting eyes.

"I came to see Mark," Fran said, as she attempted to push the man's pride aside with the force of her voice.

"He's under the weather," Mark's father returned brusquely, "but he'll be back to work tomorrow." He stepped forward, blocking Fran from further entering the ramshackle room.

"Hello, Mark," Fran called across the father. The boy did not answer. "Mark?" She called out, louder. Again, no answer.

Forcefully, she put out a gloved hand and pushed her way past Richard Clemmons, crossed the clutter, and went to Mark. Bear lay on the floor, alongside the bed; he lifted his head, beckoned to Fran with worried eyes, and whimpered. He told her that her fears were confirmed.

Fran aimlessly, affectionately tousled the dog's ears while concentrating her gaze on the sick boy. "How long has Mark been like this?" she asked Mark's mother, who now stood at her elbow.

"Since last night," she whispered. "He was outside, doing his chores. If it hadn't been for Bear barking like he did, we wouldn't have found him as soon as we did."

Fran pulled off a glove and touched the boy's forehead lightly with the palm of her hand. He was burning up. "Mark," she said, shaking him gently. "Wake up, Mark." But Mark wasn't asleep.

He was unconscious.

*F*ran spun urgently around. "We have to get him to the hospital," she ordered, frantically gathering up the meager blankets from the bed to wrap the child. "Mr. Clemmons, help me get Mark into my car."

Mark's father did not budge. "My son's not going to no hospital, Mrs. Forsythe. Mark's not going anywhere." A pall filled the room. "We don't have the money to spend on that sort of nonsense." Marianne Clemmons's muffled sobs broke the leaden silence. Fran turned slowly and deliberately like a panther ready to pounce.

"Mr. Clemmons," she seethed, "if you don't carry your son into my car this instant, then I will—and I dare you to stop me."

*M*ark had spinal meningitis compounded by pneumonia. For a week the boy was kept sedated in the intensive care unit of the county hospital. Every day, all day and into the night, Fran sat at his bedside. She kept herself busy knitting him a sweater. Sometimes she read to him, sure that somehow he could hear her. She held his hand. Whether he knew she was there didn't matter; what mattered was the chance that he might.

*F*ran was dozing in the chair beside Mark's bed when a hand gently pressed her arm. For a moment she imagined it was her son, returning from some long ago place and time . . . and then, with a start, she was awake. The boy's smile was weak, but he was smiling at her, all the same.

"Hello, Miss Frannie," he said softly.

And all her pent-up fears subsided like a wave withdrawing from the sandy shore, and she clutched the boy's hand and wept.

This time, her prayers had been answered.

Mark Comes Home

Christmas was only a week away. Fran had arranged for Doc to be Mark's personal physician, both in the hospital and after he came home. Home, Fran was determined, would be Towledge.

It was decided that Doc would speak to Mark's parents.

"The boy can't get the care he needs here," he explained to Mr. and Mrs. Clemmons at their shack. "In this instance, it is better for Mark to be at Towledge, where he can get the care he needs. Your son is not out of the woods yet."

"I told her, I told Mrs. Forsythe that my family don't take charity," Richard stormed. "She should have left well enough alone. How am I going to handle the hospital bills?"

There was a long, pregnant silence. "If she had left well enough alone, Mr. Clemmons, your boy would be dead," Doc said sternly. He took a moment to regain his composure. "Do you smoke, Richard?" The younger man shrugged his hunched shoulders. "Let's step outside for a smoke," Doc suggested.

The two men walked into the brisk night air and silently watched the white tendrils of smoke from the smoldering red tips of their cigarettes waft against the coal-black sky.

"Richard," Doc resumed. "I understand you've suffered some serious troubles for quite some time."

"Is that why you're here? So you could remind me?" Clemmons said sarcastically.

"No. I wanted to tell you a story."

Richard Clemmons took a long draw from his cigarette. "All right, how does it go? Let me guess. 'Once upon a time . . . ?'"

"Sure." Doc grinned and took another draw from his cigarette. "Once upon a time, there was a woman who lost the man she loved. They had had one child, a son, who they adored. He had grown into a fine and prosperous man; but he died suddenly at the age of forty-three, and the sorrow was too much for his father to bear. He only lived one month after his son, and the woman, for the first time in her life, was alone.

"That woman is Mrs. Forsythe, Richard, and your son has helped ease her sorrow." A look of bewilderment passed over Richard Clemmons's darkened face. "Yes, she's the woman I'm speaking of, and her tragedies happened less than a year ago. Now Mark's sick—seriously sick—and all Fran can see is that someone else that she loves dearly could be taken away from her. She can't bear it. And she shouldn't have to." Doc looked up at a single, bright star twinking in the solemn night. "Look at that star. It's all alone in the heavens, it seems. But you and I know that there are countless others that surround it, but just because we don't see them doesn't mean they aren't there."

"What are you getting at, Doc?" Richard said pensively and for the first time, without a trace of defense in his voice.

"What I'm getting at is this. You're not alone. You think you are, just like that solitary star. But everyone has troubles. And like that star, you're not alone, no matter how it seems. And there's always someone who has a heavier burden to bear than you."

"Like Mrs. Forsythe."

"Sure."

The two men gazed at the single star when the cloud cover that masked the night sky dissipated, and the heavens came ablaze with infinite stars.

Doc put his hand on Richard Clemmons's shoulder. "Richard, pocket your pride. Life is a blessing when it's shared, and a misfortune when it's squandered." Doc paused again for a draw on his cigarette, then continued. "You know, a man named Alexander Pope, who lived a long time ago, said: 'Of all the causes which conspire to blind,

Man's erring judgment, and misguide the mind, What the weak head with strongest bias rules, is pride, the never-failing vice of fools.' Richard. You're no fool, son."

"No, sir, I'm no fool. Lord knows, I try to take care of my own." The man's shoulders heaved. "Lord above, I try."

"This isn't about failure," Doc said. "This is about doing what's right. And you'll be doing as much for Fran as she'll be doing for your boy. But whatever happens, is up to you." If only, he thought, Richard Clemmons would agree to allow his son to recover at Towledge, then Mark could be released from the hospital.

For once Fran was not in her accustomed place beside Mark's hospital bed. There was someplace else she had to be, and it had taken all her Yankee courage.

She had gone to the cemetery.

It had snowed the night before, the first snow of the season. Snow carries a cushion of silence, especially when it settles over a quiet place. She stood facing a marker on which was chiseled the names of her husband and son. Fran hadn't had the final dates chiseled—not yet, not until she was ready. In her arms was a large wreath with an inappropriately cheerful red ribbon; but it was, after all, Christmas. She emerged from a haze of meditation to realize that someone was standing behind her. She wondered how long he had been there.

"Hello, Perry," she murmured over her shoulder. "I thought I told you I wanted to come here alone."

"It's not Perry," the voice returned. "It's me."

Fran turned around. Standing before her with his hat in his hands was Richard Clemmons.

Mark Comes Home

Doc drove Richard Clemmons to the hospital to bring Mark home. It was the day before Christmas Eve.

"Where's Miss Frannie?" Mark asked, as he was being wheeled out to the car.

"She couldn't come," his father replied.

Doc carried on most of the conversation during the half-hour drive back to Hardscrabble. "I'm sure you're happy to leave the hospital," Doc said over his shoulder to Mark, who was in the backseat.

"Yes, sir," Mark replied, but his reply held no joy.

They crossed the bridge over the Ossipee and down Ossipee Road, then turned off Village Road and continued along—past the turnoff to the Clemmons's drive.

"I just have one stop to make," Doc explained, "and we'll be home." Mark nodded and looked out the window. They drove down Maple Street and across Elm, past Tilt's Store and the Church. Clem Lovell was walking to the Post Office with his dog, Stan. Mark waved, and Clem waved back, a Camel dangling from the corner of his mouth, the smoke forming a halo over his head. All the houses were decorated for Christmas and so was the Church; and the Christmas tree in the Town Square was covered with brightly colored glass balls and lights that would come on at dusk. Mark closed his eyes. In his mind's eye, he was at Towledge. A Christmas tree stood in the front parlor, glimmering with colored lights and ornaments and the promise of presents from Santa. A fire blazed in the hearth, the smell of apple pie wafted through the air. The rooftop, preferred stamping ground of certain reindeer, was cloaked in downy snow. He opened his eyes. Doc had turned the car up Daniel's Hill, past the Blue Rock. . . . And they were there. They were at Towledge.

She was standing on the porch, wrapped against the cold in her blue tweed coat, adjusting a red ribbon around Bear's neck. Mark rolled down the window and shouted out, "Miss Frannie!" The old woman looked up and waved so merrily that it was a wonder she didn't shake off her hat. Bear saw Mark and, barking, bounded toward the car. Uncle Perry and Mark's brothers, who were making a snowman in the front yard, started hooting and hollering and throwing snowballs at Doc's car in a high-spirited welcome. Mark's mother was wearing an apron and waving from the kitchen window.

Richard Clemmons turned around from the front seat of the car. He was smiling. Mark hadn't seen his father smile in a long, long time.

"We're home, son," he said.

TWENTY-ONE

The Christmas Eve Pageant

"There are are many things from which I might have derived good, by which I have not profited, I dare say,"
returned the nephew: "Christmas among the rest. But I
am sure I have always thought of Christmas time, when
it has come round . . . as a good time: a kind, forgiving,
charitable, pleasant time: the only time I know of, in the
long calendar of the year, when men and women seem
by one consent to open their shut-up hearts freely, and
to think of people below them as if they really were
fellow-passengers to the grave, and not another race of
creatures bound on other journeys. And therefore, uncle,
though it has never put a scrap of gold or silver in my
pocket, I believe that it has done me good, and will do
me good; and I say, God bless it!"
　　　　　—His nephew to Ebenezer Scrooge in Charles
　　　　　　　　　　　　　Dickens's A Christmas Carol

My hands were thoroughly mittened in bread
dough when the telephone rang. As anyone
knows who has ever indulged in the therapeutic, pleasurable, productive, peaceful pastime of bread making, the
worst possible time for the phone to ring is when you've

just started kneading bread dough. It's okay if the phone rings after you've been kneading the dough for five or six minutes. By then, it's smooth, elastic and submissive because you've pounded the heck out of it to the point that it resembles—in texture, at least—a five-and-dime store rubber ball that has softened under a hot summer sun. Bread dough in its earliest stage is like the goop in cockroach traps. Once you've got it in between your fingers, on your palm, and under your nails, it takes an Act of God to get it off. Answering the phone without sliming the receiver—and doing it by the third ring—is an Olympian accomplishment.

"Hello," I said, squeezing the receiver against my shoulder while pulling a wad of dough out of the tangled phone cord.

"This is Reverend Davidson," a pleasant voice said from the other end. "Am I catching you at a bad time, Laurie?"

"No, oh, no," I lied and, to pay for my sin, I got a handful of dough stuck on the rim of my eyeglasses while trying to wipe my brow with the back of my hand. "Not a bad time at all."

"Fine." He went through a series of niceties, asking about Kip, Tommy, etc., before saying, "Laurie, I have a rather important favor to ask you." Reverend George T. Davidson could ask me to jump off the Brooklyn Bridge, and I would; and I daresay, there wasn't a person in all of Hardscrabble who would hesitate to do the same.

"The Sunday School teachers asked me to call you. You see, they are getting ready for rehearsals for the Christmas Eve Pageant and were wondering if your little Tommy would be the Christ child."

Christ child! My baby boy play the baby Jesus? I was delighted and dismayed at once. Of course it would be a privilege, but on the other hand, I was a fanatically possessive new mother and had allowed very few adults—let alone a child—to hold my son, who was now eleven months old. Having seen the pageant the Christmas Eve before, I was certainly cognizant of the fact that the players were all under the age of ten.

There was only one thing to say.

"Of course, Reverend Davidson."

And with that, three weeks of nightmares plagued my sleep. I had utterly convinced myself that the young Mary would somehow manage to drop my son on his head.

The Rehearsal from Hell

The first rehearsal was called for the following Wednesday directly after school. There is nothing more terrifying for a young mother who has studied Doctors Spock and Brazleton than to walk into a room with twenty-five screaming, shrieking, out-of-control children—especially if the room is the sanctuary of a church. Pigtails were flying, catcalls were calling; one boy was skateboarding down the aisle. Three frantic Sunday School teachers in various stages of distress were waving scripts over their heads. I held my son as close as I could without smothering the life out of him.

"Good afternoon, children." A familiar voice rose above the commotion.

"Good afternoon, Reverend Davidson," the children replied in angelic unison.

"I understand that you are rehearsing for the pageant." The boys and girls nodded their heads. "Well, that's very nice, very nice. Miss Atkinson says you are about to choose your parts. I'm sorry I can't stay, but I want you to know that I am depending upon each of you to make this the finest Christmas pageant our Church has ever seen. Good luck to you all!"

No sooner had the door closed behind him than the commotion resumed.

"I want to be Mary!" a little girl wearing a pretty Yuletide sweater yelled.

"You were Mary last year," two girls exploded. "You can't be Mary two years in a row."

"I can, too! My mother says I set a precedent!"

"Sally," Miss Atkinson said, barging her rather formidable girth between the girls. "Out of curiosity, dear, do you know what *precedent* means?"

"Of course I do," last year's Mary replied sarcastically. "It's like the precedent of the United States. It means that I am the most important person."

"No, dear, that's not quite right. I'm afraid you'll have to let another girl have a chance. You really can't be Mary two Christmas Eves in a row."

With that, last year's Mary broke into fits of tears. "My mother said I could," she screamed hysterically. "Wait till my mother finds out!"

"Lydia," Miss Atkinson motioned to one of her associates. "Take this child to the little girl's room and Calm Her Down." Miss Atkinson's expression suggested that a ruler would be an appropriate learning tool and mourned that a teacher's most effective method of discipline was no longer appropriate.

"Now, children," she continued, gathering the remaining hellions around her. "This year I am pleased to say that I have come up with a very fair way of selecting who plays which part." The children gathered with curiosity around two paper bags. One was marked "Boys" and the other was marked "Girls."

"Now," she continued, having lassoed the children's attention. "Each bag is filled with small pieces of paper. On each piece the name of a part is written. In the Boys' bag are pieces of paper for Joseph, the three kings, and the shepherds. There are twelve boys in our Sunday School, and from what I see, you, boys, are all present."

"Yeah," one of the boys muttered. "That's because our mothers make us."

"That's right, Jack," Miss Atkinson replied. "And aren't you lucky to have mothers that know what's good for you." A wave of perplexity washed over the countenances of the boys, each wondering where the luck was in that.

"In the Girls' bag," Miss Atkinson continued, "are Mary, the Annunciation Angel and, of course, the other angels."

"I want to be a sheep," one little girl cried. "I'm tired of being an angel."

"Quiet, dear," Miss Atkinson said, with a hint of impatient indifference in her voice. "Who knows? Maybe this year you will be Mary."

"Oh, could I?" the little girl beamed.

"Well, yes," Miss Atkinson replied amidst a sudden chorus of complaints, "if you pick the paper that says 'Mary.' Children, I have a couple of surprises for you. We have sheep. Two sheep."

"Real sheep?" the children asked in excitement.

"Well, no—not actually. My dogs are going to be pretend-sheep."

The *oh*s from the girls suggested they thought the idea was sweet; the *oh*s from the boys implied they thought the idea was sappy.

"What's our other surprise?" one of the boys asked.

"The other surprise is, this year we have a *real* baby to play the baby Jesus!"

At that moment, Tommy woke up and started to cry. The children had not seen me sitting in the back pew with him.

"Look! It's a *b-a-by,*" a little girl cooed, and with that, a throng came running up the aisle. "Oh, can I hold him!" "I want to hold him!" Tommy began to cry at the top of his lungs. In the wisdom that comes with the achievement of having survived raising your children to adulthood, I can now look back across the years and realize that Tommy was probably hungry—not that he was terrified by the stampede of boys and girls. Like I was.

I jumped to my feet, grabbed Tommy, and fled the Church.

A Change of Mind

As I expected, I got a call that night from Miss Atkinson. "I'm terribly sorry, Mrs. Morrow," she said. "We didn't mean to frighten you away from our little rehearsal! When the children realized we had a *real* baby to play baby Jesus instead of a doll, they were so excited. And you know how children are when they get excited."

I did not, at the time; but I was beginning to have a clue.

"I'm so sorry you didn't stay," she continued, not picking up on the vibrations I was trying to send over the phone line. "Each child seems thrilled with his or her part. Even last year's Mary. She drew the slip of paper for the Annunciation Angel. And when her mother came to pick her up— why, you never saw such a happy woman. All she could say was, 'I saw just the dress for the part in the new Filene's catalog. . . .'"

"That's wonderful, Miss Atkinson, just wonderful. I'm so pleased for you. Thank you for—"

". . . and so I'm calling to tell you that the next rehearsal is . . ."

The persistent voice on the other end of the phone deteriorated into a gurgle of superlatives about How Wonderful the pageant would be, and how it would be the Finest Ever, and how she couldn't thank me and my husband enough for allowing our adorable little son to be the Baby Jesus.

"Miss Atkinson," I said, wavering. "The girl who is playing Mary. What kind of child is she?"

"Oh, you mean Inez Watson? I think you will like her very much. If I had to pick out of all the girls the one that I thought was the most responsible and grown-up, it would be Inez. Besides," she continued, "Inez has a little brother a year or so older than your Tommy. She's very capable with babies."

I was beginning to soften to the idea when Miss Atkinson added, "I was wondering if you wouldn't mind prompting. The script is very easy to follow, and that way, if a child misses a line, you are right there to help, and the pageant will keep on moving. And you'll be close by your son the whole time."

"That would be wonderful," I replied, greatly relieved.

The Dress Rehearsal

The next rehearsal was canceled when an early winter snowstorm passed through Hardscrabble, dumping enough snow to warrant closing school for the day. With Christmas only a week away, there was time for only one rehearsal— the dress rehearsal.

The day of the rehearsal found Miss Atkinson and her two colleagues in a dither getting the children into their costumes. Barking out orders above the mayhem was none other than Marie Antoinette Hampton, who you will recall from the fishing derby as one of the illustrious judges.

"Tony helps us every year," Miss Atkinson explained. "She makes all the costumes." I waved to Tony. We had become acquainted through the Church, an acquaintence that blossomed into a friendship that has matured over thirty years to one of the fundamental mainstays in my life. Tony, as usual, was juggling two things at once—this time, with a mouthful of dress pins while explaining something earnestly to the little girl she was fitting into an angel's costume. I remember marveling at her then, and I have marveled at her ever since.

When the children were dressed and ready, Miss Atkinson called the rehearsal to order. "We don't have a great deal of time, children, so I am asking you all to listen carefully. We want this year's pageant to be perfect." The children nodded silently. "As you know, Mrs. Hampton is our narrator again this year. Let's all give Mrs. Hampton a round of applause." The children applauded. Tony curtseyed comically, and the children laughed. "Mrs. Hampton," Miss Atkinson continued, "if you will step up to the pulpit, we can begin. Children, to the back of the Church."

Tony's demeanor became professional as it always was before a performance or a rehearsal. Under a veil of subtle emotion, the retired college drama professor mounted the steps to the pulpit. For a moment, the final staircase scene of Norma Desmond in *Sunset Boulevard* flashed through my mind. The children by now had been shepherded to the back of the Church, waiting for their respective entrances. Tony took out her reading glasses and, as if brandishing a long-stem rose for a flamenco, placed them low on her nose and, with a toss of her luxurious, cropped silvery hair, opened her Bible and began to read.

I did not hear her. I was busy giving the little girl who was playing the Virgin Mary final instructions, for the twentieth time, on how to carry my child, the Baby Jesus, without dropping him on his head.

The Most Memorable Pageant Ever . . .

Finally Christmas Eve arrived. I put on my holiday best and applied a thicker than usual daub of concealer under my eyes to hide the shadows that had accumulated from all those sleepless nights. Kip looked handsome in the three-piece Brooks Brothers suit that he had worn four years before to our rehearsal dinner. "Do you think that anyone, apart from the Professor or those peculiar guests of Lila Hornbeam's at the Republican's Hideaway, have ever seen a three-piece suit before?" I asked my husband.

"Don't be silly," he said. "Of course they have. Why, just the other day, I saw old Orion dressed up in a suit, and I complimented him. Know what he said?"

"No. But then, I can't understand a thing Orion says in that Down East twang of his, anyway," I laughed.

"He said, 'Not a bad suit. Not a bad suit t'all. Inherited from my granddaddy. Got it right after the funeral was over, before they closed the lid.'"

"Oh, that can't be true!"

"No, honey," he said, giving me a kiss on the cheek. "I just made it up."

"You're terrible."

"I know," he smiled. "C'mon or we'll be late. They told you that you had to be there at six on the dot."

We indeed had been told to report to the Fellowship Room by six o'clock. Miss Atkinson was directing children and their parents like a crossing guard. The members of the Church choir kept close to the coffee machine, where they were sipping strong, caffeinated coffee for added endurance. Clem Lovell was among them. He was the choir's excellent bass. Kip was talking to one of the other parents when I wandered over to Clem to say hello.

"He's getting big, Laurie!" Clem said, tickling Tommy under the chin. "High octane coffee," he grinned, as he took a sip of the piping-hot black oil in his coffee cup, followed by a drag on his customary Camel.

"Clem," I said, "that sign over there says No Smoking."

"Yep, so it does."

"Well, then," I replied in utter disbelief, "why are you smoking?"

"Laurie," he said, taking another draw. "If there's one piece of advice I can give you it's this: 'Holidays are an expensive trial of strength. The only satisfaction comes from survival.'* I need to keep up my strength. And my vices, I'm afraid, *are* my strength." There wasn't a single person in the room that was about to deprive Clem of a single vice. He was too valuable.

After all, good basses are hard to come by.

Kip was sitting in the congregation with Tony's husband, Levis. They had come early enough to get ringside seats in the front pew. I was relieved. If anything happened, I thought, Kip could probably lunge and catch the baby if the Virgin Mary was having trouble holding him.

By six o'clock, the Church began filling up. By half-past, there wasn't a seat that wasn't taken. Harriet, the Church organist, started her prelude of favorite Christmas carols. Here and there, you could hear a voice singing softly along. A candle glowed in every window in the Church. The altar was a carpet of red and white poinsettias, and evergreen boughs with red velvet ribbons festooned the altar railing. A beautiful wreath hung along the front of the pulpit.

It was almost time. The choir, dressed in their long burgundy robes, left the Fellowship Room and filed down the

---

* Jonathon Miller.

center aisle to the back of the Church. Usually they would walk down one of the side aisles, but both were blocked by the overflow of people who hadn't the foresight to know that you have to come a full hour early if you want a seat on Christmas Eve.

It was time. Miss Atkinson, wearing a beautiful Christmas corsage, gathered the children about her. But for her beautifully coifed hair and elegant embroidered sweater that somehow suited her robust figure, she could have been mistaken for a football coach in the final huddle before sending the team onto the field.

The children were a precious lot. Tonight they were a far cry from the rollicking bunch I first encountered just a few weeks before. They lined up as they were supposed to and filed down the aisle to the happy murmur of *oh*s and *ah*s from the brimming congregation.

Reverend Davidson followed Tony, wearing a black, velvet-trimmed robe. With great fanfare, Harriet began the Processional and everyone rose to the strains of "Oh Come, All Ye Faithful." (It is, in my opinion, the most wondrous processional of all, and even the hardest heart can't help but sing the joyous refrain at the top of his lungs.) The choir processed in stately order, took their seats in the choir loft, and on the second verse, broke out into four-part harmony. The Amen resonated throughout the Church, and everyone seemed to embrace the fullness of the moment. Reverend Davidson invited those who could to be seated and welcomed the good folk of Hardscrabble, friends, and relatives—but again, I was not listening.

I was busy tucking a bottle into the brass bowl filled with gold foil–covered chocolate coins that one nine-year-old King was carrying. I had already put a pacifier in the basket of "frankincense," and just in case, an extra diaper was rolled up in the bottom of the vessel of "myrrh." Looking back, this was all utter foolishness, but at the time and to a new mother, it made every bit of sense. It is, after all, the little preparations in life that provide the comfort you hope for when you intentionally set out to thwart potential catastrophe.

Of course, the catastrophe that was about to happen was something no one had anticipated.

Oh, Holy, What a Night!

Miss Atkinson, in her enthusiasm to put on a pageant that would rival the Nativity at Radio City Music Hall, had herself constructed a prop to give the production a nuance of reality. It was an enormous cardboard box, the kind that refrigerators come in. She had cut one seam and flattened it so that its length and breadth were roughly the size of the backboard of a tennis court—well, perhaps not that big; however, it most certainly took up most of the altar. A panoramic view of the stable and the rolling hills of Jerusalem was painted in an amateur but well-intentioned hand. Taped to a tomato stake high above was the star of Bethlehem in aluminum foil and tendrils of silver gift-wrapping ribbon that radiated from each of the five points. While this may have been a masterpiece of set design to Miss Atkinson, she had been so caught up in the ferment of her imagination that she failed to figure a way to support the structure. This was the source of a great distress earlier in the day, when she was first faced with the problem. But no problem was insurmountable for Miss Atkinson—at least, not when it came to the pageant. Her seemingly brilliant solution involved duct tape, picture wire, two bungee cords, a half-dozen folding chairs, and in the end was registered in the January minutes of the Deacons and Deaconnesses meeting as a formal objection.

"A herd of stampeding buffaloes couldn't knock that

down!" I overheard her saying to one of the parents. Of course, that was a safe assumption. There were no buffaloes in Hardscrabble.

But there were children. Twenty-five of them, all of whom were about to get up close and personal to Miss Atkinson's extraordinary Christmas tableau.

The Time Has Come

Women smiled from under their feather- and fur-trimmed holiday hats. Men wore ties and white shirts under their lumberjack jackets. Lila Hornbeam, swathed in mink, preoccupied with ushering her Republicans into her pew, had misplaced her hymnal (she had stuffed it in the pocket of her coat). The time had come. Tony Hampton and Reverend Davidson were seated in the ladderback velvet chairs on either side of the altar. Tony arose like Lady Macbeth, arranged herself behind the pulpit, and looked down upon the congregation with gratified approval. She began reading:

"And it came to pass in those days . . ."

The candles reflected against the glimmering glass of the windows, and the faces of the parishioners shone with a light that came from inside them. I watched with my heart in my mouth as the little Virgin Mary made her entrance, slowly walking down the aisle with my firstborn son in her toothpick arms.

"And so it was, that, while they were there, the days were accomplished that she should be delivered."

Together, Mary and Joseph continued slowly down the aisle. Tommy was sound asleep. The little girl smiled a saintly smile; I couldn't help but smile, too.

"And she brought forth her first-born son, and wrapped him in swaddling clothes, and laid him in a manger; because there was no room for them in the inn."

Joseph and Mary climbed the three steps to the altar, and carefully, the little Mary lay Tommy in the manger, a bassinet covered with hay. Miss Atkinson was close to tears.

Then came the shepherds watching their flock by night. Tony had designed sheep costumes for Miss Atkinson's basset hounds, Bogart and Bacall—little coats and clever headdresses of faux sheep's ears fashioned from quilt batting and the cotton fleece linings from some old jackets of Levis's.

"And there were in the same country shepherds abiding in the field, keeping watch over their flock by night."

The Christmas story unfolded with Tony's beautiful diction. The angels, now, came down the aisle, one or two trying very hard not to smile; one little girl, catching sight of her parents, breaking character for a second to wave. They were wrapped in spun white gauze over lacy satin nightgowns tucked at the waist with gold braided sashes, the gowns, long put away in memory-dusted boxes in closets of grandmothers. Silver foil wrapping paper covered the wings, and wire halos wrapped in tinsel crowned each cherubic head.

"And suddenly there was with the angel a multitude of the heavenly host praising God, and saying, Glory to God in the highest, and on earth peace, good will toward men. . . ."

Then entered the Three Wise Men carrying their gifts of gold, frankincense, myrrh, a bottle of milk, one pacifier, and a disposable diaper.

". . . and lo, the star, which they saw in the east, went before them, till it came and stood over where the young child was. When they saw the star, they rejoiced with exceeding great joy. And when they were come into the house, they saw the young child with Mary his mother, and fell down, and worshipped him: and when they had opened their treasures, they presented unto him gifts; gold, and frankincense, and myrrh. . . ."

Suddenly I was awash in grace, a spiritual sensation that

has come to me only a handful of times. The Church was silent except for the rustle of angels' wings and cowbells tied around the necks of Bogart and Bacall, and the soft strains of "Away in the Manger" filtered from the organ. Still, my little boy slept. The tranquillity would not last for long.

It sounded at first like the initial rumblings of an earthquake. For a split second, I didn't know where the noise emanated from, but then it became clear. The pitter-patter of little feet had been too much for the precariously erected cardboard set. In a rare case when duct tape simply didn't cut it, the enormous cardboard prop slowly tilted forward. The first casualty was Harriet, who continued to play "Away in the Manger" as the cardboard set collapsed over her. Like a rolling tidal wave, the entire set continued to roll forward. In a feat that would have made an Olympic vault jumper proud, I hurdled over the altar railing, siezed my son from the manger, grabbed Mary by the hand, and escaped to safety just as Bethlehem came crashing down, knocking over the bassinet and scaring the bejesus out of Bogart and Bacall. Miss Atkinson raced to the rescue of her canine children, sat on the altar, enveloped her beloved hounds in her doting arms, and wept. It had all been too much.

Tony, meanwhile, had made it to the safety of the pews. After a quick glance to make certain the shepherds, angels, and lead players were safe, she did what I since have witnessed with awe on so many occasions. She adjusted her glasses and with a dramatic presence that would have made Olivier catch his breath with admiration, continued to read in a firm, deliberate voice, a voice that would have befitted Moses's wife had she parted the Red Sea instead of her husband, a voice that resonated as though from Heaven and arrested everyone with awe.

"And, lo, the angel of the Lord came upon them, and the glory of the Lord shone round about them: and they were sore afraid.

And the angel said unto them, Fear not: for, behold, I bring you good tidings of great joy, which shall be to all people. For unto you is born this day in the city of David a Saviour, which is Christ the Lord. And this shall be a sign unto you; Ye shall find the babe wrapped in swaddling clothes, lying in a manger. And suddenly there was with the angel a multitude of the heavenly host praising God, and saying, Glory to God in the highest and on earth, peace and good will toward men."

And when Tony had finished, Reverend Davidson whispered something in her ear. She nodded, took a step back and, like a shepherd herself, herded the children around our minister.

"We all know the story of the Christ child," he said. "But I wonder who among you—when you open your eyes in the morning and see that Santa Claus has come—can say that you indeed know the true meaning of Christmas."

The minister had rested his hands on the shoulders of a child on either side of him and looked out into the congregation, as if to ask his flock the same thing. From my vantage point, I could see all the familiar faces. There was Mab and Charlie Markham sitting among their children and grandchildren. Behind them were Tilt Tilton with Margie and George Allard. Mert and his wife, Marianne, were seated in the midst of several pews' worth of Hardscrabble volunteer firemen and their families. Lila Hornbeam had filled her customary pew with her precious Republicans. And Fran Forsythe sat holding hands with Mark on one side and Richard Clemmons on the other. Directly behind Fran, watching over her as he had done for most of his life, was Perry Towle with Mark's brothers and their mother. I was on the verge of tears over the newfound family when I felt Kip's hand slip gently into mine. He kissed me on the cheek, took Tommy from my arms, and cradled our smiling son in his.

Reverend Davidson continued. "I want to share with

you something that I have cherished since I first heard it spoken in a movie that was made a long time ago. I had just come home from fighting the war in Germany. My war was no different from any other soldier's. We didn't want to be there, but we knew we had a job to do, and we were going to do it. The Christmas that I spent away from home on the front line . . . well, I'll never forget closing my eyes and pretending I was with my mother and father, my brothers and sister, and all of my friends back home here in Hardscrabble. Bing Crosby had just come out with 'I'll Be Home for Christmas,' and I dreamed of our Town under a blanket of falling snow. 'I'll be home for Christmas,' the song goes, 'if only in my dreams.' And the good Lord answered my dreams. I was one of the lucky guys. I came home from World War Two.

"Which brings me to my message this wondrous Christmas Eve. I do not know who wrote this. But these words are as close to the heart of Christmas as anything I know." Reverend Davidson unfolded a piece of paper from his pocket. "It goes like this:

" 'Tonight I want to tell you the story of an empty stocking. Once upon a midnight clear, there was a child's cry. A blazing star hung over a stable and wise men came with birthday gifts. We haven't forgotten that night down the centuries. We celebrate it with stars on Christmas trees, with the sound of bells, and with gifts. But especially with gifts. You give me a book. I give you a tie. Aunt Martha has always wanted an orange squeezer, and Uncle Henry could do with a new pipe. Oh, we forget nobody, adult to child. All the stockings are filled—all, that is, except one. And we have even forgotten to hang it up. A stocking for the child born in a manger. It's his birthday we're celebrating. Don't let us ever forget that. Let us ask ourselves what he would wish for most, and then, let each put in his share: human kindness, warm hearts, and a stretched-out hand of tolerance. All the shining gifts that make Peace on Earth.' "

Everyone left the Church and walked into the holy darkness with lit candles handed to us by Harry Bixby and Tony. We encircled the wooden crèche that had seen a hundred Hardscrabble Christmases and it began to snow. High above, among the stars was the One that shone brighter than all the rest. Clem's beautiful bass voice filtered softly over the stillness: "Silent night, holy night . . ." Our voices ascended to the heavens; and in the quiet moment after the final refrain of "sleep in heavenly peace," a child was heard to whisper, "Happy birthday, baby Jesus."

৵ৣৢ TWENTY-TWO ৡৢ৵

The Wedding

*D*oris Almy's column was more confusing than usual:

It is with enormous pleasure that I announce a Very Important Marriage to be held at the First Christian Church of Hardscrabble the Saturday after next at two o'clock in the afternoon, followed by a reception at the Town Hall. I have been sworn to the utmost secrecy not to divulge the names of the bride and groom except to say that I am certain they would very much appreciate it if you were all present to witness their marriage. That is all I can say, dear friends, except to say that I myself have not been as excited about a wedding as I am about this one for years and years. For those of you ladies who would like a suggestion as to attire, let me say that I myself plan to wear my lavender satin that so many of you admired when I wore it to the anniversary tea of the Hardscrabble Horticultural Society last year or was it the year before that. And of course that beautiful ostrich plume hat that you all have told me you love just as much as Little Doris and I do. One more thing and that is instead of gifts, the happy couple wish you would bring your happiness, as that is gift enough for them. And furthermore, for those of you who have dogs that are as beloved to you as my Little Doris is to me, then do please bring them along, for the bride and groom specifically request dogs be invited, too. For this reason, the wedding vows will take place in a special tent on the lawn of the Church and not inside, just in case, as you can well imagine.

For the first time in anyone's recollection, Doris remained absolutely tight-lipped about something. No one could pry the names of the bride and groom from her lips. Speculation, of course, was rampant, and soon it was the general consensus that the wedding was, in fact, between Doris's Pomeranian, Little Doris, and none other than Professor Markham's springer spaniel, Chaucer. The fact that the Professor and his wife, Mab, refused to comment on the union only confirmed that this was so.

We had passed an uneventful winter, which in and of itself was a blessing, and Hardscrabble welcomed the lovely month of May as usual with the fishing derby, the Ladies' Guild Rummage Sale, and opening day of trout season. However, as the day of the wedding grew nearer, the excitement in the air intensified. The Ladies' Guild offered to host a bridal shower—a foil, of course, to quench their curiosity as to the identities of the bride and groom—but Doris, on behalf of the bride, gave her thanks but graciously declined. This made it more certain than ever that the wedding was indeed to unite two dogs in canine matrimony. With that a veritable certainty, the focus of each Guild member turned toward her wedding outfit. After all, if Doris Almy was going to wear that lavender number, it behooved her cohorts to appear in equally fetching ensembles, and so the competition for most elegant hat and festive frock became the focus of the older women in Town.

The members of the Lower Forty, on the other hand, took the whole thing in a more serious vein. After all, marriage was just as old Harold Gilpin had said: Once the yoke is latched on, it harnesses the couple like a pair of oxen forever. How a springer spaniel like Chaucer, a dog of sporting blood, could be bound in holy matrimony to a fluff of a Pomeranian was simply unfathomable. The members took time from their regular monthly meeting to discuss whether or not they should stand up at the part where Reverend Davidson says, "If there is any reason why this couple should not be joined in holy matrimony, let him speak now or forever hold your peace." But Tilt Tilton made a very good point when he said that Chaucer was never given the proper education to be a bird dog, which was a tragedy all by itself; and then Doc made the very astute point that even if Chaucer had the desire, it was impossible that any issue would come forth from the marriage. So the discussion was tabled.

The day of wedding finally arrived with gossip going on at the usual Meccas: Margie's Lunch, the Town Dump, and Charlie's Cut & Shave. An enormous and rather grand tent had been erected on the lawn of the Church the day before, and now a van full of flowers was being unloaded, transforming the tent into a veritable Garden of Eden.

"Of course this is all Doris's doing," the ladies said. "You know how she is about Little Doris. I wouldn't be surprised if she hired Priscilla of Boston to make the wedding dress!"

The men, of course, had their own take on the situation. "If you ask me," Major Fred Ford was saying to Mike Zalinski while Charlie gave him his usual high and tight, "Charlie Markham has been drinking a little too much of his own punch."

The time had come. It was one-thirty, and the guests had begun to arrive at the tent. Never had the Town seen such a stunning turnout. Everyone was dressed to the nines, including the men, some of who wore suits that must have been in mothballs for decades. Lila Hornbeam came with her Boxer, Brutus, and an escort of a dozen Republicans dressed in waistcoats and Hamilton collars, and several women guests dressed as though they were going to the opera. Fran Forsythe was escorted by Mark and his great dog, Bear. Stan sat between Clem and Louise Lovell. Madeline Plover, her daughter Susie, and Susie's poodle Cheré were there. A menagerie surrounded Mert and Marianne Grant with Flame, and Mike Zalinski was seated with Tess and the pair of grown-up pups from Tess and Flame's union. Ken Tibbetts and his German shepherd, Prince, sat next to George's Dog, George and Margie Allard, and Tilt. Tony and Levis Hampton had their two dogs, Tiffany and Dickens, with them and sat beside Harry Bixby and his dog, Honey. Everyone was there with their dog, including my cousin Kate and her children, who were visiting for the summer with their cairn terrier, Varmint, "the little dog with the big heart." If nothing else, this was going to be the wedding of the century in Hardscrabble, even if the bride and groom were dogs.

As the minutes ticked closer to the appointed hour, the two hundred guests took their seats in white slipcovered folding chairs under the lavishly decorated tent. Suddenly, everyone turned as limousines arrived with the bridal party. A buzz of excitement reverberated from under the tent like a flock of seagulls at low tide at the beach.

Dave Trenton stepped out of the first limousine, and everyone applauded as he escorted Ada Frump. She was wearing a stunning but simple creation that was, in fact, a Priscilla of Boston. It set off her beautiful figure—for I have failed to mention that despite her name, Ada was a gorgeous woman who bore a striking resemblance to Katharine Hepburn, and never more closely than at this moment. Judge Parker then helped his wife, Patience, out of the limousine. The second limousine pulled up, and Bert Ramsdell and his new wife, Melanie, stepped out and then Kip, who was best man. He was carrying Tommy, who was now two and a half years old. Tommy was the ring bearer, and I was the matron of honor.

That's right, Dear Reader—I've known all along who the bride and groom are. But Kip and I were sworn to secrecy, too.

The third and last limousine carried none other than Doris and Little Doris, wearing matching lavender outfits, and Professor Markham and his wife, Mab, with Chaucer sporting a bow tie. Everyone burst into another round of applause.

And then an old Range Rover pulled up. The bride and groom had arrived.

It was Jeffrey Hilton and Mary Marsh.

Everyone exploded in cheers! Jeff and Mary! And with them, Jeff's beloved English setter, Tober. For all the feigned and festive pretense, it was fitting that the happy couple would surprise the Town and, what's more, come to their own wedding together, in Jeff's cherished, beat-up Range Rover. Arm in arm, they entered the tent, waving at the crowd. Women cried, men cheered, the dogs all barked: for Jeff and Mary had been embraced, and were as much a part of Hardscrabble, as Kip and I ourselves had come to be.

Mary was radiant in a simple ivory gown that showed her off to perfection. Judge Parker kissed her hand, and Reverend Davidson gave her a kiss on the cheek, as they greeted the handsome couple at the back of the tent. Then they escorted Jeff and took their places at the head of the tent under an archway of tulips, daffodils, and English ivy.

Charlie of Charlie's Cut & Shave took out his pitch pipe and gave a C-sharp, and the Hardscrabble Barbershop Quartet began singing, "O, Perfect Love." The ushers processed, and then the bridesmaids followed in their softly draped pale yellow gowns. I turned and blew Mary a kiss before accompanying my little ring bearer down the aisle. My dress was a little different from the bridesmaids—a pale lilac blue cut fuller to accommodate the child I was expecting.

There was a pause. The quartet had finished singing. Then Mary, beaming with happiness, walked down the aisle on Clem Lovell's arm to the strains of "Here Comes the Bride," played by Linda Griffin on the harp. And when Reverend Davidson asked Clem, "Who gives this woman in holy matrimony?" Clem replied, "Hardscrabble and I do."

Clem placed Mary's hand in Jeff's and stepped back to sit with Louise. They exchanged their vows, then Reverend Davidson motioned to Tommy for the rings. He stepped forward with the satin pillow. Reverend Davidson fumbled with the satin ribbons and Tony, in her usual take-charge way, came forward to deftly untie them. It was a light moment among blissful moments. Our kindly minister told us the story of the ring: how a ring is a perfect circle, with no beginning and no end, and that is how it is with true and constant love.

Finally, it was time for the reading, which Jeff himself chose to give. He looked at his bride tenderly, lovingly, and with her hands in his, gazed into her eyes and recited what is perhaps the greatest tribute to love ever written, Shakespeare's Sonnet 116:

> *Let me not to the marriage of true minds*
> *Admit impediments. Love is not love*
> *Which alters when it alteration finds,*
> *Or bends with the remover to remove:*
> *O, no! It is an ever-fixed mark,*
> *That looks on tempests and is never shaken;*
> *It is the star to every wandering bark,*
> *Whose worth's unknown, although his height be taken.*
> *Love's not Time's fool, though rosy lips and cheeks*
> *Within his bending sickle's compass come;*

Love alters not with his brief hours and weeks,
But bears it out even in the edge of doom.
If this be error, and upon me proved,
I never writ, nor no man ever loved.

And now pronounced "man and wife" by Judge Parker, Jeff took Mary into his arms and kissed her tenderly to our shouts and tears and cries of unbounded joy by their family—the family of Hardscrabble.

George Bernard Shaw wrote, "When two people are under the influence of the most violent, most insane, most delusive, and most transient of passions, they are required to swear that they will remain in that excited, abnormal and exhausted condition until death do them part."

I know the love that Shaw extols, and if he is right—as I believe he is—then love is the most blessed state a man and woman can aspire to together engage, binding two hearts as one, two souls as a unity, two minds as a force with which to be reckoned.

Would that everyone would be so exhausted.

TWENTY-THREE

Simple Blessings

The sun had begun to gently set behind the lavendar hills as the wedding party came to an end. It had been a glorious day, more glorious than any that Hardscrabble had seen in a long time. Now it was time to go home.

Tommy was asleep in his stroller, and Kip was a few tables away, saying good night to Lila Hornbeam and the Senator. I felt a hand on my shoulder. It was Clem.

"That was a pretty wedding," Clem said. "Reminded me of mine."

"How long have you and Louise been married, Clem?" I asked.

"Let me see. . . . I've had her the longest. About thirty years."

"You mean, you've been married before?"

"Sure," Clem grinned. "A couple of times."

"Wow, you really got around, didn't you, Clem."

My old friend chuckled. "You don't know the half of it, Laurie. I was in the Navy for years, and I saw a big part of the world. Saw a lot of women, too. But the one I've got now—well, Louise, she's a keeper." He beamed across the tent at a trim, pretty, elderly lady who was glowing in animated conversation with the others about her. "I'm a lucky man," Clem continued. "And I'm lucky to live here, in Hardscrabble."

"If you've seen so much of the world, Clem, then why did you settle in Hardscrabble?"

"Well, Laurie," he said, "of all the places I've lived and all the corners of the globe I've visited, this piece of New England feels more like home than anywhere else, at least to me."

I thought a moment. "Me, too," I replied with a quiet smile.

I slipped my hand into Clem's. Together we looked around us, at our friends—our Hardscrabble family. I was home.

Clem became silent, and he took on the expression he always had whenever he was about to impart some sagely advice. "Any advice you want to share with me, Clem?" I chuckled, attempting to beat him to the punch.

"Actually, no," he replied. "I was running a few lines through my head, that's all."

"What are they?"

"First Corinthians thirteen."

"Tell them to me, Clem," I said softly.

And he did.

"Though I speak with the tongues of men and of angels, and have not charity, I am become as sounding brass, or a tinkling cymbal. ²And though I have the gift of prophecy, and understand all mysteries, and all knowledge; and though I have all faith, so that I could remove mountains, and have not charity, I am nothing. ³And though I bestow all my goods to feed the poor, and though I give my body to be burned, and have not charity, it profiteth me nothing. ⁴Charity suffereth long, and is kind; charity envieth not; charity vaunteth not itself, is not puffed up, ⁵Doth not behave itself unseemly, seeketh not her own, is not easily provoked, thinketh no evil; ⁶Rejoiceth not in iniquity, but rejoiceth in the truth; ⁷Beareth all things,

believeth all things, hopeth all things, endureth all things.
⁸Charity never faileth: but whether there be *prophecies, they*
shall fail; whether there be *tongues, they shall cease; whether*
there be *knowledge, it shall vanish away. ⁹For we know in*
part, and we prophesy in part. ¹⁰But when that which is per-
fect is come, then that which is in part shall be done away.
¹¹When I was a child, I spake as a child, I understood as a
child, I thought as a child: but when I became a man, I put
away childish things. ¹²For now we see through a glass,
darkly; but then face to face: now I know in part; but then
shall I know even as also I am known. ¹³And now abideth
faith, hope, charity, these three; but the greatest of these is
charity."

I never asked Clem how it was that he was able to com-
mit to memory something as long as I Corinthians 13, but I
know what he would have said. He'd explain that a man of
his years had plenty of time on his hands to think about the
things that mattered most. Clem lived these words. So did
the kind folks of Hardscrabble.

And so the sun rises on a new day and sets in preparation for the next. Whatever road I travel in Life, I know it
will always lead home, a spiritual home where faith, hope,
charity abide—and where surely, the greatest is indeed
charity.

Afterword

The Story Behind the Story

I went to the woods because I wished to live deliberately, to front only the essential facts of life, and see if I could not learn what it had to teach, and not, when I came to die, discover that I had not lived.

—Henry David Thoreau

Nothing is more daunting for a writer with a story to tell than to face a blank sheet of paper. If the story is true, then the task of writing it down becomes even more formidable because a true story, if it is good, ought to be told. And if it ought to be told, it should begin at the beginning.

This story has two beginnings—the first, a century ago when a boy was born in the Bronx; the second, a half century later, when a girl was born in Brooklyn. That their destinies would entwine in a faraway place called Hardscrabble was an act of fate. That the man would die knowing nothing of the woman, and the woman would live knowing everything about him, was a bittersweet human comedy that would change her life and immortalize his. They might have been lovers, had Time not kept them apart.

The man's name was Corey Ford.

I am the woman.

* * *

*O*ur paths converged in a field called the Lower Forty—
Corey owned it, I own it—in this very real, very rural,
picture-postcard New England town that he baptized and I
adopted with the fictitious name of Hardscrabble. We came
here, he and I, fifty years apart when we were eighteen—a
similarity that was one of too many to be coincidence. It
haunts me.

He haunts me.

*H*e was the stuff F. Scott Fitzgerald made heroes of—a
shining child who grew up in the heyday of the
Roaring Twenties to become the adored golden boy of New
York literary society. He was the dark, strikingly handsome
junior member of the celebrated Algonquin Round Table
who sat between Will Rogers and Harpo Marx. He christened the *New Yorker's* parvenu cartoon-mascot Eustace
Tilley for Harold Ross. He knew where to push the secret
button that would send the bootleg bar at the '21' Club
crashing into the sewer in case of a Prohibition raid. He had
women in chinchillas at the Stork Club, Scotch at the
Player's, and an invitation to every play Off Broadway, on
Broadway and, in between, society soirees and black tie
dinners. And, when Hollywood and two thousand Depression dollars a week as a contract screenwriter lured him to
the other coast, Corey packed his bags, caught the next
train, and never looked back.

In Hollywood, he was a woman's man who wore a different starlet on his arm each night of the week. He was a
man's man whose nightly nightcap at Chasen's was a holy
ritual for him and his best friend, W. C. Fields; and when
their drinking buddies Humphrey Bogart and Spencer Tracy

loaded Dave Chasen's office safe into the trunk of a taxi, Corey lent them a helping hand.

He was good to his friends that way. He gave Scott Fitzgerald a shoulder when crazy Zelda and the booze and depression kept the words from coming. He'd slip a few bucks to Robert Benchley when the liquor-moistened humorist's lips and luck went dry, and wiped Dorothy Parker's tears between one pathetic love affair and the next. He shook George Putnam's hand and gave his wife, Amelia Earhart, a last kiss good-bye before she had to fly. He urged a despairing James Thurber to see through his blindness at the genius of his essays. And when Edna Ferber threatened to sue him over his *Vanity Fair* parody of her book, *Cimarron*, Corey's apology prompted a thirty-eight-year correspondence that endured until the year before his death, when she predeceased him. He called her Smith. She called him Smith.

Corey made an enemy of Ernest Hemingway when *Vanity Fair* published "Corto y Derecho," Corey's brilliant, merciless parody of "The Snows of Kilimanjaro." They should have been friends: Hunting, fishing, war, wine, and women were common interests they each passionately pursued. But Papa stuck to his guns and his grudge right up until the day he pulled that suicidal trigger.

Burying Hemingway's rejection along with certain dark secrets he cloistered in his heart, Corey continued to craft, perfect, and lead a charmed life among charming people until December 7, 1941, when he—and the world—would change forever.

America was finally at war, and damn if Corey wasn't chafing to get into the thick of it. At forty, his age was against him, but through dogged perseverance and personal links to the chain of command in Washington, D.C., Lieutenant Colonel Corey Ford bypassed the ranks and was commissioned to chronicle the battles of the U.S. Army Air Corps. Now he was a renegade with a heart, traveling from the Aleutians to Normandy for *Look, Saturday Evening Post*, and *Colliers*. By day, in the line of fire and path of shrapnel, he wrote riveting firsthand accounts of the airmen's battles. By night, under a blackout sky lit by stars and bomb bursts, he wrote to too many mothers and fathers. He held their fallen sons close and closed their eyes after the last breath. And in his letters, Corey recounted the brave acts and conveyed the dying words, which always were: "Tell my mother I love her."

When it was all over and he saw how the world had changed, Corey realized that he, too, had changed. Hollywood no longer held any allure. Tinsel Town had become tarnished. Fields was dead, Fitzgerald was dead, and the starlets were married matrons. So he sent a couple of telegrams—one to his boss, *Gone With the Wind* producer David O. Selznick, and one to his mistress—telling them he wouldn't be back. There was only one place to go. He went home, to Hardscrabble, where he reinvented himself.

Here, at the age of forty-five, the person Corey Ford really wanted to be was born.

*T*he timing could not have been better. The front door to a bright and promising future had swung wide open, and the back door to the past was shut against the memory of the extravagant twenties, the depressed thirties, and the war-torn forties.

Corey approached the fifties—and his fifties—reincarnated as a balding, portly, pipe-smoking country gentleman. He was comfortable in his expensive, slightly worn tweed jacket and military surplus Jeep—and for the first time in his life, he was comfortable with himself. Corey was passionate about his Parker sixteen-gauge shotgun, autumn, dark trout pools, secret grouse coverts, and his English setters. He no longer wrote about the things he observed; now he wrote about the things he loved.

He wrote about Hardscrabble and its good Yankee people. He wrote about his dogs. And he wrote about his friends—a casual brotherhood of college-educated, consum-

mate sportsmen who shared a dry, devilish wit and a dedication to single malt Scotch. There was the formidable "Judge Parker" Merrow: municipal magistrate, publisher of the *Carroll County Independent* (which in *Hardscrabble* is the *Hardscrabble Gazette*) and a devout family and Labrador retriever man. There was Dartmouth College's revered secretary, "Cousin Sid" Hayward, self-proclaimed kin on the grounds that Hayward's setter was a littermate of Corey's beloved dog, Tober. The others made up the most illustrious masthead in *Field & Stream* history: chief editor Ray Holland and his son, fishing editor Dan Holland; humorist Ed Zern; and field editors Ted Trueblood and Frank Dufresne. They argued incessantly about whose bird dog was the birdiest, overstated the weight of their game bags, and exaggerated about the size of the fish they caught. Their antics became the inspiration behind one of the most popular columns in the history of outdoor publications.

The "Minutes of the Lower Forty" opened in *Field & Stream* in 1953 and immediately took on a life of its own. The hilarious escapades of the eccentric, irresponsible, irrepressible group of outdoorsmen who called themselves the Lower Forty Shooting, Angling and Inside Straight Club captivated the hearts of people who hunted and didn't, fished and didn't, laughed and cried and cherished the unadulterated honesty and warm humor of Corey's barely veiled, true-to-life stories. Readers flocked to become charter members, and over the ensuing years, Lower Forty clubs sprang up all over the world, from Maine to Vietnam, where Corey's columns gave laughter and a touch of home to American soldiers. People were certain they were kin to the scalawags of the Lower Forty and promptly tied their heartstrings to Hardscrabble. How the monthly column maintained a flawless run of seventeen uninterrupted years until its end is another story.

But end it did—with Corey's death in 1969, at the age of sixty-seven, from a stroke brought on by a lonely heart.

$\mathcal{W}$e met in carton seventeen in the Special Collections Room of Baker Library at Dartmouth College in the spring of 1993. Corey Ford had been dead almost twenty-five years. "Make an appointment," was the blunt letter I received from Dartmouth College, trustee of Corey's literary estate, regarding my request to quote a line from one of Corey's columns. Hardscrabble is perched on the New Hampshire/Maine border; Hanover, home of Dartmouth, straddles the New Hampshire/Vermont line, a drive of two and a half hours due west as the crow flies. *What a bother,* I thought. *A whole day shot just to quote a handful of words.*

I made the appointment, unaware that it would change my life.

$\mathcal{I}$knew about Corey Ford—of course I did. Everyone in Hardscrabble either knew him, worked for him, or had a family member or friend who knew him or had worked for him. Our property was adjacent to Stonybroke, the palatial stone hunting lodge–home Corey designed that was doomed to break ground a few months before Black Friday, 1929. It was so named, he would later confess, "because I was stone-broke by the time it was finished." In the 1960s, primarily to enlarge our land holdings, my family acquired Stonybroke, which included the field Corey called the Lower Forty.

Some remembered Corey as "that famous fellow with the dogs that used to write." Our housekeeper had been his. His estate manager, a Southerner you've already met named Fort Sumter Falls ("Ma daddy named me that 'cause I was born the day Fort Sumter fell") at various times taught Corey, my husband, and my sons how to shoulder a shotgun and cast a fly. Carroll Chase, the best chimney builder in the county, built one for Corey and one for me, too. We wrote for the *Carroll Country Independent*, got our water from the same gravity-fed spring, and never missed opening day of grouse season in Tinkhamtown. We bought our groceries and gas at Tilt's Store, collected our mail from Lettie Connor at the Post Office, prayed at the First Christian Church of Hardscrabble most Sundays, and got our hunting and fishing licenses at Mert's Bait & Tackle.

And we dearly loved our dogs. Corey had an extensive canine family. His childhood pup was a cocker spaniel. As an adult, he bred beagles. He brought one of the first Gordon setters into the country, doted over his Irish wolfhound, briefly had a golden retriever, thought about raising Labrador retrievers, but decided upon English setters. They were his pride, joy, and the inspiration behind numerous humor pieces published in *Reader's Digest* and *Saturday Evening Post*, such as "Every Dog Should Have a Man," and "My Dog Likes It Here."

Shortly after Corey first moved to Hardscrabble, he wrote to a friend, "Time travels slowly to Hardscrabble. Last night at Town Meeting there was a motion to send more troops to Gettysburg. Thirteen men volunteered."

Corey liked it that way, and so do I.

*J*ames Hitchcock Ford led a Gatsby life, but like Gatsby, he was shining on the outside and shattered within. Underneath that carefully crafted exterior was a vulnerable man who had loved deeply, lost desperately, and was filled with disillusion, despair, and betrayal. When he came home to Hardscrabble, he got a second chance at happiness—and grabbed it.

And here, dear reader, at the risk of sounding cryptic, and the necessity to regretfully refrain, this once, from being forthcoming, I will confide in you this: For as much as Corey Ford came to a crucial turning point at the midlife of his years, I too have come to a turning point at the midlife of mine. This is not just another similarity between us—it is the greatest single affinity we share. We were embraced as a couple of orphans, in our separate times, and adopted by Hardscrabble. We came to a crossroads and destiny pointed the way. I know the road Corey traveled and can only hope mine will too be paved in grace, with blessings. And so, I have arrived at the providential place. I am come to tell you our story.

Under a cloudless, cornflower-blue sky so typical of spring, I followed the road that hugs the Smith River and wends through one picturesque New Hampshire village after another. As the crow flies, it's the most direct route to Hanover from Hardscrabble. This was Corey's route, and he'd often stop to fish this jewel of a trout stream on his way to visit the Haywards, Hollands, and other friends who lived near the college he never attended—Dartmouth, Corey's adopted alma mater and virtually sole beneficiary of his estate. Today his route was mine.

"He who enters a university walks on hallowed ground," wrote James Bryant Conant, but I was tiptoeing on the hallowed marble floors of Dartmouth's Baker Library in a useless attempt to muffle the strident clicking of my too-high heels. The desk clerk had pointed the way down a seemingly endless corridor to the Special Collections Room.

"Go to the end of the hall," she whispered as if revealing a state secret. "When you get to the end, turn right, go to the end of that hall, and there's a door."

Halfway down the hall, a glass case displayed a first edition of *Alice in Wonderland*, and the similarities to my own, increasingly bizarre situation dawned upon me when suddenly a charley horse seized my calf. I bent over to massage the painful cramp, burst the zipper on the back of my skirt, and caught my bracelet on my stockings. "Great," I moaned, as the clock tower struck two. I half expected the White Rabbit to appear from Nowhere and admonish me that I was now late for my appointment. Pulling my torn stockings up and my jacket down, I reached the end of the eternal corridor, trotted along another, and faced a formidable, carved mahogany door. It opened, heavy and noiselessly. Sitting at a desk that would befit a Supreme Court justice and with a solemnity peculiar to people who dwell in great halls of learning, sat a slight, bespectacled, yellowish young man.

"Is this Special Collections?" I asked.

"It is," he replied. "Sign in and please give me your driver's license."

My leg was painful, my tattered stocking an embarrassment, my skirt was on the verge of defying gravity, and now I had to surrender my driver's license to a pale librarian. I felt utterly defeated and was about to explain that my driving record was clean, when the yellow young man said, "Dr. Crammond is expecting you. Take a seat, and I will tell him you are here."

I didn't wait long before Dr. Crammond was standing before me. Tall, thin, with a pleasant face and a deceivingly boyish grin that belied his middle-aged years, he visibly bore his burden as literary custodian of Dartmouth's distinguished archives of priceless treasure on narrow, slightly stooped shoulders. Behind thick eyeglasses were kind eyes that had grown weary from years of consuming small print. His handshake was strong, and I liked him instantly. With quiet pride, he led me into a small office with enormous windows that faced a tree-lined street that flanked the Dartmouth Quad. A fly rod was leaning precariously against a teetering pile of books, a well-worn fishing vest hung on the back of an old-fashioned oak swivel chair, and a dented metal fly tackle box with a missing hinge lay open on a paper-cluttered desk, revealing a generous selection of hand-tied Royal Coachmen, Hendricksons, and Duns.

"Sit down, please." Dr. Crammond waved graciously to an armless wooden chair that was not designed for comfort or long chats. "This is really the reason why I asked you to come," he said, picking up the fly rod tenderly. "And Corey Ford is the reason why I'm a diehard fly-fisherman. I read every Lower Forty column he ever wrote. Why, I still have my Lower Forty charter membership card that I got when I was a kid! You see, I was hoping you could help me."

"Me, help you?" I asked.

"Yes. . . . Oh, I see. . . . You thought you had come for permission for that quote? No. . . . I mean, yes, you have permission. You always could for just a line, as long as you credited Ford. The fact of the matter is that in the years since his death, no one has asked to look at Ford's literary archives. Then I received your letter, and when you said you owned the Lower Forty, well . . . you can understand my interest in meeting you."

"I don't understand. . . ."

"Let me explain. Corey Ford died without family. He left everything to Dartmouth—his house, his wealth, and his papers. You are the first person who's come here with even a passing interest in him, so I thought you'd take a look . . . and do something about it."

"About what?"

"About his papers."

"To do what?"

"That's just it. I'm not exactly sure."

"Can you tell me about them?"

"Well, they're in big boxes. . . ."

"How big are the boxes?"

"Pretty big."

"How many are there?"

"Sixty-two."

"That's a lot of boxes."

"Yes. Ford was very prolific. He left Dartmouth his entire body of work in hopes that it would be of perpetual benefit to the college, but no one did anything about it. You could. You're a writer. And you own the Lower Forty."

"Sixty-two boxes of papers could take up the rest of my life," I pondered.

"Of course," Dr. Crammond said as he began tying a fly onto the tippet of his beloved five-weight rod. "After you leave, I'm going to slip away and play hooky. I'm anticipating a Hendrickson hatch at my secret trout pool," he nodded confidentially. "You know what Corey used to say. 'There are some things a man will share—his car, his tobacco, and just maybe even his wife. But you never ask a man to share the whereabouts of his secret trout pool!'" Dr. Crammond turned his attention back to his fly, and I dissolved into my thoughts. This was a helluva deal. I didn't come to Dartmouth prepared to make a decision that would affect my future. This was a crapshoot, but I knew enough to know I'd get just one chance. I said, "Tell you what. I'll pick a number. Let me see that carton. I'll reach in and pull out the first papers my fingers touch. If what I find sings to me, then

I'll do as you ask. If not, it wasn't meant to be. I don't believe in signs, but that's all I've got to go by."

"Follow me," Dr. Crammond said, quietly pleased. He leaned his treasured rod against another precarious pile of books stacked on the floor like the Tower of Pisa and led me back into the mahogany-paneled, grave-silent Special Collections Room. He motioned toward a library table in a dark corner of the room. On it was a lamp with a green glass shade. It cast an eerie light on the polished wood. "Gerald," Dr. Crammond said to the keeper of my driver's license, "Mrs. Morrow would like to see a carton from the Ford Archives. Box number . . ."

"Seventeen," I interjected.

"Good. Gerald, will you bring up carton seventeen?" Gerald nodded earnestly and withdrew, for all I knew, into the White Rabbit's tunnel that led to the archival labyrinth. "When you are through," Dr. Crammond said, "come see me in my office. We should have a little time before I have to head out, and I would like your philosphy on fishing caddis nymphs at first light." And with that, he, too, disappeared.

I was alone in a cocoon of carved paneling and stained glass. Staring critically from atop carved Corinthian columns were marble busts of Poe, Webster, Longfellow, Frost—New Englanders all. If only they could speak. . . . I was lost in that thought when Gerald appeared, struggling under the weight of an enormous carton. "Seventeen," he huffed, as he set the carton down on the table with a thud, obvious relief, and a pale smile.

"If you will excuse me," he whispered, and he returned to the labyrinth for what I assume was an invigorating, much-needed cup of tea. Once again, I was alone.

The lid of the carton was sealed with dust, the talcum of time, and came off reluctantly. I closed my eyes and spoke to the silence. "All right, Corey. What shall it be?" and reached gingerly in. My fingertips touched a fragile sheaf of brown papers. The dry, crackled edges turned to dust. I almost moved on, to find something less delicate, but something told me to stop. I separated the fragile sheets and carefully pulled them from the carton. The handwriting was in pencil. . . .

How Corey was only thirty-one years old, at the peak of his success and in the throes of a nervous breakdown, determined to get through it alone, somehow. He had come home, to Hardscrabble. In a minuscule handwriting, he told me his story. . . .

. . . of how he had gotten into the habit of taking a walk every day, just before dusk, to the end of the road—our road—to a private place, a cemetery that is hidden in a copse and surrounded by a stone wall, like the Secret Garden. There, under the mantle of dusk's fading light, he would sit and "contemplate my great sorrows"—sorrows, I would later discover, that would cripple most men. One such day, Corey found the caretaker was still at work, cutting grass. He went up to the old man, and after brief pleasantries asked, "How long after a man dies before he is forgotten?"

And the old man replied, "A man is never forgotten as long as he is remembered."

Remember me. . . .

The words drifted on a breeze from the past, and a chill went down my spine.

Do not forget me. . . .

Then Corey went on to describe a far corner of the cemetery, where "stones with little lambs mark the graves of children who did not live to see twelve-month."

The paper was dated August 23. Tears stung my eyes.

A newer grave lies alongside those olden headstones crowned with lambs. There lies my infant daughter, Elizabeth, who died the day of her birth—August 23—fifty years after Corey expressed his own grief in the papers I held in my trembling hands.

I understood now why I had been summoned to Dartmouth.

*W*eeks turned into months as I returned again and again to Dartmouth. I embraced the archives with abandon, absorbed in the world of the most engaging, intelligent, witty man that I would, alas, never meet. The deeper I got into the archives, the greater the coincidences between Corey's life and mine. About our "shared" life in Hardscrabble, yes—and stranger coincidences. Corey's parents, for instance, rest in a cemetery that had been my family's farm until the Civil War. His friend, Humphrey, was my grandfather Bogart's cousin and childhood playmate.

And so, spring turned into summer as I continued to piece together the increasingly perplexing puzzle of Corey Ford's life. The more intimate I became with the man, the more concerned I became that he had been gay. This began to hinder my work and impinge upon my enthusiasm for what I was beginning to view as a project instead of a passion. It had long been rumored that the lifelong bachelor, who appeared more frequently and more comfortable in the company of men, led a double life. By August, I was convinced this was so, though I had no proof, and I decided to give up the archives. To me, this wasn't about alternative lifestyles. It was about my inability to write about a person who had lived out his life as a lie. At first, I vacillated. Ultimately, there was nothing for it but to explain to Dr. Crammond that I had decided to throw in the towel.

Then, the evening before my final trip to Dartmouth, I sprained my back. So searing was the agony that I became semiconscious from pain. My family sat with me until I drifted off to sleep on the sofa, then went upstairs to bed.

In the haze of slumber he came to me. He was not tall or short, young or old, and he spoke no words, but I understood what he was saying. For the second time, Corey Ford was reaching out to me, across the past.

Do not forsake me. . . . Do not forget me. . . .

And when I awoke, he was gone. The pain was gone.

But I had not changed my mind.

The following day, I brushed the soil from a modest, long-forgotten gravestone, placed upon it a nosegay of wildflowers, and prayed. Chiseled on the marker, simply, was JAMES HITCHCOCK FORD, 1902–1969. The flowers were from the Lower Forty. It was the day of the twenty-fifth anniversary of Corey's death. The day was warm and beautiful. At that moment, the clock tower of Dartmouth College struck twelve.

It was a good time to say good-bye.

After I left the cemetery, I went to see Dr. Crammond. "You may have to wait. He's in a staff meeting, and these tend to go on," my friend Gerald, the yellow young man, explained. To pass the time, I asked him to bring me one last carton. He had brought me all of them over the past months and had gotten used to carrying them. Remarkably, his complexion was no longer yellow, and his shoulders seemed broader. Gerald had developed a keen interest in my work. What's more, he never asked for my driver's license again—a check, I had learned, that people take nothing from Special Collections, which is not a lending library. For the second and last time, I gave Gerald a random number.

Twenty-three. . . .

It was a familiar carton, one I had worked on many times, but this time, I thrust my arm until my fingertips touched the bottom. Something was wedged in the corner of the box. I pulled out a fistful of tightly packed file folders and uncovered a brittle, black leather book—a diary. I pried open the lock, and his secret. After all these months, Corey's diary had somehow escaped me, until now.

It was all there. The clandestine confidences he revealed to no one but himself—and to me.

I will never hear his voice or look into his eyes—not in this lifetime, at least. I will never feel the touch of his hand or the breath of his whisper in my ear. Yet I know that I can never leave him. No, it is not enough. But it's all I have.

And at least for now, that will have to do.

It has been called the greatest outdoor story ever written, and yet Corey Ford never saw it published. Not until his death did the then-editor of *Field & Stream* remember the dust-covered manuscript that the magazine's most popular columnist had sent him seven years earlier; only then did he recall how time and time again, Corey begged him to publish the story. "It's the best thing I've ever written," but the editor demurred. "Our readers won't get it."

It was published, finally, falsely proclaimed to be Corey's swan song—a blatant lie. Nothing would have delighted Corey more than to have seen the enormous outpouring of love for his story. But he would never know, and now the world knows why. I found the original copy in one of those cartons. It had been edited. I put it back together. This is the way Corey meant for it to be.

Now maybe you will understand the things I have told you.

The Road to Tinkhamtown
BY COREY FORD
(Reprinted with permission of Dartmouth College)

The road was long, but he knew where he was going. He would follow the old road through the swamp and up over the ridge and down to a deep ravine, and cross the sagging timbers of the bridge, and on the other side would be the place called Tinkhamtown. He was going back to Tinkhamtown.

He walked slowly, for his legs were dragging, and he had not been walking for a long time. He had not walked for almost a year, and his flanks had shriveled and wasted away from lying in bed so long; he could fit his fingers around his thigh. Doc Towle had said he would never walk again, but that was Doc for you, always on the pessimistic side. Why, here he was walking quite easily, once he had started. The strength was coming back into his legs, and he did not have to stop for breath so often. He tried jogging a few steps, just to show he could, but he slowed again because he had a long way to go.

It was hard to make out the old road, choked with

young alders and drifted over with matted leaves, and he shut his eyes so he could see it better. He could always see it whenever he shut his eyes. Yes, here was the beaver dam on the right, just as he remembered it, and the flooded stretch where he had to wade, picking his way from hummock to hummock while the dog splashed unconcernedly in front of him. The water had been over his boottops in one place, and sure enough as he waded it now, his left boot filled with water again, the same warm, squidgy feeling. Everything was the way it had been that afternoon. Nothing had changed. Here was the blowdown across the road that he had clambered over and here on a knoll was the clump of thorn apples where Cider had put up a grouse—he remembered the sudden roar as the grouse thundered out, and the easy shot that he missed—they had not taken time to go after it. Cider had wanted to look for it, but he had whistled him back. They were looking for Tinkhamtown.

Everything was the way he remembered. There was a fork in the road, and he halted and felt in the pocket of his hunting coat and took out the map he had drawn twenty years ago. He had copied it from a chart he found in the Town Hall, rolled up in a cardboard cylinder covered with dust. He used to study the old survey charts; sometimes they showed where a farming community had flourished once, and around the abandoned pastures and under the apple trees, grown up to pine, the grouse would be feeding undisturbed. Some of his best grouse-covers had been located that way. The chart had crackled with age as he unrolled it; the date was 1847. It was the sector between Kearsarge and Cardigan Mountains, a wasteland of slash and second-growth timber without habitation today, but evidently it had supported a number of families before the Civil War. A

road was marked on the map, dotted with Xs for homesteads and the names of the owners were lettered beside
them: Nason, J. Tinkham, Libbey, Allard, R. Tinkham.
Half the names were Tinkham. In the center of the
map—the paper was so yellow he could barely make it
out—was the word Tinkhamtown.

He copied the chart carefully, noting where the road
turned off at the base of Kearsage and ran north and
then northeast and crossed a brook that was not even
named on the chart; and early the next morning he and
Cider had set out together to find the place. They could
not drive very far in the Jeep, because washouts had gut-
ted the roadbed and laid bare the ledges and boulders,
like a streambed. He had stuffed the sketch in his
hunting-coat pocket, and hung his shotgun over his fore-
arm and started walking, the old setter trotting ahead of
him, with the bell on his collar tinkling. It was an old-
fashioned sleighbell, and it had a thin silvery note that
echoed through the woods like peepers in the spring; he
could follow the sound in the thickest cover, and when
it stopped, he would go to where he heard it last and
Cider would be on point. After Cider's death, he had put
the bell away. He'd never had another dog.

It was silent in the woods without the bell, and the
way was longer than he remembered. He should have
come to the big hill by now. Maybe he'd taken the
wrong turn back at the fork. He thrust a hand into his
hunting-coat; the sketch he had drawn was still in the
pocket. He sat down on a flat rock to get his bearings,
and then he realized, with a surge of excitement, that he
had stopped for lunch on this very rock ten years ago.
Here was the waxed paper from his sandwich, tucked in
a crevice, and here was the hollow in the leaves where

Cider had stretched out beside him. He looked up, and through the trees he could see the hill.

He rose and started walking again, carrying his shotgun. He had left the gun standing in its rack in the kitchen, when he had been taken to the state hospital, but now it was hooked over his arm by the trigger guard; he could feel the solid heft of it. The woods were more dense as he climbed, but here and there a shaft of sunlight slanted through the trees. "And the forests ancient as the hills," he thought, "enfolding sunny spots of greenery." Funny that should come back to him now; he hadn't read it since he was a boy. Other things were coming back to him, the smell of the dank leaves and the sweetfern and frosted apples, the sharp contrast of sun and the cold November shade, the stillness before snow. He walked faster, feeling the excitement swell within him.

He had walked all that morning, stopping now and then to study the map and take his bearings from the sun, and the road had led them down a long hill and at the bottom was the brook he had seen on the chart, a deep ravine spanned by a wooden bridge. Cider had trotted across the bridge, and he had followed more cautiously, avoiding the loose planks and walking the solid struts with his shotgun held out to balance himself; and that was how he found Tinkhamtown.

On the other side of the brook was a clearing, he remembered, and the remains of a stone wall, and a cellar hole where a farmhouse had stood. Cider had moved in a long cast around the edge of the clearing, his bell tinkling faintly, and he had paused a moment beside the foundations, wondering about the people who had lived here a century ago. Had they ever come back to Tinkhamtown? And then suddenly, the bell had stopped, and he had hurried across the clearing. An apple tree was growing in a corner of the stone wall, and under the tree Cider had halted at point. He could see it all now: the warm October sunlight, the ground strewn with freshly pecked apples, the dog standing immobile with one foreleg drawn up, his back level and his tail a white plume. Only his flanks quivered a little, and a string of slobber dangled from his jowls. "Steady, boy," he murmured as he moved up behind him, "I'm coming."

He paused on the crest of the hill, straining his ears for the faint mutter of the stream below him, but he could not hear it because of the voices. He wished they would stop talking, so he could hear the stream. Someone was saying his name over and over. Someone said, "What is it, Frank?" and he opened his eyes. Doc Towle was standing at the foot of the bed, whispering to the new nurse, Mrs. Simmons or something; she'd only been here a few days, but Doc thought it would take some of the burden off his wife. He turned his head on the pillow, and looked up at his wife's face, bent over him. "What did you say, Frank?" she asked, and her face was worried. Why, there was nothing to be worried about. He wanted to tell her where he was going, but when he moved his lips no sound came. "What?" she asked, bending her head lower. "I don't hear you." He couldn't make the words any clearer, and she straightened and said to Doc Towle: "It sounded something like Tinkhamtown."

"Tinkhamtown?" Doc shook his head. "Never heard him mention any place by that name."

He smiled to himself. Of course he'd never mentioned it to Doc. There are some things you don't mention even to an old hunting companion like Doc. Things like a secret grouse cover you didn't mention to anyone, not even to as close a friend as Doc was. No, he and Cider were the only ones who knew. They had found it together, that long ago afternoon, and it was their secret. "This is our secret cover," he had told Cider that afternoon, as he lay sprawled under the tree with the setter beside him and the dog's muzzle flattened on his thigh. "Just you and me." He had never told anybody else about Tinkhamtown, and he had never gone back after Cider died.

"Better let him rest," he heard Doc tell his wife. It was funny to hear them talking, and not be able to make them hear him. "Call me if there's any change."

The old road lay ahead of him, dappled with sunshine. He could smell the dank leaves, and feel the chill of the shadows under the hemlocks; it was more real than the pain in his legs. Sometimes it was hard to tell what was real and what was something he remembered. Sometimes at night he would hear Cider panting on the floor beside his bed, his toenails scratching as he chased a bird in a dream, but when the nurse turned on the light the room would be empty. And then when it was dark he would hear the panting and scratching again.

Once he asked Doc point blank about his legs. "Will they ever get better?" He and Doc had grown up in town together; they knew each other too well to lie. Doc had shifted his big frame in the chair beside the bed, and got out his pipe and fumbled with it, and looked at him. "No, I'm afraid not," he replied slowly, "I'm afraid there's nothing to do." Nothing to do but lie here and wait till it's over. Nothing to do but lie here like this, and be waited on, and be a burden to everybody. He had a little insurance, and his son in California sent what he could to help, but now with the added expense of a

nurse and all . . . "Tell me, Doc," he whispered, for his
voice wasn't as strong these days, "what happens when
it's over?" And Doc put away the needle and fumbled
with the catch of his black bag and said he supposed that
you went on to someplace else called the Hereafter. But
he shook his head; he always argued with Doc. "No," he
told him, "it isn't someplace else. It's someplace you've
been where you want to be again, someplace you were
happiest." Doc didn't understand, and he couldn't
explain it any better. He knew what he meant, but the
shot was taking effect and he was tired. The pain had
been worse lately, and Doc had started giving him shots
with a needle so he could sleep. But he didn't really
sleep, because the memories kept coming back to him,
or maybe he kept going back to the memories.

He was tired now, and his legs ached a little as he
started down the hill toward the stream. He could not
see the road; it was too dark under the trees to see the
sketch he had drawn. The trunks of all the trees were
swollen with moss, and blowdowns blocked his way
and he had to circle around their upended roots, black
and misshapen. He had no idea which way Tinkhamtown was, and he was frightened. He floundered into a
pile of slash, feeling the branches tear at his legs as his
boots sank in, and he did not have the strength to get
through it and he had to back out again, up the hill. He
did not know where he was going anymore.

He listened for the stream, but all he could hear was
his wife, her breath catching now and then in a dry sob.
She wanted him to come back, and Doc wanted him to,
and there was the big house. If he left the house alone, it
would fall in with the snow and cottonwoods would
grow in the cellar hole. There were all the other doubts,
but most of all there was the fear. He was afraid of the

darkness and being alone, and not knowing the way. He had lost the way. Maybe he should turn back. It was late, but maybe, maybe he could find the way back.

He paused on the crest of the hill, straining his ears for the faint mutter of the stream below him, but he could not hear it because of the voices. He wished they would stop talking, so he could hear the stream. Someone was saying his name over and over. They had come to the stream—he shut his eyes so he could see it again—and Cider had trotted across the bridge. He had followed more cautiously, avoiding the loose planks and walking on a beam, with his shotgun held out to balance himself. On the other side the road rose sharply to a level clearing and he paused beside the split-stone foundation of a house. The fallen timbers were rotting under a tangle of briars and burdock, and in the empty cellar hole the cottonwoods grew higher than the house had been. His toe encountered a broken china cup and the rusted rims of a wagon wheel buried in the grass. Beside the granite doorsill was a lilac bush planted by the woman of the family to bring a touch of beauty to their home. Perhaps her husband had chided her for wasting time on such useless things, with as much work to be done. But all the work had come to nothing. The fruits of their work had disappeared, and still the lilac bloomed each spring, defying the encroaching forest, as though to prove that beauty is the only things that lasts.

On the other side of the clearing were the sills of the barn, and behind it a crumbling stone wall around the orchard. He thought of the men sweating to clear the fields and pile the rocks into walls to hold their cattle. Why had they gone away from Tinkhamtown, leaving their walls to crumble and their buildings to collapse under the January snows? Had they ever come back to

Tinkhamtown? Or were they still here, watching him unseen, living in a past that was more real than the present. He stumbled over a block of granite, hidden by briars, part of the sill of the old barn. Once it had been a tight barn, warm with cattle steaming in their stalls and sweet with the barn odor of manure and hay and leather harness. It seemed as though it was more real to him than the bare foundation, the empty space about them. Doc used to argue that what's over is over, but he would insist Doc was wrong. Everything is the way it was, he'd tell Doc. The present always changes, but the past is always the way it was. You leave it, and go to the present, but it is still there, waiting for you to come back to it.

He had been so wrapped up in his thoughts that he had not realized Cider's bell had stopped. He hurried across the clearing, holding his gun ready. In a corner of the stone wall an ancient apple tree had covered the ground with red fruit, and beneath it Cider was standing motionless. The white fan of his tail was lifted a little, his neck stretched forward, and one foreleg was cocked. His flanks were trembling, and a thin skein of drool hung from his jowls. The dog did not move as he approached, but he could see the brown eyes roll back until their whites showed, waiting for him. His throat grew tight, the way it always did when Cider was on point, and he swallowed hard. "Steady, boy," he whispered, "I'm coming."

He opened his eyes. His wife was standing beside his bed and his son was standing near her. He looked at his son. Why had he come all the way from California? he worried. He tried to speak, but there was no sound. "I think his lips moved just now. He's trying to whisper something," his wife's voice said. "I don't think he knows you," his wife said to his son. Maybe he didn't know him. Never had, really. He had never been close to his wife or his son. He did not open his eyes, because he was watching for the grouse to fly as he walked past Cider, but he knew Doc Towle was looking at him. "He's sleeping," Doc said after a moment. "Maybe you better get some sleep yourself." A chair creaked, and he heard Doc's heavy footsteps cross the room. "Call me if there's any change," Doc said, and closed the door, and in the silence he could hear his wife sobbing beside him, her dress rustling regularly as she breathed. How could he tell her he wouldn't be alone? But he wasn't alone, not with Cider. He had the old dog curled on the floor by the stove, his claws scratching the linoleum as he chased a bird in a dream. He wasn't alone when he heard that. They were always together. There was a closeness between them that he did not feel for anyone else, his wife, his son, or even Doc. They could talk without words, and they could always find each other in the woods. He was lost without him. Cider was the kindest person he had ever known.

They never hunted together after Tinkhamtown. Cider had acted tired, walking back to the car that afternoon, and several times he sat down on the trail, panting hard. He had to carry him in his arms the last hundred yards to the Jeep. It was hard to think he was gone.

And then he heard it, echoing through the air, a sound like peepers in the spring, the high silvery note of a bell. He started running toward it, following it down the hill. The pain was gone from his legs, it had never been there. He hurdled blowdowns, he leapt over fallen trunks, he put one fingertip on a pile of slash and floated over it like a bird. The sound filled his ears, louder than a thousand churchbells ringing, louder than all the heavenly choirs in the sky, as loud as the pounding of his heart. His eyes were blurred with tears, but he did not need to see. The fear was gone; he was not alone. He knew the way now. He knew where he was going.

He paused at the stream just for a moment. He heard men's voices. They were his hunting partners, Jim, Mac, Dan, Woodie. And oh, what a day it was for sure, closeness and understanding and happiness, the little intimate things, the private jokes. He wanted to tell them he was happy; if they only knew how happy he was. He opened his eyes, but he could not see the room anymore. Everything else was bright with sunshine, but the room was dark.

The bell stopped, and he closed his eyes and looked across the stream. The other side was basked in gold bright sunshine, and he could see the road rising steeply through the clearing in the woods, and the apple tree in a corner of the stone wall. Cider was standing motionless, the white fan of his tail lifted a little, his neck craned forward, one foreleg cocked. The whites of his eyes showed as he looked back, waiting for him.

"Steady," he called, "steady, boy." He started across the bridge. "I'm coming."

*H*e had been sick when he wrote "Tinkhamtown," sick in body and soul, for a long time. Corey was sixty-seven that summer when, while traveling in Ireland, he developed an aneurysm that required immediate attention.

They flew him back home, to Mary Hitchcock, a stone's throw from his house, where he had an operation, and it was deemed a success. He was recuperating in Dick's House, a brick mansion dedicated to ailing members of the Dartmouth family; Corey was surely family, considering all he'd done for the college—founding a boxing squad, the rugby team, helping boys financially through college.

He called home.

"Bring me Tober," he said, meaning his English setter, the son of Cider. But in the few minutes it took for one of the boys to get Tober to Dick's House, Corey had suffered a crushing stroke.

He was half paralyzed. The doctors determined there was nothing they could do, not anymore, so he went home where his housekeeper and a nurse could care for him, and the boys could come in and out and keep him company.

One morning he made it known that he wanted to go to the bathroom to shave, alone. A couple of the boys carried him in and closed the door. Shortly after came the crash. Corey had suffered a second stroke, this one devastating: He was in a coma.

The ambulance came. It was a short distance to the hospital, and they put him in a private room. Meanwhile, one of the boys had followed in Corey's car with Tober. He would want Tober. A couple of boys were outside Corey's room. They gave their mate the signal, and he led Tober up the fire escape. When the coast was clear, they took Tober into Corey's room.

He lay there in a coma. Tober saw Corey and jumped on his bed and set down beside him. The setter put his head on his master's shoulder.

And in the coma, Corey Ford raised his arms, put them around his beloved dog's neck, and died.

A year to the day, despite a loving home, Tober followed his master to Tinkhamtown.

Is Tinkhamtown a real place? Yes, of course. Everything is the way Corey said it was, down to the lilac trees. Majestic elms surround the cellar holes, vestiges of homes that were once alive with people; but the elms died, too, from disease. The summer of the twenty-fifth anniversary of Corey's death, I went to Tinkhamtown. The dead elms were alive again with new, green growth and new life sprouting from saplings and branches thirty feet up.

I once brought someone to Tinkhamtown, the only time I ever did. When we came to the bridge, he stopped. He refused to cross.

He said it was not his time.

But then, how will we know when it is our time to cross the bridge?

And So, Farewell and Adieu

"This is the [Hardscrabble] of the past and present, and of the future, who shall speak? But whatever may betide— and if it be ill may we not be here to see it—the mountains will still keep a stately watch in their changing garb of green or russet gold or white, with the lakes spreading below in sparkling blue or armored ice. What man has created here can pass away, but the beauty with which God dowered this beloved corner of our great land will remain forever, even as it dawned upon the vision of that first white explorer three hundred years ago."

—Dorothy Peck Chapman

We have come to the end of our journey, and it is time to part. Do not say good-bye. Just say so long. We will meet again, and then, as Joe Gargery said to Pip in *Great Expectations*, what larks we shall have! In the between time, remember Hardscrabble; remember all the things you've been told and seen and heard. . . .

Whenever you hear the breast-bursting song of the first robin of spring, or whiff the sweet autumn perfume of rotting apples settling on a mossy bed of fallen leaves . . . When the deep blue of a bottomless summer's lake has the cast of a sapphire, and a trout breaks the surface and flashes his tail in the sun-glinted water . . .

Think of us. . . .

For Hardscrabble will always be just down the road apiece and as far away as a thought; as eternal as a memory, and evermore sheltered in the safekeeping of your dreams.

And now, dear friend, Godspeed.

From the Hardscrabble Cookery Book

When it comes to cooking, New England's culinary legacy consists of apples, cinnamon, molasses, pumpkins and squash, baked beans, corn bread, venison, trout, and grouse.

Here are some of my favorite recipes. I hope my stories gave you a taste of New England. If not, these recipes will.

CAROL MAYHOFER'S CALICO BEANS

As I told you earlier, no New Englander worth her—or his—salt would think to use canned beans. However, if time is a factor in preparation, you'll be forgiven if you used the canned variety when you prepare this delicious recipe. You can substitute salt pork for bacon and, if you prefer, use molasses instead of brown sugar. You'll find that baked beans allow plenty of variation. In fact, barbeque sauce instead of ketchup makes a nice variation. You can even add bite-size pieces of frankfurter, to add to the meat presence, or increase the quantity of hamburger you use.

The baking method suggested here is the quick version. Ideally, you'd pour the beans that you soaked the night before into an old-fashioned covered baked bean pot—the kind, alas, that you now find in antique stores for hefty prices, though a good neighborhood hardware store is likely to still carry them next to the canning jars. Simmering beans on the top of a wood cooking stove is the best slow heat, but you have to be extremely careful that the firebox doesn't get too hot, or you can overcook the beans, and they will come out hard and inedible. If the stove is hot, move the bean crock to the middle or extreme opposite side of the stove from the firebox, where its cooler. That's how the old-timers used to turn a stove down, since there are no dials or digital instruments on a wood cookstove! Ideally, the thermometer on your wood cookstove should never get hotter than 400 degrees, so feed the fire a stick of wood at a time and always check the liquor to make sure the beans do not dry out. Stir frequently with a wooden spoon.

Frankly, the ideal method in this modern day and age is to bake beans in an electric Crock-Pot; first, on high, but after the mixture bubbles, on low all day long. Again, be sure to add water and stir thoroughly with a wooden spoon so the bean gravy remains moist and rich, and the beans are always covered. Baked beans can last three or four days in the refrigerator. They freeze very well in freezer bags and afford a quick and easy dinner when you reheat them.

1/2 lb. bacon, cut in 1–2" pieces
1 large onion, chopped coarse
1/2 lb. hamburger
1 can butter beans, drained

1 can kidney beans (do not drain)—
  or, one cup of dry kidney beans, soaked overnight,
  and parboiled till soft but firm
1 can pork and beans (do not drain)
1 cup ketchup
1 tsp. dry mustard
2 tsp. vinegar
1/2 cup white sugar
1/2 cup brown sugar

Preheat oven to 350 degrees.

In a large skillet or 8-quart pot, sauté bacon and onion till onion is transparent, then add hamburger. Brown lightly. Drain any excess fat. Add beans and stir with a wooden spoon. Set aside. In a bowl, combine ketchup, mustard, vinegar, and the sugars. Fold these with a wire wisk until the mixture is smooth. Add to the meat and beans. Pour in an ovenproof casserole, and bake for 45 minutes. Delicious served with Boston brown bread warm from the oven and a crock of herb butter.

SWEET POTATO CASSEROLE
An Old Hardscrabble Favorite

You can substitute winter squash for sweet potatoes in this deliciously simple recipe. However, squash has more water content than sweet potatoes, and you should drain and reserve the vegetable liquor to add, as needed, during the cooking process.

This is an excellent accompaniment to pork dishes and is a special favorite at the Thanksgiving feast, on the sideboard alongside the turkey. This dish neither keeps nor freezes well, but it is so delicious that it's doubtful you'll have any left over.

Preheat oven at 350 degrees.

Pare sweet potatoes and cube. In a covered saucepan, boil the cubed potatoes in two inches of water plus one tablespoon of butter on high heat, being careful to turn the potatoes frequently so they do not stick and burn on the bottom of the pot. Add water if necessary until the potatoes are fork-tender. Remove from heat, and drain and reserve excess liquor. Add butter, salt, and pepper to taste, a touch of nutmeg and cinammon, and a little heavy (not whipping) cream until the mixture is smooth, being careful to add just enough so it is neither watery or too firm. You may want to use a food processor or Mixmaster so that the potatoes are velvety smooth. Pour into an ovenproof casserole. Top with seasoned bread crumbs that you have tossed with a little melted butter and, on top of this, sift a thin layer of brown sugar. Bake until the casserole starts to bubble and lightly brown, about 20–30 minutes. If the casserole bubbles but does not brown, put under the broiler, watching very carefully that the bread crumb crust does not burn.

MISS FRANNIE'S SHERRIED BEEF

3 pounds stew beef, cut in 1" cubes
1 can sliced or button mushrooms
1 envelope dry onion soup
3/4 cup sherry
2 cans cream of mushroom soup

This was a favorite quick dish of Miss Frannie's that she often used for last-minute entertaining. The cut of meat is important—if it is too tough, you can either marinate it overnight in olive oil, balsamic vinegar, and pepper to taste, or you can slow-cook the stew in an electric Crock-Pot during the daytime, or in a low oven (275 degrees) for 31/2–4 hours, being careful, as always, to add a little beef bouillon or broth to maintain a nice gravy.

You can serve this dish over mashed pototoes or rice, but Miss Frannie used to serve it over wide Pennsylvania Dutch–type noodles that she had tossed in unsalted butter, since the meat dish carries enough saltiness and gives a nice contrast to the noodles.

You can freeze the Sherried Beef in an airtight container or freezer bag. When you reheat, use a large saucepan, add a little water, and stir constantly with a wooden spoon to avoid scorching. Then cover over low heat and let the steam defrost and cook the beef.

Preheat oven at 325 degrees.

Brown the stew beef in a little olive oil in a hot (but not spitting hot) frying pan. Set aside. In a casserole, combine mushrooms in liquor, sherry, and the onion soup. Stir well, then add the two cans of cream of mushroom soup. Add beef, and turn with a wooden spoon until it is well-coated. Bake 3 hours. Serve over wide egg noodles.

TUTTI-FRUITTI FRUIT PUNCH

1 box or small bag frozen strawberries
1 large can frozen orange juice
1 large can pineapple juice, undiluted
1 jar Maraschino cherries
1 liter ginger ale

This is a Bogart family favorite that my mother always served as a nonalcoholic alternative at our Christmas parties. We've never tried adding spirits to this because it is so delicious. Tutti-fruitti Fruit Punch is such a favorite among the children who we entertain here, at Hazelcrest, that I usually wait for the children to arrive before preparing it. They love helping—and being the first to taste this Hazelcrest holiday classic. Even though my sons are now grown up, they still stand around the punch bowl with their cups on the ready for the first swill!

The day before: Arrange the strawberries in a decorative metal Jell-o mold or ring (do not use ceramic, porcelain, or glass). Fill 3/4 full with water. Freeze.

Shortly before your company arrives: In a punch bowl, combine the orange juice with the pineapple juice, pouring a little of the pineapple juice at a time until the frozen orange juice is fully defrosted. Add the liquor from the jar of Maraschino cherries. Just as your company begins to arrive, add the ginger ale, slowly. Stir gently so that the punch does not froth. Add Maraschino cherries. Remove strawberry ice from the mold by topping it with a plate, turning it upside down, and running it under hot water in the kitchen sink until the ice mold gives. Float it on top of the punch for a festive holiday or summertime drink that is popular the year long.

VENISON MINCEMEAT FOR PIE

There was a time not long ago when deer hunting season made the difference between a full larder and a slim one. Deer hunting remains important to many people in Hardscrabble, but today it is out of tradition more than necessity. Still, not a single hunter hereabouts takes a deer without afterwards offering a prayer to his brethren of the woods, thanking him for giving his life in order to nourish the hunter and his family. It is an old belief that dates back to the time when the Indians roamed these hills and dales, and likewise offered thanks to the great whitetail deer.

This was not always the case, however. The invention of

the repeating rifle, compounded by the lack of regulations that limited hunting season and the quantity of game a person could take, depleted the New England forests of white-tail deer. Mert Grant and Orion Brooks, who were born and bred in Hardscrabble and probably never have been more than fifty miles outside its borders, remember seeing their first deer when they were teenagers, back in the '30s.

That's why hunters today are called the original conservationists. Hunting licenses generate the lion's share of funds that support conservation—seven dollars out of ten, in fact.

And the respectful hunter still will murmur a quiet prayer over his brother of the woods.

This recipe is ideal for lesser cuts of meat that benefit from being ground. Remember that venison has very little fat, and beef fat must be added when the meat is ground. Alternatively, many people prefer to add one pound of 75 percent lean hamburger to two pounds of venison, to give it the necessary moisture for cooking.

> 9 cups ground venison
> 18 cups apples, cored, and ground with the peel
> 41/2 cups molasses
> 9 cups granulated sugar
> 3 tablespoons cinnamon
> 11/2 teaspoons cloves
> 11/2 teaspoons salt
> 3 teaspoons nutmeg
> 41/2 cups cider vinegar
> 1 cup white raisins

In a large pot, brown venison thoroughly and drain fat. Add apples and the rest of the ingredients, and turn with a wooden spoon until thoroughly mixed. Cook until apples are tender but not too soft. If the mixture becomes too dry, add a little water. Cool. Prepare piecrust and bake, as usual. If you are not using the mixture immediately, store in airtight containers for up to two days or freeze in freezer bags, being certain to collapse the bags of all air.

How to Properly Cook Venison

Venison is a very delicate meat. The backstrap is the choicest selection. Overcooking this is committing a culinary crime! The secret to cooking venison properly is to use a good oil, preferably virgin olive oil, and watching the heat, sauté in a frying pan two minutes or so on each side, depending on the thickness of the cut, and then a little less on the other side. A few slices of onion or a touch of garlic goes a long way. A sherry or red wine helps keep the meat moist and provides a delicious stock that you can thicken with a little flour or cornstarch for gravy.

Some venison can be tough, especially if it is from an older animal. In this case, slow cooking for a long time in a covered casserole under minimal heat with a good beef or wine stock, a little olive oil, some onion, salt, and pepper, will make a beautiful stew. Add potatoes, carrots, celery, and other vegetables that complement a red meat stew.

HARDSCRABBLE DINNER ROLLS

1 cup warm milk
2 packages or 2 tablespoons yeast, dissolved in the milk
    with 2 teaspoons sugar sprinkled on top to activate the
    yeast. Allow to proof in a warm, draft-free place, about
    10 minutes. (Don't leave too long or the yeast will
    crust. If this happens, mix gently with a fork to be sure
    it will proof again.)

1 teaspoon salt

2 tablespoons melted butter

21/2 cups flour

Preheat oven to 350 degrees. After the yeast proofs, add salt, butter (be sure the butter is not spitting hot! Cool a little, or the heat may kill the yeast), and slowly add flour, mixing with a wooden spoon until it becomes stiff. Then, knead until the dough is smooth and firm. Put in a warm, draft-free place for 45 minutes or until it doubles in bulk. Pull apart dough, about the size of a ping-pong ball, and twist into the shape of a Parker House roll. Set 2 inches apart on a greased cookie sheet, and allow to rise again, about 15 minutes. Bake 10 minutes. For a golden crust, brush a little butter on the top of the rolls when they're done, turn off the oven, and let them sit for another minute, watching to be sure they do not overbrown. Or, separate a yolk from the egg white and beat a little water into the yolk till smooth. Use this to brush on the top of the roll. Brush the batter in layers of thin coatings, allowing a little time between each layer so that the batter doesn't puddle and soften the top of the roll. Serve immediately. These do not tend to keep, so freeze them in a freezer bag if there are any left over.

HARDSCRABBLE CORN PUDDING BREAD

11/3 cups yellow cornmeal

1/3 cup flour

1 teaspoon baking soda

3 tablespoons brown sugar

11/4 teaspoons salt

1 cup milk

2 eggs

1 cup sour cream
1 can creamed corn
2 tablespoons melted butter

Our first Thanksgiving, I turned over the turkey because I thought you had to. Of course, it didn't occur to me that all the stuffing and the juices would fall out. I've come a long, long way since then. Living in rural New England on a tight household budget inspires extraordinary creativity in the kitchen. Were I to think which recipe was my first real success, it is this. It was inspired from a cookbook given to my mother as an engagement present a long, long time ago. I varied it, added to it, and came up with this. Like a soufflé, monitor your oven temperature, as that could make all the difference between a light, airy cornbread and a solid brick. Another tip: If you separate the whites from the yolks of the eggs, beat the whites until they are frothy, then fold them into the batter gently with a spatula, it will have a delightful lightness about it, like a soufflé.

Preheat oven to 425 degrees.

Sift dry ingredients together. In a separate bowl, mix eggs, sour cream, creamed corn, and melted butter until the mixture is creamy. Slowly pour this into the dry ingredients and mix well with a wire whisk or on low speed in a Mixmaster until the batter again is smooth. Pour slowly into a large buttered Pyrex baking pan. Reduce oven heat to 350 degrees. Bring the pan to the oven. Very slowly, pour the cup of milk right down the middle of the pan. DO NOT MIX! Carefully put the pan in the oven. Bake approximately 35 minutes or until done. Done is when the milk forms a pudding and the bread is moist. This must be served hot. Hardscrabble Corn Pudding Bread neither keeps or freezes. Plan to make it about an hour before serving dinner. This is absolutely delicious with New England boiled dinner (see below), baked beans, or any main dish where the meat is pork.

New England Boiled Dinner
the Hardscrabble Way

1/2 lb. salt pork, cut into cubes
1 3-lb. piece of corned beef
1 package dry onion soup
2 cups apple cider vinegar
1 tablespoon dry English mustard
8 medium-sized potatoes, peeled and quartered
2 large white onions, quartered and separated
1 head green cabbage, quartered
3–4 parsnips, peeled and diced coarse
1 turnip, peeled and cubed
4–6 carrots, peeled and diced coarse
1 bay leaf
Salt and pepper to taste

The New England boiled dinner is a time-honored tradition and is delicious and so easy to prepare. This is a fall and winter favorite, but a little too hot and heavy for the warm times of year. When you come in from the cold to an enormous pot boiling on the wood cookstove and an apple pie cooling on the topmost shelf—why, there is no aroma in the world quite like it.

This is my own recipe, which I've changed over the years and, to me, is pretty close to perfection. The beauty about this dish is that you can add or take away and still end up with something extraordinary.

You will need a very large covered pot for this dish. "The gang's all here" quantity that I suggest will feed a large family or a houseful of guests. You can have it, if you're cooking for fewer people.

Cut the vegetables, as suggested above. Under medium-high heat, brown the cubed salt pork in the pot and turn frequently with a wooden spoon until the fat is transparent. Add corned beef, turn, and brown the outside. Then add the dry onion soup and continue to turn with the wooden spoon, coating the meat. Add vinegar, stir, and then add the mustard. Stir again. Gradually add the vegetables, turning them so that everything is well mixed. Fill the pot with water, covering the stew right up to the top, add the bay leaf, and season with salt and pepper to taste.

Simmer at least four hours at a gently rolling boil. Once the water has boiled down to half, add only enough to maintain this level. Turn the stew every so often so that all the vegetables cook thoroughly.

Grandma Bogart's Apple Pie

The quintessential New England dessert is hot apple pie, served with vanilla ice cream, whipped or heavy cream, or raisin sauce. Apples are the fruit most associated with New England. It is virtually impossible to walk through the rural parts of Hardscrabble, the unremembered cemeteries, the overgrown fields, the farms, and even some of the yards of the village houses and not find apple trees. A young tree that has taken root will last for decades, if not longer. Properly pruned, it will produce copious amounts of sweet fruit for autumn picking. Even trees that are overgrown and forgotten will bear fruit in the topmost branches, year after year after year. When the first whiff of apple perfumes the air, then you know that autumn is just around the corner.

Most recipes for apple pie are pretty much the same. It's just one of those things that, if you get fancy with added ingredients, you're simply gilding the lily. The secret to magnificent apple pies lies in the apples you use. You want an apple that is tart, not sweet. It should not be firm-fleshed, like a Red Delicious, which is purely an eating apple. You want an apple that will bake down into a flavorful, tender (but not mushy) pie. Cortland, Winesap, Granny Smith, Jonathan, and Rome Beauty are popular baking apples.

Another secret is to use a deep-dish pie plate and to stack the apples quite high, slicing them thin and creating a dome before you apply the top-crust. Shallow pie plates result in skimpy pies. When a deep-dish pie is served hot out of the oven, you will need a knife and serving spoon in order to heap the portions on the plates! Once fully cooled and chilled, the pie becomes firmer and less of a challenge to serve.

One word about piecrusts. Making a perfect piecrust from scratch is an art, and if so, none is better than the one you can make by simply following the instructions on a can of Crisco. For as much as a true New England cook never uses canned beans, she or he never buys a premade piecrust or makes one from a boxed mix.

Here I have a confession.

The best pies I have ever made have crusts that have come from a box of piecrust mix. Its easy, flaky, and light. There is nothing more depressing in the kitchen than to fight over a proper piecrust. Unless you have the talent to make one from scratch, get a couple of boxes and forget the hassle. Making a good pie is, like bread making, "kitchen therapy."

Preheat oven to 350-degrees.
Prepare piecrust.

1/2 cup granulated sugar
1/2 cup brown sugar

1 teaspoon cinnamon
1/4 teaspoon allspice
1/4 teaspoon nutmeg
1/4 teaspoon salt
8–10 large peeled and cored apples, sliced thin
A generous amount of butter

Process the sugars through a sifter, blender, or Mixmaster so that the mixture is fine. Add the spices and salt, and once again process until the mixture is fine and thoroughly blended.

Grease the pie plate with Crisco (not oil; rather, that solid shortening) and line the bottom with pie pastry, rolled with your rolling pin to an 1/4-inch thickness, being sure to let at least two inches come over the side all around the pie plate. (This will give you plenty to play with when you crimp the piecrust.) Spread a layer of apple slices, overlapping slightly, until the layer covers the bottom completely. Sift the mixture over the apples, covering it completely, then dot with snippets of butter. Spread a second layer of apples carefully and again sift the dry spiced sugar generously on top, dotting once again with butter. Repeat this process until the apples are stacked high, but not so high that they are going to teeter over like the Leaning Tower of Pisa. Remember that these will reduce as the pie bakes. The slices of apple should have piled into a rounded dome. Gently center a large round of piecrust for the top layer and lay it over the dome of apples. Carefully adjust the crust so it is centered, and press it lightly into the dome of apples. With a kitchen scissors, trim away the extra dough so that you have a little over an inch in diameter beyond the outside edge of the pie plate. Using the prongs of a fork that you'll hold upside down, form the piecrust by turning the excess back into the pie and pinching the crust between your thumb and forefinger. Then, depress with the prongs, allowing the fork to make little holes where it comes in contact with the top crust. The prongs make a decorative edging. Go all the way around.

Some people will use the juice of a fresh lemon to make apples that may be too sweet a bit tart. Others cut the amount of sugar and dribble a little honey on the apples. Some people do not use brown sugar at all. You'll develop your own recipe over the years. That's the splendor of New England cookery—it's creative, always appreciated, and you can adjust the recipe to your tastes, your larder, and your needs.

A Word About Pumpkin, Cherry, Mincemeat, and Blueberry Pies

A real apple pie must be made from fresh apples that you pare and core and slice yourself. Jars of ready-to-bake fillings just don't bear comparison.

The same does not apply, however, to pumpkin, cherry, mincemeat, and blueberry pies.

You certainly can make these from scratch, no question. However, over the course of the decades that I've lived here in Hardscrabble, none of my homemade efforts have equaled the delicious prepared pie fruit that you can get right off of your grocery shelf. Why, even Tilt Tilton stocks jars of pie fillings at the Hardscrabble Village Store—that is, all except for apple. "I'd just as soon go hungry than to stick my fork in a piece of apple pie from a can," he says.

Making a pumpkin pie from a pumpkin is tantamount to deciding to build a house and going into the woods with an ax. Preparing a pumpkin is enormous work. There are times when I have had to cut a pumpkin with a handsaw, it's such a physical job. Then, you have to remove the seeds and sinew. Bake the quarters in the oven over a pot of water *and* baste the pulp frequently to keep it from drying out. Then you have to remove the pulp from the hard shell, boil the pulp, season it to taste, put it through a sieve to remove excess water, and then as it bakes, pray that it doesn't have the consistency of the ground during mud season.

HARDSCRABBLE SOUP

There are hundreds of recipes for soup, but the simplest, most delicious and most filling of all is Hardscrabble Soup. The old-timers also call it Whatchagot Soup, because the ingredients consist of whatever you have in the refrigerator and pantry. Some of the best soups are made up of the last three or four potatoes in the bag and cleaning out the crisper of the last of the onions, carrots, zucchini, mushrooms—almost anything you keep in the crisper. Add an inexpensive cut of meat, and you've got the makings of a soup fit for a king.

The secret to a good Hardscrabble Soup is common sense, a notion of what makes a good combination of flavors, and a delicious broth base that is made purely from beef or poultry. Leafy vegetables such as broccoli and cauliflower, and those with high water content, such as asparagus, zucchini, and summer squash, are delicious as vegetable soups all on their own, and oftentimes are pureed. However, when you mix these with meat-based soups or stews, they cannot withstand the long hours of simmering and deteriorate into a mush that doesn't really contribute much to the soup stock or its consistency. Also, these tend to lend an acidic taste to stock. You can, however, add these vegetables to a thick soup—just parboil them in a separate pot with a pinch of salt till they cook up a little softer than al dente, and fold them into the soup at the last minute.

The greatest tool in making a good soup is time: the longer it simmers, the better it will be.

Simmer is a very important word in making a soup or stew. Never boil a soup or a stew! A high boil will make the meat tough and destroy the delicate and subtle combinations of flavors.

In Hardscrabble, what we call a stew is what you probably would describe as a thick soup with meat. A chowder is a thick soup with fish. What you call a stew—a combination of vegetables and meat in a gravy—is known in Hardscrabble as a casserole.

Venison is a popular soup meat. Just as in most venison preparations, however, you have to add a little fat. Brown cubed venison or venison burger in a little salt pork and include the salt pork in the soup. You can remove the excess fat after a soup has cooled and the fat solidifies when it rises to the top.

The best beef-based soups come from the cheapest cuts of meat. Here's a hint: Instead of buying stew beef, buy a pot roast and cut the meat into one-inch cubes yourself. You'll find that the meat is a better grade and less expensive. With beef, you tend to use potatoes. With chicken and turkey soups, rice or noodles are good companions. However, do not add the rice or noodles at the beginning of a long simmering process. Rice should be added about an hour before serving; noodles should be cooked in a separate pot with water that's at a rolling boil, then folded into the soup at the time of serving. Otherwise, these are starches and they get soft and, well, starchy.

Soups that simmer all day long need to have water added from time to time to keep the soup from boiling down. It's always a good idea to have a jar of bouillon around, and add a tablespoon (or 2–3 cubes) or so to taste of beef bouillon in veal or beef stocks, and chicken bouillon in chicken or turkey stocks. Another secret stock ingredient is apple cider vinegar. A cup added to the pot adds a rich taste and tang that can't be beat. (Do not use red wine or balsamic vinegar—it's too heavy.) As for herbs, that's a very personal taste and frankly, I stay away from these. I find that even the smallest amount of herbs can get in the way of the natural flavor of the meats and vegetables. This being said, purely vegetable soups do benefit from an herb that brings out their natural flavors—for example, a little basil and oregano with a tomato soup is delightful; chives with a leek and potato soup is a must; and tarragon with a cold summer squash and zucchini soup is delicious. Always add salt and pepper to taste. Use sparingly, as these can make your soup a disaster with the flick of a wrist, and there's no way of undoing a soup that's got too much salt added to it!

A well-made soup is served with bread. If the soup is rich, bake a simple yeast-rising white or wheat bread. If the soup is clear, a cold soup, or a vegetable-based soup such as zucchini or broccoli soup, a batter bread with rich flavors stands up better. Soup can be as extravagant as a filet mignon. At night, enjoy soup along with a good glass of wine or a cold glass of beer.

Cheers!